# the last good paradise

## tatjana soli

St. Martin's Press  New York

THE LAST GOOD PARADISE. Copyright © 2015 by Tatjana Soli. All rights reserved. Printed in the United States of America. For information, address St. Martin's Press, 175 Fifth Avenue, New York, N.Y. 10010.

www.stmartins.com

Designed by Steven Seighman

The Library of Congress Cataloging-in-Publication Data is available upon request.

ISBN 978-1-250-04396-2 (hardcover)
ISBN 978-1-4668-4230-4 (e-book)

St. Martin's Press books may be purchased for educational, business, or promotional use. For information on bulk purchases, please contact the Macmillan Corporate and Premium Sales Department at 1-800-221-7945, extension 5442, or write to specialmarkets@macmillan.com.

First Edition: February 2015

10  9  8  7  6  5  4  3  2  1

the
last good
paradise

## also by tatjana soli

*The Lotus Eaters*
*The Forgetting Tree*

*For my mom, who taught me to follow my heart always*

*I am tormented with an everlasting itch for things remote.*
—M ELVILLE, *Moby-Dick*

# *Porca Miseria!* Pig of Misery!

## *(The Sorry State of Things)*

*All men live enveloped in whale-lines. All are born with hal-*
*ters round their necks; but it is only when caught in the swift,*
*sudden turn of death, that mortals realize the silent, subtle,*
*ever-present perils of life. And if you be a philosopher, though*
*seated in the whale-boat, you would not at heart feel one whit*
*more of terror, than though seated before your evening fire with*
*a poker, and not a harpoon, by your side.*

—MELVILLE, *Moby-Dick*

A 7.1 tremor had been felt throughout the Southland that morning, the epicenter somewhere out in the hinterlands of Lancaster, unnerving residents, but the offices of Flask, Flask, Gardiner, Bulkington, Bartleby, and Peleg were seemingly immune. Ten floors up in the sybaritic conference room, the air conditioner purred; the air was filtered, ionized, and subtly scented of cedar. Ann looked out the plate-glass windows at the expansive, gaseous hills of West Los Angeles as a contemplative might look out of her meditation temple. Smoke was pouring from a Spanish Colonial Revival house halfway up a nearby manicured hill, and as she watched, toylike candy-colored fire engines curled up the narrow canyon roads to put it out. The glass was proofed; no siren sound reached her. She was protected from the ninety-degree heat outside, the fume-laden gridlock below, the merciless sunlight above that leeched color from the landscape.

"You drowned my twenty-year-old bonsai collection," Mrs. Peters accused the neighbor she was suing.

Her client was blowing it. Catlike, Ann leaned over and whispered in her ear. "Picture where you want to be a year from now."

The client, Mrs. Peters, the fourth wife of a major Hollywood producer, was not hearing no; her husband was a prime client of a senior partner at the firm, Bartleby, and he had told Ann to "nuke the nuisance suit" in arbitration.

Ann, junior partner, was smartly dressed in an expensive, Italian-cut skirt suit, low-heeled Blahnik pumps, and black-framed eyeglasses that she didn't need but used for effect. The firm's philosophy: Big fish eat little fish. The lesson to be derived? Make sure you are a big fish. She meant to exude big-fishness, but she had been mostly silent for the last fifteen minutes of the meeting, causing Mrs. Peters to think she had been handed down to the office dud.

The defendant's attorney, obvious small fish Todd Bligh from his own one-man, eponymously named firm in Marina del Rey, was wearing jeans and flip-flops. He looked like he should be a bartender on a beach somewhere. For the last fifteen minutes, he had been droning on about soil erosion, mudslides, environmental degradation, and acts of God. Blah, blah, blah.

Ann ran a fingernail along the condensation ring of her water glass on the waxed Brazilian rosewood conference table. The endangered species table had been purchased illegally by the Flask brothers precisely because it was politically incorrect, proving how badass and above the law the firm held itself. Out the window, the Spanish Colonial was being delicately licked by flames.

"Acts of God," Ann said dreamily.

"Yes," said Bligh.

"I've been to your property, Mrs. Brenner. It's stunning. So well groomed. Your gardener . . ."

"Avelino."

Ann pretended to check a piece of paper, although she had the gardener's name, immigration status, and driver's license memorized. "Yes. Mr. Avelino Aragon is quite skilled."

Mrs. Brenner perceivably relaxed at this acknowledgment. "He's been working for me for ten years. He's invaluable."

"So skilled and experienced in fact that he advised you it would *not* be a good idea to remove the cinder block retaining wall that had been in place twenty years, reinforcing the hillside."

Silence in the room, and now Mrs. Peters was the one smiling, albeit tightly. She had insisted on going ahead with her scheduled preholiday chemical peel, and she exuded a bruised, melted beauty, like a middle-aged Barbie.

Ann sighed. "Mrs. Brenner, didn't he also tell you it wasn't a good idea to bring in two truckloads of topsoil, spreading it on top of a clay hillside to plant flowers for an outdoor party? That it would run off in a rain? Straight into my client's patio, choking her prize, exotic plant life. Yes?" Again, the faked note check. "A rare imperial, eight-handed bonsai imported directly from Takamatsu, Japan, replacement value in the five-figure range."

Todd Bligh now had beads of sweat rolling down his face despite the cool air blowing on him.

Ann did not mention the crucial and probable cause of the lawsuit— that her client had been snubbed and not invited to said party. "Just as an aside, when I looked into your tax records, I did not see withholdings for Mr. Aragon. Ten years, plus penalties. Also, in case this goes to trial and is reported in the press, can you confirm or deny your absence from the residence during the landscaping work while staying at Voyages Rehabilitation facility in Malibu for an OxyContin addiction?"

It was a dirty, shower-inducing job, but someone had to do it. No, correction, she was being paid to do it; it was her specialty, to land the eviscerating mortal thrust. As the settlement papers were drawn up in the firm's favor, Bartleby dropped in and shook Mrs. Peters's hand, effectively taking credit for the outcome. "Tell Jerry to call me for tennis this weekend." He gave Ann a terse nod and was gone.

When Todd Bligh left with his client, he refused to make eye contact with Ann. He appeared visibly shaken, smarting from the hardball she had just served. She heard the slapping sound of his defeated flip-flops as he walked down the hallway. He would be happier as a beach bartender.

After the others had all left the conference room, Ann closed the door, locked it, and turned off the punishing fluorescent lights. Rumor was senior partners from decades before had installed the lock in order to conduct liaisons—the only glass looked outward into the lozenge of golden, poisonous air. A design psychologist claimed that the fishbowl effect so popular in most conference rooms, suggesting openness and transparency, was detrimental in a city of entertainers, who when observed did what came naturally: they acted. Once the walls became concealing solid maple, settlements skyrocketed.

Ann threw off her pumps. She unbuttoned the back of her skirt and unzipped it a few inches, rolled down her control-top panties, freeing her bloated stomach. A small moan of relief like a burp escaped from her diaphragm. Sweat had broken out on her forehead. Bloating, pimples, swollen breasts and feet, and a fine mustache on her upper lip were the fun part.

After the clomiphene failed to induce pregnancy, the doctor had switched her to hormone injections. The drive to the doctor's office was too difficult with an eighty-hours-a-week work schedule, so Richard gave her the painful shots as she bent over the bathroom counter, fighting back tears. This was not what she was supposed to be doing with her husband while bent over the bathroom counter, but even though she must have been dropping eggs like a goose, the effect of the drugs made even the idea of sex horrific in her present crazed, engorged state. Its main effect was to hone her bloodlust at work, as she had just so ably demonstrated (the OxyContin bomb was a scorched earth tactic, but she was tired and wanted a quick kill). Only when she wrote out the monthly exorbitant checks to the fertility clinic, which was not covered by the firm's cut-rate health insurance, did she feel like getting her money's worth. Then Richard and she had sad, porno-inspired sex. Maybe they should have adopted.

Ann opened her briefcase and pulled out her stash of Mars bars, the only food she craved, even though she had promised Richard she would save herself for dinner. She ripped the wrappers off and dropped the bars into her mouth, opening another before she devoured the first, an obscene assembly line of gluttony. Only when her mouth was crammed full of chocolate did she at last feel a glorious calm descend. This was her true shame and infidelity: the sugary, waxy, acrid grocery-bin chocolate she was addicted to. In disgust, Richard threw them into the trash every time he found a stash. Food snobbery was the price to be paid for marrying a professional chef.

"How can you?" he'd say, his lips twisted as if forced to taste something fantastically bitter. He gave a tight nod—a tic that drove Ann up the wall—then stoically forgave her. "Sweetheart, you know that crap messes up your palate."

But Ann didn't want his gourmet Felchlin Gastro 58% Rondo Dark Chocolate that puddled on the tongue like silk, that left an aftertaste of cassis. She wanted her *nostalgie de la boue*, love of the gutter, an attraction to what was unworthy. Exactly.

She rooted around in her briefcase and found the book she had stayed up late into the night reading, *The Moon and Sixpence*, the story of a Gauguin-like figure who runs off to Tahiti. She rewarded herself for tasks done by sneaking away to read a few pages. Today she deserved a chapter at least for settling the case. She unfastened the top buttons of her blouse to cool off. If only she could get her prickling, rashed skin dry for a second. Soon her blouse was off, and there she stood in her new mom-bra. The polished rosewood beckoned like the glassy face of an ocean. She lay down on it under the wash from the air-conditioning vent till the cold cedar air raised goose bumps on her arms. Her breasts ached, but she wouldn't go so far as to unhook her bra. Her chest size had gone from flat A-cup to grapefruit-sized D-cup, and was just one more thing Richard wasn't getting to enjoy.

Savagely, she ripped open another candy bar wrapper. One of the new age ideas was that failure to conceive was a proactive reaction to the body's not being ready. The prospective mother developed a kind of allergy to the father. What she needed to do was visualize her future baby to make herself user-friendly. Although Ann had thought the idea abysmally simpleminded, she was surprised that this ended up being her favorite fertility activity: she pictured cute baby girls with blond hair and pink cheeks, boys with Richard's brown eyes who bounced on their chubby legs like puppies. The happiness she experienced in these fantasies gave her a wan assurance that she might make an okay mother someday.

Of course she wanted a child, but since it had not happened naturally, she was oppressed by the likelihood that she would have hormone-induced twins at the least, possibly triplets or quintuplets—what were they called when the number went even higher?—while she was daunted by the prospect of even one baby. A biological clock had gone off, but she wasn't sure it was inside her; rather, it seemed outside, in everyone else. Newspapers, magazines, TV talk shows, her girlfriends, her mother, celebrity baby bumps on the covers of tabloids in the grocery store line. Even her gynecologist of twenty years had joined in. Fertility was the new über-lucrative specialty compared with plain-vanilla gynecology or obstetrics. When Ann put her feet in the stirrups—in the early years worrying mostly about STDs, then about trying *not* to get pregnant— she now was assaulted by pictures stapled to the ceiling of babies dressed like cabbages. The Fertility-Industrial Complex, she joked with Richard until they found themselves inside of it, when it became distinctly less funny. Since when had procreation turned into a job?

A knocking on the conference door shook her out of her reverie. "Ann, are you in there?"

She said nothing, swinging her feet into a nearby leather swivel chair. Candy wrappers littered the table and floor like spent condoms.

She heard another voice. "Maybe she's in there with someone."

"The Scorcher? She's probably playing alone. After devouring her mate. The lady praying mantis. She's ruthless. The Peters case was settled in an hour. The Brenner woman ran out of here crying. Dolan crushed."

"Have fun in there." The smirking voices moved off.

This was why she deserved partnership over the other junior partners—because unlike them, she knew that the seemingly solid, soundproof conference room doors had been specially hollowed out so that private negotiations could be overheard. Yes, she'd won. Her consolation prize. But they were wrong. She wasn't ruthless; she was just trying to be a big fish. Things would get better. They had to. Today was her thirty-eighth birthday.

Richard was determined to test-run a few new recipes before he baked Ann's cake for dinner that night. It was his favorite time in the kitchen, before Javier and everyone else showed up, and he opened the back door onto the alley, enjoying the whiff of sea breeze. He put on Pavarotti's Neapolitan songs, and set a pot of Yukon Golds to boil. When the phone rang, it was yet another credit collection agency asking for Javier. "He's on vacation," Richard said and hung up. He needed to work on his potato-and-fennel au gratin—he still hadn't gotten the right mix of creamy and sharp cheese. As a substitute for pedestrian Gruyère, he was thinking of maybe a Cantal or Reblochon? Or finding a source for a salty, buttery, earthy L'Etivaz?

The delivery buzzer rang, breaking Richard's thoughts. He slapped at the intercom with floury fingers. It was UPS.

"Where from?"

"Overnight from Lodi."

Shit. The rabbits. Richard and Javi's brainchild. Hardly a restaurant in the LA basin served rabbit—just hole-in-the-wall ethnic places in the Valley—yet in Europe it was a well-respected staple. He would explain on the menu that rabbit was lower in fat and higher in protein than chicken. The challenge was overcoming the bad image. Richard's solution was to substitute it in some well-known recipes. He would transform coq au vin to lapin au vin. Rabbit Abruzzi in a sauce of tomatoes, olives, and artichokes. Then he would feature one French classic such as *lapin aux pruneaux*, rabbit with prunes. But the delivery—a box of fryers for experimenting—wasn't supposed to be till tomorrow, overnighted on dry ice from a free-range rabbit farm in Northern California. Should he dare try making a dish for tonight?

Richard took delivery and put the box on the counter, grabbing a pair of bone shears to cut the plastic binding. His palms were just the slightest bit sweaty. When he took off the lid of insulating dry ice, the sight that met his eyes set him back years. Not anonymous, cut-up fryer pieces sanitized in plastic but four whole, furry white bodies funereally laid out in the interior. Unskinned. Was this a joke? Was the supplier some kind of sadist? He put the Styrofoam lid back on, spinning away and stumbling over a chair, his shirt soaked in flop sweat.

A throbbing engine stopped in the alley. Richard staggered toward the door to close it to keep the fumes out. It was Javi behind the wheel of a new silver Corvette convertible.

"What are you doing in that?"

"Leased it."

"With what?"

"Almost the same as the Honda." Which in Javi-speak meant double what the Honda cost.

"Creditors have been calling all morning. Not about my gnocchi."

"Want to take a ride?"

Richard thought of the leporid sarcophagus and the unpleasant task ahead of him. "Give me a minute." He shoved the box in the walk-in refrigerator and fled.

It was way past noon by the time Richard and Javi made their way back to the restaurant, arms fraternally around each other. They'd gone up the coast highway, the day so spectacular they had decided to continue all the way to Malibu, and once in Malibu they couldn't *not* stop off for a quick seafood lunch of *fritto misto* and beer on the pier, and then they ran into a chef friend who staked them to a round of *reposado* tequila. The only blip in the afternoon occurred after Richard bought yet another round of drinks for the group and his card was declined, but he laughed it off as having overspent for the restaurant and paid in cash.

It was late by the time they returned, and he went to check messages in his office—electric company, credit card company, linen supplier, bank. The only call he returned was from the car dealership verifying Javi's employment and a salary that was more wishful thinking than reality. When he arrived back in the kitchen, Javi had the box of rabbits out, butcher paper spread, with a splayed white body in the center.

"Looks like the Easter Bunny arrived early."

Richard forced himself to look at the matted fur. He lost it at the sight of the delicate, folded-back velvety ears. All the blood in his body sloshed down to his feet so that he had to hold on to the counter to keep from falling through the floor.

"Whoa, you okay, partner?" Javi asked.

"Not feeling so good."

"Why don't you leave this to me? Start on Annie's cake."

"I almost forgot." Richard went to the bathroom and splashed cold water on his face. What had happened to him? Unheard of—a chef with an aversion to cooking meat. The idea of stockyards made him faint. Boiling lobsters made him queasy. The easy acceptance of *foie gras*, roasted whole baby lamb, and, his own undoing, rabbit paralyzed him. He looked at his blotchy face in the mirror and considered googling "psychotic breakdown."

His shins itched to the point of him scratching himself raw; his doctor had diagnosed stress-related eczema. He had developed a tic under one eye that at random moments made him appear to be winking. Earlier that day in Malibu, it had happened in front of a toned young woman in spandex who, thinking he was being lewd, gave him the finger. Now he swallowed half a bottle of probiotics, washing it down with copious amounts of Pepto-Bismol in an attempt to curb the chronic indigestion, PUD (peptic ulcer disease), and irritable bowel syndrome that had started during the last few months and threatened to ruin the upcoming evening.

The enormous strain of trying to make the opening a success and at the same time cover for Javi's threatened implosion was wearing him down. On top of that, he felt guilt over Ann's working so hard and in good faith handing over all her money to him for the restaurant, some of which he had to hand over to Javi to keep various collection agencies off his back so

he would concentrate on designing the menu. Now Richard had to tact-
fully broach the matter of new car payments that were out of the question.

The itching grown unbearable, his medicated cream at home, in despair Richard headed back to the kitchen for olive oil to slather on his
raw skin. When in doubt, olive oil. Javi was on his cell phone, and when
he saw Richard, he scowled and went outside for privacy. Often Richard
wished he could invite Javi to live with them; just do away with the pre-
tense that the man was a fully functioning adult and treat him like the
willful, tantrum-prone five-year-old Freudian id he was.

As Richard finished up Ann's cake (Javi having mercifully taken over
the "rabbit issue," creating a fricassee with cilantro and onions as an
appetizer for that night), he had a stroke of inspiration and whipped up a
bowl of crème Chantilly. He had not had time to buy a present, but what
kind of present would it be anyway, with them both knowing it was Ann's
money that bought it? He went into his chaotic office, shoved whole stacks
of paperwork out of sight, and spread a long tablecloth for ten on the sag-
ging sofa, the ends puddling nicely. Standing back to assess the makeshift
effect, he raided the supply cabinet for votives and set them on every surface: the room itself turned birthday cake. He placed a butane Iwatani
brûlée torch at the ready to light them for Ann's arrival.

Ann let herself in through the front entrance of the restaurant. The
beauty of the dining room consoled her, despite the fact she was
tired and had a stomachache from all the Mars bars. It was her baby,
designed from scratch from notes she had taken from their favorite places
over the years. Instead of the modern, antiseptic dining spaces then in
vogue, theirs would have a rococo feel. The room had deep-red velvet
walls with chocolate-brown wood accents and was hung with ornamen-
tal mirrors in heavy gilded frames. On the center of each virginal white
linen tablecloth stood a small crystal vase, which would be filled with
choice blooms spotlit from a halogen light in the ceiling. The tables would
not have candles, which were an inefficient use of limited table space, but
hundreds of votives would be lit on shelves projecting from the walls.

Ann wanted each customer to feel like a prized truffle nestled inside a Valentine box of sweets.

That was the future. Right now she wanted nothing more than to go home, put on a bathrobe, and hole up in bed with a thick novel, but there stood Richard, inexplicably winking at her. He took her hand and led her to his office, the fiery room fragrant with melted wax and burned sugar. A rubber bowl of whipped cream stood on his desk.

"Strip," he said softly, "my sexy thirty-eight-year-old goddess."

She giggled.

"Where's Javi?"

"I sent him for ice. An hour-long ice trip to be exact."

The lit candles heated the room more quickly than Richard would have thought possible. Stripped down to his undershirt and boxers, he suddenly realized that the room was a classic firetrap. As he led Ann to the sofa, he tried to recall exactly where the new box of fire extinguishers had been stored.

Meticulously Richard basted her arm in a coat of whipped cream that he then licked off. "No fair!" Ann laughed, and he fed her dollops off his fingertips. He couldn't help himself—as much as he loved Ann, the whipped cream was making his throat so acidic he felt close to throwing up. He moved to another position, licked spoonfuls off her inner thighs, but the angle made his neck crick. He drove himself on, denying the pain, moaning to release some of the agony, which Ann mistook for passion, prompting her to grab his head and cant his neck at a forty-five-degree angle of torture as she kissed him. He buried his head in her cleavage to hide the tremoring like a Mexican jumping bean beneath his eye.

They made love. It was nice. Friendly. Comfort sex. She had the sense that Richard was clenched inside; his mind seemed far away. Because he had seemed to enjoy it so much, she grabbed his head again and gave him another hard, bad-girl kiss. Afterward Ann felt a purring contentment as she got dressed, as well as a stickiness under her clothes that she couldn't wait to go home and wash off. She was still wearing her good suit from the office—she had come straight there from another ten-hour day—but it seemed petty to complain when Richard was trying so hard. He was under such strain, she was surprised he even remembered her birthday. A dry cleaning bill and a potentially ruined wool skirt. Life could be worse than being desired by your husband under a mountain of whipped cream.

T hey sat in the restaurant's new kitchen with its gleaming stainless steel appliances, its spotless linoleum floor—within weeks the kitchen would never again be as quiet and pristine. Richard and Javi had cooked up a special five-course dinner and dragged a small table in from the dining room, complete with tablecloth and tapered candles.

Richard had pulled out a 1974 Louis Roederer Cristal Brut Rosé champagne, known for its silky bite and salmon color. They toasted.

"Did you braise the sirloin tips?" Javi asked.

"No, I thought the main dish and roasted broccolini would be enough." Javi winked at Ann. "Carrots scream, too."

They polished off Javi's rabbit appetizer, then a Roquefort-and-sautéed-apple quesadilla, an organic baby greens salad with hearts of palm, and then a mango ice as palate cleanser. Javier, the mad-genius chef, had created a new dish in honor of Ann's birthday: soba noodles with pink Florida prawns, braised bok choy, miniature scallops in soy sauce, rice wine, and serrano chilies. Richard's broccolini was brought to the table as an afterthought.

Javier's reputation for achieving culinary ecstasy had the tables booked up for two months solid from opening night. Every restaurant critic from Santa Barbara to San Diego planned to make the pilgrimage to their obscure location on the wobbly border of Santa Monica and Venice, braving chronic lack of parking and the abuse and urinary insults of homeless people, the indigent, and the belligerent who haunted the canyons of urban blight west of the 405. There were rumors of national foodies from *Esquire*, *Travel & Leisure*, etc., booking under aliases.

Javier's fiery temper, moderately good Latin looks, vulgar mouth, and lewd behavior toward anything female created an outsize personality that fit perfectly in a profession where chefs were under the onus of not only cooking delicious meals but also having that magic celebrity "it" factor promising that just around the corner the Big Break would happen, which would render same-week reservations a thing of the past.

The fire from the serranos was delightfully unexpected, but after the initial surprise one realized the taste was not quite right.

Richard's aversion to cooking meat was becoming a problem. It had started when he was a teenager, but then abated at CIA, Culinary Institute of America, where he had to learn how to french-cut a rack of lamb, divide a pork loin into chops, carve steaks, and grind meat and sausage. The constant pressure to perform prevented him from dwelling on the meats' previous incarnations—that is, until the master charcuterie/butchering course a year after he met Ann. It was an honor to be invited, and he was flown coach to France and put up at a youth hostel in the Marais, with a bathroom down the hall that had never seen a scrub brush. They couldn't afford the airfare for Ann to join him, and besides, she had just started at the law firm. Still, it was Paris. He was young and in love with food.

The pig slaughter set him back years.

Everyone knew it. The French were cruel eaters: *foie gras*, veal, live-boiled lobsters. Their philosophy affected all dishes, and all of it bothered Richard. Even tomatoes were blanched, peeled, cored, seeded, and whatever remained was then pureed and strained until all tomato essence had been deracinated. If there was a God, how could people peel asparagus? He considered switching to the pastry track, but the truth was that for all his modesty, his "Aw, shucks"-ness, his love of the anonymity and camaraderie of the kitchen, he wanted Emeril Lagasse superstardom. There had never been a celebrity vegan chef in the history of the world for a reason. One didn't open a restaurant on the strength of puff pastry and ganache. In the testosterone-filled world of chefdom, pastry was for pussies. So he cooked meat and suffered in silence.

When Javi left the table and disappeared after the main course, Richard grabbed Ann's hand and pressed it against his chest. "This is the happiest time in my life. Or it will be soon when we open. And it would mean nothing if you weren't by my side."

Ann wiped at her eyes. The serranos were killing her.

"You've sacrificed a lot. It hasn't been easy. Pretty soon it will be your turn."

"Her turn for what?" Javi yelled, out of sight, deep in the bowels of the walk-in refrigerator. "You two will finally have babies and make me an uncle?"

"My turn to go to art school," she answered. "A solo gallery show. Then children." Because even after the financial sacrifice of law school, the ungodly hours that hopefully soon would come to fruition in an offer of full partnership, Ann already had the sinking knowledge that this was not the life she wanted to be pursuing for the next thirty years. She was ready to spit the bit of family tradition.

Richard scowled at Javi's eavesdropping. He shrugged and gave Ann that goofy, lopsided grin that still had the power to charm her—he was her big, helpless, fuzzy puppy. "With the help of a little whipped cream?" Richard whispered.

The whipped cream foreplay had started during their days of courtship while he was still at culinary school. He was in downtown St. Helena during a sudden thunderstorm when he ducked under the overhang of a building to get out of the rain. Cowering in the corner was a thin young woman with the most intense green eyes he had ever seen. Inexplicably, she was wearing a pink satin dress and matching shoes that were drenched. She looked like a fairy gone bad. He said hi, and she bit her lip. He saw she was shaking.

"Can I help?"

"I'm scared of thunder."

Amazing. This Richard could do. He took off his jacket and wrapped her up, put his arm around her for warmth, then led her down the street to the best bakery in town where he fed her floury, raisin-studded sweet rolls and coffee while telling her cooking stories until the rain stopped. She was not a defrocked fairy, he found, but was in town for a wedding that she had now missed. Hours passed, and next thing they knew the sun was out.

"Can I cook you dinner?" he asked.

Back at his apartment, as he unpacked groceries, she opened his refrigerator to confront four shelves piled with cartons of whipping cream. He was on dessert rotation, and overachiever that he was, he practiced at home.

"But what do you do with bowl after bowl of whipped cream?" she asked.

She dipped her index finger deep in the bowl and swirled it. Then she raised her creamy finger to her lips and licked it clean. Slowly. She dipped and swirled again, dabbed it on Richard's lips until he caught on and began to lick her finger. The girl was afraid of thunderstorms but not calories. After that night, they flew up and down the state to see each other whenever a night opened up. By the time his dessert rotation was finished, they had both gained ten pounds, Ann's skin was milky soft, and they were in love.

N ow she leaned over to return Richard's kiss as Javi began singing. They stopped before their lips touched, turning toward the gaping refrigerator door where he stood holding Richard's cake of green-tea ganache between layers of rosewater-scented sponge cake, which blazed with candles as the room plunged into darkness. Richard joined in singing "Happy Birthday" and then "Feliz Cumpleaños."

The bonfire of flames in the sudden darkness blinded Ann. She felt grateful even though all this fuss embarrassed her. She took a huge breath, closed her eyes, and dreamed that soon her life as a painter would start, or her life as a mother, or as co-owner of a successful restaurant, even if she kept her law day job, which was really a day-and-night-and-weekends job. At least she had delivered Richard safely to a success that he so wanted. Ann felt that happiness rubbed off, like newsprint but in a good way. Once the restaurant took off, she hoped to finally quit the firm and work the front of the restaurant. At home she would convert the extra bedroom into a studio looking out over the canyon. Real life would finally begin. She wouldn't allow for the thought that perhaps she didn't have the talent, because why would someone have a desire for something that she wasn't good at?

Every firm Christmas party, Flask Sr. put his canvases up for the charity auction, and under his vengeful eye the rest of them were forced to bid. By playing it safe, had she already proved that she wasn't the real thing? But one had to eat, right? After all, wasn't that what all the last years of denial had been about? To achieve Richard's dream first, and then parlay his success into her own? Was that too crass? She couldn't imagine van Gogh or even Pollock thinking like this, but being an artist in the twenty-first century was financially becoming more and more a hobby, like poetry or scrapbooking. She closed her eyes and blew the candles out in a single hopeful puff, and they were plunged back into total darkness.

The truth was, she would settle for being the first face people saw when they came to the restaurant. She loved the idea of making people happy, even if it was as temporary a fix as a good meal.

"You can turn the lights back on," Richard said.

"I didn't turn the lights off," Javi said. "You did."

"Shit, a fuse," Richard said.

"Don't spoil the mood," Ann begged.

More candles were lit, a slightly lesser bottle, a 1998 Philipponnat Clos des Goisses Brut, was opened, and Ann made a prophetic toast: "May this restaurant's success be everything you two deserve."

"May it make us famous," Javi added.

Richard and Javi made a sloppy vow that they would remain lifelong friends. Running a restaurant wouldn't sunder that, as it had the relationships of so many of their peers from CIA.

"Besides," said Richard, stifling a belch, "I don't need to be the star."

A moment of uncomfortable silence opened into which Ann rushed to exclaim about the deliciousness of the cake because the truth that all three of them acknowledged, separately and in various combination, was that Richard wouldn't be a star even locked in a room by himself. Among his quiet charms, charisma was not one of them. He had no choice but to hitch his wagon on the psychopathic joyride that was Javi to even have a chance of creating culinary buzz. A restaurant was about more than just food, sacrilegious as that sounded. It was about branding, cloning copies across the gastronomic map in San Francisco, Honolulu, Las Vegas, New York, Miami, with the goal of later branching out into cookbooks, signature tableware, maybe even a show on the Food Network, etc.

They talked and drank another hour. Ann would later look back and consider that night the death knell of her innocence.

"I love you guys," Javi said, the alcohol turning him maudlin.

"Time to get home." Ann yawned. "I'm exhausted and have to be up early for a briefing."

"The little lawyer," Javi said, hugging her so hard that her shirt stuck to her sticky back. "You smell like *dulce de leche*."

"Let me fix that fuse first." Richard jumped at the chance to go outdoors in privacy and release some of the noxious gases building up inside him. The chilies were burning his esophagus, and there was a scary liquid rumbling in his stomach. He got a flashlight and went out to the alley.

Alone, Javi stared at Ann in the candlelight, his eyes made dreamy by too much alcohol.

"Stop it," she said.

"I'm remembering you also tasted like *dulce de leche*."

Richard came back in. "That's funny—nothing flipped." In the dim candlelight, he couldn't detect Ann's flushed face.

"Probably something electrical. I'll call someone in the morning," Javi said. "You two go on home."

"Are you sure?" Ann asked.

"Go be lovebirds."

But the next morning when Richard (recovering from last night's dinner with a panade of aspirin and antacids) got to the restaurant, Javi was still sitting at the table in the middle of the kitchen, drinking out of a bottle of their best tequila. A large ceramic cutting knife lay on the table in front of him, although so far he had only used it on limes. Clearly he had not been home yet.

"Did they fix it?"

"Seems I forgot to pay the bill. I put it on my credit card this morning."

"You could have written a company check."

Javi's handsome face darkened. Now it was Richard's turn to look at his partner more closely. He did not like what he saw. Purplish circles under his eyes, the eyes themselves bloodshot, not to mention his breath, which was both sour and alcoholic and vaguely canine. Richard worried about lighting a match too near him.

"Have you slept?"

In answer, Javi, ham actor, pushed a pile of bills across the table.

"Tell me it isn't as bad as it looks. Do that. Tell me," Richard said.

"It's fucking Armageddon!"

It was an acknowledged fact that if you knew Javi, you knew he was a spendthrift. Richard's mistake was in not learning the true scope of his debt before going into a partnership, which was in every bad way akin to a marriage without even the conjugal perks. As he flipped through the bills, his temples began to pound, his skin was drenched in a malarial ooze, and then Javi made it worse.

"Inez, that greedy sow, is suing me for more money. She says I lied and hid income. They froze the restaurant's account."

Javi had always been the wild playboy with women problems all through CIA. After he married Inez, Ann and Richard thought he'd calm down, especially after the baby was born, but he still stalked the pretty young sous chefs, the hostesses/wannabe actresses. Javi joylessly womanized all through his divorce, and this pile of bills was an ugly diary of debt for back alimony, child support, health insurance, workers' comp, rent, credit cards, utility bills, car payments, and a whole slew of unpaid disasters going back to and including student loans at Culinary Institute, going back even further to student loans for his first year of medical school, which he dropped out of, going all the way to the primordial debt of UC Riverside undergraduate. The ex-wife had sued and filed an injunction to freeze the restaurant's accounts, claiming he had misrepresented income, although the money was Ann and Richard's life savings, earmarked for a year's worth of rent, payroll, purchase of kitchen equipment, dining tables and chairs, china and stemware, cutlery, the services of an interior decorator and florists, all of which had already been contracted out. They had committed to a five-year lease, signed with personal guarantees. In the parlance of the food industry, they were cooked.

Things were so dire, Richard was actually roused to action. "I'll talk to Inez. I'll explain it's our life savings. She'll understand."

"Maybe not."

"Inez likes us."

"I might have misstated things, like that you embezzled money from me."

That Richard didn't even blink at this admission was an admission itself of how deep the trouble was.

"Just so you know, I need to leave town for a few days."

"Now?" Richard was going to kill him with that ceramic knife.

"I borrowed from some loan sharks to keep us afloat."

"Us?"

"And I took the rest of the petty cash to the casino last night. Guess what? I lost."

"That's the thing. I could win betting that you would lose."

Javi took a slug from the Cabo Uno Anejo. "Javi says, 'Let them eat blinis.'" He cackled, the careening laugh, hysterical and threatening, then veering over into self-pitying sobbing.

"They can't do this," Richard said, now considering using the knife on himself. "Ann will never forgive me. She'll leave."

"Ann will never leave you. Trust Javi on this."

Richard's insides had now gone to the last stage—hot, molten lava in danger of erupting any moment—the divergent tectonic plates of Javier (why was he suddenly referring to himself in the third person?), Ann, divorce, failure, penury, and possibly a future bout of shingles tearing him apart.

After Richard called Ann at work, she consulted with the only senior partner still there on a Friday, Flask Sr. Waiting while he finished up a phone call on a long, tubular Bang & Olufsen phone that came out from his ear like an ice pick, she stared at his latest artwork hanging directly behind his head on the wall—a grove of arthritic eucalyptus trees that looked as if they had a bad case of infectious skin disease.

"So before we start, since we are fellow artists, how do you like my new plein air piece?"

Ann nodded appreciatively, searching the canvas for something non-career-threatening to say. She was furious her artistic aspirations had somehow leaked out, and especially to a senior partner, who might use it to deny her the partnership that she didn't want. "It's like . . . I can actually smell the trees."

Of course. There had been a stupid morale-booster seminar months ago in a downtown hotel ballroom. Each of them had to stand up and tell what his or her hobby was, which was essentially a joke because, except for the senior partners, no one had time to sleep, much less have hobbies. "I'm a painter," Ann had said. "I mean, I'd like to be. Paint on weekends, that is. Someday. When I'm not working." She had kept on standing there, qualifying, like a punctured tire slowly leaking air.

When Flask got off the phone, she outlined the basic parameters of her "friend's" situation: the account had been frozen due to pending legal action, which could take *years* to resolve. Flask frowned. "What kind of friend are you?" He laughed, so Ann immediately backpedaled and tried to minimize the situation's severity. He informed her the creditors could indeed freeze the account if it was opened as a legal partnership. Of course she knew this, but she was looking for some kind of insanity loophole, covering the possibility of your partner losing it and proceeding to ruin your life.

"It's unfair," she said.

"That's the law, honey."

Now literally she was in the client's Italian-designed seat, and the view was very different. She knew only too well how she could be messed with, the agony and lack of ecstasy of interminable litigation, a long, slow bleed that won by attrition. Was this one of those karmic retribution things like in the movies? She felt deep remorse for causing Mrs. Peters's victory the day before. She reddened at the memory of the OxyContin gambit. Shame, *shame* on her.

Outside the senior partner's heavy, closed mahogany door, with its raised gold lettering that spelled out his name, Ann stood, realizing with a sense of premonition that she would never be behind such a door with letters spelling out *her* name; that the plush gray Berber carpet, the paneled walls, the tastefully spotlit artwork that had given her such a sense of permanence and security working there were *not* actually there for her at all. They were to instill awe and respect among clients, who were billed astronomically, by the hour, as they sat on those deep, ergonomically designed sofas in the waiting room, or enjoyed the espresso-pod coffee brought over by the discreetly sexy receptionist; the intention of the furniture, the offices, the fine accoutrements of lawyering was to lull, to make believe that the law had some weight to it, that the clients weren't at the mercy of chance, that their fates weren't left to the vagaries of interpretation. These partners, who were so tastefully and expensively dressed, whose whole presentation shouted success, were not saviors or even guides of the legal system; they were enablers. Like in Las Vegas, the house always won, and the Flask, Flask, Gardiner, Bulkington, Bartleby, and Peleg partners—mostly male, quickly walking, making adjustments midstride to go around the marooned and stationary Ann in the hallway—were sharks who kept moving, kept litigating, or died. Ann had made a terrible, terrible mistake, thinking herself a shark, spending all those years in law school honing a bloodlust she had no appetite for. Now, after a decade practicing law, she had to admit she didn't understand the first thing about the law; it was beyond right or wrong or justice; it was about hours billed and petty vendettas, and the lawyers were paid mercenaries sent out to do unfair battle. The last time Ann felt she had truly ministered justice was as a five-year-old, when she presided as judge over a friend who had stolen her toy: "Guilty," she had pronounced, "but still innocent." Ann hadn't gotten any smarter since. Drifts of briefs like snowfall blanketed her desk, covered and muffled every good intention. She could not bear the thought of growing old inside these walls; she had worked there ten years and did not have a single person whom she could truly call friend, if "friend" meant someone she could tell of her unhappiness in being there. The embarrassing truth was that she wanted to be loved, and people hardly ever loved, or even liked, their attorneys; they were a necessary evil, like dentists or hookers.

Mrs. Peters, riding high on her bonsai win, had sent a Swedish, pink-leather, hammered-silver cocktail shaker with a big "A" embossed on it as thanks. After Richard's call, Ann had stared at the extravagant accusation of it on her desk and then broken down in tears.

And then the revelation. It occurred to her that the court order might not yet have arrived at the bank. In a daze, Ann drove to the local branch and told the teller she needed to get a cashier's check for the entire total in the account. House down payment. To hide her shaking hands, she clutched her cell phone. The teller had been there only a week and was impatient to close up her window and get to her salsa class, all of which she told Ann as she processed the paperwork.

"I've always wanted to learn to dance," Ann said, light-headed, black spots floating in front of her eyes. "We're buying a second house in Mexico, and they demand all cash."

"Really?" The girl did it without question, impressed by Ann's expensive handbag, her expertly highlighted hair, the glasses that clarified nothing.

For the first time in her good-girl life, Ann got the adrenaline high of being on the wrong side of the law. She simply stole what was about to be stolen from her, but the cashier's check was a hot potato because any claim on the payee, Ann, would render it void. Her only option was to cash it somewhere fast. The only person she could call was her loyal, unprincipled best friend from law school, who also happened to be a kick-ass class-action attorney, Lorna Reynolds. Lorna would get off on the risk and, if necessary, handle any legal ugliness that arose.

In her less kind moments, Ann thought Lorna had lately turned a little neocon in her politics, but she preferred to remember the two of them as they had been a dozen years before, smoking pot and listening to rock music. Lorna's irreverence had saved her through a dark period.

According to Ann's family, becoming an attorney started with having to go to the right school. Her father and sister went to Yale; her brother rebelliously opted for Harvard. Ann had dutifully applied and gotten into both, with UCLA as her backup. Her siblings were back east when her mother was diagnosed with breast cancer. Ann could not, would not, leave her alone with her father, who, although not unkind, was incapable of transcending the cool logic of his profession. Exhibit A: He was incapable of boiling an egg. Exhibit B: He rose from the dinner table in the certain knowledge that the dishes somehow always made their way back to the cupboard clean without him. Ann's compromise was accepting the backup and living at home.

All families have their peculiarities, but it was impossible to describe to outsiders how shaming her decision was to them. Her father could barely look her in the eye; her siblings distanced themselves. They all thought her weak—everyone except her mother. Fifteen years later, her mother was fine, and Ann never once regretted her decision. But it was Lorna who got her through.

They used to joke about dropping out of law school and becoming groupies to some of the bands they were enamored of like American Music Club, the Talking Heads, the Red Hot Chili Peppers, the Rolling Stones, the Wallflowers, U2, Guns N' Roses, and Prospero, especially the lead singer, Dex Cooper, whom they met one night stone-cold drunk at the Troubadour. They were there pretending to be bad, wild girls and not buttoned-down law students. After plying them with whiskey sours (Ann's first), he invited them both to come back to his place, provided they could drive him since his license had been revoked courtesy of a DUI.

As luck would have it, Ann was driving. Dex promptly fell asleep in the backseat. She remembered getting lost as they wound up into the steep, overgrown canyons of the Hollywood Hills. The house was a throwback to the '50s, a glass-and-stucco bachelor pad at the top of the hill. As they walked to the front door, Ann noticed the yard was weed-choked. Inside, it smelled of cats, although none were in evidence. Dex quickly went to the bar, backed up by a plexiglass panel into the pool, very James Bond. Ann rolled her eyes at Lorna. Dex poured gigantic drinks and then took off his shirt.

"So what do you girls do?" he slurred.

"Go to school," Lorna said, gulping down her drink.

"Which high school?"

The girls dissolved into laughter while Dex patiently drank.

"Where's the bathroom?" Ann asked and made her escape.

The bathroom, along with the rest of the house, was filthy. It seemed Dex was camping rather than living there. She poured her drink down the toilet. When she came back to the living room, Lorna was French-kissing Dex on the sofa.

"I need to get home," Ann said.

"Curfew?" Dex asked. "Want to get high first?"

"No!" Ann said.

Lorna sat up and straightened her blouse. "Don't bother. Ann's a prude."

Dex nodded. "That's too bad."

Once they reached the driveway, they fell into each other's arms giggling.

"Oh my God," Lorna said. "Oh my God!"

"I know!"

"Dex Cooper!"

"You kissed him!"

"I would have given him a BJ if you didn't barge in."

"Lorna!"

"Dex Cooper!"

"Still."

They broke down in laughter all over again.

Later, Lorna said she was holding out for her number one, Axl Rose, as unlikely as that was to happen. Ann claimed to have always preferred Eddie Vedder, but it lay as an unspoken truth between them that Lorna had passed the wild test while Ann failed.

With the hot-potato check, Ann drove aimlessly in her Toyota as she dialed Lorna. "You won't believe the shit that has just covered my entire life."

Lorna directed her to go to the nearest branch of her bank, which she

GPS-ed on her iPhone, and told her to put the signed-over check in the night deposit box, directed into Lorna's account. "I'll figure the rest out. Lie low. I've got contacts at my bank. Come by my office tomorrow, and I'll give you cash. Then get out of town for a while so you can't be deposed. Out of sight and the limits of jurisdiction, out of mind."

The previous April, Ann and Richard had been to their first and only session of couple's therapy, courtesy of a social acquaintance Ann knew through one of her professional women's groups. The problem, as Ann saw it, was that she hardly knew her husband anymore. For the last ten years, they had both worked so hard they never saw each other. She had deferred her dreams of being a painter to first creating a successful restaurant for Richard, and that required earning money as an attorney, while what she wanted—a happy life with Richard—was moving further and further away till it was just a blur on the horizon. She was tired of catering to her spoiled clients, people who had either inherited their wealth or earned it too easily, dealing with children in the guise of adults for her livelihood. As she sat in the office, she realized the miscalculation of being there. She did not need to pay someone to tell her what was wrong. She needed a new life.

She knew the therapist, Eve, from her Women Ethically For the Environment (WEFE) group that met monthly at various trophy houses on the Westside, and served organic vegetables paired with expensive imported alcohol. Eve's style had impressed Ann, and the monthly WEFE meetings had made improvements in her life that made her feel nominally better, such as: she now recycled, ate organic and grass-fed, and wrote out checks (albeit for small amounts) to various international NGOs to make clothes and furniture out of recycled garbage.

At Eve's office, they sat marooned on a Balinese opium bed carved from sustainable teak.

"Should I take off my shoes?" Ann asked, uncomfortable and unhappy. Through Eve's eyes, Ann was aware that Richard appeared slump-backed and slope-shouldered, that his potbelly topped his belt like a muffin rising over its tin, or, in Richard's case, a brioche. Eve's husband, Guy, who attended black-tie environmental events with her, was a former B-list actor who now worked strictly as an activist, allowing him free time to spend every day at the gym maintaining his six-pack abs. He was on the correct side of open land, clean water, sustainable farming, and baby seals. The only thing that sustained Ann through her present mortification was that years ago, at an event, Guy had put his hand on her ass and made a pass, a klutzy move that she had deflected. Richard would never do that.

"Shoes on, shoes off. Ann, do what makes you feel comfortable."

Which was impossible, because leaving the room was the only thing that would accomplish that. Ann dropped one pump, and then the other, with a loud clatter on the Saltillo tile floor. "Nice floors," she said to cover the noise.

"Eduardo is the best. I'll give you his number," Eve said. "He's a wizard. We just came back from a design trip to an island in French Polynesia. We discovered exotic woods. The heat and the light. The place is pure sex."

"Did Guy like it?" Ann asked.

"He couldn't come. So let's get to work. Now what I'd suggest is for you and Richard to lie side by side and close your eyes."

Ann, grateful for the privacy of closed lids, felt herself burning with shame. It drove her crazy how Eve repeated their names back to them, as if reading off index cards, as if they might forget who they were. Too late, Ann saw the conflict of interest in discussing one's personal issues with someone one ate canapés with. Someone who took her floor man to the South Seas. She would have to quit the environmental group and find another cause. A waste because she didn't believe in therapy—in fact, prided herself on being the problem solver for others—and this exposure made her feel doubly humiliated. Thank God for the small favor that Eve had revealed that Guy had cheated on her numerous times (this *after* the hand-on-the-tush incident), and had come to see *her* a year ago about a divorce that never materialized.

Eve coughed and spoke in a soft voice. "Now, Ann and Richard, I want you two to picture where you want to be a year from now."

Ann moaned, her eyes still closed, poisoned by her own words used against her. This was the question she had posed to Eve the year before, her standard for divorce cases. Eve had stolen it. Apparently the answer for Eve ended up being staying with Guy, whom she claimed had re-formed. The law had shown Ann that people rarely changed. At best, the behavior went inward, underground, where lust carved out a dark and dangerous hole in one's heart.

"See," said Richard. "Always a negative, knee-jerk reaction."

"Could I have some water?" Ann asked.

"Of course," Eve answered. "Flat or sparkling?"

After Ann downed the full glass in a few gulps, Eve continued.

"I'll have to use tough love with you two. I'm sending you on a trip alone together. Tell me the first thing that pops into your mind, Rich-ard, for a romantic place."

"Romantic?" Richard repeated, seemingly stumped by the meaning of the word, as if he were on a quiz show. "Something French?"

"Good! Now, Ann, a landscape that speaks to you."

"A desert," she said, to be contrarian. Fat chance they were going anywhere with the restaurant about to open. They had no money to go on vacation, but she wasn't about to admit that either.

"Now we're getting somewhere!" Eve was so excited she clapped her hands. "You're building a vision of the future together. Let's refine. Richard?"

"Desert? You hate the desert—"

"No, Richard, please," Eve said. "No judgment."

But both of them knew judgment was all that was left.

"Okay," he said, narrowing his eyes in an effort to undo Ann's choice. "Ocean."

"That pretty much leaves Algeria," Ann said.

"Okay, okay. You're making it tougher," Eve conceded.

"A desert island!" Richard yelled.

"That's it! Perfect!" Eve shouted. "I know just the place. Picture water the palest blue. Sand blinding white. The breeze is warm and caressing. No crowds, no kids. It's like the world has disappeared, and it's only the two of you. With thousand-count Sferra cotton sheets and the best French wine. Here," she said.

"What?"

"Open your eyes."

Ann saw a brochure with pictures not unlike the tropical screen savers she drooled over in her office. "It's lovely," she said.

"It's required. Don't come back till you've gone."

Ann and Richard never went back to therapy.

I t was the beginning of high season in the South Pacific. Although there were still plenty of vacancies at the bigger resorts, Ann had her own reasons for seeking out the most isolated, lonesome destination she could find, preferably sans telephone, WiFi access, or electricity.

She had been obsessed with islands since she was a child. Had it started with *Treasure Island*, continued through *Gilligan's Island* reruns (while her friends debated whether they wanted to be Ginger or Mary Ann, she had always wanted to be the Professor)? Had it ignited with that treacly remake of *The Blue Lagoon* with Brooke Shields? All the endless incarnations of *Mutiny on the Bounty*? Had it solidified through multiple viewings of *Swiss Family Robinson* and *Island of the Blue Dolphins* (she preferred the book)? Her obsession wasn't even diminished by the depressingly realistic Tom Hanks movie *Cast Away*, although the relationship with Wilson, the volleyball, was a disturbing glimpse into the void.

Sure, she had the same triad of tropical island screen savers as everyone else, except for everyone else it represented a vacation, with the promise of alcohol and mindless sunbathing. For Ann, it was something without which her life would remain unfulfilled. These were not the ideal circumstances to live out this fantasy, but really, when would it be ideal? No man was an island, but maybe a woman could be.

She charged the whole trip on their last credit card that still had room on it and then went out shopping for the most expensive flip-flops she could find—beautiful Italian ones with jewels and buckles sewed on the thin, butter-soft leather straps. That she couldn't afford them seemed even more reason to have them now.

When Richard came home from the restaurant and saw the sales receipt, he pounded his fist on the desk till his skin was bruised.

He was at the vertigo-inducing, ruthless edge of defeat that he'd stepped back from so many times before. It had finally gotten too hard. Richard was tired to death, his body going rogue on him, exhausted by the relentless, penny-pinching life that had befallen them. He revolted from the cheap therapist psychobabble optimism of Eve: things would probably *not* get better. They were screwed. He would not utter the lie that things would work out because actually it looked like the Dark Horseman of the Apocalypse himself had ridden up. Richard clutched his chest, worried that he might be having a heart attack that their shitty piecemeal insurance would not cover. So be it.

Then Ann showed him the bag of their stolen, about-to-be-stolen-from-them money.

"You could be disbarred," Richard whispered.

"I'm tired of the law," she countered.

By bedtime the next night they were on a plane, hurtling over the vast light grid of Los Angeles, the plane flinging itself into the darkness of sky and ocean that was farther west. Ann knew enough about the law to know they weren't worth pursuing out of the country. Criminal intent in this case was a comfortably gray area.

Ann looked around and wondered, did other people have a fantasy of how life should be lived? Would any of them pick up and change their circumstances if given the opportunity? She had the fantasy part down, but did she have the guts?

They clinked umbrella-stabbed cocktails at thirty thousand feet. "Think of it as our first vacation." Ann took another sip of her drink.

In the old days, California was the end of the line, but now, with the forces of globalization, one could just keep flinging oneself farther and farther west, hopefully landing somewhere that fulfilled one's dreams of happiness before one ended up back in the place one started.

# Unnamed Atoll Somewhere in the Tuamotu Archipelago

*Queequeg was a native of Kokovoko, an island far away to the West and South. It is not down in any map; true places never are.*
—MELVILLE, *Moby-Dick*

The water surrounding the atoll was the green that green would be if it were drained from a bowl and only its ghost residue remained against the white porcelain. The memory of green, a promise of green. From the plane, the water appeared so translucent as to be almost invisible. The concept of a desert isle became concrete in Ann's mind. After all, that's what she specialized in with her clients—turning emotions into concrete plans. Sometimes it was enough just to have a plan. Which this wasn't. This was pure impulse.

Looking down on the bleached, arid white of her doughnut-shaped future, conveying as it did a terrible sense of solitude, isolated and alone in its universe of water, she was afraid the concrete would not work for Richard and herself. What was this thing, the pursuit of happiness, that moved out of reach as you approached it? Was the emphasis on the wrong word? Was it simply about pursuit? Did said happiness evaporate when one got within proximity of it, moving off to lure one from yet another difficult, forward location? A fata morgana of the soul? Or, as in their case, did the chance at happiness just take a headlong dive off a cliff?

They climbed out of the small plane and crawled unsteadily off the wing, cramped legs and aching backs from the long flight from the coast, the longer overnight stay in crowded, noisy Papeete, where they had sat in the sweltering cab, stuck in traffic on the lagoon-side road, diesel fumes spewing from the truck in front. The buildings were defeated and ratty, patinaed by weather. Oily and trash-strewn water lapped at the docks. Tourists moved in bored raids on the stores. It could have been a particularly ripe neighborhood around San Pedro or Long Beach. Paradise seemed very far away.

As soon as they landed, Richard's cell had begun ringing—Javi.

"Don't answer it," Ann said.

Richard looked miserably at the flashing caller ID screen, then switched to vibrate, and every time it did, he winced. Finally, Ann grabbed the phone and flung it out the window of the cab. It bounced on the sidewalk and plopped into the viscous water.

"We can't afford roaming charges," she said.

That night they couldn't get to the restaurant the hotel chef had recommended (a matter of honor in the profession that he sent them to a true foodie place) because the main streets in Papeete were shut down, protesters clogging the thoroughfares, choking traffic to a standstill. They waved signs and banners in French with drawings of what looked like nuclear mushroom clouds atop palm trees: MORUROA E TATOU, ARRETEZ NUCLEAIRES, VERS UN MONDE SANS NUCLEAIRES, PROTEGEZ NOS ENFANTS, NON PLUS SECRETS, COMPENSATION, RESTITUTION.

"Didn't they stop testing decades ago?" Ann asked the driver, who was from the Philippines.

"These people spoiled. Keep showing cancer and three-headed fish, tourists stop coming. Then how happy will they be?"

Blocked, they turned back and ate an overpriced fifty-dollar hamburger at the hotel.

The next morning on the way back to the airport, they had the taxi stop at a downtown bank specified by Lorna. Ann went in and came out with her tote bag perceptibly heavier. The island-jumper to Rangiroa in the more remote Tuamotu Archipelago was only an hour flight, but they sat stranded on the tarmac for three hours while the details of a possible strike by the airport personnel were hammered out. Ann had read about sun damage and mosquitoes, and wore cargo pants, a shirt, and a base-ball cap made of SPF-treated fabric, which she now had to roll up as she sweltered in the cockpit.

"Don't you have any luggage?" the American pilot, Carl, asked when they handed him Richard's backpack.

"We travel light."

But Ann was staggering under the weight of her tote bag, which she kept glued to her side.

Since they were the only passengers, Carl propped open the passen-ger door for a breeze, pulled out some cold beers, and offered them a round. He was in his fifties and had a weathered, castaway look. He flew the plane barefoot.

"Don't worry. Things will straighten out," he said.

"Does this happen often?" Ann asked.

"Yup."

Ann was used to timing not only her lunch breaks but also her bath-room stops. The casual disregard of a schedule unnerved her. She couldn't remember the last time she had nothing to do. In LA, everyone worked themselves to death, to exhaustion, to hysteria, for the day when the phrase "I'll have my people call your people" was not ironic. The new status symbol in the first decade of the twenty-first century was lack of time, and the more people you employed to do the everyday mundane, the more you rose among your peers, so Ann's clients employed not only maids and gardeners, pool men and personal assistants, nannies and au pairs and private chefs, but also hairdressers and facialists who came to their houses, along with yoga and Pilates instructors, personal wardrobe buyers, astrologists and nutritionists, pet walkers and masseuses. There were even rumors of a man who went around the Westside and adjusted all the manual clocks in one's house to compensate for daylight savings time. Ann had neither time nor people.

Carl was a former army pilot who'd flown scores of missions in the Middle East. "Done with that life," he said. "This is paradise. You'll get used to it." Still undecided, the air tower finally allowed their small plane to leave while holding back the larger Airbuses. "See, I told you things would work out. And if they didn't, at least we got beer."

When they landed on the deserted coral airstrip, there was no one to greet them.

"What happens now?" Ann asked.

"Your boat ride to the main resort, then on to your final destination. That place is as remote as it gets. I never thought Loren would get any business." Carl shrugged and began checking the engine, ignoring them.

An hour later, a small motorboat trailing a black fan of smoke roared up to the dock. A tall, gaunt man, shirtless, skin turned the shade and texture of ironwood, waved his arms at them as if in long-lost greeting.

"Loren, you SOB. Where've you been?" Carl shouted.

"Here and there, my friend."

"Your guests are here and now. I have to pick up a fishing charter in two hours on Mooréa, and I'm late. How about that?"

Loren jumped over the side of his boat and tumbled face-first into the water.

The pilot cracked up laughing. "Yeah, man, you've been here and there in a good bottle of rum."

"Where's their luggage?"

"They travel light."

Loren turned to look at Richard and Ann.

She shrugged. "It's not a crime."

Loren swept out various debris from the boat, and hauled out a few plastic garbage sacks. He and Carl exchanged desultory local gossip in French.

"Put the sacks in Cleo's Dumpster while I keep her busy." Loren went inside the customs building/grocery store/petrol station/restroom.

Ann pulled Carl aside. "Is he okay?"

"It's hard to dump trash. Can't bury it—the ground is too water-logged. No place for a dump on an atoll."

"I meant his drinking."

Carl pondered the question as if it might be valid. Tourists were their lifeblood, and locals had to stick together. Still, Loren didn't make it easy. "Oh, he's drunk all the time. Perfectly safe. Frankly I'd be more worried if he was sober." He looked Ann over and liked what he saw. So would Loren. Carl still had the rigidity and squareness of being military, and he found Loren's open debauchery distasteful. "A word to the wise—he likes the ladies. If it's female, he'll try to jump it." That should set Loren up for a fun, tense little vacation.

"I can take care of myself," Ann said.

When Loren emerged from the building, he squinted at her. She looked like a hazmat worker getting ready to defuse a bomb. "No good. You must change for the ride. Much waves and water." He motioned with his hands, water flowing down his face and over his chest, which he pushed out in an approximation of air breasts. "Wear the hat and shirt for sun over the bathing suit. Sandals so that the coral does not cut your feet." He gave her a tired, worn smile, his eyes distant, the same transparent blue-green as the surrounding water.

"What's that smell?" he asked, coming close to her.

"DEET."

"Hand me your bag," he said.

"That's okay."

"Ah, one of those angry American fem-lib types."

She carried the bag into the customs building to change, turning just in time to see Loren retch over the side of the boat.

They were supposed to go straight across the lagoon and then on to the more remote *motu* where their lodgings were, but Loren mumbled about difficulties getting supplies. Ann had overheard Carl mention a burned-out engine and saw money exchange hands. They were comped a night at the fancy main resort, and would meet up in the morning to continue out.

Beyond jet lag and on their way to serious collapse, Richard and Ann agreed, grateful to be stationary with the prospect of a night's uninterrupted sleep.

Ann stood looking down at their aquarium coffee table, surveying the rocks, coral, and fish suspended in the water below as if in blue amber.

"What are we doing here?" Richard asked, not expecting even the effort of an answer. He flipped on the flat screen and searched for the Cooking Channel. "We could at least be in Paris or Nice. Eating to die for."

"I'm sick of food."

"Oh, that's nice."

When she had first met him, Richard had been wire thin and passionate about being a great chef. They would eat at restaurants, and if he approved, he would bang his hand down on the table in approval. She found his excitement sexy. Now he had what was commonly known as "chef's slump." A combination of too much tasting and too little time out in the sun doing things like jogging. The extra pounds gave him a ponderous, rolling gait and fallen arches.

"I'm sick of fancy food. I'd be fine if I never touched another mole again." Oaxacan Mole Negro was Javi's signature dish. Ann had turned cruel.

Despite all the water and humidity, the billowing pink clouds on the flat horizon, there was a great impression of dryness on the islands that made her parched. She downed the small green bottles of mineral water in the minibar one by one.

"You know those are ten bucks each? A dollar a swallow," Richard said, reading the in-room menu.

He felt sorry, culpable for his own part in the restaurant fiasco, but still he couldn't stop himself from complaining. He wanted to get back to LA and somehow fix things. Maybe Javi could explain the situation to the bank, or better yet to Inez. Maybe the loan shark would be interested in having a personal chef to work off the debt? Even if it took another ten years to set things straight, that was better than standing still, there, which was basically nowhere, the end of the earth, doing nothing. "We could go home tomorrow. Return the money. Start over. I mean, what's the plan here?"

"The plan is to not have a plan right now."

Had she really just said that? She had told the human resources person at the firm that a family emergency had come up, and she would be out of town indefinitely. If this wasn't an emergency, she didn't know what was. If her actions were discovered, she might be fired. Even if she wasn't dismissed, the hint of impropriety would blow her chances of making partner.

They picked their way gingerly across the narrow beach of crushed coral, under a scraggly row of desiccated palms. The place gave off the ramshackle aura of a B-movie set. Felled, diseased coconut trees were scattered throughout the beach, victims of the last hurricane, poisoned by the salt water. Neat little pyramids of coconuts were stacked here and there, resembling rusted cannonballs or shriveled heads, some already splitting open, sprouting shards of neon-green leaf.

At the hotel bar, they sipped drinks prickling with more paper umbrellas. Ann's stock-in-trade irony, her anger-tinged sarcasm, had been declared strictly verboten on this trip as per Richard. It almost killed her to not make a quip about the European diver set sprawled around the hotel, wearing Speedos the colors of tropical fish, sporting long, unkempt hair, pierced and inked body parts, trying for the vintage Richard Gere, Mick Jagger, Steven Tyler looks of the '80s. She felt like a downed electrical wire, bouncing, snapping, smoking, useless.

After another round of drinks, they held hands, giggling as fish passed under the glassed insets in the floor. Ann remembered, as if she had forgotten, that she really did love Richard, and that it was just bad luck and contrary fate that had estranged them.

"Let's go have a feast," she said.

On the way to the dining room, the concierge waved them over with an urgent message. Richard blanched as he read the note. "It's Javi. How did he know we were here?"

"Lorna might have told him." She was disappointed that their secret was already out. She had wanted to make Javi suffer even as she told Lorna to look after him.

"He's says he's taking care of things." Richard blinked. "He says he loves us."

"Oh."

"Let's try to be happy tonight. Keep it light."

"What do you say we try the tuna carpaccio?" she said as a peace offering.

"Sure."

Their courtship had been a gastronomic whirlwind. Food their lingua franca. He had courted her through all the great winery-restaurants of Napa, courtesy of his school connections, teaching her to pair a zinfandel with an heirloom tomato pasta sauce. They visited San Francisco and the great kitchens in Chinatown dedicated to dim sum, where she sampled rice noodle rolls, egg tarts, and chicken's feet. When she was swamped with work, they stayed in LA, trying the unique fusions of Cal-Mex, the mysteries of blood-orange margaritas and grilled mako shark tacos. It wasn't until she met Richard that Ann understood that food could be sexy.

The tuna came, ruby fleshed, on a bed of emerald arugula.

"Are we a couple?" Richard asked as his fork hovered over a bite of tomato-and-caper-topped fish.

"Of course," Ann said. "Yes, definitely. Yes, yes, yes," she said, but it came out, *Shush, shush, shush.*

"Okay."

"Are we on the lam?" She giggled, drunk beyond the abilities of mere alcohol.

Outside, across from the pool filled with fluorescent-suited children, stood Loren, tattered shorts the color of driftwood riding low on his narrow hips, talking with the hotel manager. Ann didn't care for his type, or the type he seemed to be: a hustler, maybe a dissolute, once-upon-a-time gigolo? Blasted good looks. Unlike the tourists—doughy white and sunburned pink, swaddled in garish tropical prints—Loren's dry, weathered self blended in naturally on the island. And yet, in the middle of all the high spirits of tourists on vacation, the laid-backness of the natives and expats who lived there, Ann sensed that for the three of them—Loren, Richard, and herself—things were deadly serious. Loren's sepulchral gaze across the pool alarmed her. She was pretty positive she didn't want him as their host.

L oren had had it with Steve, the manager. Loren's collection of huts *rustique* had a loose reciprocal agreement with the main resort. Alone, the place was too financially unviable in its remoteness to be kept supplied, despite the steep price tag for the eco-experience of existing without electricity—as in no light, air-conditioning, TV, computer, WiFi (yes, he did have to explain that)—and with the ban on cell phones equipped with long-range GPS satellite, as well as children under eighteen. They had worked out a symbiotic relationship because Loren did provide an *expérience sauvage*, and there was a certain clientele that hungered for that exclusive, minimalist luxury. Ironically, two decades before, Loren had had the real experience he was now selling on these same beaches, minus the mosquito-net canopy beds, plunge pools, and gourmet dinners. For him it had just been the magic of grilling fish over a fire and sleeping on a mat.

The problem was that Steve wanted to tack on another 10 percent for groceries and alcohol.

"You're killing me," Loren said.

"Listen, my costs are going up. If I don't pass them on, I start losing money."

"Occupancy has been bad. I've had to refurbish some bungalows. Bad timing."

Steve frowned. Steve was a prig. In his thirties with salt-and-pepper hair and a soft voice, he could have passed for an English butler except for the Polynesian shirt and flip-flops.

"I'm not running a charity for you out there."

"How long have you been in the islands?" Loren asked, knowing beforehand the answer. "Let me explain to you. I am your bling. Your celebrity bait. I'm what brings out the travel writers for their castaway experience. Without me, you're just another tiki lodge with second-rate food and a fake pearl farm with low-grade product brought in from the Philippines. No Lindsay Lohan, no Sarkozy. No *New York Times* travel spreads, no *Travel & Leisure* awards, no *Le Monde*, not even TripAdvisor. *Comprenez-moi?* Do you hear me?"

Steve's face had gone boiled-lobster red. He resembled a balloon under pressure of bursting.

"I've been here over twenty-five years," Loren said. "I'll be here long after you've packed up your bags and gone back home. What I require is loyalty. And I repay it. Otherwise I cut you off. I'll get you fired. It will be so bad, you'll never want to see sand again the rest of your days."

"I'm going to take a loss on everything I give you," Steve squeaked out.

"I'm glad we have this understanding. If you ever get a lady friend, the stay's on me. On your next pickup from the airport, I need you to give Cooked's brother, Teina, a lift."

"Where's he been?"

"He just got out of prison in Papeete. Long story you would rather not know."

"Wonderful. You want me to be your mule and run drugs, too?"

A beach ball rolled up and bounced against Loren's ankle. He picked it up and tucked it under his arm while he finished talking with the manager, who appeared to be suffering sunstroke. The children in the pool waited in a hushed silence. Ann, too, held her breath, expecting . . . what? A deflating slash with a long knife? Before she could say anything to Richard, the teak face cracked wide again, flashing teeth, and Loren high-stepped like a comical bird straight into the water, holding the ball overhead. The children raced, joyfully screaming, to the other side as he lobbed it across and then proceeded to play catch.

Ann laughed.

"What's funny?" Richard asked, deep into his study of the menu.

"Our host," Ann said. "Get a lock for the bag."

On their way through the lobby to the gift shop for the lock, there was a commotion at the front desk. A man was being carried out on a stretcher.

"What happened?" Richard asked.

Steve shrugged, restored from his run-in with Loren by a change of clothes and a stiff shot of whiskey. "Bends. He was an experienced diver, but he stayed down too long. Rushed the decompression."

"That can happen?"

"They get carried away."

"I had no idea."

Steve gave his official smile. "We give a complimentary first diving lesson."

"Not for this guy," Richard said.

"Polynesia is all about what's under the water. The land part is only a glimpse of her real beauty. If you're careful, nothing will happen. This is the safest place in the world."

Unless, Steve thought, you are unlucky enough to get tied up with grizzled old-timers like Loren. Steve liked this couple despite the fact that they came without luggage, which boded poorly for tips. They had not slipped him a hundred to get upgraded to the sunset side of the over-water bungalows. Besides that, he was being forced to comp their stay tonight and (if you factored in Loren's discount) everything they ate and drank when they got to Loren's *motu*.

"What do you think?" Richard asked Ann. "It is free." It became suddenly imperative to squeeze every last dime of value out of this trip.

"Go," she said, and to her surprise he did.

A nn escaped back to their air-conditioned bungalow and dropped on the bed shrouded in white mosquito netting. Alone. In the world's honeymoon capital. Absurd that she was disappointed; they were as far from the circumstances of romance as could be imagined. It seemed impossible that their whipped-cream-seduction birthday dinner was less than a few days in the past. Why shouldn't Richard be signing up for each and every thing that brought him a moment of escape? Still. In the old days, he would have eagerly followed her back.

On their first night together, Richard had inexplicably left the bedroom before they made love to go check that the doors were locked, the windows bolted, the gas on the stove turned off, and then he tested the smoke detectors. Odd, but Ann liked a guy who took care of things.

When she came out of his bathroom in his old T-shirt, he was lying on the bed, naked except for a towel neatly draped across his hips. She had giggled. Why the towel? Modesty? To protect her purity? Surely not. Nuzzling his ear, she decided it was more like those fancy restaurants where they bring your entrée under a silver *cloche*, set it down in front of you, and then fling the cover off before your eyes. *Voilà!* Even though you already knew perfectly well what you ordered.

She had never dated a man who fed her so well. Food was love, and Richard lavished it on her, brewing her espresso in the morning and making her freshly baked brioche. Sometimes Dutch pancakes, sometimes Mediterranean omelets. He packed her off with a lunch bag of Parisian-ham-and-arugula sandwiches with olive tapenade, pistachio *cantucci*.

Now, their life in tatters, he went off diving. Where had her protective, nurturing Richard gone? Amusing himself despite her torment. Ten years, every year since law school, lopped off. Ann worried because she knew from long professional experience that relationships only continued on some basis of parity, to be determined by the two parties. Where was that parity now?

The deep dark unspoken reason that she couldn't entirely blame Richard was that she, Ann, ruthless lawyer to the stars, aspiring big fish, had not done due diligence on Javi as a business partner because he was Richard's best friend, his best man at their wedding, the intended godfather of future children that they could probably no longer afford to have—and of course because of The Lapse, although she had banished it from being a factor in her thinking. Or had she? The 101 of law school: In business, you have no friends. She had known better, yet obviously she had not.

Richard came back hours later, lips and fingers pruned, exhilarated. "You have no idea! The fish!" He promptly lay down and fell asleep.

Ann dozed until midnight, then was wide-awake. Jet lag and worry made rest impossible. Perhaps she had been too hard on Richard—didn't he deserve any break from the tension that he could get? What was so bad about being underwater, looking at Technicolor fish, if it helped you forget your problems? She tugged on him, nibbled on his shoulder, but he swatted her away, unwilling to rise back up to consciousness.

She rose and stepped out on the deck, closing the glass door behind her to seal in the coolness. Better that Richard didn't wake, that she didn't make her desperate effort at intimacy. The air lay hot and close, heavy as if she were in a sauna; the lagoon a pellucid blue under the moon, inviting as one of those azure martinis they served in the hotel bar. Richard had compared it to drinking pool water, but Ann topped him, claiming it was like drinking antifreeze. She climbed down the steps of the ladder and dipped her toes, surprised at how deliciously inviting it felt.

They had both known what a wild card Javi was—brilliant and passionate and petty and malicious and, on top of it all, careless. Was it even possible that she once had thought she loved him, that she had considered leaving Richard for him? That was years ago, in the way past. Javi and she had put it behind them, yet this betrayal stung all the worse for it. Wasn't there still some love, some protectiveness for her? For Richard, whom he supposedly loved as a brother? But she knew deep down in her heart that Javi was hurting the worst of all.

The scariest thing was that a secret part of her rejoiced at the news of Javi's profligacy, the restaurant's demise, her professional ruin. It forced her to do what she had been too cowardly to do otherwise: crush family expectations, risk the censure of friends and colleagues, endure her own guilt over failing Richard financially. She might very well have plodded on until retirement on the unhappy path she had picked. That was all over now.

Ann pulled her nightgown over her head and slid naked into the water, which had a refreshing bite to it once she was fully submerged. Underwater, rocks and bursts of coral appeared like dark clouds in the distance. The world turned topsy-turvy. She went on her back—the stars overhead hung ripe and heavy like fruit. Time passed, unmarked, as if she had fallen asleep, dreaming of floating, or floating while dreaming, when something slippery, cold, and bone-crushingly powerful brushed underneath her bare back, lifting her ever so slightly up out of the water. Out of nowhere came the image of Loren, teak chest and narrow hips, pressing against her. She pushed the thought away, dutifully replaced it with the matrimonially sanctioned image of Richard, before she flipped over on her stomach, looking down into the water in time to catch the pound of something dark throbbing away through the water even as she reached out her hand to touch and caress the danger at her fingertips.

She lifted herself to the bottom step of the ladder and sat shivering in the moonlight.

A mistake to have left the firm citing a personal emergency, handing her caseload over to a coworker who would undoubtedly bad-mouth her now. This would be seen as weakness. One of the senior partners, Peleg, whose wife of thirty-five years died of cancer, managed to put in a half day after the morning funeral. No mercy would be shown to Ann.

She didn't always hate the law.

During her summer breaks from law school, she interned for eccentric Professor Faucett, who drove a beat-up old VW van and lived in a shack in the shabby part of Silver Lake, brilliantly defending clients against corporations. Ann spent all-nighters, all-weekenders, with a group of a half dozen other idealistic types known as the "Faucetts," who literally ate and slept in order to come to work, driven by the passion he inspired to do good.

Faucett had bad teeth, frizzy gray hair, and irregular laundry service, but none of that mattered because he was beating up the bad guys. After taking out living expenses (minimal), paying alimony (hefty) to a wife in the Palisades, who was not about to wait for the meek to inherit the earth, and child support (hefty) for their daughter, who attended private school and drove a BMW convertible, Faucett plowed every remaining last dime into defending the defenseless.

Ann was as in awe of Faucett's selflessness as she was appalled by the wreck of his personal life. From his example, she, too, longed to do good. That summer she liked feeling that what she did mattered. She loved bolting out of bed in the morning like a legal knight in shining armor. But everything around her, from the expensive clothes in the

Beverly Center to the big houses in Bel Air and Brentwood, suggested that the direction Faucett had taken was a fool's path, one not capable of being followed, as impossible to replicate as trying to imitate Mother Teresa.

Just as in med school, where all the first-years professed a desire to help mankind and by the fourth year were clawing for specialties in dermatology or plastics, Ann noticed during the last year of law school that the aspirations of her fellow Faucetts underwent a seismic shift. Gone was the talk of pro bono work and public defenders. Now they were trying to guess the needs of the big firms: Patent defense? Estate planning? Now it was the address of the firm, the view from the office, the make of one's car that determined one's choices.

She never got in touch with Faucett again after being hired by FFBBP because she couldn't bear confessing that the summer had been the equivalent of a moral one-night stand. She had sold out when the concept was still a valid one. Now guilt over selling out was as quaint and old-fashioned as knitted doilies, what with A-list actors hacking sheets through Kmart, and famous lawyers making cameos on TV shows. She joined the ranks of the dissatisfied, hating her job and dreaming of the day she could retire early and follow a passion—painting, or producing artisanal cheese, or deoiling penguins.

Ann was climbing back to their deck to towel off when she heard the snap of a door closing nearby.

In the harsh morning light, Loren, hungover, watched Ann come out of the hotel and walk down to the dock in a somber brown one-piece suit that looked proper for a grandmother taking a pram walk on the cold, rocky coast of Normandy. The suit flattened her breasts and covered every inch of derriere. A crime. An oversize straw hat hid her face, the zinc oxide 50 SPF sunblock giving her a Kabuki-like ghostly glow underneath.

If he didn't know better, he would have thought her coldhearted, but he guessed she was merely unhappy, like many of his tourists. In the old days, if she had been single, he would have had her in bed within a day. If married, two. She was his type: good-looking but not flashy, intelligent but not dried out. Out of his league in the States, but all was possible in the islands.

One discovered interesting things about people when they were on vacation. Loren would take out a high-powered, arrogant businessman on a diving trip—the kind of guy who wouldn't give anyone the time of day back home, insulated by at least three levels of assistants—but stick an oxygen tank on his back and drop him in shark-infested waters, and he'd become as docile and compliant as a puppy.

Couples were trickier. Other than lust-besotted honeymooners, one either had two partners who were sick to death of each other or two strangers who hardly knew each other, suddenly thrown together with no distractions. Always a volatile mix.

Droves of Westerners flew to the islands with some variation of cast-away fantasy. He got a high percentage of honeymooners, who were the best because they stayed in their *fares* most of the time, only coming out for food and alcohol, and they rarely complained. The second biggest group was the retireds—wrinkled, tired, unsure, bewildered by their sudden release into leisure. They would stare at the overpriced menus in the tourist hotels, wondering if this was what they had worked so hard for, saved for so parsimoniously, to waste money like this. An existential question for sure. They complained about everything because nothing could measure up to their impossible longings. He was sympathetic, but these weren't his bread and butter. The last group—the unhappys—these had been Loren's specialty.

The sun rode hard and yellow against the thin green sea. Richard and Ann got into the boat with their two small bags while Loren was still carrying on supplies of groceries and gasoline. After a few boxes, he stopped, exhausted, to wipe his face and light up a cigarette. After ten minutes of inaction, Richard got out and began to load boxes himself. Loren idly watched with neither thanks nor a request to stop. Finally he stubbed out his cigarette and helped. By the time they were finished, every square inch was packed, with barely enough room to sit. It was disconcerting to see everything they would be eating for the next week or so loaded around them in the hot sun. In true third-world style, the can of gasoline nestled next to the grapes, mangoes, and pineapples they would be eating; bottles of bleach cozied up to the meat and bread; plastic cartons of milk sat unrefrigerated.

"Make sure you have gone to make pee-pee. The boat trip is an hour and a half, with lots of bouncy-bouncy," Loren said. He enjoyed the grimace on Ann's face as she turned away. He found it amusing how squeamish Americans were at the mention of bodily functions. Didn't they understand that all humankind was mere flesh, animated by spirit, if one were so inclined to believe? "We are riding the pass into the lagoon. Twice a day a big tide comes in and out, bringing many animals: the sharks, the porpoises, turtles. We will come back for diving."

"I took my first dive yesterday," Richard volunteered.

This was another of Richard's traits that irked her—how he tried to befriend everyone he met, even this condescending Frenchman.

"Yes?" Loren said.

"Did you say sharks?" Ann asked.

"I loved it," Richard said.

"Many, many sharks," Loren said. "The sharks in Polynesia outnumber the people. Mostly safe to swim in the lagoon in the daytime. They have so much food. Unless they are hungry. I will take you to feed them—give you the thrill of the deep." Loren looked at Ann. "Never swim at nighttime, though. That's when they feed. It's very dangerous."

Ann turned a shade whiter under her zinc oxide. The memory of the dark shape underneath her, taking her measure, proving that it was master, that it chose the time and place of mortality before swimming away, spooked her.

The ride, as promised, was long and bumpy. Loren rode at a fast clip, carelessly plowing the nose of the boat into each wave crest, dousing them with spray. Wind whipped the water from blue to green and back to blue. In every direction, the world spread out—a horizontal, watery desert.

Under the roar of the engine, Ann whispered into Richard's ear: "I think this is a mistake."

Richard shook his head. He hated this about Ann, how she took a headstrong position and then reversed herself. "It's paid for. We're doing this."

The truth was that Richard had been so stressed by the restaurant opening he was on the verge of a nervous breakdown, but now that the obstacle had been removed, he felt . . . empty. What did one do without crushing pressure every waking moment? The lack of tension scared him, but there was a moment yesterday while he was deep underwater when he had felt curiously at peace, as if the pressure of the water both held him down and together; without it he was in danger of flying apart. He still hadn't processed the experience and was shy to describe it.

He had never imagined the sun from underwater, had never seen such brilliant tropical fish—not in a pan, or even baked whole—but alive, swimming. It was a mystical experience to be at the source of one's food, swimming in the same element it did. For twenty minutes, he forgot about everything, including, blissfully, the disaster of his career. Not quite true. Underwater, the words of his hero, Brillat-Savarin, came to him and made sense for the first time: *The universe is nothing without the things that live in it, and everything that lives, eats.*

He was so mesmerized that the dive master had to bang on his tank and angrily signal for him to ascend. It was a moment as pure as his first discovery that food could be something more than mere sustenance.

Richard's parents were first-generation immigrants from Ireland. They had squatted down in a nondescript suburb of Stockton, California—his father, a mechanic; his mother, a schoolteacher—and never looked up again. Richard's childhood was a long, devastating rotation of Hamburger Helper, Wonder Bread, Jell-O, and tuna melts blanketed in Velveeta cheese.

His parents took no joy in eating. Food was simply ballast. Taught by their parents to prepare for a rainy day (and all the days in Ireland were rainy), Richard's parents felt the necessity of building a fortresslike nest before starting a family. First they saved to buy the garage Richard's father worked in (becoming a small-business owner was the holy grail they had come to America for). Then they decided they needed to own a house. Substantial savings were essential, and after that a college fund, which ended up half filled by the time Richard was finally born to now very middle-aged parents. As a teenager being raised by the near elderly, gray hair and bad knees the norm, Richard himself developed a preternatural maturity about him. At fourteen, he monitored his salt intake and watched *The MacNeil/Lehrer Report* every night, wedged on the couch between them.

Going back to Ireland during summer vacations, Richard confronted the dark sources of his parents' parsimony. His grandparents had slogged through a carb-laden adulthood in a postwar Europe marked by lack. The apartment they lived in all their lives was dark, with small, high windows that blocked the cold, as well as air and sunlight; the place had the permanent odor of root vegetables and things kept beyond their prime. His grandmother tortured him with an unimaginable repertoire of family recipes passed down through the Dolan generations: mutton broth, nettle soup, rarebit, white pudding sausage, cabbage-and-bacon pie, skirlie, boiled or fried or baked boxty, potato champ, more potatoes, potatoes on potatoes, on and on. A sadistic, starchy, leaden nightmare.

But salvation finds us wherever we are hiding.

Back in Stockton, new neighbors moved in across the street: a professor at the local college with his FRENCH! wife, Chloe, and their son, Claude, who was the same age as Richard. Richard's first meals over at their house, as Claude's new best friend, were remembered more fiercely, were more formative, than his first sexual experiences: melted Brie on a toasted baguette with fresh arugula on top, for dessert meringue over a plain vanilla custard. The first time he tasted Chloe's baked zucchini—topped only with extra virgin olive oil, *fleur de sel*, pepper, lemon juice, and Parmigiano-Reggiano—he felt the force of religious conversion. The transubstantiation of simple ingredients into divine, gourmet manna convinced him that there was more to life than he had previously guessed. He went home, walked into the pantry, and threw out his mother's green can of Kraft Parmesan Cheese.

Chloe was much ahead of her time in the '70s, searching out local farms and backyard enthusiasts to purchase produce directly, a precursor to the ubiquitous farmers' markets of today. Richard went with her and learned to buy only fresh brown eggs; to hunt out heirloom varieties of lettuce such as Red Deer Tongue, Bronze Mignonette, and Black-seeded Simpson; to smell tomatoes and cantaloupes for their sugar level. He never looked back, and long after he had lost touch with Claude, Richard and Chloe continued to exchange recipes and food gossip. She was the proudest person at his graduation from culinary school. Unfortunately, she was also the person responsible for his meat aversion.

Chloe, like all dedicated gourmands, insisted on close contact with her food at its source. It was one thing to get vegetables at the farmers' markets, or even search out eggs and milk at nearby farms; it was an entirely different thing to go to an old-fashioned butcher. Richard, middle-class, sheltered teenager, had never thought of beef, chicken, and pork past the fact that they came in neat little sanitized packages of Styrofoam and cellophane. At the worst, there was the absorbent pad underneath that would be pinkish when you lifted up the meat, giving off a sour whiff of mortality, but that could be quickly buried away in the garbage. Chloe had wanted special parts not available at S-mart, and so she researched and found a local butcher operation.

As they walked through the door—Chloe in her bulky, lumberjack hiking boots that she wore bare-legged with shorts decades before it became fashionable—Richard broke out in a sweat. The chilled air had a heavy mineral smell of blood. Oblivious, Chloe went to the case and began to talk with the owner about offal, oxtails, baby lamb, and the possibility of French cuts such as *roti, cotelettes, jambon, jarret.* She was excited as they were ushered to the back, a warehouse filled with wooden tables and a sawdust floor. The walk-in meat locker had the expected upside-down carcasses of cows and pigs, but also the grayish body of a dog-sized baby lamb. Richard looked at its head, saw the curled-back lips revealing teeth the size of corn kernels. He felt dizzy and concentrated on not upchucking in front of the skinny man with the mitt-sized hands. Butcher's hands.

Suddenly he hated Chloe for her casual cruelty, her toned, pale legs that disappeared into the netherworld of her faded denim shorts. A pig carcass had been hauled in and set down on the table. A bone saw lay next to it, with a disembodied swine's head, which, to Richard's horror, Chloe had ordered to make *fromage de tête*. He ran out of the place, bawling like a little kid. They drove home in silence, Chloe chewing on her lower lip, her paper-wrapped plunder hidden in a liquor box in the trunk.

At Culinary Institute, talented but plodding Richard almost immediately fell into the orbit of Javi of the mercurial temper, whose dishes vacillated between sublime and inedible. Javi had satyric dark good looks, and didn't wash often enough, but women lined up. Teenagers, middle-aged housewives, wealthy tightened socialites, all were after him. When Richard confided to Javi his dad hadn't been thrilled to find out his only son wanted to be a cook, Javi laughed.

"Your pop's a philistine. Cook, my ass! We are food artists!"

Richard knew, however preposterous it sounded, it was also true— nothing could describe that first zucchini experience except art. Chloe had led him to his vocation, but Javi sealed the deal. Ann had understood his passion intuitively from their first date. But now time had done its dirty work to them all.

The boat slammed down hard on a wave, almost pitching Richard overboard. Loren drank from a bottle of cognac and offered it around. Ann prissily declined and was shocked when Richard nodded. Loren dug out a new bottle, handing it back. "What made you choose my resort?"

Richard shifted, turning his back to Ann's sullenness. He knew that embracing this experience was the right thing simply for the fact that his eye twitch had stopped. "A friend gave us your brochure. Eve Capshaw."

"Evie." Loren nodded. "A crazy one. She and her boyfriend, Eduardo, fought like animals. Everyone heard. Then they made love. Then fought. They exhausted us."

Richard blushed. "Eve's husband's name is Guy."

"My mistake," Loren said. "I must have the wrong Eve."

Loren gave a lewd wink to Ann that she ignored.

"The travel website said your place was the most remote," she said.

"Ah, so you two can feel the fire of romance?"

Neither Ann nor Richard uttered a word.

"We attract a quixotic clientele," Loren said, leaning back and steering only with his fingertips. "Only people with special reasons come this far. You are surprised I use such a word? From *Don Quixote*, the knight who tilted at windmills, thinking they were giants. There is much time to read here."

"My favorite book in the world is *Robinson Crusoe*," Ann said.

"You never told me that." Richard turned back to look at her.

"You never asked."

By the time they reached the *motu*, they were more than ready for solid ground. Loren cut the engine, but the noise still drummed in Ann's ears, deafening her. They climbed out and waded, knee-deep, to shore. A sturdy young Polynesian woman waited, holding two flower leis, which she held out to them with a small bow.

"*Maeva*," she said. "Welcome."

She lifted a tray of pinkish fruit juice. She had the broad, square face and black eyes of a Gauguin figure.

Ann felt like she had stepped into a painting. She bent and kissed the girl's cheek.

Loren took a sip from a glass of the juice and grimaced. "Oh, cut the crap, Titi. These people are cool. Put rum in it."

Titi's face turned dark as she stalked away. As was fast becoming habit, Richard helped unpack supplies and ferried them to the kitchen while Ann, crestfallen, stood looking at the place: the ring of white sand beach, gently rising ground that led to a pate of coconut trees in the center; six *fares* and the main communal kitchen and dining area. Exactly what the brochure showed, but the reality disappointed nonetheless. In her desperation she had entered a kind of magical thinking where place would take care of situation, but this place, so free of distraction, seemed to threaten the opposite.

Under a palm tree sat a bearded man reading a book. Next to him, under an umbrella, a woman knitted. They both looked up at the new arrivals, but when Ann lifted her hand in greeting, neither waved back.

"I'm thirsty," she said.

"Titi!" Loren yelled, clapping his hands. "Where the hell are you?"

In the kitchen, Titi stood over the tray of guava juice, fuming. The juice, icy cold when she'd poured it, was lukewarm already. What to do? Dump it out and pour more? She couldn't waste like that with Loren's penny-pinching. Should she drop ice cubes in and dilute it? Loren was getting worse about tanking up the guests right away, trying to keep them high and happy, which translated to less work for him. Cooked's plan was to multiply that to give Loren a scare. She had decided to ignore Cooked, but Loren was pushing her to her limit. Maybe he deserved scaring.

Titi wondered again for the umpteenth time if Cooked was right. She didn't feel particularly oppressed, she earned good money compared with her cousins in Tahiti, but still she resented the easy, careless lives of these tourists, resented Loren's loafing and lechery, leaving all the work to her and Cooked while he holed up in his shack. None of their family could ever afford to vacation there, and that seemed wrong.

She pondered the brown bottle on the shelf. Local moonshine that should knock the new guests off their feet for days, although when she had used it on Dex and Wende they had asked for a refill. Cooked said it was long past time to start making trouble. Trouble was what probably had got his brother in jail so long. Titi used Teina as a cautionary tale to keep Cooked in line. She poured all the juice into an ice-packed cocktail shaker, then held the brown bottle over the frosty canister, lost in indecision, when she again heard Loren's sour yell for her. She was just about to pour when she heard him tell the new guests of her family's claim to fame: Titi's mother, Faufau, had been one of the great beauties of the islands, descended from royalty. Her grandmother had greeted Thor Heyerdahl when he landed on the shores of Raroia on the *Kon-Tiki*.

A few years before, Titi had been paid by a publicist to be on the same beach when the explorer's grandson Olav re-created his grandfather's expedition sixty years later. Hearing the story always pleased her, but she still would have poured if the new lady guest hadn't kissed Titi's cheek when she held out the lei. The lei stuff was Hawaiian tradition, started up for tourism, but since Loren insisted, what the hell? But the kiss had touched her. This lady didn't deserve to drugged, with a wicked hangover to boot, for Loren's crimes.

Titi had bigger concerns. Cooked was on his way to big trouble. He lectured her on how the islands were like the children of France—the neglected stepchildren—much like the two of them were the neglected children of Loren. Loren had won the islet in a poker game from an old Frenchman long dead, while Titi's family had grown up, made love, married and had children, worked and died on these islands, generation after generation slowly forced to sell off their family lands to survive the rising costs brought by these foreigners. On top of that, there was Moruroa, the leaking of radioactive poison into the waters. Cooked's involvement in protests put him on a police list of troublemakers.

Like a fist, she, too, felt the pressure to fight. Newly resolute, she was about to tip the bottle into the shaker when Cooked whistled through the window to her. When she looked up into his face, she could tell he was amorous. He had placed a hibiscus flower behind his ear to lure her. It would be a full afternoon of lovemaking, and she didn't want to risk sick guests interfering with that. She stuffed the cork into the brown bottle and put it back on its shelf, splashed some of Loren's expensive dark rum into the shaker, swizzling with her index finger and licking off the drops as she poured. She winked at Cooked. Revolution could wait another day.

A fter they toasted their arrival, Loren, Richard, and Ann, still clutching her tote, made their way to a thatch bungalow, what they called a *fare* on the islands.

"List of amenities—sun, ocean, sand. No electricity. No refrigerator, no phones, no computers, no WiFi, no radios. No exceptions, don't ask. Welcome to paradise."

Loren plopped Richard's light backpack down on the teak wraparound lanai and tucked his hands against his lower back, as if the minute-long walk had strained him. "You're in luck," he said. "Only two other couples here. Automatic upgrade to the Royal Kahuna Suite. Everyone else canceled."

"Why is that?" Richard asked as Ann pushed past him and walked into the room, pleased with the open-air lava rock shower, the grass-bottomed plunge pool with flowers floating on top. So this was what white-collar exile looked like.

"They predict a few raindrops." Loren looked up to the spotless sky and shrugged. "What do you think?"

"I don't know."

"It's better this way . . . too much trouble. Let the damned tourists stay in Papeete and go shopping."

"We're tourists," Richard said.

"That reminds me. The main resort got a delivery from the airport." He brought out a battered FedEx envelope from his canvas bag. "This cost a small fortune to get here. It must be important."

Richard and Ann stood back as if the thing might bite. Finally, she took it and ripped it open the way one ripped off a Band-Aid, fast, to cause the least pain. It was an expensive Iridium sat-phone, like those used in documentaries about climbing Everest, where mountaineers conveyed heartfelt final words in a tent in a blizzard on the vertical face of the southeast ascent. She turned it on and saw 278 missed calls from Javi. She turned it off and for good measure threw it in the plunge pool.

Loren raised his eyebrows.

"We came here for an unplugged retreat. We do not want to be connected."

"Then you are in the right place after all."

As they stood on the lanai, Richard wondering if Loren was waiting for a tip, they could see a couple snorkeling in the lagoon. They surfaced, took off their masks, and kissed. Not just a peck but a deep, long, breath-stealing suck that made the watchers on the lanai suddenly feel like voyeurs. The two cavorted in the water like a pair of lusty porpoises, and then, with a scream, the girl swam like crazy for the beach. The man chased after her. Ann felt a cold sweat break out under her arms, remembering the dark throb of the shape beneath her in the lagoon at the hotel. How appropriate that her vacation began with her witnessing a shark attack.

When the girl reached the beach, she tumbled, laughing. She was tanned, topless (this was a French protectorate, after all), her breasts perfectly round like plastic fruit, powdered in sand. The man rolled over her. Her thong was like a piece of blue ribboned floss between her buttocks. Loren and Richard stared, dry-mouthed.

"Loren!" the girl yelled, revealing a high-pitched, girlish voice and the fact that they had known they were being watched, had in fact been performing for their audience. "You should have seen the sharks following your boat! It was crazy!"

"It's always that way," Loren yelled back. "They wait and hope for the pretty girls to fall in."

"Amazing," Richard whispered.

"What?" Ann said.

"Nothing."

"Then they take a big, juicy bite," Loren said.

The man standing beside the girl was tall, skinny, and cadaverously pale, spider-webbed with tattoos over his arms and legs.

"That's Dex Cooper. A rock singer. Too much trouble. And that's his naked little friend."

"Dex Cooper?" Ann had never chronicled for Richard the infamous noninterlude with Dex.

Alone in the bungalow, Ann struggled to find a satisfactory hiding place for the money bag. The room was a simple thatch box, with a canopied bed, an armoire of rattan, and a wicker table and chairs. Everything open, no locks on the doors or windows, so that she despaired of hiding it and considered digging a hole outside. Did they have wild animals there? Boars, monkeys?

Richard pointed out that the water table was so high it might soak the money. "Carl said that's why they can't bury bodies on atolls," he said.

"Who's Carl?"

"The pilot. Traditionally they either burned bodies on raised pyres, sent them out to sea, or ate them."

"Thanks."

"We could ask if there's a safety-deposit box."

"Why didn't I think of that? Do you think he has a dozen? Do you think it would look suspicious?"

In a panic she stashed the bag on top of one of the overhead beams, gambling on the unlikeliness of the location, while Richard unpacked and wiped down all the surfaces with his antibacterial sheets. Later Titi congratulated her for using the typical native storage system—slinging a rope over a rafter and hoisting a bag overhead. Ann decided the *motu* was small enough that, statistically, the thief would be found out. But what about the risk of rain, wind, insects, and who knew what else? There was always the unforeseen lurking. What if she and Richard drowned or got eaten by sharks? What if they were killed for the money, their bodies disposed of in any of the myriad ways Richard had just described? What then?

"You're being paranoid. We haven't done your hormone shots for days," Richard said.

"I threw them away." On the last night in Los Angeles, she had stood in her bathroom with the package of syringes and ampoules and thought, no more. One could only endure so much, and she needed to feel like herself again. Maybe she would start over when they returned home. Or maybe she wouldn't.

Although Richard wouldn't dare show it, he was relieved. Giving the shots had been oppressive, and enduring Ann's moods even more difficult. "So now what?"

"I haven't gotten that far," she answered.

At sunset the group was called to the beach for the shark feeding. Not knowing the ritual, Ann peeked outside as Cooked blasted away on a conch. On the right side of his bare chest, a descending series of triangles were tattooed from shoulder to waist, continuing on under his only clothing, a loosely wrapped pareu. He looked like a travel bro-chure. In fact, a year before, Cooked had been paid to do an ad for a local soda, and his likeness on posters over all the islands caused a flood of fan mail and a big boost of orange soda sales. Titi had torn the fan letters up.

He waved at Ann. When Richard and she reluctantly made their way to the beach, Loren invited everyone into the water, then went to the kitchen for the feed. The bearded man and the knitting woman were nowhere in sight. Only Richard and Dex stepped forward, shaking hands as they stood waist deep in water. The girl had put on a bikini top so skimpy that it seemed more an accessory to her nakedness than a cover. A wrap clung around her hips. A belly button ring with a pendant spelled out WILD in diamonds.

"Hi, I'm Wende," she said. "With an '*e*.'"

"Ah," said Ann. "Yes, you are."

"Oh my God," Richard screamed. "Something's bit me!"

Dex bent down and looked through his mask. "It's just a gray saying hi. He bumped his nose against you."

Ann looked away, embarrassed for her husband. Standing beside Dex, it was hard not to make unflattering comparisons. Dex had that uncanny rocker juxtaposition of not being physically handsome and yet being achingly sexy. No, it was more than that. His fame overwhelmed the reality of him. One had to concentrate hard either on who was in front of you or what you knew about him. Putting the two together was as head-splitting as wearing 3-D glasses.

"Please, Ann, Windy, go in," Loren yelled from the kitchen.

"He refuses to get my name right," Wende whispered.

"What if a shark attacks?" Ann asked.

Loren picked up a rifle from behind the kitchen door and waved it. "Boom, boom. Dinner."

Ann frowned. If she feigned sickness, would they be entitled to a refund? Maybe they could still go on to New Zealand or Thailand.

"I thought Polynesia was all about peace and love," Wende said.

Ann nodded in sympathy. "Looks can be deceiving. What about Cook, Crusoe, cannibalism?"

The men put on snorkeling masks and waded out into chest-high water, then squatted down. Again, Loren high-stepped like a comical bird straight into the water as he had at the hotel pool, this time holding a basket of fish remains. Ann saw this was his shtick, how he entertained people. The blade of a black fin rose and then submerged along the surface of the water. She closed her eyes.

"I'm glad another woman is here," Wende said. "All this macho crap." She thumbed the lagoon, the sharks.

"What about the other couple?"

Wende frowned and shook her head. "Nonstarters."

Dex's band had been big when Ann was in high school in the early '90s. They had plateaued by the time Lorna and she had found him drunk at the Troubadour. Wende didn't look a day over twenty. It must have been lonely to be stuck there with the geriatric crowd. Not that Richard and she were in vacation mode.

"I was in Prospero's last video, 'Buy My Freedom,'" Wende said. As if that would clear Ann's puzzled expression. "I'm his muse."

Ann laughed out loud. "That seems a very old-fashioned word."

"Did I use it wrong?"

"It's the perfect word."

"It really just means we get drunk, stoned, and have sex. Then Dex works all night. I don't do anything. Pilates, yoga, swim. I guess that's what a muse does."

"You're young. You'll grow out of it." Indeed, being Dex's groupie was exactly what Ann could have done that night at the Troubadour, and if she had had a child from that union, Wende could conceivably have been the product, give or take a few years. All the girl had to do now was finish college and go on to grad school, work herself to death for the next decade, and then lose the fruits of that labor to an unscrupulous ex-lover/business partner, and then she could be said to have outgrown it like Ann. The self-pity was welling up in her; she forced it back down.

During the time they were crazy about each other, Ann and Richard had wanted to travel, but, deciding to be responsible, they had moved that goal off into the future. Like a mirage, it had remained always just beyond their reach. Now it was too easy to imagine washing up on the shores of fifty or sixty—tired, worn out, indifferent, having fulfilled none of their dreams. Maybe being a muse was as good a thing to be as anything else.

The water in front of them suddenly exploded. Richard bobbed up like a rocket.

"That was amazing!"

Loren looked pleased.

"Ann, did you see that?" Richard yelled.

"I didn't see anything. It happened underwater."

But that was not the entire truth. She had seen the fin and later the surface bubbling with motion. Richard was down there, his helpless white, flabby body as bait, but what could she do to prevent the steamrolling of fate? So she faked nonchalance.

"You could at least pretend to take an interest." Richard sulked.

After dark, the absence of electricity shrank the island to the size of the dining area. Loren sat at the head of the table and entertained, keeping the party lively. He drank copiously but picked at the food. During dinner, the bearded man, who Loren hinted was a quasi-famous writer, said nothing, simply studied them through his thick glasses. He was traveling under a pseudonym, his real identity only just found out because of a message sent from the main resort—his agent trying to contact him about a film deal—had given away the game.

Ann knew the heavy frames were a hiding mechanism. Try as hard as she could, she could not think of his name, although he seemed vaguely familiar; it was one of those three-part ones that always stumped her.

"I'm a big reader," she said, in her best cocktail-party mode. "What are the titles of your books?"

He gave her an appraising look. "I write about the universality of the human experience, using the devices of thinly disguised autobiography and increasing brevity. Long books are as passé as the missionary position."

"Oh."

"My debut, *Colossus*, was a hundred and twenty-nine pages about a boy's awakening sexuality and realization that he is a genius. I was awarded a Genius Grant for it. My second book, *Lunch*, was eighty-nine pages about a little-read genius novelist deciding what to eat for lunch. It won a major prize you've probably never heard of, and got me labeled a 'writer's writer' by the *New York Times*."

"What does the novelist end up eating?" Richard asked.

The writer stopped for a moment and squinted at Richard, trying to decide if he was being ridiculed or Richard was just stupid. He decided the latter, and went on.

"Currently I'm writing my third, *Sand*, which should run sixty-seven pages about a novelist so brilliant no one reads him so he goes to a desert island to write a book about it with his homely wife who supports him. The woman's money emasculates the man so he betrays her."

No one said a word.

"He betrays her with the comely, nubile, sexually promiscuous young girlfriend of an embittered, washed-up, immature pop singer. The writer's lovely new mistress begs him to take her away and use her as his muse."

Ann coughed. She was mistaken. She had never heard of him, nor did she want to. "You don't have any of your books with you, do you? For sale?" His lip curled; she was deeply sorry she had asked.

"It would be a bit 'used-car salesman' to carry one's own books around, no?"

"I always wanted to try to write a book."

"Yes, and I always wanted to try to do brain surgery in my spare moments."

Ann was drowning in a toxic swamp and needed a lifeline. "Is this your wife?"

He leaned forward so that Ann was prevented from extending her hand to the woman.

"Hello," the woman mumbled over his extra-large, balding, genius head.

"Enough gossiping!" the writer said.

"Hold on," Dex said. He had been talking with Loren and only half listening. "You aren't *the* John Stubb Byron?"

The man actually flushed in pleasure.

"Man, I had no idea. You haven't said two words to us the last week.

*Colossus* is one of my favorite novels of all time. It changed my life. *Lunch* is pure poetry. This man is a genius!"

"Please," he said, staring into his goblet of wine. "I try to pass through the world anonymously in order to observe its truth without the distorting lens of my little fame, thus the nom de guerre."

"If only I had my copies here for you to sign," Dex said.

"I can probably dig some up in my suitcase." He turned to the woman. "Go. Bring a copy of each and my Sharpie."

For the rest of the meal, the satisfied writer was silent and openly contemptuous of the whole table except for Dex, giving his wife significant looks until dessert was served, which the two promptly carried away to their *fare*. The two remaining couples lingered in the oasis of oil lanterns.

"Love it here," Dex said.

"How long have you been at the resort?" Richard asked.

Ann knew that Richard had never heard of Prospero, but even if he had, it would have made no difference. One of the things she admired in him was his absolute imperviousness to the seductions of celebrity outside the culinary world. He was just on his usual friend-making mission. She thought Dex sensed it, too, and that's why the two men hit it off.

"A month? Longer? It's so good I lost track of time," Dex said.

Wende rolled her eyes.

"Really?"

"Thinking about buying my own *motu*. No offense, Loren, but you charge pretty steep."

Loren smiled. "What is paradise worth, my rich friend?"

On a speck of coral halfway across the vast Pacific, the conversation degenerated, as it did between most Californians, to speculation about real estate prices back home. The popping of the real-estate bubble into the ugliness of the mortgage loan crisis was an unprecedented loss of innocence for most Golden State residents.

"But the high-end is okay," Richard said, trying to be upbeat.

"My Holmby Hills place, the Montecito ranch, the hideaway in Palm Springs, the duplex in Venice—all upside down. Can't unload a one. The property taxes alone are eating me alive," Dex said.

Ann wondered how fast they could dump their fixer-upper starter house, fully furnished, if they had to. It felt like divorce, thinking this way. The house had been the symbol of their early marriage. One of the casualties of being an attorney was seeing houses, furniture, cars all reduced to their base value. Their life reduced to an equation of location times square footage, totally ignoring the fact it was a charming old Craftsman bungalow with a deep backyard lined with royal palms and walls covered in bougainvillea. It had been the place they had dreamed their dreams. In the beginning, they devoted their weekends to refurbishing it: painting walls, replacing moldings, laying down vintage-style tile. They splurged installing stained glass to replace the glass in the transoms above the doors. Just as they had finished the wide-plank, distressed pinewood floors, Richard and Javi, tired of working for others, had decided to open a restaurant.

The house fell into a spell of neglect that Ann assured herself was only temporary. The kitchen remodel would have to wait. Weeds appeared in the backyard, the pool turned green, Optimistically, Ann still shopped flea markets—a French wire egg basket, a needlepoint stool—a habit she had developed with her mom when times looked bleak. As she would have argued in a court of law, they still had a dream—it had just been postponed.

During the chemo and radiation treatments, her mother suddenly had decided that the house needed remodeling. This from a woman who allowed her husband's frat house sofa to be in the den years after they married.

"Are you sure?" Ann asked, not wanting to ask the obvious: Did she have the energy for that kind of undertaking?

Each day they drove to antique shops and estate sales, studied books to learn about period furniture, zeroing in on French. They discovered parts of Los Angeles they had never been to before. They stopped for breakfast and lunch at places no one they knew went to. It was their first adventure together. The house transformed from casual '70s-style ranch house to bohemian Parisian apartment.

When they hauled in a particularly large toile French settee, her father took her aside. His eyes, magnified by thick lenses, appeared anxious. "I just don't understand this furniture obsession, do you?"

"I don't know . . ."

"What happened in Paris?"

A nn understood that houses, like marriages, were about process, that one was never truly finished. Finished people, as per her clients, usually sold, divorced, or died. So Ann was fine with the empty bedroom that would one day be a studio. She bought a used easel at a garage sale and set it up in a corner; she stacked canvases against the back wall. All in the service of someday. Another bedroom, furnished with only a futon for Javi's sleepovers, was the future nursery, although neither of them discussed that right now. It was at this juncture that Ann had to force herself to stop thinking. This was the point beyond which she could go no further. Beyond this point, there be dragons. The whole thing now threatened to have to be sold bare bones, dream-stripped.

S o what do you do?" Dex asked Ann.
Silence.

"Ann is an attorney," Richard volunteered.

His answer was truncated, unsatisfactory. It was too little. A pause opened up for her to fill, which she emphatically chose not to.

Why did Americans always insist on asking about occupation, as if what you did was who you were? In other cultures it was considered rude, like asking someone's income or weight or age. Or maybe it was Ann's hypersensitivity to *her* profession, being pigeonholed. The silence echoed with the pain of a thousand lawyer jokes that had rained down on her over the years:

*Q: What's the difference between a jellyfish and a lawyer? A: One's a spineless, poisonous blob. The other is a form of sea life. Q: How many lawyers does it take to screw in a lightbulb? A: Three. One to climb the ladder, one to shake it, and one to sue the ladder company. Q: What does a lawyer get when you give him Viagra? A: Taller. Q: What's the difference between a lawyer and a vulture? A: The lawyer gets frequent-flier miles. Q: If you see a lawyer on a bicycle, why don't you swerve to hit him? A: It might be your bicycle. Q: What's the difference between a lawyer and a leech? A: After you die, a leech stops sucking your blood. Q: What's the difference between a lawyer and God? A: God doesn't think he's a lawyer. Q: How are an apple and a lawyer alike? A: They both look good hanging from a tree. Q: How can a pregnant woman tell she's carrying a future lawyer? A: She has an uncontrollable craving for bologna. Q: How many lawyer jokes are there? A: Only three. The rest are true stories. Q: What are lawyers good for? A: They make used-car salesmen look good. Q: What do dinosaurs and decent lawyers have in common? A: They are extinct. Q: What do you call twenty-five attorneys buried up to their chins in cement? A: Not enough cement. Q: What do you call twenty-five skydiving lawyers? A: Skeet. Q: What do you call a lawyer gone bad? A: Senator. Q: What do you throw to a drowning lawyer? A: His partners. Q: What is brown and looks really good on a lawyer? A: A Doberman. Q: Why did God make snakes just before lawyers? A: To practice. Q: What's the difference between a lawyer and a herd of buffalo? A: The lawyer charges more. Q: What's the difference between a tick and a lawyer? A: The tick falls off you when you're dead. Q: How was copper wire invented? A: Two lawyers were fighting over a penny. Q: Why does the law society prohibit sex between lawyers and their clients? A: To prevent clients from being billed twice for essentially the same service. Q: How can you tell a lawyer is lying? A: His lips are moving. Q: Why did New Jersey get all the toxic waste and California all the lawyers? A: New Jersey got to pick first. Q: Why don't lawyers go to the beach? A: Cats keep trying to bury them. Q: What do you call five thousand dead lawyers at the bottom of the ocean? A: A good start. Q: What's the difference between a dead skunk in the road and a dead lawyer in the road? A: There are skid marks in front of the skunk. Q: What do you call a smiling, sober, courteous person at a bar association convention? A: The caterer. Q: Why are lawyers like nuclear weapons? A: If one side has one, the other side has to get one. Once launched, they cannot be recalled. When they land, they screw up everything forever. Q: What do lawyers and sperm have in common? A: One in three million has a chance of becoming a human being. Q: Why won't sharks attack lawyers? A: Professional courtesy.*

Ann felt sick to her stomach.

Dex was a celebrity, a rock star. No one asked what he did. He looked like what he did, even if one didn't know his band or his music. Wende was a muse. Loren, a hotelier. A darker realization came to Ann—soon she wouldn't even be a lawyer. One couldn't possibly introduce oneself as an ex-lawyer. It was a little like explaining one *used to be* a genocidal dictator. Once . . . always.

"I'm a chef," Richard said.

"A chef? Whoa, I *love* that."

"We own a restaurant." Richard downed his wine in one swallow and poured another glass to the brim.

Ann looked at him, startled, then pleased. Under the table she squeezed his knee.

Richard had upped his alcohol consumption considerably since leaving Los Angeles, and yet he felt surprisingly peppy. His stomach had stopped its fierce gurgle; his hives had calmed down. "It's called El Gusano."

"Seriously? Too funny." The men high-fived. "Where is it?"

"Venice."

"I live there! Part-time."

"It's opening in a month." Richard took a big swallow of wine.

"Ah," Dex said. "Resting before the storm?"

"You got it."

"What kind of food?"

Richard paused. "Mexican-French fusion. We don't want to be stuck with labels."

"Fuck no! My kind of guy. Why do you think I'm hiding out? Out of reach of those corporate bloodsuckers. I'll be at El Gusano. With friends. Famous ones. Reporters will come. Get you a write-up."

Richard nodded. He was close to tears.

The lie had been a necessary one. The restaurant was still alive to both Ann and Richard; admitting its demise was like a death. They needed time to adjust to their new circumstances. In their imagination El Gusano, The Worm, had taken the place of their house as the locus of their idea of who they were. Imagining its possibilities occupied every spare minute. Ann, who kept away from the kitchen, obsessed over the look of the place. She studied the effect of stemware, silverware, plating. It was their creation, especially precious after all the years of slaving in someone else's space, following their rules.

Titi made a last pass around the table with coffee and cookies. In a spasm of coughing, Loren excused himself, and she finished the service alone. A look relayed its way around the table. After drinking a bottle of wine at dinner, Loren had faded quickly. Still early evening, but the island was already shut down. Dex brought out his guitar and a ukulele he had ferreted from Cooked, and played back and forth between the two instruments.

"Ask Cooked to come play drums," he said to Titi, but she shook her head no.

"He's tired."

"You are exhausting my drummer." Dex smiled. "Go on. We'll close shop."

Prior to Richard and Ann's arrival, an informality had descended on resort service that would remain in force. For the money they were paying, Ann wouldn't have minded a little more pampering.

A cigarette hung from Dex's lips while he played; he removed it only to drink alcohol. With his long hair and tattoos, he reminded Ann of a child who had outgrown his Halloween costume.

"I know you," he said, strumming his guitar while Richard, whose spirits had miraculously picked up, played checkers with Wende in her short shorts and halter top.

"I don't think so," Ann said, staring out at stars that were eerily large. It felt like being in outer space. She could sense the immense night around them, the buffer of thousands of miles of watery emptiness between them and home. Dex went away, then came back with a bottle of tequila and two glasses. He poured; Ann drank. She considered the capriciousness of happiness, how all those years ago this moment would have been the high point of her life. Instead she had hidden in the bathroom, Lorna had French-kissed him, and the possibility had vanished.

"'For as this appalling ocean surrounds the verdant land, so in the soul of man there lies one insular Tahiti, full of peace and joy, but encompassed by all the horrors of the half known life.'"

"Impressive," Ann said.

"Melville. I've been reading from Loren's library. Trying to get into the spirit of the place."

Behind them, Wende squealed, laughing. "No fair!"

"You live in LA." Dex took a drag from his cigarette. "I bet we met at the Troubadour or the Whisky."

Ann downed her shot. "Not in this decade."

"Could've sworn."

Ann walked away to the water, her skirt dipping in the surf as a rogue wave washed up around her, the soaked cloth manacling her ankles. Dex was harmless, but she didn't need to have the past rear up now. She was having enough trouble dealing with her present. What were the odds that Dex Cooper would be there? Part of her wanted to get on the phone to Lorna and gossip. The withdrawal from not being able to connect to any electronic devices felt like rehab. It made her as jittery as giving up coffee.

She stretched out on the cool sand, hiking the sodden fabric up on her thighs. Wende, having won at checkers, plopped herself down next to her.

"Boring, boring. It's, what, nine o'clock? I'm bored to death."

Ann nodded.

Seashells scuttled back and forth in the darkness, hermit crabs drunk-driving.

"You've got nice arms and legs. Any tats?" Wende asked.

"Excuse me?"

"Tattoos. I did some of Dex's. You should let me do you."

"I'll think about it," Ann said.

"I thought we were going to Bali. Nightclubs. Or Phuket. No offense, but you two coming has been the most exciting thing to happen."

"None taken." The girl was unformed, a hard, unripe fruit who in a strange way reminded Ann of herself at that age—never able to rest in the minute, always looking for more. "Tell him to take you someplace else."

In college, Ann dated a theater major, drank Manhattans, and wore black—a nonrebellion by other people's standards but outrageous by her family's. Her father had been a patent attorney, and when he retired, he taught theory at the law school. There was never a doubt that her older brother and sister would study law. The household lived, breathed, and ate jurisprudence. Around the dinner table, they talked of nothing else but the latest article in *ABA*. Outside interests and hobbies were considered an eccentricity.

Her mother, though, was mutinous. She and Ann would hole up in the den and watch foreign films. From her, Ann discovered the possibility of a secret life—doing what was expected of you on the surface while the subterranean you bubbled along underneath.

Wende snorted. "Dex thinks this is great. Just snorkeling, eating, and getting laid. Writing new music. No fans bothering him. I don't mind the fans. Fans are fun." Wende looked over her shoulder, then leaned over. "Between us, he's a little old for me."

"Why'd you come then?"

"I know what you're thinking—dumb groupie from Idaho. Yeah, and a father fixation. It's simple: I love his music. My mom played it all the time when I was growing up. I just admired him so much. But up close, his insecurity, his drinking, his using sexuality as a substitute for intimacy, as a marker for masculinity, well, it wears on you. I didn't sign up to be his mom."

"How old are you?"

"Twenty-four."

Going on thirty-eight. Ann had been wrong. This girl was far more together than she was now.

"I have my own CD. It was my dream back in Idaho. But seeing the business up close, I'm having second thoughts about spending my life that way. Having my image manipulated by a corporation sexing up my work for their profits, being at the mercy of a young, unsophisticated, fickle public. Yuck, you know?"

"Sure."

"Being here has got me thinking about doing something with the environment. Engaging my passion, but not in a self-involved way. Being of service, you know? Like sharks."

"Sharks aren't self-involved?"

Wende giggled. "They are being overharvested, and no one cares because of their bad PR image. *Jaws* and so forth. I'm sorry, I'm talking way too much."

"Listening to you makes me feel young again."

"That's what Dex says. I think he uses me as his base target demographic. Until I met him, I'd never been out of the country before, except Cabo. I want to experience things before I settle down like you and Richard."

"We're settled all right."

"I see how he looks at you. In love, like he's afraid you'll disappear."

Was that true? On top of all his other worries, did he have to worry about her? "He knows I'm not going anywhere."

"An outsider sees things. My mom says I have the sight."

Ann got up and dusted the sand off, pleased despite herself. Although she didn't believe a word, it was falsely reassuring, like a good fortune cookie.

She headed back to the *fare*, looking forward to seeing Richard, maybe apologizing for being a little too hormonal, too type-A lately, but when she got there, the room was dark and he was asleep.

She woke early to the sound of a boat engine. Outside, John Stubb Byron and his silent knitting wife hurried onto the boat as if they were making a getaway. Cooked waved at Ann, and she waved back vigorously, as if to say, *I see you, I see you.* The boat motored out of the lagoon.

Later at breakfast, Ann asked about the couple.

"They say it's too crowded here." Loren lifted his thin shoulders and dropped them in a noncommittal way.

Only Ann and Richard showed up for breakfast. Mango was served, a splendid thing—voluptuously split open, orange flesh shiny under Ann's spoon. She never ate mangoes at home; she didn't know why. She avoided them at the grocery store. They seemed exotic, difficult with their thick greenish-yellowish-red skin bruised like a sunset, and the large pit pinioned down within its fibery strings. A mystery how to prepare one, but here the fruit was opened, diced, ready and willing. Here mangoes were lovely. She promised herself that, from now on, she would eat them at home to remember being on the island. While they lingered over a third cup of coffee, Loren brought Ann a fax from the main resort. It was yet another note from Javi:

*Spent the night in jail. Lorna bailed me out. Don't worry— everything will be fixed. BTW, Lorna's not as stuck up as she used to be. Hope you don't mind me asking her out.*

She balled up the paper, but there was nowhere to throw it, so she stuck it in the pocket of her cover-up. Titi glared impatiently at their empty plates, willing them to get up. As Ann and Richard poked along the beach, they saw her and Cooked disappear into the trees.

It was strange to go from full-throttle panic to having nothing to do but worry about one's tan lines. Should they have stayed back home and stuck it out? Should Ann even now be sitting in the prison of her job? Richard couldn't bear the thought of his stillborn kitchen. Leisure time yawned in front of them, and without email or Internet, much less TV, Ann thought this might not have been the best idea to get their minds off things after all. Richard had not asked to see the fax, but now, alone, he hinted.

"That from Javi?"

"Yes."

"Anything I should know?"

"He says, 'Don't worry.'"

Richard gave his irritating tight nod.

W hen Cooked came back from his morning "nap," he offered to take the two couples over to a nearby deserted *motu* for snorkeling. Ann declined.

"Are you sure?" Richard asked. His voice wheedled like a young boy's asking permission to go play, not wanting to give away his excitement.

"Go enjoy yourself," Ann said.

Richard hesitated, knowing solidarity was what was called for, but why couldn't Ann go along with the program just this once? He craved the release of being back underwater.

She took his hand. "We can't just sit and stare at each other, right? Nothing is going to get decided today."

"Can you remind me again what we're doing here?"

"Assessing our options."

"It's not criminal, though, what we did, right? It was our money."

"It has more to do with intent. The truth is slippery sometimes." Answered like a true lawyer.

Wende came out in a tiger-print bikini, wearing oversize dark glasses. She tiptoed, as if too much motion hurt. Cooked's eyes grew big, grinning at the invitation that was Wende as she climbed into the boat. Titi stood in the kitchen doorway, sulking.

"Is there any way I could get some breakfast to go?" Wende asked.

Now Cooked climbed back out and waded through the water to the kitchen. Titi huffed inside. Sitting at the table, drinking coffee, Loren read his newspaper, ignoring the whole thing as if he were just another guest.

The previous night they had been kept up by the rapt, orgasmic sounds of lovemaking coming from Dex and Wende's hut. It had woken Richard from his exhausted slumber, and Ann and he had lain side by side in bed, listening. They snickered at the obvious showmanship, although the truth was that it made each of them mourn the disappearance of lust in their own lives. Why couldn't they have had the island to themselves so that they could concentrate on healing through nature, communing with the solitariness that was the essence of the desert island ideal, or at least be with civilized people who muffled their cries of pleasure in their pillows?

As they waited, Dex came out in long baggy swim trunks, whistling.

When Cooked carried out a paper bag of fruit and folded pancakes, Wende called across the water: "Thanks, Titi. You're the best."

Titi shrugged, not sorry in the least that she had spit on the pancakes. She watched the girl untie and shed her top as soon as the boat took off.

When it was gone, Loren looked up, surprised to find Ann still sitting on the sand, nursing a coffee she had cadged from the kitchen.

"You don't go to swim with the fishies?"

"I don't like water."

Loren laughed. "Perfect." He stared at her a moment. "I didn't at first either. It scared me. But that's why I eventually went in. I will make a picnic for us later."

"I came for solitude. I can entertain myself quite well."

"I'm a selfish man—I would like you to keep me company. If you change your mind, let me know."

The boat motored out across the blue lagoon, and soon it was easy to forget that there was even such a thing as land—it seemed the entire earth was covered with this limpid, body-temperature bathwater. The sun overhead scalded, and Richard felt his skin starting to tingle from burn. He'd forgotten Ann's sunblock. Although he tried to concentrate on the watery view ahead, Wende was slathering oil all over her lovely, bare brown self, smelling of coconut, and it was difficult not to be taken in by the display.

Dex had been pouting over the sudden departure of John Stubb Byron, especially without even a good-bye or the promised signed books. "But I get it," he said. "Artist to artist. Mano-a-mano. We blew his cover, his anonymity. He couldn't be the observer but became the observed. It's an artist thing."

"You always want people to recognize you," Wende said.

That's when Dex feigned sleep, wedged into the back of the boat, propped up on the life jackets that no one wore. The islands were very French in their disdain for safety regulations.

Richard knew how unworldly, how adolescent it was, but how did the French handle this topless thing? Their everydayness about it made it all the more erotic. Or maybe it was the other way around; maybe the puritanical streak in Americans made any sighting of off-limits flesh all the more seductive. His parents had been affectionate with each other, but he still marveled at the fact of his conception, as prudish as they were around the house: a peck on the cheek or an embarrassed hug passing for intimacy.

When Cooked, their instructor and safety monitor, dropped anchor at a picturesque cove, they put on flippers and masks, then jumped into the water while he waved them off and took a nap.

They paddled to a huge coral forest, watching clouds of parrot fish swim by. As beautiful as the sea life was, even more beautiful to Richard were the mermaid flutterings of Wende, her hair a halo around her. At one point, he grew so bold as to grab her ankle to point at a glorious burst of angelfish behind her bare back. She nodded in pleasure. He longed to place starfish over her perfect breasts, if not his own outspread, starfishlike hands. After half an hour, Dex signaled that he was ready to return to the boat. Wende went with him, but as much as Richard missed her company, he found he didn't mind being alone. He was never alone in his regular, workaday life; working in a kitchen was a team activity.

He could not describe the sensation of being underwater, but if anything, this time was even more intense than the dive lesson. It put the car-crash reality of his life in perspective. The closest he had come to this kind of experience was when he was in the hospital five years before after lifting a too-heavy crate of steaks.

Richard never allowed himself to relax. Always he felt pressure. His life was a constant round of being late, hustling, making do, and catching up. Even on the rare occasions when he was ahead of schedule, he would prep in advance for future chores so that eventually he forgot what it meant to unwind. Even in his sleep he dreamed of chores he had done during his waking hours so that his entire twenty-four-hour day ended up being an endless treadmill of anxiety. In the hospital, nothing had been expected of him except sleeping and eating; the pain was a minor inconvenience. He had the unprecedented luxury of sitting on the toilet for a leisurely bowel movement instead of straining while someone pounded on the door with a delivery that waited for his approval. Technically, that had been his last time off till now.

If he could have only imagined that a place like this existed. Underwater, there was no blame. Underwater, there was no possibility of talking with Ann about their troubles. Underwater, the possibility of Ann leaving him became more remote. A relief. All one could do underwater was marvel at the perfection of the world that one normally let pass by. Like Wende's breasts. Floating facedown in the ocean, his ears stoppered by water, he joined the fish in their fishy daydreams.

The truth was this leisure made him feel guilty because during those long ago summer days with Chloe, learning about the joys of French food, Richard had found his bliss, and he had pursued his love of cooking all these years, cocooned away from those who worked just for money. People, for example, like Ann. Just because he followed his bliss didn't mean he should have allowed Ann to support his dream. It wasn't as if that bliss kept Richard from having to hustle, kept him from getting tired and discouraged. Kept him from doubting if it was worth the price he was paying. Everyone encouraged one to "live the dream," but no one talked about how to pay for it.

Floating above a particularly spectacular growth of coral, Richard would have exchanged it all to be a fish—just not one fated for his own frying pan.

He was learning the hard way that even divine cooking didn't make one immune to being unloved. Sadly, food wasn't always enough.

Toward the end of what he would call his Summer of Food, Richard had gone over at the preappointed time to Chloe's to practice a *pâte brisée*. Claude was away at baseball practice. He found Richard's interest in cooking with his mother a little freaky and now made himself scarce.

The kitchen was empty. Sun streamed in and filled the air with floury dust motes. Richard made himself at home, sitting at the kitchen table and thumbing through Larousse's *The Best of French Cooking*. Time passed. He looked up from the recipe for a complicated *torte ganache*, and his head was hot from the sun beating through the window. How long had he been there? He got up and filled a glass with water from the sink when it occurred to him that he had heard no sounds from upstairs. Was the house empty? Had Chloe forgotten? Suddenly he felt strange, as if he were trespassing. What if her husband or Claude came in and found him?

"Chloe?" he called up the stairway.

Nothing.

He should have left, gone home. Even years later he could not say why, but he stayed. Instead, he climbed the stairs and entered the room he knew was the master bedroom. It was the one Chloe always came out of dressed in her Capri pants and sleeveless shirts, trailing musky perfume, ready to cook.

The bedroom was disappointingly ordinary, not the French boudoir of Richard's nighttime imaginings. No flocked wallpaper or gilded mirrors. The realization that he had been picturing it startled him. He looked hard at the king-size bed, memorizing for later its chenille spread, creepily like the one on his own parents' bed, trying to picture Chloe's brown hair splayed on the pillow. Somehow he knew she slept on the right side, by the window. He walked to the dresser, ostensibly to look at the wedding picture of the professor and Chloe, but even as he bent to compare the younger Chloe with the one he now knew, his hand was yanking the handle of the top drawer. There, as he'd hoped, were her undergarments. He clutched at a lacy bra and brought it up to his nose—it smelled of Chloe's signature perfume mixed with her skin, only more so. Then he saw underwear—in flesh tones and black—not skimpy and shiny and candy-colored, like glimpses he'd caught of girls' at school, but not the big beige granny pants of his mother either. He felt a flush through his body—intense pleasure and discomfort combined— utterly unlike anything he had experienced alone in his room at night. He picked up the underwear and balled them under his nose, feeling the stiffness of the crenulated lace waistband, but they smelled only of detergent and line drying, a soft powdery baby smell that did nothing to encourage his fantasies. He held the panties up to the sunlight, imagined Chloe's narrow, boyish hips in them, the Bermuda triangle of her dark pubic area. He spread the panties and examined the cotton insert at the crotch. Pristine. Inexplicably he brought the fabric to his tongue, tongue against dry cotton, and felt another fierce shudder. Just at the moment he was ready to sink to the ground to relieve his unbearable tension, he heard a watery slosh from the bathroom.

Impossible. His heart hammered up into his throat. "Pervert" would be the kindest of labels. Chloe would tell his mom and dad in the guise of concerned parenthood. He would be expelled, grounded, ridiculed. He was doomed. He threw the underwear back in the drawer and slammed it shut with a bang, and then tiptoed back to the bedroom door. Clearly, he had lost his mind.

"Chloe?" he said, his repentant voice weepy. He was dead meat.

Nothing. A minute later, another watery thump.

He walked to the bathroom door and knocked. "Everything okay in there?"

Nothing. Then the softest of moans.

There was the disgrace of being discovered snooping in Chloe's bedroom, more specifically in her underwear drawer, or the larger cosmic catastrophe of doing nothing. Wasn't this one of those moments you read about in books, a character-defining moment that could screw up your life forever if you chose wrong? He opened the door.

Chloe lay naked in the bathtub, her knees and breasts and head forming islands in the filmy grayish water. Her head rested on the lip of the tub, but she didn't open her eyes at his entrance. On the bath mat was an overturned amber vial of pills.

"Fuck, fuck me," Richard breathed as he bent down to touch her skin, which could only be described as feeling like a refrigerated piece of raw chicken. The water, gone cold, rippled with her shivering. "Did you take these?" he yelled, his Mrs. Robinson suddenly morphed into the senior hearing-impaired, but she shrugged him off in her deep slumber. He had no idea what to do. He tried to lift her out of the water, but her previously lusted-after, lithe body was now as heavy and unwieldy as a sack of ancestral potatoes. He put a sneakered foot on the tub rim for lever-age, but that didn't work either. Finally, thinking all the while how he was going to catch hell for getting his shoes wet, he stepped in with one foot, trying to brace under her arms and lift, his fingers oblivious to the fact that they were brushing against nipples, but he almost slipped, nearly braining them both. If he let go, he worried, she would slip beneath the water and drown. *Oh my God. Fuck. Me.* Now he stepped in with both feet as Chloe's weight started to burn the muscles in his arms. With his outstretched foot, in a balletic feat that almost cost him his hamstring, he yanked the chain of the plug, then squatted down as her head lolled on his shoulder and the soapy amniotic water around them drained away.

Now he was slimy wet and cold. He bit his lip to keep from crying. From that moment a strange twinning of sex and safety lodged itself in his unconscious.

He maneuvered around and rested Chloe as comfortably as possible in the tub's bottom while he stepped out and ran to what he hoped was the linen closet, water squishing in his shoes, and pulled out an armload of towels. He paused before he covered Chloe, feeling a tenderness (he had never seen a naked middle-aged woman's body before, certainly not his puritanical mother's). Her breasts were small and high, slightly con-cave on top, the nipples darker and more pronounced compared with the small, pink, puppy roundness in magazines his friends passed around. Even at his young age, he recognized that the images in the porn mags were not the real deal, but fetishistic, consumerist fantasies that encour-aged the substitution of anatomically supersized body parts for attrac-tion, a paid voyeurism of man-made boobs, airbrushed crotches, inflated inner tube lips. Chloe's body was real. Slim and toned, it contained a history. Her stomach, although flat, was soft, the lower belly pouched. Her rear end was gloriously full—one could see its contours even under clothes—with tiny ribbons of stretch marks around the hips. He wor-shipped this woman and, given the chance, would have married her a thousand times over the silly girls his own age.

When Richard had used all the towels from the linen closet—under

her head as a pillow, wedged underneath her body for warmth, on top
for modesty—he at last felt safe enough to leave her. He ran into the
bedroom, grabbed the phone, and called his mother.

Sarah Dolan, née Donnelly, was the third daughter, fifth child, of a
large alcoholic Irish family, and the appearance of one overdosed
woman in a bathtub did not greatly perturb her. She did want to know
what part her Richard had in this, but first things first. She took the
pulse of the stylish Frenchwoman, a woman who had snubbed her and
instead befriended her young son. She slapped her awake, then asked
her a barrage of inane questions like name, date, and current president,
determining that if Chloe had taken enough pills to kill herself, the job
would already have been done. When she mentioned calling an ambu-
lance, Chloe became so agitated it was clear that she didn't need one, or
the attending scandal that would follow. Sarah hunted around the medicine cabinet until she found the ipecac, then forced a dose down Chloe's
throat. She got her out of the tub and into underwear, a robe, and tube
socks.

"Where is Claude?" Sarah yelled into the bedroom.

"Not here," Richard mumbled.

A cloud darkened Sarah's prim blue eyes. This, too, would have to
wait. "Go make a pot of coffee and bring us a cup," she said, to get her
son out of the room and preserve whatever innocence he had left.

Sarah sat on the edge of the tub while Chloe hugged the toilet, retch-
ing out the last toxic remnants of her stomach. Periodically Sarah got
up, once to fish around the drawers for hairpins, which she used to pin
Chloe's bangs back, and another time to find a washcloth, which she repeatedly wet, wrung out, and handed over. After the toilet had been
flushed a last time, Chloe put the lid down, laid her head down on top
of it, and began to sob. The lavishness of her grief impressed even a stern
Irish girl. Now that the danger was over, Sarah was getting impatient to
leave. She had left the dinner preparations in midstream—uncooked
hamburger in the pan, frozen corn in its boiling bag.

"Dear, would you like me to call the professor?"

A loud wail came up out of Chloe's chest as she stood up, her robe gaping open and revealing her body once more just as Richard came through the door with the cup of coffee.

"That piece of *shee-ittt*. *Merde*. He's left me for his little *pute* secretary. He's such a cliché, he can't even be original in his choice."

"Richard, go find alcohol—vodka or gin—and pour a glass for Mrs. Arnoux."

"Claude's father sleeps with the mother of Claude's first girlfriend. The girl my little boy lost his virginity with. It will make him sick in the head."

"Richard!" His mother yelled down the stairs. "Bring the bottle and two glasses."

After her own family's boisterous drunken example, Richard's mother was a teetotaler who sipped only enough wine to make toasts on special occasions, so this was a big deal.

Richard went to the cabinet that he knew from long habit held the liquor. During sleepovers, Claude and he used to sneak into it, watering down the alcohol until the remainder was the color of pale tea. All he could think of was that Claude had done it with a girl and not told him, a major breach of best friend etiquette. He was not anxious about Chloe despite the horrific events of the afternoon. Truth was his mother was the person you most wanted in charge during times like these.

When Richard was six years old, it had seemed an excellent idea to steal grass clippings out of the garbage can, add flowers from the garden, and pour bottled salad dressing on top, just like his mom's salad. Then eat it. Out came the ipecac.

Calmly his mother kneeled and held his tiny shoulders as he vomited in the wastepaper basket, dabbing his lips with Kleenex, washing his forehead with a damp cloth nonchalantly as if this were the most ordinary thing in the world to happen—your son eating grass.

"Mama's little cow," she crooned.

He slept through the afternoon, night, and next morning, finally waking at noon. No mention of school missed. She brought him his favorite, grilled cheese sandwiches with the crusts cut off, not once scolding him, figuring rightly he had already suffered enough. She was mystified by her son's precocious love of cooking but defended it, especially against her husband, who called him a sissy. A good Catholic girl, she believed it was a mysterious gift that demanded to be used by its recipient.

Now, as Richard sat on the stairs at Chloe's house, Sarah made a call to the family doctor, explaining the situation in as vague terms as possible, not using names, although it would be common knowledge soon enough. He said the only responsible thing to do was take the woman in question to the hospital, where she could be monitored. That, or have her personally supervised.

The hospital wasn't an option—Chloe had made that much clear—but she was surprisingly willing to live with the Dolans. She moved into the guest room while Claude shared Richard's room in a kind of extended sleepover.

"How come you never told me you did it?" Richard whispered.

"If you ever tell anyone about this, I'll say you were banging my mom," Claude hissed back.

For the next week, Richard's parents lived in terror.

Chloe stayed up all night, playing cassettes of Edith Piaf and Nina Simone over and over. She drank profusely, although the doctor had strictly forbidden it, and smoked her black cigarillos like a chimney. Smoking wasn't allowed in the house, but his mother said nothing, instead choosing to focus on keeping the house from being burned to the ground. Brown-rimmed holes scorched into the fabric of the sofa revealed the white eyes of stuffing. Years later, the faint reek of tobacco still hung in the curtains.

Chloe spent her days and nights in her bathrobe, unwashed, crying. Sarah sat next to her in silence and listened to long drunken tirades against the professor. Many times Chloe switched to French to more easily utter a particular obscenity in regards to her husband, and Sarah, grateful for her lack of fluency, was able to muse over what a melodic and romantic-sounding language it was. She would buy tapes, she thought, and teach herself a second language.

The whole week, the family took shifts, making sure someone was always there to watch over Chloe and potentially douse the house, although Sarah never left Richard alone with the woman, sensing that some potentially disastrous relationship between the two had been narrowly avoided. Claude distanced himself from the whole fiasco and spent his time at school or at other friends' houses. At the end of the week, realizing her welcome was coming to an end, Chloe took a shower, put on her raisin-dark lipstick, and gave them sloppy hugs on her way out. A week later, a moving van pulled up.

Richard and Chloe kept in touch through letters, exchanging recipes and finds of rare ingredients, such as Calabrian chili-infused oil, tangy raw-milk French cheese, or Japanese *umeboshi*, salt-pickled plums. They never referred to that day, just as they avoided mention of the visit to the butcher.

A year later, Richard received a photo of Chloe in a white skirt suit, a small, insouciant pillbox hat perched on her head, standing in front of a Gothic church on the arm of the man who was her new husband. His mother shook her head and *tsk-tsk*ed, but he guessed she was impressed at Chloe's resilience. After that, Richard received postcards from exotic places: France (of course), but also Spain, Morocco, India, Thailand, and Japan. The notes always centered on food. At Christmas he would receive packages: herb bundles from Provence, a tea set from Japan, Turkish delight from Istanbul. Chloe was his proof that second acts were possible.

Getting into CIA had been a culmination of everything Richard had worked for starting from those Chloe days, but for Javi it was a reprieve, an escape, a place to chill out. The housing department had put them together simply because Javi's last five roommates had moved out of the apartment within a month's time. Javi cultivated a constant party atmosphere. Strangers could be found wandering the rooms at all times of the day and night. Because he was a lady's man, there was always a couple of mournful women in tow—women who cleaned the place and brought flowers, trying to win his heart. As often as not, Javi would go straight from CIA to some other party and would never show up at home at all, and these women fell into Richard's sympathetic orbit.

Was Richard taking advantage? Was he a cordial predator? He had a certain desperate, grateful charm. They were all beautiful in his opinion—women he wouldn't have been brave enough to talk to in any other circumstance—but there they were in his apartment, alone, jilted, and he was willing to pour them wine and listen to their heartache. Usually he was rewarded. He realized years later they were probably in all likelihood simple mercy beddings, but you had to start somewhere.

Afterward, he would take these lovelies, wrapped in his old bathrobe, to the kitchen and begin his true seduction. Perhaps a simple apple-and-sage *croque monsieur* toasted in the oven? Maybe a *salade frisée aux lardons* with poached egg and bacon fat? Or maybe a basic roasted-cherry-tomato-and-feta omelette, accompanied by an appropriate wine? He would try to make another date as they finished the last forkfuls, almost never offering to share. They adored his food but warily stood at the front door like loyal dogs waiting for the return of their prodigal master, deflecting his efforts at getting their number. Future meetings would be left vague. Already he knew they would not return to clean the apartment or to warm his bed. As they kissed him on the cheek good-bye, it was always with the same words: "You should really open a restaurant. Please tell Javi to call me."

That all changed when he met Ann. When she came to the apartment, it was only for him; she was not even aware of Javi's existence. On their first date, while his famous *coq au vin* was simmering on the stove, he snuck downstairs and left a bread bag tie on the mailbox, his and Javi's signal that the apartment was romantically occupied. The tie stayed in place the whole weekend.

When Richard took off to go snorkeling with the other couple, Ann sat under a palm tree and pouted. She admitted it—she was angry that he was taking it all so well. As if in fact they were on a vacation instead of hiding out. Why did she want him beside her—to beg her forgiveness, plead for her to be a little happy? Richard was being Richard. He tried to be sympathetic, to act like their mutual problems were mutual, but he easily reverted to his perpetual Zen state where all he thought about was food. Even after all this, his mistress was still the kitchen, and he longed to be back with her. It was like infidelity, but in a more subtle, unfightable form.

Despite her best efforts, Ann could not hold on to her pique. The island took care of that. She looked across the beach at the gently spooling waves and thought, this is what paradise means. Her dream. What struck her was that there was so very little to it. It was characterized by lack, like a minimalist painting. How could you paint it and not have it turn out like a souvenir-shack paint-by-numbers? How to convey the fullness of the experience rather than emptiness? She thought she was on the verge of an original composition—a band of land and sea, with the majority of the canvas filled with sky—but her first impulse, rather than to try to find supplies to paint it, was to call Lorna or Javi to talk about it. Until she realized she couldn't.

Another technology withdrawal pang. Nomophobia. The fear of being out of mobile phone contact. Maybe she would write down what she was thinking on a piece of paper and text it as soon as she got to the airport or to a decent connection, but that seemed like cheating. Social networking was about spontaneity, and having what amounted to a prepared statement seemed disingenuous.

She loved paradise. But how in the hell would she last two weeks unplugged?

For the next three days the pattern repeated: Cooked took Dex, Wende, and Richard out for snorkeling and diving. Ann stayed on shore, reading, napping, and eating lunch alone.

The searing silence of the place poured into her. Her thoughts slowed, then slowed some more, until there were gaps where she was only aware of sun and wind, the sound of the surf that was like her own breath. Although her annoyance at Richard might have daily increased, the reverse happened—time away made her want to see him more. She looked forward to hearing about his underwater adventures precisely because she had no intention of joining in.

"It's just so mind-boggling down there," Richard said, his Wende-sparked lust fueling detailed descriptions of fish and coral he had seen.

"You seem to really be into it," Ann said.

"It's . . . otherworldly."

"Wow. Fish."

"I wish you were down there with me."

"Why?"

Why? Because he loved his wife and was desperate to transfer Wende's hotness to his longing for Ann. He reached out and touched the strap of her dress.

They made love without the aid of whipping cream.

Afterward, Ann lay on her back and stared up at the dark cloud of their money bag suspended overhead.

"I can't believe the restaurant is gone," she said.

And like that, all the euphoric diving and sex chemicals pumping through Richard's body washed away, and he was miserable again.

When asked how she spent her days, Ann was evasive. Her experience, or lack of it, was so indescribable it was . . . indescribable. She sat on the beach all day. She stared at the water and the clouds. The changing colors of the lagoon slowed her heartbeats. There were moments when it became hard to believe that the rest of the world existed—Los Angeles, San Francisco, New York seemed imagined places, filled with imagined importance. Even harder to believe was the struggle that she had been consumed by these last years, a struggle that now seemed so insubstantial it could be lost in the break of a wave. Time stretched elastic like a rubber band, became wobbly at its edges (only an hour passed? an afternoon?) and infinite at its molten core. The likelihood that FFBBP had fired her for absenteeism, if not for outright embezzlement, didn't greatly trouble her. The longer Ann stayed on that beach, the more she was convinced that it was the only place she had ever truly belonged. But what did that mean?

A resort couldn't serve as one's spiritual home. Solitude at this level was prohibitive. Besides being totally fake. Maybe Richard and she could find their own island, rent a small hut? Surely there was someplace where they could go native, become recluses, live off the land? Could this technically be called an early midlife crisis?

On the morning of the seventh day, she was worried over the distinct possibility that she was going a little nutty in her splendid isolation.

Loren was fiddling with a telescope he had brought out. When she asked him about it, he said it was for the Transit of Venus that would occur in two weeks.

"It won't happen again for another hundred years."

"We'll be long gone from here by then. Two more weeks. What would that cost?"

As she prepared to leave for another day of beach watching, Loren stopped her.

"When we sent the latest charges, they were refused. Your card is maxed out. Can you give me another one?"

A pause.

"Is there a discount for cash?" she asked.

He looked at her quizzically. "We'll work something out."

"Is that offer of a picnic still good?"

They waded around to a sheltered cove the color of jade on the other side of the *motu*. Ann lagged behind, slipping on the algae-draped stones. After watching her grow more and more frustrated, Loren set the basket high on a rock and returned to help her, cupping her elbow and directing her steps.

"Don't put your weight down till you feel around with your foot for a secure hold."

She rested her hand on his shoulder and followed his footsteps.

Leaving her to read in the shade under a tree, he spearfished in a deep tidal pool. Although Cooked was supposed to catch something that day, if what Loren caught was big enough, it would serve for dinner. The last few days Cooked had come in empty-handed, besotted by their busty guest, and upsetting Titi, who then lagged at her work. At

least that distraction was better than his messing in politics. A good
boy, but in that direction lay only doom. When had truth and justice
ever coexisted for any length of time?

If Loren could get them to marry and settle down to work the resort,
Cooked would forget the rest. That was why he turned a blind eye to
their long nonworking afternoons. His wedding present would be the
title to the property upon his death. Wasn't there a lovely, poetic justice
in that? A small enough present with the huge debt owed and the dwin-
dling revenues, but that was in the future. Loren had more immediate
problems to keep him occupied, and what he longed for that moment
was to get his mind off everything.

Her eyes were green, mocking. Eyes that her husband no longer looked
into? Was that the problem? She made him feel unsure, self-conscious,
alive. Not the type to be pushed around. Seduction was a great game he
never tired of, like hunting the most elusive reef fish. A thrill when the
spear impaled it, but also an immediate sorrow. Once caught it was not
the same thing at all.

The hideous khaki walking shorts made her look like a British female
birder. They ballooned up around her legs and hips like a bun smother-
ing a hot dog, denying her figure. He imagined the shape of her ass
underneath like a sculptor shaving away layers of marble to uncover the
masterpiece waiting to be revealed.

She looked up from her book, Stevenson's *South Seas Tales*. She always read thematically on trips, although this once she was woefully
underprepared (having reread *The Moon and Sixpence* four times already)
and was at the mercy of the communal library, where her current read
had been stashed away among the donated pulp thrillers and romance
novels of past guests. Loren was crouched still as a statue, resembling
a huge egret; his whole body tensed as he watched what lay beneath the
water.

Her agreeing to lunch was partly embarrassment at the denied credit
card. She sensed it might be best to make him an ally, but also she real-

ized she had judged him unfairly. He was not the shallow, beachcomber gigolo she had labeled him. At dinner he made intelligent and witty conversation, but it was when he felt unobserved that she was most interested. Then his face took on a deep melancholy, making it clear that he was more than his circumstances. Just as she wanted to amount to more than hers.

A true host, he took his cue and made her comfortable by their mutual silence. Neither of them was a talker. Time passed so slowly and peacefully that by two in the afternoon, Ann was starved for both food and conversation. When she went with Richard anywhere, he exhausted her by not being able to sit still, always reaching out for lifelines—eating, searching for restaurants, talking to chefs, even grocery shopping—anything to avoid inaction.

"Ready for lunch?" she shouted.

"Thought you'd never ask."

Loren opened a nice bottle of Montrachet. As he plied the corkscrew, she noticed the first joint of his ring finger was missing.

"Fishing accident?"

"Polynesian rite of mourning," he said.

She waited, but he said no more. She spooned out shrimp-and-papaya salad. The trip was turning out to be altogether not a poor exile. Luxurious. Not like poor Crusoe eating his goats.

A real gadfly, Loren entertained her with tales of the stupidity of local politics in Tahiti, which he knew plenty about, and misbehaving guests, including Eve. He enjoyed her laugh.

"You have found a good life here."

He nodded.

"Was it hard, leaving everything behind?"

He didn't know her well enough to say that in his experience what people left behind ended up being much less important than they thought. It was a kind of ego, imagining one's life irreplaceable and unique.

Loren had long practice at framing his story so that it both amused and obscured. People came to the islands to ditch reality at least for a few days. They did not want a sad-sack story. Nor did he intend to provide it.

"In Paris, I worked as an artist briefly. Sometimes I miss that."

"An artist?"

Loren shrugged. "I fell in with an avant-garde group. I needed money, so I thought I could pull off installations like others were doing. It worked for a time. But when I came here, no regrets."

"Do you still do art?"

"The urge has left me."

"Can it just go away like that?"

"It's an appetite like any other."

"I lied earlier. We're escaping, running away from trouble. The credit card issue won't be resolved, but I have cash."

Loren waved off her apology. "I came here to escape also. It worked for me—perhaps it will for you."

"What a relief it would be. Escape. I already feel healthy just not being connected." Lightning should strike her for telling such a pointless untruth.

Ann had gone alone into the plunge pool the night before and felt around the grassy bottom with her feet till she retrieved the satphone. She had overheard Dex say how waterproof they were, and indeed, when she snuck down the dark beach and called Lorna, she answered on the first ring.

"So how is it?" Lorna said.

"You'll never guess who is here."

After they had exclaimed over Dex, Lorna admitted that things were not going well.

"Javi's ex hired a barracuda. They are slapping all kinds of charges together against the three of you. Collusion, fraud, etc. Harassment, plain and simple. I'm trying to settle this thing. Get some dirt on her. Sit tight. It might take some time."

"How's Javi holding up?"

"Out of his mind to talk to you guys."

A thought occurred to Ann that she realized was the real motivation for her call. "Don't sleep with him. He's fragile."

"It's been ten years since your fling. Statute of limitations. Bye."

N ow Loren started to put away the picnic things. "You are enjoy-ing your unplugged vacation? How is your husband enjoying himself?"

"He likes watching fish apparently."

"He seems a lost soul."

That stung. She blinked and looked away. "We've been under stress." She gave a dry, dissimulating chuckle that she would have disliked in someone else. "Somewhere along the way we forgot how to be happy. Can we talk about something else?"

Loren hesitated, then decided to take the gamble. "I saw you swim the first night at the hotel."

Her face went blank, unreadable. Professional training kicking in. "That must have been amusing."

A mistake, but there was no turning back. "I couldn't look away."

"Why are you telling me this?"

The idea of being watched infuriated her, but she pretended to not care. Caring meant you showed all your cards. After all, she had guessed his secrets already. When he bent over at dinner the previous night, she had seen the ugly bedsore-like bruises along his hips. In the firm's minus-cule pro bono work, all done for publicity, always dumped on the associ-ates, she had been routinely assigned clients who didn't have the insurance to cover the financial ravages of AIDS on themselves and their families.

"I'm telling you in order for you to know me. So I'm not a *perverti*. Otherwise I'd have an advantage over you. In a friendship both people must be equal."

She smiled, her words out to haunt her again. "You could still be a pervert. A gentleman wouldn't have looked."

The gamble had paid off. Sometimes risk made one appreciate the goal even more. He wanted this woman's friendship more than he'd wanted anything in a long while. "I'd rather *not* be a gentleman than *not* to have looked."

Ann laughed. She had forgotten that delight could come so easily.

After lunch, Loren climbed back to his tidal pool. Going after one particularly tricky eel, he slipped and scraped his leg on a long branch of volcanic rock.

Ann jumped up and grabbed a towel. "Let me clean it."

"No!" He put his hands out to stop her coming closer. The diversion of his game was now gone. He had functioned well for years, but his health was giving out. His reality was to quarantine himself until he was down to this island, to dismiss all his lovers and become a celibate as some kind of penance, but the course of his illness was relentless. The fact was that soon he would lose even this—palm trees, lagoon, ocean, sunset, self—when he could no longer work. Cruel fate would not even allow this one chaste conquest. "Stay away!"

"Loren, I know."

"You know nothing." He bowed his head, sweat beading on his forehead. "Hand me the towel."

After he wrapped his leg, he hobbled back to the compound in silence, leaving Ann to fend for herself while carrying the basket. She had to fight her instinct to pester him with questions, force him to a responsible course of action.

There had been a time in her youth, in high school, when she had been too timid to ask questions, afraid of revealing what she did not understand. Later, in law school, she blossomed, grew provocative, argumentative, a know-it-all, intent to prove herself. But during these last years, she had settled back down into that familiar silence, comfortable in her not knowing until the information, ripe, fell into her lap. She would allow Loren to ask her for as much or as little as he chose.

When Titi saw Loren and the blood-soaked towel, she ran for the first-aid kit and rubber gloves. Once he was bandaged, she joined them to eat dessert on the beach. Their conversation didn't interest her, so she merely nodded her head to the rhythm of their voices and ate most of the custard and cookies herself.

"It's like having a shark bite your leg," Loren said. "The leg is gone, but your mind cannot believe the reality. The old reflexes go on."

"How long?"

Loren shrugged. "The symptoms, only in the last year. I pretended to myself that they were nothing. Years ago I had the fever. Then it was gone. I forgot. Maybe it disappeared, I thought. A year ago I started to have problems. I went to Papeete for treatment. But I can't stay there . . . My kingdom needs me. The drugs make me sick so I stop taking them. Next time they don't work as well. It goes on."

"Wouldn't it be better to go to the States or France?"

"I'll die wherever I am. Please say nothing. No one will come if word gets out. The story of me being a drunkard is much more picturesque."

There was nothing Ann could say. How badly she'd misjudged him that first day.

Loren took a stick and drew shapes in the sand.

"Which do you prefer?"

She frowned. "The circle, I guess."

He nodded. "I thought as much. It is better than the square, more loving. But I prefer the squiggle—the wild, the unknown. For that I am paying."

The next morning, Loren did not come out. Titi made her *tsk–tsk*-ing sound when questioned at the breakfast table, implying that it was due to overindulgence. When Ann went later to question her, Cooked was sitting at the kitchen counter, Titi hand-feeding him pieces of peeled fruit.

"Tell me what's really happening."

"He never takes the pills. The alcohol is very bad."

Determined, Ann walked to the remotest corner of the resort, where Loren's hut was secluded behind bushes, set back in the jungle on a slight elevation. It had not been refurbished as the others had, the island's punishing climate revealed in the brittle, rotted thatch, the bleached and cracked floorboards. A sign above the door read:

DO NOT COME IN. YOU HAVE NOT BEEN INVITED.

PRIVATE. OFF LIMITS.

YES, THIS MEANS YOU.

Ann knocked.

"Go away," Loren said. She tried the door and found it unlocked.

Coming from the harsh sunlight, she waited a minute for her eyes to adjust to the dimness of the room. Pandanus mats against the windows blocked both sunlight and fresh air. The room echoed her first impressions of the island's emptiness; its few pieces of furniture were scattered as if they'd been left where they washed ashore. Incongruously, one of those pieces was an ornate French sleigh bed that had seen better days, pushed into the corner. Loren was settled in a lair of pillows and sheets.

"Guests are forbidden here."

Although the walls were empty, one door was covered with curled sketches and watercolors of palms, the ocean, a few sunsets, all hastily but expertly done. The paper was yellowed and split along the edges, suggesting they were not recent, yet it was hard to tell for sure. Everything aged prematurely in the tropics.

"Are these yours?"

"Get out."

She narrowed her eyes at him now that she could see in the gloom. The sight was not a good one. Loren's gaze was cold, mineral, reptilian. This is how he'd learned to keep people at a distance. "You don't scare me anymore, you know, with that whole snooty French bit."

"Tourist and native, never the two shall meet."

"We're way past all that now, don't you think?"

"Since you refuse to leave, can you at least get me a bottle from the chest?"

Ann made a face.

"I'll let you stay only on the condition you promise to stop the Florence Nightingale routine."

Ann went to the wooden seaman's chest and pulled out a bottle of absinthe.

"Do people still drink this? I thought it was banned."

Loren hissed out a laugh, which turned into a cough. "*La fée verte*, the green fairy. An old French vice. Will you share a drink?"

"Titi said you shouldn't."

"Titi is a young girl. She doesn't yet accept hopelessness. Besides, we've already reached ten in the morning."

Ann uncorked the bottle and searched for glasses.

"On the windowsill."

The tumblers were dusty; she dipped the corner of her wrap inside for a quick wipe.

"No. For your first time, we should drink from the right glasses. Go to that cabinet."

Ann found small, delicate glasses with ballooned bottoms.

He directed her on the amount of water to pour into the absinthe, watched as it clouded.

"Oscar Wilde said of drinking this: 'After the first glass, you see things as you wish they were. After the second, you see things as they are not.'"

They drank in silence.

"I admire you," she said.

"Hopelessness as a lifestyle?"

"You're not caught up in all the crap. Given it all up, out here, unplugged. It's impressive."

"It's not that simple."

"It is, but it isn't. You charge exorbitant rates and give us *nothing* . . . except peace. Because we're paying so much, we think *nothing* is exclusive. If it was free, we might think it was a gulag."

Loren downed the drink and held out his glass for another. "To things as they are not."

Ann stretched out next to him, propped against the curving headboard.

"Do you have family we can call?"

"I had two daughters. I have no one to call."

All her ready-made answers and platitudes wilted; she could only pour the next drink.

"Some would have been unhappy, but being here saved me."

Ann took Loren's hand and brought it to her lips. "You are my monk of the South Pacific. My ascetic."

Loren's face relaxed, the alcohol taking the edge off.

"Monks are just followers. The sheep. The mystics are the wild ones, searching for the truth. They are the bad boys, the rock stars of religion."

As they clinked glasses, Richard stuck his head in the door. Squinting, he froze seeing them together on the bed.

"Everything okay?" he asked.

"How could it not be? You have a lovely wife."

"Yes, I did," Richard said, his cheeks puffing as if to add more, then deciding against it.

"*Did?*" Ann said.

"Do. I do. Have a lovely wife. We're about to leave for snorkeling. Coming?" He abruptly closed the door before she could answer.

Ann stood up and straightened her clothes. The absinthe had made her seriously drunk. "Do you know the story of the scorpion and the frog?"

Loren remained silent. He was in love.

"The scorpion asks the frog to carry him on his back across the river. 'But you will sting me,' the frog says. 'If I did that,' says the scorpion, 'we would both drown.' That makes sense, so the frog puts the scorpion on his back and starts swimming. Midway across the river, the scorpion stings him. 'Why?' the frog says. 'Now we will both drown.' 'I cannot help myself,' the scorpion says. 'It is my nature.'"

"Are you calling me a scorpion?" Loren asked, enchanted.

Ann giggled. "And I'm a shark. What a pair we make."

When she came out, Richard pounced. "What were you doing in there?" he said, pinched, as if he smelled something bad. He did that tight nod thing she hated, then did it again, like a schoolmaster or a judge.

"It's the 101 of human relations. What he wants, I can give."

W as Ann one of the unhappys, after all? Impossible to tell. Loren himself had been. Married five years, a father. When he and Matilde, his wife, amicably separated, he looked forward to moving from Lyon to Paris to explore what he thought was his true life. A life that required the anonymity of a large city with lots of like-minded partners. The gratifications of his body were unimaginable after being suppressed so long. Equally unimaginable was the loneliness of divorce. He missed his children. He needed men and loved women. A doomed hybrid lover.

When his life as an artist took off, it was as much a surprise to him as to anyone. Success came too easy. It felt like stealing. No matter what he put up, if he told the right story about it, people accepted it. He did paintings of the interior of his closet. Then his real closet reconstructed in the gallery to compare with the paintings. A collage of photographs of movie stars and singers and girls from school who had provided inspiration while he had masturbated at age fourteen. For an important museum show on obscenity, he had a freshly slaughtered cow hauled in and put on a large white dais. A new cow forklifted in each day to comply with health department regulations. Newspapers condemned it, people protested it, but Loren maintained that killing millions of anonymous animals in stockyards was the true obscenity. His work developed a certain cachet, became in demand to the select. He had found his same hunger in others, and by answering it he fed them both. For a time, his future looked promising.

Then his wife married a local man in Lyon known for his drinking and his foul temper.

Loren asked for custody of his daughters, Bette and Lilou. Although his wife had been understanding of his reasons for the divorce, although they still spoke on the phone, she coaxing intimacies from him—Loren admitting to the ecstasy of a certain partner, or how a man he had lived with three months got up one morning and punched him in the face—now she used all these facts against him. An unfit father, a depraved lifestyle. Loren hired a lawyer. During visits suddenly circumscribed by a conservative judge, he noticed bruises on his ex-wife's arms and legs.

"Why do you allow this, Matilde?"

Her eyes had deadened like spent coals. She turned her back on him. "Have the girls back at five, or even that will be taken away."

The price of his freedom had become too dear. When he saw a bruise on Bette's shoulder, heard the child's rehearsed lie of falling off a chair, Loren took the girls and fled. A long time ago.

The happiest time in his life—standing on the deck of a copra boat, the roiling blue-violet ocean off the Marquesas, the green rocky vertical islands. His children asleep like puppies in the nest of coiled ropes at his feet. An intoxicating, rare mix of freedom and love. Life was not so much easy out in the Pacific as it was empty, so empty it made it possible to start over. What was the myth of the South Pacific about if not escape?

He ended up in Papeete and took a series of menial jobs in hotels and restaurants. Nothing was too demeaning because at the end of the day he got to go home to his girls—their kinked, silky hair and milky breath. It felt as sacred as being in church to watch them sleep, the sight of their tiny delicate feet.

The house he rented was a bungalow at the end of a dirt road lined with pepper trees, backed against a coconut grove and the ocean. Two prehistoric-looking flamboyants anchored the small front yard. Bougainvillea smothered the house, so the girls were only half-lying when they told people they lived inside a flower. He hired a Tahitian grandmother, a large, kind-faced woman, to care for the girls. They developed golden tans and strong muscles from playing sunup till sundown on the beach with the woman's granddaughter Titi and other local children.

Loren didn't touch a drop of liquor, or touch another man or woman.

In the fall, he enrolled the girls in a French private school. They cried at having to force their feet into shoes again. When the nuns at the school requested school records, the authorities tracked him down and took the girls. Lilou screamed, and Bette bit like a feral animal, but the grandmother kept rocking in her hammock. Although tears ran down her face, she was too familiar with white men's unfairness to protest.

After getting out of prison, Loren got into brawls at the local working-class bars, letting loose a rage that had ballooned inside him, indulging in vices he had been too diplomatic to indulge in before, until finally he rescued himself by escaping to the more uninhabited outer islands. He worked plantations on Tahiti Iti, Bora-Bora, Mooréa, learning the hard business of copra, vanilla, potatoes, noni. He ran a cattle ranch in Fiji. After a time, the lushness of the islands bored him, and he went farther, to the remotest archipelagos—bleached, skeletal atolls precariously floating mere inches above the ocean, guarding womblike lagoons. The sky overwhelmed, stars burned, the Southern Cross flared. It felt like the beginning of the world, and it suited him. The more that was subtracted, the more powerful what was left became. Over the years, the past gradually erased itself. Sometimes he wouldn't see another white face for months, and yet he felt at home. He would never return to the confining society of France.

He had broken free.

But as with most liberations, there were lapses. Little had he guessed that his tastes would be accepted on the islands, with little rancor or shame. Beautiful brown-skinned men offered themselves without guilt. Later he also began to indulge in European women, but that was more for intimacy than lust.

He hoped when his daughters grew up, they would come back to him, and he would prove he was not a bad man, not an uncaring one, despite appearances to the contrary.

Every morning of his new life he swam in the warm, baptismal waters and thanked God for giving him this second life that was so removed from the first as if not to belong to the same person. One night he played poker, and his life changed again.

A week into living on the island, something strange was happening to Ann. Nothing seemed able to disturb her calm. This felt beyond strange to a person accustomed to being buffeted by her emotions this last year. After Richard found her on Loren's bed, he had stalked off to the boat and a long day with nubile Wende. Certainly Ann felt sad it had gotten to this point—her husband jealous of a homosexual hotelier and flirting with a beach bunny—but it was what it was.

Ann looked forward with guilty pleasure to another day spent alone. She went to the kitchen and loaded her beach bag with a half bottle of wine, a sandwich, and fruit. She dumped in sunblock, a paperback, and the sat-phone *just in case*, but much like her attitude toward Richard, her need to confer with Lorna became less and less compelling. Even the menacing scenarios that might conceivably be hers in the future—fired from the firm, bankrupt, foreclosed house—only made her philosophical. If she allowed these thoughts in, she would be gloomy, making it yet one more lousy day. She was a hopeless, doomed rat on a treadmill of misery because, face it, there was no fixing this particular existential dilemma. So why hurry? At two thousand dollars a day, not including VAT taxes, she couldn't afford to waste another single, precious minute of paradise.

Ann walked along the shoreline, looking for a good spot to spend the glorious afternoon, absorbed in the sensual details around her. The beach was picture perfect—white sand with a rosy pink mixed in, coconut trees leaning out over the water. She considered taking a picture with her phone, but why? What she should do was go beg some paper and pens off Loren and sketch the scene. But having to compare her own inevitably amateur efforts with the perfection in front of her, not to mention Loren's talent, would destroy the happiness she felt in the moment. Better to just laze.

The sun was so penetrating, her skin felt infused with light. She sat down and reapplied a slather of sunblock. Despite her best precautions, her skin was darkening to a pleasing gold that she had not had since her teenage years, when she basted herself poolside, oblivious to sun damage two decades down the line. The demarcation line between the exposed skin and the skin under her old brown bathing suit was startling. Pulling the straps of her suit down over her shoulders to apply lotion, she sat still, allowing the sun to touch the stark white. She glanced around—her stretch of beach would remain deserted all day. Why not? She pulled her bathing suit down so it bunched around her waist, close enough to pull back up if needed. It was the most freeing sensation imaginable—the sun and air on formerly cloistered skin. With no witnesses, even witnesses who were used to the sight of bare-breasted women and nonchalant about it, Ann felt a primal lack of restriction, as if she were truly a child of nature, freed of her awful self-consciousness. Even Richard's familiar loving gaze upon her would have made her shy.

Usually she only looked at her naked self in the mirror in order to find fault and then quickly cover up. At home, Ann felt she was existing under siegelike conditions of a particularly impossible notion of beauty that made low self-esteem a constant. The billion-dollar beauty industry battered one to insecurity month after month from magazine covers, TVs, movies, clothing stores. Men unconsciously held the swimsuit edition of *Sports Illustrated* as an ideal—a D-cup, six-feet-tall, one-hundred-pound, anorexic eighteen-year-old. No real woman—much less an approaching-middle-age woman, much less a working woman with an eighty-hour workweek, no personal trainer, and no plastic surgery—had a snowball's chance in Tahiti of competing. Ann knew this whether she chose to acknowledge it or not.

She flung herself back in the hot sand, liberated. Nonetheless, as she closed her eyes, she put a straw hat over her face because, liberation or not, sun on the body was one thing but on the face, no way; it led to premature wrinkling, wiping out the last five years of her retinol regimen.

It felt splendid, the heat on her body, the slight breeze, which caused her nipples to harden. The effects of the hormone shots were diminishing, and her small breasts felt like her own again. Was it possible that the very dream she had been pursuing was the thing that had been blocking her happiness? She fantasized about being kissed on her mouth, her neck, down to those nipples that were now definitely erect. She couldn't make out exactly who was doing the kissing. Was it Richard, Loren, or Javi, or more likely some combination? Or none of the above?

Then the unimaginable happened—she fell asleep.

Asleep as in an hour of deeply passed out. Only the rising tide nibbling the soles of her feet ("Richard?" she mumbled) woke her up. She sat up and was briefly scandalized to find herself bare-chested—who did that?—until she remembered. The tender white virginal flesh was now flaming pink. When she tugged her suit straps back up, the friction made her cry out in pain. Damn.

She scuttled backward to the shade of an overhanging palm, pulled her suit back down because the press of spandex stung, and took out her lunch. Pulling the cork, she drank straight out of the bottle. The joys of solitude. She ate the whole sandwich in big, unladylike chunks, wolfed through the fruit, spitting pits and seeds into the sand, and then glugged down the rest of the wine. Her head buzzed pleasantly as she watched the white-foamed surf ride in on green waves, heard the percussive roar of breakers on the reef. She felt literally at the edge of the earth, alone, and reveled in it.

After twenty minutes, she got a little bored and decided to pull out her paperback.

One longed for the Robinson Crusoe experience only to a point. Spirits picked up considerably when the character Friday showed up. No fun at all to be shipwrecked with nothing: no food, no clothing, no communication, no companionship. What Ann had was perfect—a day alone, topless, and then a gourmet dinner, a luxurious bungalow, a companionable-enough husband. It was the precarious balancing act between solitude and community that made perfection. She got to her feet, leaving her string bag behind for later. No one would steal it. Another part of the Crusoe experience: the lack of crime. It was as if you were president of your own country. Forget that—the president had hardly any control over the country. Instead you were benevolent dictator, king, or, better, you were a god, little *g*, over your terrain, and could make it over to your own liking.

A swim would be perfect—the water would be deliciously calming on her burning skin. She did a strong breaststroke parallel to the shore, the straps of the pulled-down bathing suit dragging like an underwater parachute, bunching uncomfortably between her legs. Why not go for the full experience?

She did a sidestroke perpendicular to shore and bodysurfed till her stomach scuffed against sand, hesitated, then unpeeled herself from the suit as if it were an old dead skin. In many ways it was harder for Ann to take off her bathing suit than to give up being an attorney—she had never seen herself as a lawyer, but she thought she knew what kind of woman she was, and that didn't include being a nude woman on a beach. Neither assumption ended up being the whole story.

Fearing the incoming tide, Ann wadded the suit into a ball and threw it back into the tree line so that it wouldn't get swept out. She took a mental snapshot so that she could find the suit again—a clump of five palms, some boulders, more trees. The interior was so repetitive one could circle the island without ever realizing it. The key was to face out and memorize the shape of the cove—hers was heart-shaped.

Only a few days ago, she had been waylaid by the sight of a partially clad Wende, and now look at her. Filled with pure animal good spirits, she ran, kicking up the sand (she may have even let out a little victory howl), and jumped into the surf, splashing up drops of water that briefly sparked in the sunlight before gravity recaptured them. Then she dove deeply into the salty embrace of the lagoon.

The green fairy incident in Loren's bungalow had set off an estrangement between Richard and her that she was at the moment not at great pains to fix. As much as she loved her husband and wished to protect him, Ann admitted to a dark streak of wanting to shake him up.

Although she was mildly jealous of his lust for Wende, she wasn't jealous enough for the simple reason that she knew Richard wouldn't act on it. The reason for nonaction had less to do with fidelity than with a basic tentativeness on his part, a timidity that extended from his personal life to his professional—Richard simply didn't believe in himself enough to have an affair. Ann had always suspected that this was why he got swept up by Javi; they were so clearly opposites.

After Ann and Richard had been dating about a year, he went through a period Ann later called his depression. It coincided with a master class that included a trip to France to learn butchery. Ann had just started to work, and there was no way she could leave for a month. Javi had already moved to LA to work as *commis* at a famous restaurant; Richard would join him once the course was over.

Richard came back changed, and the only logical conclusion was that it was due to meeting a girl. Ann waited for the announcement that he was breaking up with her, but it didn't come. Instead Richard worked at the restaurant longer and longer hours. When he came home, haggard, he went straight to bed. Their sex life sputtered out. Ann figured he was too nice to break up with her, or didn't know how. When he began talking about apprenticing with a famous pastry chef in Paris, that was the last straw.

Ann called Javi up and asked him to have a drink with her after work. She needed to run something by him.

She waited for him at a trendy Westside bar he chose. Ann felt guilty and out of place to even be in such a place without Richard knowing. It was happy hour, and she had been elbowed off the bar, and crowded at her table, and one by one her empty chairs had been removed by adjoining parties. She feared that if she went to the bathroom, the table would be gone on her return.

When Javi walked in—jeans, black T-shirt, wetted-down hair— men and women turned to stare. Javi had charisma; he looked like someone whose name you should know. A chair miraculously reappeared along with a menu. The cocktail waitress whom Ann couldn't flag down for a glass of water was now all attention while he ordered shots of a little-known brand of exclusive tequila. Then he turned to Ann.

This was Javi's great gift—when he directed all that magnetism, charisma, and wattage on a poor single female entity, said entity felt so grateful. Now Ann fumbled over how she would inform him she was breaking up with his best friend and wanted his help.

His dark eyes pooled themselves into hers. He hunched over in his seat and held her hand in both of his, almost like a confessional.

"You want to dump Richard?"

"How did you know?"

"How could I *not* know? Question to you: How did you last this long? Richard's messed up, man."

Ann hung her head in guilt and, worse, started crying. Smeared black raccoon eyes. "I'm a terrible person."

"He doesn't see you, *mi amor*. He is too caught up in his own shit."

The classic pot calling the kettle black, but she didn't know it at the time. "He's good-hearted."

"And hardworking. Blah, blah, blah. Pour me another."

The waitress hovering nearby made eye contact with Javi, nodded, and shot away like a hunting dog for more tequila.

"He's a talented chef," she said, digging in. "Better than you."

To his credit, Javi nodded his head at this blow. "I'll give you that. Maybe. But it's about more than dry technique, isn't it? Where's the passion? He doesn't like to sweat. Answer me: Does he take care of you?"

Ann was startled out of her tears by the question.

"You know." He ran his index finger along her wrist.

"I don't care—"

"You don't care?!" he said with such force that people at other tables turned to look at him. "It's a crime! Beautiful woman such as yourself. Leaving you at home every night while he goes out for a beer with Alicia. Nice girl, but not a thought in her head. Just 'You're the bomb, Richard.'"

He had said the magic words to release her (although didn't the very act of choosing lacy, special-occasion La Perla lingerie that morning indicate premeditation on her part?). Half an hour later, she was at Javi's place with said lacy underwear around her ankles. He was on his knees, making her feel as if she had never known what sex was before. Multi-orgasmic, no-strings-attached sex. Afterward he gave her an affectionate peck on the forehead. No talk of love or a relationship in the future. Only years later did he also admit there had been no Alicia.

Javi's cool professionalism as a lover balanced nicely against Richard's maudlin tenderness, his recent postcoital crying in bed, his lack of initiative pretty much all the time. But somehow Ann put off breaking up with Richard even as she continued to sleep with Javi. She rationalized that this technically was the definition of a transitional stage.

One day Richard came to Ann's office unannounced at lunchtime. "Grab a bite?"

"Sure."

On the drive to Richard's favorite gourmet hot dog stand, she said nothing, fearing that he had found out about the affair.

"I've been fired," he said as he took the first bite of his grilled cipollini onion, horseradish-mustard-slathered veggie dog.

"Why?"

"I told them I wouldn't work with *foie gras* or veal any longer. I told them my preference was that they be taken off the menu. These meats in particular are harvested using inhumane methods."

"Oh, honey."

"I have to stand up for what I believe in. It's been killing me. You are the reason I get up every morning, and I hurt you like this."

"Oh."

If only she could take back the last month, but that genie wasn't going back in the bottle. Guilt for betraying Richard, *who loved her.* More guilt for enjoying her afternoons with Javi so much. Guilt for not breaking up with Richard, *or* with Javi, for that matter.

"I was going to propose when I got promoted to line chef."

"Oh."

"Now what?"

"How about opening your own restaurant?"

Richard nodded. "That's my dream, but not yet. We don't have the money or experience."

"Then what?"

"I don't know."

Richard was excited by the prospect of his own place but scared at the reality. Ann didn't know enough about the business to help. That's when she thought about Javi. The next afternoon while in his bed, she brought her plan up.

"You need what he offers," she said.

"What about us?"

"Us ends."

But not before a last afternoon-into-the-early-evening of *amor*. She chastly kissed Javi on the forehead as she left.

Armed with a master plan, Javi and Richard moved to a new, high-concept restaurant chain and quickly went through the ranks from *commis* to sous chefs. Richard, with Javi covering for him during really noxious duties, did all the rotations, spending extra time (no Javi) as *garde manger*, *legumier*, *potager*, and *entremetier*; less time (50 percent Javi) as *friturier*, *grillardin*, and *rôtisseur*; no time (all Javi) as *boucher*. Surprisingly he excelled as *saucier* and was promoted to sous position ahead of Javi, but Richard was nothing if not loyal. Ann did her part by working long hours at FFBBP to raise capital.

Ten years later Ann's memory of being with Javi was as unthinkable as incest. Not quite that bad, but knowing Javi and his history with women had cured Ann of ever being tempted again.

Hours passed. Ann swam and walked farther than she had ever gone before around the island. The solitude was so complete she couldn't imagine it being broken. Her thoughts, instead of heading as usual to fixing the disaster of their life back home, stayed right on the island, right in the moment. Even though a week before Richard and she had been on the brink of the success they had so struggled for, today she couldn't summon much sadness for its passing. How could a sacrifice of ten years be wiped away in a week and not matter? What was wrong with that picture? Did they know that the restaurant would be a success? What if El Gusano turned out to be just another type of prison? Was she becoming gun-shy of commitment of any kind? It felt like she had only done the prep work and skipped the climaxes of her professional life—partnership at the firm, running a restaurant. Already she was at the denouement. For the first time in her carefully planned life, the future remained opaque.

Surprisingly, it didn't feel as bad as she thought it would.

She was gazing up the beach, feeling like some cross between a castaway and a mystic, when she saw it. A sight that literally stopped her in her tracks and took her breath away.

Her head pounded. The first thing that came to mind was the scene she had read in *Robinson Crusoe*—when after living alone for many years Crusoe found that single human footprint in the sand of his deserted isle. Far from making him happy, it terrified him. Granted, cannibalism was a problem she thankfully didn't have. This was a twenty-first-century footprint. She felt dizzy, and then the reality of her nakedness occurred to her. One arm went across her breasts; the other covered her pubic area. Her chest went concave, as if she were less visible that way. Ann turned and ran, realizing, too late, that her bare ass was in full view.

It took her half an hour to scour the beach backward toward the resort for the heart-shaped cove and clump of five palms, where she found her string bag but no brown bathing suit. When she had retraced her steps to said cove for the fifth time with still no bathing suit in sight, she gave up and scurried to the resort. Her previous confidence and joy in her nakedness, her oneness with nature, had evaporated, replaced by the primal terror one had in dreams of appearing naked. Except she wasn't dreaming. What were the odds—the first time she had done such a thing—that this would happen? Chastened, she was frantic to hide all evidence of her lapse.

The dive boat had returned and was tied up at the dock, but thankfully no one was in sight. She hid behind a palm for a minute, surveying the empty path, then made her run for her *fare* on the other end of the beach. Behind her a door slammed, but she did not dare turn, just barreled straight ahead, determined on invisibility. As she jumped on the lanai and placed her hand on the doorknob, she distinctly heard a wolf whistle. She did not look back.

The scuba diving ménage à trois had taken an interesting turn that day. Before they took off, Richard as usual checked the gas level in the boat, made sure there was an extra can of petrol, established that the radio was operational. Cooked was much too lax. Earlier Richard had talked Loren into teaching him how to check the gas levels in the scuba tanks and inspect them for leaks. On his own initiative, he gave the mouthpieces a quick antibacterial swipe.

A pattern had developed over the previous outings: At first the three of them would take off and look at things together. Then Dex and Wende would swim away, and Richard obligingly swam in the opposite direction to give them privacy. The first time he was alone, he heard a crunching sound, like someone eating cereal. He thought he was hallucinating when he spotted its source: a beautiful green-and-blue fish, munching on coral. Sometimes Richard was so still, fish came and nibbled on him as if he might be edible. He liked these nibbles and never shooed the fish away. Afterward his skin would have small purplish bites like miniature hickeys. Richard was growing to cherish these times when his mind was so concentrated on the sights around him—lacy fans of white coral; clumped brain coral in magenta, apricot, and green; clown fish; manta rays; sea turtles; blue starfish—that he literally lost himself until either Cooked or Wende swam to get him.

Needless to say, he greatly preferred Wende's visits: the halo of blond hair floating, the flipper-elongated mermaid legs, the sparkle of belly button ring. He even liked how her lower jaw and mouth looked under the mask, like a goofy Muppet, making the beauty of her whole face less intimidating. Her running joke was to sneak up behind him and pull on the elastic waistband of his swim trunks, then let go, snapping him. When, lost in his fishy daydreams, he startled and sputtered in his mouthpiece, she found this hilarious. She would tap on his air gauge, indicating it was time to surface, and then they would ascend side by side, air bubbles promiscuously mixing, their heads finally breaking above water, masks crowning their foreheads.

"Don't do that," he said, mock angry even as their thighs brushed while treading water. "Naughty girl."

Each day after lunch on one or another deserted atoll, Cooked and Dex lit up a joint, and soon both would be conked out. Although in truth Richard wouldn't have minded a nap himself, Wende was wide-awake and, for his intents and purposes, alone.

Under normal circumstances, Richard would have put himself out of temptation's way. He would have toked with the guys, then napped. He'd had years of practice turning a blind eye to pretty waitresses, hostesses, and even the occasional femme fatale chef. But the recurring vision of Ann propped up on that sarcophagal sleigh bed, sopping down that disgusting snot-green drink with Loren, burned behind his eyelids. So when Wende called, he went.

The first time this happened, they decided to explore a bird sanctuary on one of the islands. As they crawled up on the birds, trying to keep quiet and not scare them away, Richard put out his hand and laid it on her sun-warmed shoulder. He inhaled deeply. She smelled like good soup.

Another time, guiding her around a rocky shore, he held her hand. Even these chaste acts racked him with shame, as if the two of them were having wild crazy sex orgies each afternoon. He was a swine, a typical horny guy dry-humping as soon as an attractive young woman walked by, and yet . . . Wende *was* pretty, Wende *was* well built, Wende *was* young, sweet, unironic, worshipful, and, most important of all, Wende *didn't* see him as an utter loser.

Although the demise of El Gusano, the fact of Javi's profligacy, and Richard's own carelessness in allowing things to come to this unforgivable pass were soul-shattering, what could be done now? His solution was to go back to work. Things would either straighten themselves out or not, but he didn't envision no longer cooking. Richard cooked, therefore he was. This is where his guilt came in: Ann hated her job. She did it for them, and her sacrifice was on the verge of being wasted. How long would it take Javi to pay them back? It would never happen. There was nothing Richard could do about any of it, and so he lusted after Wende.

This last week had been revelatory. He had forgotten what normal people did with the empty hours of a day, how long and voluptuous said hours could be when wrapped around pleasure. His usual day started at six a.m., when he rose to accept deliveries at the kitchen, continued to cleaning and prepping, then cooking, ordering, managing staff, and at the end of a long day, two a.m. on average, falling back into bed exhausted. His view of the bigger world was out the kitchen's back door to the alley. Of course his body was enjoying this leisure, but his soul was restless. The knowledge that he had done his best to be what Ann wanted and failed tore him up.

On that particular day's rock-star-boyfriend-less excursion, Wende stubbed her toe, and Richard offered to massage it. She sat on the sand and put her shapely foot in his lap, oblivious to the fact that she was exposing the metallic-gold isthmus of thong bikini between her legs, or that her pumiced heel was pressing down on his groin.

"I love your hands," Wende said.

Richard, mystified, looked down at his scarred, callused cook's hands that he only noticed when they were damaged and got in the way of his work.

"I cook," he said. "Escoffier said that good food is the foundation of genuine happiness."

"I want a man who loves me like you love Ann."

Had she really just said that? Richard smiled, a look he worried was mincing rather than seductive. Was this a test?

"Dex is such an old man, you know?" Wende said.

He ground his knuckles into the ball of her foot, then kneaded the tendon along her arch. Her toenails were frosted pink like the icing on a cupcake, and he surprised himself with the fantasy of putting one of her little toes in his mouth.

"Not that old," he said.

"It's his attitude. Like a father almost."

"I could be your father."

"Almost."

"So why are you with such an old man?"

"I don't believe in the limitations of age. I'm an old soul."

Despite lusting after her, Richard had to bite the inside of his cheek not to smirk. "So the money didn't attract you?"

She shook her head and flung herself back on her elbows. He tried not to notice that her breasts bulged out invitingly from their little gold lamé triangles of shelter. Forget soup. The *sillage* from her skin was of coconut, apricots, caramelized sugar.

"It's more of a hassle than anything else. It attracts these hangers-on. People Dex shouldn't be around. I came for the music. I stayed for the music. He's a major talent. I worry about him being on his own, but I'm still young. I can't be his mother. I want to find real love like you two have."

Richard's mind was an utter blank. You two? When it came to him that she meant him and Ann, it was like a pail of cold water. "Us!" He flung Wende's foot off his lap and jumped up. "You should be fine now. Let's go back."

After all these years of faithfulness, Richard had for the first time (second time if you included fantasies of the Spanish sous chef Alicia, which he had never acted on) been willing to flirt with the idea of another woman, and yet he—stupid, stupid—had been unaware, blind to the fact that time was passing, had passed in fact, and that he had reached that critical stage where a man is no longer attractive on his own to younger women. Youth would no longer carry the day. He had to face the fact that the receding hairline and the pot belly and the hair sprouting out of his ears were not just aberrations, things that could be fixed or hidden away, but instead were precursors to the fact that Richard was on his way to turning into a middle-aged lech desiring but not getting the pootie. And what did a young woman want with a middle-aged lecherous man unless he was rich, glamorous, or preferably both, like Dex Cooper?

"You should go home to your parents."

Richard just prayed that Ann would get over her infatuation with the cadaverous Frenchman.

Wende stuck out her pink tongue at him. "Who are you? My dad?"

She said it in such a snotty, schoolgirl tone it was all he could do to not bend her over his knee and spank her. That he kind of liked the idea mortified him. When they arrived back at the boat, she went aboard and put on a T-shirt, totally ignoring Richard. Had he angered her that much?

Dex didn't open his eyes. "Cooked's been telling me about the drift dive. It's wild. We gotta do it."

"Great," Wende said, clearly indicating it was not. She stretched her arms above her head and arched her comely back while giving Cooked the hard, appraising look of a hungry person standing in front of an open refrigerator, desiring to be tempted. Her eyes scanned his triangular tattoos, slowly trailing down his torso (conscious of this ravenous gaze, he sucked in his stomach).

Cooked burst out into a big stoned grin, intuiting Richard's flirtation was at an end.

"How about some beer?" Dex said, and stood up unsteadily just as Wende switched seats away from Richard to sit next to Cooked, teeter-tottering the boat. As if Dex had changed his mind and wanted to dive instead, he bent over the side of the boat and pitched in headfirst.

From underwater, Wende's screams made the same scratching sound as the parrot fish Richard had heard earlier. Dex was in a dead man's slump, oblivious to the fact he had fallen overboard. Richard grabbed him around the waist and kicked upward, thrilled that, despite his panic, his old Boy Scout training had sprung back into use. With Cooked's help, they hoisted an unconscious Dex onboard, and Richard went to work. In the restaurant biz someone had to learn CPR, and Javi had been uninterested, so Richard had taken the course alone.

He bent over and blew in Dex's mouth. His only practice before was on a rubber dummy. He had never had contact with a man's lips; of course it was his fate that today, instead of Wende's lips, he should be touching Dex's. Now Dex opened his eyes, and they stared at each other for a long intimate moment before he turned away and retched out a cupful of lagoon.

Ann didn't bother to shower off but threw a shirt over her sticky, burned skin, tugged on her khaki shorts, and stalked to Loren's hut. When she reached his lanai, Titi was blocking the door by sitting in a lounge chair as she braided her long hair.

The sight was stunning. It made Ann want to ask if she might sketch her later. For a second, she wondered if Loren might have some pastels or oil paints to lend her, but then she remembered her righteous black cloud of outrage and pushed on by.

"He's tired," Titi said.

"Sorry, but I must." Ann jumped over the end of the lounge and used her shoulder on the door, flinging it open. Loren was in bed.

"You lying bastard!"

"Can I help you?"

"I can't believe that you would do something like this."

"You will tell me any minute what 'this' is?"

"Robinson Crusoe island? Back to the primitive? While you have a camera setup like some creepy reality show? You *are* a *perverti*."

"You did venture far today."

"So you are responsible? Leaving it all behind. Mr. Buddha here."

"*You* called me those things."

"You accepted being called those things."

Ann had been in a transcendent state when she came to that particularly picturesque cove, and it didn't register at first sight—the six-foot aluminum pole or the camera bolted at its top. After futilely searching for her bathing suit, she had snuck through the trees and watched the camera's movement—it seemed stationary, rotating neither left nor right but focusing straight ahead on the last fifteen feet of sand and the ocean beyond it. When Ann literally turned tail and ran, she had not been filmed in all likelihood, but the spell had been broken. She felt violated. On the way back to the resort, she no longer communed with the sand, water, and sky; no, she was looking for likely hiding places of more cameras because the reality of one presaged the likelihood that the whole island was being surveilled.

Loren sighed. "It's a very long story."

"I have time."

"It was started for my daughter. It's become popular. A million regular viewers around the world."

Ann's eyes grew big as the implications sunk in. As she looked around the room, her glance stopped at the door papered in watercolors. She moved toward it.

"No, Ann. Please."

She gently opened it. Inside was a desk upon which sat a huge Apple monitor. File cabinets lined the wall. Computer, printer, modem, cell phone, everything a tech geek could desire to hide out on an island and still be *totally plugged in*. Above the desk was a large world map with little colored pins stuck all over it. Was there a term yet for technological infidelity?

"Bastard! You are such a supreme hypocrite!"

Loren said nothing.

Ann came back, stood at the footboard, hands on her hips.

He sighed. "Aren't we being self-righteous? What do you think—that this is a real experience? Ann? Talk to me. This fantasy of escape that comes with *premier cru* French wine and vegetables flown in from Australia? You're sleeping on Frette sheets, for Christ's sake. *Vous êtes une femme folle.*"

"You're right." Anger leaked from her quickly.

What was her grave disappointment about? Loren had called her out. Meek Richard let her get away with more than was good for either of them.

"I run a resort. I need to contact Papeete, the parent hotel across the lagoon, potential customers. Emergency services if need be. I have to live in the modern world, *non?*"

"Of course."

She felt defeated, and worse, her fantasy shattered. She needed the island to be pure to validate her choice in coming there. Truth was, her confidence at the wisdom of having dumped her job was crumbling. She was scared. She was burning through money like no tomorrow. If she flew back and begged the senior partners, went on her hands and knees to that windbag Flask, would they take her back? She had a crush on a gay hotelier who might be a pervert and certainly got off on spycraft. She was probably *not* going to have a baby. Her husband might have stopped loving her in favor of an uncomplicated nymphet. *Une femme folle*, indeed.

Ann was hardwired into the American dream, and, by necessity, she saw every tick downward as a temporary aberration, a pit stop, a state from which she would roar back to triumph. Unthinkable that she would go down in the world and then stay down. Un-American.

"Tell me the truth about one thing: Do you have cameras on us? In our rooms, on the beach?"

"I swear . . . just the one."

"So what's it for?"

Loren broke into the sly smile of a ten-year-old boy playing a fast one. "It's my masterwork. During my best years at the gallery in Paris, maybe a few hundred people saw my work. Too avant-garde, too obscure, too expensive. It appealed only to snobs—and people too embarrassed to admit they didn't understand it so they praised it instead. It's like those nightclubs that are exclusive only because of who they keep out. I've finally done something that reaches hundreds of thousands of people."

"Are you making money?"

"No, no," he said, as if the idea was distasteful. "It's anonymous. It's a website of nothing except the empty beach. It's on all the time. The only interaction possible is to leave comments. There is a visitor counter. Thousands of repeat visitors. Some people go regularly every day. Some go only when they are in crisis, to calm themselves. Death of a parent, spouse, child, or pet; divorce; loss of job; illness. Ended romances. Like the Buddhist explanation of the universe—Indra's net. It's like the most fantastic dream—to be part of all these lives."

"I'm . . . speechless."

Loren sat back, pleased. "Imagine a spiderweb with drops of dew along each strand. Each drop reflects all the others. Then each reflected drop reflects all the other reflected dewdrops. On and on forever. Pour us some absinthe."

"How do people find out about it?"

"Word of mouth. I will not do press. No ads. I want no one to find out where the actual beach is or about me. The privacy and anonymity of the experience are essential. That's part of the magic. Promise?"

"But you could charge."

"I don't want to profit—it's a memorial."

"To who?"

"I don't wish to say."

Ann nodded at the incongruity of an anonymous memorial. "Show it to me."

It was a huge relief to sit in front of a computer again, staring into a screen. In reflex, her hand curled itself around the mouse like holding a lover's hand as Loren brought the site up. There it was. Kind of. A strip of sand and then the ocean. There was sound so that you could hear the surf. Ann watched it a few minutes and had to admit it was peaceful. But one didn't see the beautiful palms behind the camera; one couldn't feel the burn of the sun or the silk of the breeze. No bite of salty ocean. No way to convey that infinity of space.

"Did my visit get recorded?"

Loren wagged his head and scrolled down the comments.

"People thought they heard footsteps, then a woman's voice cursing, then running that faded away. It caused a bump in viewership. People asked to have it replayed. That's against the rules."

"Whose rules?"

"Mine."

"Unbelievable." Ann paused. "What do you call it?"

"*Plage*. Beach."

"That's imaginative."

"It's about pure experience. Not my interpretation of that experience."

"How do you know it's not accidentally visited by people looking for beach party videos? Or bikini watchers?"

"They'll get bored."

"But you want to attract the people the site was meant for? Right? Otherwise, what's the point?"

"How would that happen?"

"Call it 'Robinson Crusoe.' If you put 'South Pacific,' they'll be looking for hula girls."

Loren frowned. "Too much like Mickey Mouse. Disneyland. They'll want some castaway staggering around on the sand, eating a live fish."

"No. It's the solitude. That's the experience people want. That's what we spent the money to come here for. That's why I'm here. Give them that gift."

As frail and tired as Loren had looked before, now his eyes lit up. The prospect of bringing new life to the webcam got him out of bed. When Titi came with fruit juice, he drank his down without a thought and shushed her away. He jostled Ann out of his chair, then went about purchasing his new domain name, waving to her as she left to get ready for dinner.

Hours later, Loren hosted dinner but left before dessert. Dex started the nightly concert, announcing he would play a new song he had just written. Richard sat alone with his beer, glowering as Wende bent over Cooked beating out a slow rhythm on his *to'ere* drums. Then she took his seat, latching the big drums between her lithe thighs, as Cooked bent over behind her, his arms over hers, virtual Polynesian nesting dolls, and they tapped out a rhythm together. Unbearable. He looked away, just in time to observe Loren rejoin the group. He leaned over Ann and whispered in her ear. Great. Ann broke into a huge smile and hugged Loren, reaching up to kiss his cheek.

His wife's burgeoning affair.

Only later would he understand that success, even anonymous, could be a wonderful medicine.

# Rock 'n' Roll Will Save Your Life

*For all men tragically great are made so through a certain mor-*
*bidness. Be sure of this, O young ambition, all mortal greatness*
*is but disease.*

—MELVILLE, *Moby-Dick*

Dex got into it like everyone else—for the girls. A license for pussy.
Beautiful girls and ones tending toward plain, tall and short, fat
and skinny, smart and slow, with every combination in between, and
they had all become inexplicably available. Rock music was the last refuge of the misfit, which Dex considered himself at age sixteen; ditto,
the unathletic. Musical ability was a ticket out for guys who were pale
and thin-chested, smoked pot and skipped classes. Grow your hair, get
some tattoos, and start learning to play that guitar that you cradled at
first mostly as a prop, and magically, everything that formerly labeled
you as a loser—lack of social skills, lack of education, lack of a good
future—converted to cool. You didn't even have to wash regularly.

Dex had lost count of the number of days they had been on the island.
Northward of two months, he guessed, but he didn't want to know. He
had this idea of falling outside the confines of time, and avoiding the
calendar and not wearing a watch were part of that plan. Loren was cool
about not making them feel like they were on the meter. In fact, the
astronomical charges that Dex got when he finally read the statements
months later came as a kind of betrayal, showing just how unlaid-back

the whole arrangement was in reality. The fine print stated categorically that "inclusive" included a two-bottle-per-day limit on alcohol, after which huge, nasty surcharges began to sprout up for such things as extra booze, as well as requests for special food or service outside of regular dining hours. Ditto for Cooked's supply of pot, billed under miscellaneous.

"Just charge the Visa when you need a bump," Dex instructed, and boy did they.

The six months before Dex arrived at the island had been a hell of touring town after town, or rather auditorium after auditorium, because after a while he didn't bother finding out the names of the towns or even the states they were in. The band members, especially his lead guitarist, Robby, and he were fighting, arguing about the music, the schedule, the recording contract, even about the drug supply at each stop. They had turned from being the bad-boy conquistadors of rock into little old ladies bitching over the sandwiches at a bridge lunch. The only thing they did not argue about was the need to earn more money because the band had become its own animal and needed constant feeding.

It was the first time in twenty-five years that it felt like a job.

The usual high he got from playing had gone MIA. The songs tasted like leather in his mouth. As short of the true experience as jerking off was to making out with the love of his life, currently Wende. Or, rather, the pyrotechnics, the glitz and glam, the selling of CDs, T-shirts, bumper stickers, and hats almost made the real-live musicians beside the point. Although they refused, their label would have preferred Prospero lip-synching for a more foolproof performance. The goal was to imitate the record instead of improvising and keeping the music alive and changing. It had become de rigueur for many bands. Generic, zombie boy bands were drawing bigger crowds with their fake, manufactured, forgettable sound. Dex swore before he stooped to Milli Vanilli–ing his music he'd quit. Attitudes such as this led to the perception among corporate that he had grown "difficult."

The audiences, disappointingly, did not seem to register the empty, hollowed sound in the music. They were enthusiastic as always. Grooving. In almost all ways, they were the best part of the concerts. Even when Dex insisted on throwing in a few blues pieces—moody fuckers—fans tasted it, then howled and begged for more. Maybe the change was just in his mind. So he compensated with the drugs, which left him totally strung out by the time they came off the road. The band members scattered in different directions immediately like opposing politicians who had been forced together for a photo op.

W ende and Ann had taken off in the boat for a shopping trip in town with Cooked, so Dex was alone for the first time in months. He didn't like being alone, but today it was half okay because he was still riding high from the day before. He lit up his morning budski. He was proud of going cold turkey from the heavy drugs on arrival, and sweet Wende had nursed him through that ugly first week. Now he was on a rigorous regimen of alcohol and weed only, and he felt like a million bucks. Frisky as a teenager, and the song ideas had started coming again. He had not written a new piece in ten months, and he was in fear that he had gone dry, but no, he had simply abused the muse. Some roadie had given him a book of Buddhist teachings, and he had read it—proof he was going soft in the head, but it had forced him to see the error of his ways.

Yesterday in the boat, while Richard and Wende went off to check out birds, Dex had heard a whole damn song delivered entire in his head. A gift. It made him feel drunk, bottled up with magic, and he was in some artistic fugue state when he fell overboard. When he came to, he looked up into Richard's eyes overjoyed that he *hadn't lost the song*. Dex hardly talked on the trip back, scared that it would leak out of him. Without a word to anyone, he jumped out of the boat and ran to his *fare*, slamming the door behind him, and grabbed a pen and paper. For the next couple of hours, he was in heaven. The lyrics flowed in his ear, and he wrote like a possessed *vodoun* priest because one misplaced word and the whole shimmering house of cards would come crashing down. Then he grabbed his guitar and notated the riffs, the change-ups, not entirely but enough so that there was the skeleton of a song.

As he had with his former addictions, Dex now craved a phone for the first time since they had been on the island so he could play it for Robby. A peace offering. More than that, a golden egg because the band had had enough hits that Dex could smell one, and this was a winner. The lodestone to anchor a new album. He felt spent, expansive, like after the best sex, a high beyond where any drug could take you. Drugs weren't for the music; they were for getting through the periods without the music. And yet . . .

Was creation just another addiction? Didn't the Buddhist stuff talk about the illusion of all worldly success? Which turned out to be especially true once the band finished paying the label back their advances; gave another cut to their business manager, their producer; took care of rehab expenses (nonrecoupable), houses, wives, kids, mistresses, and shrinks. At forty-plus years old (he was as cagey about his age as some long-in-the-tooth soap-opera actress), hadn't he been there, done that? Illusion, no shit. He had a deep suspicion of himself—that this detoxing, dropping off the grid, the monogamy with Wende was really just about process, like that of a boxer in training. Was it possible that all Dex really wanted was a new hit single? How could he prove to himself the purity of his intentions?

He didn't even want to go there with the fact that, besides Wende's most excellent boobs, what really turned him on was her most excellent ear. Untrained, she could pick out a particularly sweet riff in a sea of demos. She intuited the real players from the pretenders. It didn't hurt that she also fell into their most important demographic. After six marriages, two to the same woman, Dex swore that he had finally found his soul mate.

With Ann's suit gone, she had borrowed one of Wende's bikinis. Richard's eyes narrowed as he watched her walk across the sand and into Cooked's waiting craft for the trip to town. She skipped her usual sunblock and instead greased herself up with Wende's monoi oil. The men had not been invited and would stay behind.

Outcast, Dex and Richard stood on the beach, waving to the women as they sped off across the lagoon. Richard thought he saw Cooked place his hand on the small of Wende's bare back, but he said nothing. Titi moaned and returned to the kitchen.

In the small tourist trap of a town, Wende led Ann to a tattoo parlor and convinced the sullen staff to let her work on her friend. The owners were unsmiling, but not nearly as unsmiling as Ann. Wende gave Cooked a hundred and told him to get beers for everyone, and the mood lightened.

"I'll make sure all the sterilization procedures are done," Wende whispered.

"You should be a diplomatic envoy . . . someplace that needs it, like the Middle East. Your talents are wasted here."

"I'm a semi orphan," Wende said. "I've learned to be resourceful."

"You said you had a mom."

"I do. She was living on a commune when she met my dad. She never really got over being a hippie. We kind of self-raised. Then dad froze to death in his car. *David Copperfield* kind of stuff." Wende swabbed down the needles with alcohol. "Where do you want it?"

"On my shoulder?" Ann asked.

It had seemed a good idea the night before when they all got drunk celebrating Dex's new song, but now she wished she hadn't agreed to it.

"I know just where. And what. Trust me."

As Wende worked on the inside, tenderest part of Ann's thigh, Cooked joked with the workers who stood watching and drinking beer. He regularly stole looks at Wende. After what seemed like hours, Ann couldn't stand the pain any longer. "Enough! We'll finish it later." She looked down and saw the front half of a shark—looking either as if it were cresting out of the water or as if it had been bitten in half. When it was done, it would appear to be circling around and around her thigh.

"What do you think?" Wende asked.

A slow smile spread on Ann's face. "I'm not the kind of woman who does this."

"Maybe now you'll have to become her."

"It burns."

"Yeah."

"Let's go have a drink."

Wende and Cooked exchanged looks. "Cooked wants to take me on a tour for a couple of hours."

Along the main street of the place, Ann found a shabby café with outdoor tables, and she rested in a chair, nursing her stinging thigh by drinking down a carafe of house white. It had not occurred to her to find a phone or computer to contact anyone. Only when she read over the care brochure from the tattoo parlor, which clearly read *Do not drink alcohol during or immediately after*, did she begin to feel paranoid. When had she become this reckless woman?

In front of her was the turquoise lagoon. Across the street between two low-slung buildings, the violet pounding ocean. Could such cutting beauty become mundane? The locals passed through it with hardly a glance. What was it that Loren found here all those years ago? Perhaps as easy an answer as that it was the furthest thing he could imagine from his former life.

Without Richard the beauty of the place would crush her.

She knew his little infatuation with Wende had ended, but what if it hadn't? She was too mature to say that she couldn't live without him, but life without him would lose its flavor. Why was it that while separated she felt her love most clearly? He was her *pain au chocolat*.

On the beach, fishermen stretched their nets, knotted tears, shouting back and forth to one another, laughing so much that the progress regularly came to a stop. A man paddled a pirogue, the brown curved hull cutting through the pale green water like a blade. A woman, draped in a coral muumuu, walked down the sidewalk, stopped, and clucked to a scabby, nut-colored dog trailing behind her. The scene could be a painting by Gauguin.

Ann felt a pang of remorse that she was not brave enough to leave everything behind as the great artist had. Would he have been as great if he had stayed in Paris? His life was mythologized because it was such a hard thing to do. Wasn't Gauguin's renunciation of everything what finally had allowed him to paint as he had? In Paris he had been a stockbroker—almost as bad as being a lawyer. Easier that he was in a loveless marriage. She still loved Richard, but was love enough? Gauguin left behind five children. He took up with a fifteen-year-old Tahitian girl and had four more. He painted a paradise that was more fantasy than reality. Fantasy for all the poor saps back home not brave enough to make the leap. He was a selfish bastard and a genius. Ditto Picasso, Pollock. Women didn't act like that. How much damage was Ann willing to wreak on those around her? How dare she—lowly associate at FFGBBP—think she could ever remake her life at this late date?

The summer before law school started, Ann's mother insisted on going to Paris before chemo. Her father opposed the idea. He pleaded a heavy workload, but then he always pleaded a heavy workload. The one time her parents had gone to France had been a disaster, and Ann suspected that was his real reason. Usually, if he traveled at all, it was on educational/cultural tours arranged through his alma mater. Trips that were an endless round of lectures, museums, and hard drinking with alums. Kind of like being back in the frat house. Ideally, he liked spending the entire time speaking English, minimizing his contact with local people. Her mother hated these trips and refused to go. Her idea of travel was to wander, to get lost, to talk to strangers, to live life spontaneously, every last thing her father disliked.

So Ann and her mother went without him.

August in Paris was hot and dusty; the city abandoned by locals. Her mother took her to all the sights she remembered from her first trip, places discovered while alone—walking along the Seine, stopping along bridges, the Promenade Plantée, the Tuileries. They ate at romantic restaurants at ten at night, a dining time her father would have found scandalous, and finished entire bottles of wine.

On their last full day, instead of sleeping in, her mother went out to have her hair done. She returned carrying a new dress in a plastic sleeve. She had been eyeing it at a nearby boutique all week long but only now had made a decision. It was cotton, sleeveless, a frivolous deep red that she would usually deem impractical. By the time Ann had showered, her mother had put makeup on for the first time during the trip. She wore heels and perfume.

"What's going on?" Ann asked.

"We're going to visit a friend."

This was news because they knew no one in Paris. It was half an hour by Metro across the city. They took a cab to a nondescript, middle-class neighborhood. The cab stopped at an old square with an oversize fountain in the center. A movie theater anchored one side, a Gothic church the other. Restaurants crowded the sidewalks with outdoor tables shaded by umbrellas.

Ann's mother stood unsure.

"Is this the right place?" Ann asked.

"Joanna!" a man's voice called out.

His name was Marc. He had been an exchange student and had befriended her mother in college. Later Ann would try to recall his features—silver hair, aquiline nose—but could not. It wasn't that he was unattractive. His features were transformed as he looked at her mother, and that was only the half of it.

Before her eyes, this mother that she swore she knew everything about turned unrecognizable. The tightness, the tentativeness, the somberness dropped away. The woman who took Marc's arm was relaxed. She glowed.

One of the restaurants was his, and he seated them at a table by the fountain. Waiters brought a bottle of champagne, and Joanna, who never drank in the daytime, toasted.

The day passed like an alternate reality, another life her mother could have lived instead. Marc had his car brought, and he drove them to his house in the country for lunch. The car was a convertible, and Ann scrambled into the tiny backseat while her mother tied a scarf over her hair. As they drove out of the city, the open fields and rolling hills eased the scary constriction Ann had been feeling. For the first time she acknowledged fear over her mother's illness. Up front, Joanna looked like a '50s movie star, oversize sunglasses and head flung back to let the sun warm her face. Even though Ann was an adult, she felt every child's dismay at the evidence of her mother having had a life, and apparently a lover, before Ann existed.

The old stone farmhouse was at the end of a lane in a small village. When they got out of the car, people surrounded them: Marc's three grown children, two daughters and a son, their spouses, and a handful of grandchildren. It was the birthday of one of the grandchildren, and neighbors had come to celebrate. Ann helped the oldest daughter carry food outside from the kitchen while Marc led Joanna around the property.

"He was so excited about her visit," the daughter said. She had a dark beauty that Ann guessed was the mother's. The elegant dress she wore was protected only by an apron.

"So was she," Ann said, although of course her mother had told her nothing about it.

"He told me Joanna was his first love. Before he met our mother."

"Is she here?"

"She passed away. It's been hard on him, so this visit is good."

Lunch was served under the trees at a long wooden table. The children sat on blankets scattered across the lawn. Marc sat with Joanna beside him at the head of the table. From where Ann sat, she would have sworn they were a couple, had always been together; they fit each other so naturally. She had never seen her mother like this, had never before seen her in love. Compared with this table, their life back home paled.

As each dish was passed, Marc put a spoonful on Joanna's plate and then served himself. He carefully arranged a bit of cheese and a fig and fed it to her. Ann's eyes stung. Her father would never have thought of doing such a thing.

When they returned to their hotel that night, Ann questioned her: "Why did you never mention him?"

"He was the first man I fell in love with. You don't talk to your children about that if he's not their father. How could I uproot my life and live in France? He went home and married. Later I met your father—"

"But you knew the difference."

"Who I loved. Every person we love changes us."

Wende was nowhere in sight, and Ann's thigh stung. The waiter was eyeing her for occupying the table so long. To hell with it—she ordered more wine and a sandwich to go with it.

The thought of returning to her windowless office—reward for being promoted from junior to senior associate—filled her with despair. Hadn't Napoleon bragged he could make grown men die for little bits of ribbon? She had spent years of her life to win those cubic feet of gloomy office space with the mushroomy-smelling ventilation system blowing down on her head. On her cluttered desk, Mrs. Peters's hammered-silver monogrammed cocktail shaker in pink leather was waiting to be taken home to join a cabinet full of similarly expensive useless gifts, which the firm regularly doled out at holidays and birthdays and which clients gave in gratitude: designer nut trays, monogrammed silver ice tongs, crystal jam pots, expensive scented candles in their own Italian terra-cotta jars. The kind of uselessly lavish things that one immediately thought of regifting. Ann took a big sip of wine.

Richard was moping at being left behind back at the resort. Was she taking out her anger on him? They could not keep going on this way. At the very least, they would burn through all of their money. Eventually they would have to either go forward or go back; one couldn't tread water forever.

Richard was sweating.

The day was hotter than previous ones—the air heavy with rain, although the sky was immaculately cloudless. The women had deserted. Ann had been distracted and distant when she left that morning. From long years of marriage he recognized that dormant-volcano quality she had when about to make a declaration, and he dreaded the inevitable explosion. He needed to talk, to hold hands, to cuddle, and yet on this empty island the only time they spent together was at night in bed, and so far every night Ann had turned her granite back to him and slept like the dead. What was she so tired from anyway?

Loren, his rival, scowled when he invited him to a game of chess.

Alone, Richard drank a morning beer and sat down to read, but the slapping of the waves against shore, the boom of the reef beyond, the floodlight glare of the sun on the white sand beach made it impossible to concentrate.

Above a clump of palms, tiny puffs of smoke appeared. Gratefully, Richard threw down his book to go investigate, thinking maybe Titi was preparing one of those Polynesian earth ovens he always wondered about. As he rounded the shoreline, the sight in front of him stopped him in his tracks.

Dex sat cross-legged in front of a large bonfire. In the blazing daylight, the fire appeared fake, like pretend flames in a stage play, harmless and funny. Tears tracked down Dex's pocked, sharp cheeks as he swayed back and forth, chanting something. Listening more closely, Richard decided he was singing—maybe the new song from the night before?—although he couldn't be sure. His first instinct was to retreat, but his overriding second one, honed by years in the Scouts up to the level of Eagle Scout, was to help. He was fairly fluent in crazy due to Javi and knew the best offense often was none at all.

He strolled at a leisurely pace up to the fire and flopped down on the sand. It was too disconcerting to look at Dex's face, twisted in agony— bad drug trip?—so instead Richard stared at the flames, their orange tongues leeched of threat under the pounding sun.

"Hot mother today, huh?"

Dex wasn't swaying after all; he was trembling. He wadded another piece of paper and fed it into the flames as if he were performing an ancient sacrifice.

"What you got there?" Richard prodded.

"Illusion," Dex said.

All his long career as a musician he had been hoarding these inspirations, trapping them down on paper or recording them on tape, scrawling words on his own arms, on receipts, cocktail napkins, paper towels in grubby nightclub bathrooms. Once he even used a Sharpie on a groupie's back, a single phrase down her spine, and took her to his hotel to copy it down in his spiral notebook because there was no agony like losing these whiffs of magic (he'd gladly write them in his own blood if he had to). He lived under the constant worry that the source that gave so freely might turn capricious. It was like being the worst kind of junkie—the kind no one wanted to cure. Maybe—he was going slow here—just *maybe* he would decide to never write another song again. It was conceivable. Could he be happy just being a regular guy? Maybe he would stay on this island, away from the temptations of civilization. Was he strong enough to give it all up? Nah, he could never give it up. He loved the music too much. Or did he?

In a daze, he looked over at Richard, who had saved his life. This last week he had hardly talked to the guy, although Wende and he had grown thick as thieves. But now that they were alone together, Dex realized he missed being around his band, around other dudes. Loren wasn't the hanging-around type, and Cooked was always busy.

"Compadre!" Dex leaned over and hugged him.

"You okay?" Richard squeaked, the strength of Dex's vise-hug emptying the air out of his lungs.

With his thin, ropy arms and legs, his dyed-black hair sticking up at all angles, the black-and-blue bruiselike effect of his tattoos, Dex didn't look healthy in daylight.

"I'm glad you were here for this."

"Me, too. That a new song you're singing?"

Dex shook his head. "A chant from the Tibetan Book of the Dead. The Great Liberation Through Hearing in the Bardo."

They both watched the last ball of paper crumble up and turn black.

"You feel like playing some volleyball?" Richard asked.

"Sounds good." Dex stood up and dusted off sand. "I'll herbalista us up some smoke."

"Okay," Richard said.

"That's my man! Let's doade."

When Dex started playing in the early '80s, it had been fun. He played lead guitar and performed vocals at every dive in LA, joined any band that would have him, traveled around the country broke and high, and loved every single swarmy last minute of it. He was already a seasoned journeyman musician when Prospero came together in Robby's garage. The band members found themselves with a hit single nine months later and then came the record contract. It had never let up since.

All the attendant ills of the business hadn't really affected Dex because he'd already been around long enough to be inured to them. His refuge was the music, playing it, writing it, recording it. The perks of the lifestyle were . . . interesting. It was crazy to land in a town and a few hours later have prime women willing to bed you. That very availability, combined with the boredom of the road, made short-term relationships easy. Women used him for their bucket lists. Did a rock star: check. Long-term relationships, on the other hand, were next to impossible, which didn't prevent him from marrying a few of these women—among them Robby's sister, a compound disaster when Robby then caught Dex cheating on her while on the road. A few of the wives thought they could outsmart the business by touring with the band, but the relentlessness of touring and the endless supply of those bucket-list women eventually wore them down. Dex survived because he was nurtured by the music. Each time onstage energized him. Until recently.

The band was like family. Dex's closest relationships were with its members, but over the years strains began to show. Usually it was a band member's perception that he wasn't getting his due. He would talk of going on his own. Girlfriends fed the fire; wives threw gasoline on it. The music went from being a pure thing to just a way of paying bills. That was getting more difficult, too. Robby, an accounting major before he dropped out of USC to join the band, had gone over the books and found that they were earning less on each album, less on each tour.

"Maybe we've peaked," he said. "Ten years ago. And no one told us."

Dex was, as usual, so buried in writing songs for their current album he hardly registered Robby's concern. "We're still earning fine."

"Don't you notice at concerts, they always want us to play 'best of'?"

"It's just a natural cycle."

"Yeah, downward. We're jumping the shark."

But what if that was part of the cycle of progression? Dex now wondered. You couldn't stay at the top of the mountain forever—newer, younger bands were constantly coming up. Maybe one had to resign oneself to the fact that eventually everything—countries, governments, houses, lovers, bands—begins a long, inevitable slide toward obsolescence, which made it no less lovable to those who had been along for the ride. Otherwise, why did Aerosmith still tour?

Even though the groupies were still fine backstage and at the hotels (notwithstanding that he himself didn't partake as regularly as he used to—he needed sleep, had to finish a song, or just wanted to veg out and watch the play-offs), when he looked out at the first row or two at concerts (all you could see with the glaring lights), he was confronted by a sea of middle age. Thickening waists, guys with gray hair or none at all. The women were still beauties, but they weren't hot teenagers anymore: they were the mothers of those teenagers. Maybe some of those very teenagers had been conceived while listening to Prospero songs. The circularity made Dex dizzy. He then had the mortifying thought that those middle-aged people in the audience were his age—or, rather, he was their age, and if they had aged gracefully, if they looked fulfilled and happy grooving out there in the audience to music they remembered from their youth, then wasn't Dex the one who was age-inappropriate? He was still living like a teenager, albeit a rich, indulged one. What was age-appropriate for a rock star, anyway? The rock 'n' roll persona was a uniform; one conformed by nonconformance. There were exceptions, but they proved the rule. Blues guys—Muddy Waters, John Lee Hooker, Bo Diddley—didn't have this problem. Perfectly acceptable to be a fat old grandfather and still able to get down with the blues. Dex's nightmare was to watch those commercials late at night where they featured the "Best of a Decade" music—a whole parade of one-hit wonders, a slew of "Whatever happened to . . . ?" Would there come a day when Prospero took its place on a Best of the '80s or '90s with the others? Their only salvation might be that, by then, downloading and pirating would have made those commercials obsolete.

Dex had a secret fantasy of changing his name, disguising himself, and going to play blues anonymously. It was one thing to be old; it was another to be a has-been.

Fact was, as much as the fans purported to love you, they didn't forgive you for being mortal. They looked at Dex like, *"What happened to you?"* As if he were to blame for time's ravages. Did they look in their own mirrors? But they had a point. Rock 'n' roll was about youth forever, and so, too, should be its players.

Dex stood inside his darkened *fare*, scrambling in his suitcase for the stash of *pakalolo* that he had scored off Cooked. His swim trunks were sandy, so he pulled them off, to put on a clean pair of shorts. As he hopped around, trying to get his leg through, he bumped into a chair, and his foot, jammed inside the shorts, got stuck. Down he went in a great heap on the ground. Lying there he caught a glimpse of his sad self in the mirror and gave himself THE LOOK. This was his regular method of self-examination, used before each and every concert to ground himself, and now he was severely questioning what he had just done by burning the song. He knew he was a little bit of an egomaniac—it came with the job—but what he had just done was plain-and-simple stupid.

Outside, Richard gave a delicate cough. "You okay?"

"Couldn't be better if I tried."

It came down to this: live with the music, including the pain of the business that surrounded it and enabled it, or give it all up. He had enough money if he was careful. This stunt out on the sand had been an offering in that direction. He had felt freer and happier than in a long time, until the last piece of paper became ash, and then the void yawned open. What had he done? Throwing back a gift like it was a spoiled fish? What if the universe now revenged itself on him? Reneged? Withheld? Went constipated? Glued its knees together like a pissed-off old girlfriend?

"Dex?" Richard called.

Dex opened the door and walked out on the lanai. Richard sat on the stairs, gazing out at the water, wondering what his escaped wife was up to in town. When he turned and saw all of Dex, he went pale. Why was he wearing no clothes? His mouth opened, but no sound came out.

"I think I've just messed up bad," Dex wailed.

Wende kind of felt bad for Dex, but not enough to *not* do what she was planning with Cooked. Dex had been alive for a lot longer than she had. In the decade before she was even born and while she was growing up, how many women had he been with? How many would come after her? As far as she was concerned, she was owed a day off. Her loyalty toward him consisted of keeping the details of their relationship private, publicly allowing him to appear as the stud, but it did not extend to her remaining a muse, a.k.a. nursemaid, to his moodiness, insecurity, overdrinking, and overindulging in drugs, most notably weed, and underperforming in bed due to all of the above. Let Richard babysit for a few hours.

The sole benefit of the island was that there was no one else he was likely to try to sleep with—although Ann was hot, she definitely would not go for him—but Wende didn't care about that anymore. Let him find someone else. Guys like him needed inexperienced, naïve girls like her former self who didn't know enough to make demands, who were dazzled by all the flash. For a while. And then needed to be replaced.

It was good walking down the street with someone her own age, someone not famous, someone Polynesian. Would this technically qualify as going native? They held hands and ate ice-cream cones and giggled. Tourists gave them dirty looks.

Cooked had been eyeing her for the last two months, but only since the almost-drowning incident yesterday had that interest ignited her curiosity. Dex was so caught up in his creativity/destruction music crisis he didn't notice the balance had shifted on the boat—granted he had been unconscious for part of the time. Playing his song the night before, he didn't see that Wende paid no attention and instead beat out a rhythm of lust on Cooked's drums. Dex should have heeded the fact that back in their *fare* for the night, she had shaved and depilated and made herself satiny ready, and then turned her back on him for a full night's rest.

Cooked went into the town's single grocery store, owned by friends, and borrowed a Vespa. Wende climbed on back, winding her arms around his muscled stomach. Ten minutes later, they were at his family's village. Where the first town existed to cater to tourists and European tour workers, hotel staff, etc., this place was strictly local. Along the beach, piles of trash smoldered in the sun and were pushed back and forth in the waves. Empty cans, diapers, broken junk. When they walked through the trees, Wende's eyes grew large at the sight of neatly planted rows of marijuana as tall as she was. It reminded her of Christmas tree farms in Idaho. A handmade sign read, WELCOME TO PARADISE.

"That's our best cash crop. Spending money," Cooked said.

He introduced her to about twenty women from his immediate clan who were working on various projects around the compound. His mother kissed her on the cheek, greeting her in French, which Wende did not speak. Then Cooked led her to his bedroom and closed the door. He dropped his shorts.

"They all know we're in here!"

"It's okay. It's cool, lady."

"Wende."

"Windy."

"With an 'e.'"

Cooked's English-language skills were not advanced so she tried not to be critical. His single bed had dirty sheets; the room was a pigsty. He was basically a twenty-something teenager like herself. He also wasn't terribly romantic. They smoked a joint, and he got down to business. Apparently, kissing wasn't big in their culture, but he was young and indefatigable.

Afterward, bed-rumpled, glowing, they came out into the kitchen, and two dozen adults and children smiled and giggled at the lovebirds. Within minutes she was a member of the family.

Wende didn't want to be so creepy, imperialistic, or colonialistic as to ask Cooked if this was an everyday occurrence—bringing home a *popa'a* tourist for a little afternoon nookie. She wasn't going to turn mushy—was she special? No, the whole clan seemed genuine in their kindness and in their lack of surprise.

Cooked's mother opened up some cans of Punu Pu'atoro and fried the corned beef up with onions, then served it with roasted breadfruit, coconut bread, and *po'e*, baked papaya in banana leaves. Afterward, Cooked led her back to his bedroom, where they started all over again.

Wiped out, Wende fell asleep squashed against the wall and woke up when the late-afternoon sun glared through the window. "Hey, we need to go! Poor Ann."

Cooked grunted and tongued her knee.

It was when Wende was reaching under his desk for her shorts that she saw the pictures of the babies with horrendous birth defects, some of an unidentifiable jellyfish-like appearance.

"What is this—?"

"I must confess to you," Cooked said solemnly. "I am a revolutionary."

Wende had not traveled enough to understand the faked, tabula rasa quality of the resort compared with real island life. Her whole life was tabula rasa, and she was dying to experience the authentic. Traveling made her feel like an anthropologist. Wherever she went, she tried to picture living there. What would her life look like in Cooked's village? It was certainly poor, dirty, and chaotic, but it was alive in ways that the resort could never be.

Cooked had grown up hearing the adults talk about injustice. His own father had been lured from their village to Papeete with the promise of high pay in construction work on military and government buildings. The whole family moved with him, leaving their large hut that they'd built themselves on family land, to live in a subsidized apartment in a bad part of town. For the first time in their lives, they did not know their neighbors.

Cooked remembered how ashamed he was when he saw his mom and dad smiling, scraping, and humbling themselves in front of the French. Only in the privacy of their apartment could they pretend to talk back. There they boasted; they preened. So it was natural when Cooked became a teenager that he'd admired the gangs that formed, that took power through fear. They had renamed him from his birth name, Vane, to Cooked, legacy of a long campaign of oppression. But Cooked didn't want to terrorize his own neighborhood. He admired the activists that were fighting the outsiders.

"My parents were servants. I'm a servant. Will my children and their children be servants also?" He told Wende about the dual ravages of economic inequality and the aftereffects of decades of nuclear testing on his family. His brother Teina was on his way to becoming a minor thug. "Instead I want to lead a revolution."

Wende's eyes were wide open. This was, bar none, the best date she had ever been on.

"We're wage slaves. We protest, wave signs, and are ignored. I want to wake them up. I want them to start paying attention."

His sense of purpose excited her more than his lovemaking, and as he told her his plans, all she could think was *Yes, yes, yes yes yes yes.*

The truth was Wende had been attracted physically to Cooked but had found him boring until this moment. Suddenly he transformed before her eyes from a Polynesian Justin Bieber to a Polynesian Che Guevara. She pulled him back down on the bed one last time. Revolutionaries could be sexy! She'd had no idea.

She said good-bye to Cooked's bedridden aunt, Etini, who had leukemia. Although there was government health care, it was hard to access. The island had only a primitive clinic with basic services. Staying in Papeete was expensive and lonely. Being sent to France for advanced therapy was unthinkable. Etini was too ill to work. A class-action lawsuit for the poisoning had been stalled in the courts for years as the victims died off. How did the resort and tourists look from Etini's window? All of it made Wende even angrier with her current stupid, frivolous life. Sacrilegious thought: Did the world really need another pop song?

As little as Cooked's family had, comparatively, they seemed more content than the resort's guests. Or was that a Gauguinesque projection, wishful thinking by dissatisfied, exploiting colonists? The clichéd dream of the happy native? She'd given gladly when Cooked asked to borrow some cash before they left. In full view of everyone he gave all five twenties to his mama with a kiss. Wasn't that kind of sharing, giving to those in need, what it was all about? Maybe her mother's commune idyll had rubbed off on her?

Wende hummed "Road to Nowhere" (her favorite song from the retro '80s music scene that she obviously liked—for example, her crush on Prospero—but which drove Dex crazy), and buried her face in Cooked's warm shoulder on the ride back to town.

If Richard had told his friends back home that he was hanging out with Dex Cooper, he would have been envied, but the reality was something else.

Dex brought out a supersize spliff, which they smoked down to a nub; they started in on alcohol next.

"Maybe we should get some exercise?" Richard asked, realizing he sounded way too goody-two-shoes.

They proceeded to lazily lob the volleyball back and forth in the saunalike temperature. Titi came out and watched them, grinning, estimating they'd suffer from heatstroke within minutes, and went back inside. Soon they were stretched out under a palm.

"Ah, those look yummy," Dex said, pointing at the cannonball coconuts right above their heads.

"Loren told me getting hit on the head with those is the leading cause of injury here."

"Nah, I'm sure it's more like getting eaten by a shark."

"No."

"Doesn't matter. It's paradise here," Dex said. He began grappling up the slick trunk of the tree. "Help me."

"No way," Richard said.

"Come on, bro. Let me stand on your shoulders to get a leg up."

Richard knew it was stupid. One of them would probably end up getting hurt, but he did weigh a lot more than Dex, and after all, he *was* getting to be Dex Cooper's buddy.

They scrambled for long minutes before Dex finally gained purchase on a ridge of bark and shimmied up to his goal. Richard limped away, afraid he'd dislocated a shoulder. His skin was abraded by Dex's toenails digging in.

"View's fine up here."

"Shake them off and get down."

Richard moved away as coconuts rained on top of him.

Titi came out, cross. "You come down."

As Dex tried and failed to reverse his course, his former ease vanished. He was hugging the tree for dear life. "Easier said than done."

He made the first rappelling move downward and came flying off the tree, landing with a thud. Titi and Richard ran to him.

"You okay?"

"I burned it."

"He's delirious," Richard said. "Get Loren."

"The *song*."

"I don't understand."

"On the beach. It felt righteous, but now . . ."

Richard shrugged. "Write another one."

"This was the big one."

"Okay . . ." Richard was exhausted. This felt a few degrees beyond even Javi's neediness. "Write it again."

Dex opened his eyes. "Will you stay with me? You're my good-luck charm. You saved my life yesterday, man. I can't manage it alone."

Midwifing the birth of a rock 'n' roll song. What if this was the next "Satisfaction" or "Imagine"? Richard felt a tightening in his chest. They'd morphed from buddies to bromance. "I'd be honored."

They locked themselves up in Dex's *fare*, which Richard discovered was twice as big and much fancier than his and Ann's, and ordered Titi to play bouncer, keeping everyone out and a steady supply of booze and food coming in.

At first Richard felt uncomfortable in his role as witness. "You sure you don't want to be alone?"

"I need you here. You saved my life, man."

The unkind thought passed through his mind that he wished Dex would stop mentioning the rescue. He didn't want to be reminded of the disturbing mouth-to-mouth, or that maybe he was being befriended because of his CPR technique and not for himself. But what American male had not at one time or another fantasized that he was a rock star up on the stage—torn jeans, sweaty and grubby, pounding away, jabbing with the none-too-subtle phallic symbol of electric guitar at groin level? This was beyond a dream come true to watch the music being made. Richard took a slug of dark rum and passed the bottle over.

Dex's creative process was deceptively unorganized. He wrote words on a notepad that Richard thought weren't exactly literature:

> *The White Whale*
> *Wanted it so bad and got it*
> *Didn't know what to do and burned it*
> *Who knew it had such deep, deep, sharp teeth.*

But as Dex started playing chords, the words grew meaning beyond themselves. Chords exploded, changed key. A melody in the beginning disappeared, then returned, transformed, deepened. It was about something unknown in the singer's life—if Richard didn't assume it was this afternoon's disaster of burning the song and falling out of the tree—but also about more than that.

> *Went down that pole of darkness*
> *Hit the earth and went on in*

The words became beside the point. Richard thought about the music he had loved as a teenager—Poison's "Every Rose Has Its Thorn," Zeppelin's "Kashmir," Nirvana's "Smells Like Teen Spirit," Guns N' Roses' "Welcome to the Jungle"—realizing he had never questioned the meaning of those lyrics. The essence was inside the music, and it was clear that Dex had the magic, was able to weave lyric and melody with a genius utterly unexpected from the person he had observed during the previous week. It took four straight hours of playing before perfectionist Dex was satisfied, and an exhausted Richard could tell no difference between each version, but he could hear the difference after every tenth playing—a subtle refining process, an accentuation of improvisatory riffs. Even after a hundred repetitions, the final time Dex played the song brought tears to Richard's eyes. He didn't care if it made him a wuss: he had just witnessed a genuine birth. Something new and beautiful existed in the world.

"Did you get it back?" he said after waiting a respectful time till the last chord faded away.

Dex shook himself as if he had been in a trance. "It's better than the first time."

"Cool."

The two men walked out victors into the roseate island sunset.

The women returned to the resort as the horizon faded to purple. The group toasted the end of the day with rum punches. With a sphinxlike smile, Ann showed a mystified Richard her half-shark tattoo, then swaggered to their *fare* to change for dinner. Wende's lips were kiss bruised. Cooked jumped out of the boat and moored it to the dock. Dex felt sick to his stomach when he heard him humming an approximation of "Road to Nowhere" as he carried a small battered valise to one of the vacant *fares*. On his neck was a purpled love bite.

Titi stood at the kitchen threshold, scowling, waiting for Cooked to notice her. When he did, she turned her back to him and stomped inside.

What have you guys been up to?" Ann asked. She was surprised at the sudden camaraderie of the two men after they had mostly ignored each other for the past week.

"You have no idea." Richard grinned.

Titi moved around the table, banging down bowls and plates so they jumped. When Wende looked up at her, she saw her diamond WILD pendant suspended from Titi's ear.

"Hey, that's mine!"

Titi smiled. "I thought we were sharing everything, Polynesian style."

Wende bit her lip as Dex buried his head in her neck.

"Oh, baby, it was awful," he said.

She stroked his back, distracted. "You fell out of a tree?"

"I thought it died. But it's back. The best."

"The tree?"

"The song."

Wende rolled her eyes at Ann, with an I-told-you-so expression. "That's great. Let's eat."

"This song changes everything. If only Robby could hear it."

Ann looked pointedly at Loren, who kept passing dishes and offered nothing in the way of assistance.

Finally she got up. "Come with me," she said.

The two couples went to Ann and Richard's *fare* (Richard embarrassed that it looked almost threadbare in comparison with Dex and Wende's), and they pointed flashlights into the plunge pool while Ann poked around the grassy bottom with her foot.

"Here it is," she said, pulling up the dripping sat-phone. Thank God Javi had thought far enough to get a waterproof one.

"You could probably store it in a drawer," Richard said.

Dex called Robby, and they talked briefly. Once Robby turned his recorder on, Dex played his guitar and sang into the phone. They all clapped at the end.

"Let's celebrate!" Dex howled. "Where's my herbalista? Cooked!"

The next morning they lounged around the breakfast table hungover. Loren had deigned to make an appearance after avoiding the partying the night before. He wanted to see Ann, but she had not come out yet.

"I'm bored," Wende said.

"Do you know about the island's cannibalism?" Loren asked her.

Field trip. Everyone would go, with Titi and Cooked bringing lunch later. At the last minute, Ann canceled, deciding to stay in bed for the morning. Loren took them the clockwise route around the island, slyly dodging the camera by turning inland and walking a few hundred yards into a palm grove in which stood a rubble of stones and a large cut block. He was irritated that he wasn't seeing the one person he planned the trip for.

"What's this?" Richard asked, brushing away dead leaves. He snatched his hand back as an eight-inch-long banana-yellow centipede went scurrying for cover.

"Be careful," Loren said. "Those are poisonous."

The place was clearly not on the list of must-sees for the resort's regular clientele. Loren used a fallen palm frond to clear off the overgrown debris. The stone dais was big—the size of a mattress. On top were carved figures, the largest a whalelike fish on which there were cup-sized depressions.

"This is where they did human sacrifices. Those were used to collect the blood."

"Yuck." Wende turned away, hot, pocked with mosquito bites, sorry she had come. Why hadn't she stayed on the beach, drinking like Dex wanted? But then she felt ashamed. That was the old Wende. She turned back and forced herself to stare into the stone cups, imagining them full.

"Real live cannibals?" Dex said.

"On the Marquesas. The last owner of the island had this brought here."

"Why?"

"He bought it cheap from a chieftain over there. But then things got confused. He wasn't allowed to send it out of the country to the museum that paid for it."

"So he left it?" Richard asked.

"Yes. He left it. There was a lawsuit when he lost the island to me. The government forgot about it. Then he died. End of story. Ready for lunch?"

To "make nice" with Richard after the tattoo, Ann agreed to go out on the boat for a day of diving even though she was loath to lose a day full of solitude. Wende joined the men in the water, and all three came back with tales of black-tipped sharks whipping by.

Cooked assured them that the sharks were harmless. "They just check you out. Bump, bump," he said, grinning at Wende.

When they motored to a sheltered cove for snorkeling, Ann still would not join in.

"Don't be scared," Wende said. "I'll protect you."

Ann bit her lip, not wanting to mention the unresolved shark circling her thigh that very moment. Wende seemed a bit weak in the execution stage. They finally convinced Ann to float in the shallowest part, but every moment in the water she was on the lookout for an approaching dark shape and didn't rest until she was back safely in the boat. She missed the mysterious largeness of a day spent alone on the beach— the description of what paradise should be. What was Loren doing? She smiled, thinking he was undoubtfully grateful for the reprieve of an afternoon without entertaining.

Back on shore, evening came in another blaze of violet.

It was understood that Cooked and Titi were betrothed to each other from childhood and would marry in the future. It was also understood that Cooked fell for the tourists once in a while. As per custom, both were allowed to have outside casual relationships before marriage, but Titi had already had her experience and wanted no more. She pretended Cooked's excursions didn't bother her, but this time, especially, Wende did.

The locals working the hotels were used to coddling tourists like spoiled children. Foreigners had the most outlandish ideas about life on the islands, as if it were some kind of paradise, another Eden. As if Tahitians didn't have all the regular problems that existed back home and then some. On vacation, tourists loved it when you fussed over them, brought them their favorite fruit all cut up and served in a pineapple boat for breakfast as if they were small children. Not only did they smile, but then they tipped big. They wanted you to stroke and pamper them in luxury. They pretended to want to know the history of the islands, but they did not want to know the reality. The businessmen from Papeete came and built, destroyed the ecosystems of land and water, made money and left. They drove the gods away. Some of their own people betrayed them, profited by pretending development meant progress. Instead, their home had become a ghetto in paradise. So why was this girl so nosy?

This was the first time Cooked had taken a tourist home. Taboo. Even if it was just to get away from the crybaby Dex, he had crossed an unspoken line. He had told the girl everything and included her in his crazy schemes that even Titi refused to have anything to do with. Why would a big-breasted blond American girl get involved in their trouble? It made no sense unless—Titi swooned—she had fallen in love with him. Women did crazy things for their men.

As much as Cooked complained about how the French cheated, he was flattered when one of the foreign women found him attractive. Besides everything else, this was bad for business. Titi was the one who charged on the manna line of Dex Cooper's credit card every week. The nice lady's bag of money grew smaller each week. He was keeping them open. Other tourists would be more demanding.

Titi had first started at the resort as the maid after being a poli-sci major in college. Cooked was the boat driver and dive instructor; he had been studying for a phys-ed degree. Now they also had added the chores that Loren had dropped over the last year. She became concierge, bookkeeper, and cook. She was even thinking of taking an online course in web design to build a new website for the place. Cooked took on the work of handyman and now, apparently, gigolo. What couldn't be replaced, what Loren did expertly, was entertain foreigners. When he discovered Cooked's plan, he would be furious. Titi had to stop it without getting Cooked fired, or causing the foreigners and their money to leave.

Loren had been drunk almost every day for the last five years she worked there. Sometimes he disappeared for days, and they covered for him as best they could. This sickness was a new complication they couldn't keep hidden for much longer. What to do? Titi recalled Bette and Lilou from when they were all children together, playing on the beach. Her grandmother told her that one of the girls, Bette, had died from a disease. She supposed it was true because the only letters that had ever come over the years were from Lilou. None had come for a very long time now. Was it time at last to make amends for the past?

Titi stared into the refrigerator, unable to come up with yet another meal. Usually she prepped and served for Loren but didn't make the fancy foreign dishes from start to finish. Under Loren's supervision, the cooking had been good, if basic, but with his absence, meals had degenerated into fruit, yogurt, and sandwiches served by a lovesick Titi.

She decided to chop fruit and make ambrosia salad for the fifth time in a row. She sliced the baguettes from Cooked's love trip to town and jabbed salami and pickles into their fluffy insides. Their people were not jealous like the Westerners, but still . . . Titi chopped harder and harder, castrating mangoes, gutting pineapples, shaving the salami paper-thin, putting sharp little gouges into the cutting board that dulled the blade of the knife.

Cooked was making a fool of himself. She knew of his secret dream to be like the great and mighty Temaru, to stand up to the government, to foment revolution. Titi even suspected he wouldn't mind being imprisoned for a short while to add to his street cred (he was still famous mostly for his soda ads). What infuriated Titi was that he complained so loudly about the foreigners and then let himself be the plaything of an American girl. How could any of them be strong with a leader like that?

She was tempted to throw up her hands and take the boat to Papeete. Her cousin was having a baby, and there would be celebrations. Maybe she would meet someone new, someone unlike Cooked, who cared more about politics and foreign women than he did about her. If it came to that, their vows could be undone.

After dinner she would go to Loren's room and describe what was happening, what Cooked was planning, and avert disaster. Cooked would hate her. Things would change for better or worse. Maybe, just maybe, she would start her own revolution.

When the dishes were cleared, as usual Dex picked up his guitar, Wende and Richard set up their checkerboard, and Ann relaxed in a hammock. Once everyone settled, Titi made ready to go to Loren, just as Ann rose theatrically and stretched, arms overhead, then made the trip to his hut herself.

A nn lay on Loren's bed while they drank their green fairy nightcap. Loren chuckled. "Oh, how I would have liked to have had you."

"Really?" Ann downed her shot. They were kindred souls; he saw the artist in her that no one else did, or else, at least he didn't see the lawyer in her. She got up and swayed back and forth at the foot of his bed. The tattoo ached, and since she had already broken the prohibition against alcohol while healing, she saw no reason to now stop. At least the pain was numbed. The absinthe made her invincible, or was it Loren's words? Or was the tattoo already wreaking its talismanic effect?

"We would have been good together," he said.

The past tense of his desire, the implied hopelessness of his present, threatened to start tears that she would not allow in front of him. At one of their monthly WEFE cocktail parties, Eve had suggested volunteering at a hospice in order to feel she was contributing to the community and counter her disgust with the law. Even after completing basic training, the staff found Ann bawling away at the bedside of patients. "You are depressing the dying," they said. One of the nurses had puffed her lips, disappointed. "You're a crier." She was fired from the volunteer position.

Now she worried over how to distract them both. She unbuttoned her shirt and swayed to the faraway strains of Dex's guitar, channeling her thinner, early-twenties self (although she had never done anything remotely like this back then), pulling the fabric slowly down over her arms, her approximation of what a low-key striptease might look like. The shirt looped over her head in a slow circle, a lasso of lust. Wearing only Wende's bikini, she drowsily danced around the bed, moving her hips, holding the bottle of absinthe.

"We can have this. I can give you this," she said.

She pulled at the string around her neck, felt the pieces of fabric fall away from her breasts. Of course, toplessness didn't really count for the French, but still. The shock of her nakedness made her hesitate. Unable to look down, she looked into Loren's eyes; his delighted gaze gave her confidence to continue dancing, newly emboldened.

Loren reached for the bottle, and as she came close, he ran his hand up the inside of her leg, touching her tattoo.

"Ouch!!"

It burned as his fingers touched the outlines of the half shark, and the physical contact broke the spell. She motioned with her hands water flowing down her neck and over her breasts, throwing her head back, a backstroke with her arms as she danced away toward the door and the night beyond it, escaping straight into the disapproving bulk of Titi, who stood there.

"Oh!" Ann said, her arms covering her breasts, an unequivocal confession of guilt. Was that Wende's pendant dangling from Titi's ear?

The whole world has gone mad, Titi thought. She was so furious she turned and stalked out.

The next day, Dex and Richard cannabized and played volleyball while Ann sulked in her hammock, depressed at the twinned dark fates of Loren and herself, and read *Moby-Dick*:

> . . . *that one most perilous and long voyage ended, only begins a second; and a second ended, only begins a third, and so on, for ever and for aye. Such is the endlessness, yea, the intolerableness of all earthly effort.*

On the salty, hot wind she thought she smelled a coming storm. She felt the approach of a calamity: Loren's slowly losing battle with his mortality made everything around her seem too fragile to be trusted. Every few hours she rose and made her pilgrimage to Loren's hut to check on him. Each time she left, Richard smashed the volleyball into the net or into a nearby coconut palm. When it got stuck, Cooked had to shimmy up the trunk to lob it out. Dex had been forbidden to go near a tree. For differing reasons, each person pretended to not notice Wende and Cooked slipping away into an unoccupied *fare*.

Each night, Richard and Ann had to endure the awkwardness of being alone in their *fare* before going to sleep. Their early intimacy on the island had once again retreated. Richard, stoically virtuous after his dismissal by Wende, was boiling over.

"How's Loren?"

"Fine."

"You two are chummy."

She blushed for him. "You're not jealous?"

"No, of course not. Yes."

She wasn't going to tell, but then she did. "He's dying."

Richard felt a embarrassing mix of pity and elation. "Really?"

"I wouldn't lie about a thing like that."

And then, like the well-oiled machine that was every long marriage, they effortlessly rolled on to their regular workaday argument.

"We've been here a week and a half. Ten days times how much per day?" Richard asked.

"What does it matter?"

"It matters because in a few more weeks we'll be broke and back home. Then what?"

"I don't know."

That stopped him. Ann always knew, always had a plan B, if not C, D, and F. His only conclusion was her plan didn't include him, and she was too polite to mention it.

"Are you sure you don't know, or you don't want to say?"

"Lorna said stay away."

The island's library consisted of a one-room building with glass walls on two sides facing the sea. The rusty jalousies stayed cranked open to catch the breezes and only were closed for rain. The back two walls were filled floor to ceiling with books. Five freestanding bookcases took up half the room, filled with discards from guests, mostly cheap paperback thrillers and romances, except on one shelf where Ann found four signed copies each of John Stubb Byron's *Colossus* and *Lunch*, dated the day before he left. Ann frowned and took one of the copies to keep. One wall consisted of Loren's extensive collection of history and fiction centered on the South Pacific. In the front of the room, facing the beach, was a rattan sofa, and here Ann spent long hours reading. She was alternating between a history of Captain Cook and *Typee* by Melville, but at the moment both were splayed in front of her while she napped.

The smell of cigarette smoke woke her. She sat up so abruptly, spots flew before her eyes like flushed-out birds.

Dex was shuffling along the back shelves, puffing away as usual.

Claiming to be suffering a serious case of island fever, Dex had begged to join Loren on a grocery-buying trip to town once he verified that Cooked was going along also. At least for those hours, Dex was free from imagining what Cooked and Wende might be up to. He also wanted to sneak an hour at an Internet café.

"Sorry I woke you."

She moved to get up.

"Stay." He came and sat down on the sofa next to her.

"You okay?" she asked.

He didn't look okay. His skin was waxy; dark circles pooled under his eyes. He didn't look like a guy who had been on vacation for the last two months. The trip to town had undone him.

He shrugged.

She lifted the book he had laid down. "Shakespeare?"

"I think it's here for *The Tempest*. The plays soothe me. They were my best subject in school."

She took a moment to absorb the unlikeliness of this. "Your new song is great. Are you looking forward to recording it?"

"I'm thinking of burning it up again."

"Why?" She didn't bother pointing out that the threat's impact was considerably lessened by the fact that it already existed on Robby's recorder in California.

"Richard saved my life. I should give something up for that."

"Why not look at it from another angle? Did you ever think you were saved to play music?" Why was it so easy to see destiny in others' lives but not one's own?

His face twisted. "I've been betrayed."

"I don't think Wende—"

"Robby."

"You've lost me."

"My lead guitarist. 'Who having into truth, by telling of it, / Made such a sinner of his memory / To credit his own lie, he did believe . . . ' In other words, I got fucked. Robby was supposed to take over business for a while so I could go off to write songs and recuperate. I was burned out. I'd done the same thing for him a few years ago. But now he acts like I've died. Instead of 'and' for a contract, I agreed to change it to 'or' to make things easier. His word is enough."

All the legal alarms were ringing in her head. "Why would you agree to that?"

"I trusted him like a brother."

*The 101 of law school: In business, you have no friends.*

Dex was inhaling so hard on his cigarette, she thought any minute he'd suck the whole thing in.

"He did a long interview. It's on the Internet. I watched in town. Said I had personal problems, drugs and stuff. That I'd gone into hiding on an island."

It was like someone falling off the wagon in AA, the tech binge.

"So go and take back control."

"The band's over."

Ann thought the most diplomatic response was no response, but then couldn't help herself. "You *are* hiding on an island."

"I should have hired a lawyer like you."

"You should have."

"Could still."

"I'm a recovering lawyer." Ann was silent. "A freebie: You shouldn't have played that new song for him till you dissolved the band. Since it was created under the umbrella corporation of Prospero Inc., he's entitled to it. He has artistic control over its licensing, I'm guessing?"

Dex's face had grown longer and longer. He looked at Ann now almost as if he were in a trance. "Fuck."

"You've got to dot those *i*'s and cross those *t*'s before you have your tantrum."

"Richard said you were a cold one."

"Just saying." It stung that she had been talked about.

Another perfect day. Flat blue despite the fact that rain was forecast. As was her new habit, Ann got up early and walked to the far side of the island where the camera was. She sat behind it and stared at the view that it stared at, a veritable Alice behind the looking glass. It was reality and virtual reality simultaneously—or, rather, it was both the real thing and its abstraction. She felt she was on the verge of some grand truth while being suckered at the same time. She could have gone to another stretch of beach almost identical *without* a camera, but somehow the very act of the scene being recorded made it easier to concentrate. Immensely restful to be alone but at the same time with thousands of other alone people staring at identical waves. It had the same swampy communalness as sitting in a matinee movie theater crowded with strangers. Of course she was privileged to be there in person, but she imagined when she got home she would also log on to this view. It represented a kind of genius on Loren's part.

She was sorry to admit that while waiting for Cooked and Wende's delayed return in town, she had bought a blue pareu for its camera worthiness. In every way that mattered, the spell of escape was broken. It was broken for others also.

I've had it here," Dex said. "I want to go back to the main hotel. Get back to LA." Visions of Robby hijacking the band haunted him.

Panicked, Wende looked around for Cooked. She had thought they'd have weeks, if not months, to settle plans.

Ann decided to say nothing about seeing him take off with Titi earlier. She worried that if the other couple left, Richard would want to leave as well. That would effectively close Loren down.

"Anyway," Dex complained, "the food's going downhill."

Richard agreed. "Loren's not up to his duties."

"He's not feeling well," Ann said. She knew how to press Richard's buttons. "Why don't we take over cooking? Don't you miss it?"

It was an old lawyer's trick—never ask a question you don't already know the answer to.

"Maybe I could whip something together tonight." Richard grabbed at the chance to investigate the kitchen that Titi so zealously guarded. Returning from a quick reconnaissance, he announced there would be a feast that night to use the supplies in the refrigerator that were about to spoil. "Instead of snacks, we could have been eating like kings these last days. What's needed is a little know-how."

Something was up with Wende. That afternoon, she appeared wearing a sensible one-piece from her high-school swim team. When not in the water, she covered up in T-shirts and shorts. Her hair was tied back in a ponytail. For the first time, she looked like the girl from Idaho she was. She volunteered as sous chef for Richard and chopped vegetables. To Ann she confided that she felt guilty about Cooked and would not sleep with him again.

"I'm not some kind of home wrecker, you know."

"Did you give Titi your WILD pendant?"

"Reparations." Wende frowned. "I've matured. There are terrible injustices in the world. Not everyone lives in a resort, Ann."

"That's true."

"There are oppressed people," Wende said under her breath. "I want to make a difference."

What surprised Wende the most after all these years playing muse was how much spare time she had when she was no longer under the onus of being "hot." While she wasn't going to make a federal case out of it, everyone underestimated what it took to be her, or the former her: the

WILD hot young thing, muse, groupie, aspiring actress/singer/model of her ex-Wende incarnation. An unimaginable relief to be rid of that burden. For example: the hair. On the island, she allowed it to go au naturel, but back in LA she had a standing semimonthly appointment for highlights with her colorist to get that perfect sun-kissed carefree look. Then there were the hair extensions, which cost a fortune and only looked right when styled by a professional, so she went in every other day to her hairdresser for a shampoo, blow-dry, and finger-curl. Then the face. Facials involving equipment with electrodes, lasers, and pulsed-light gadgets out of *Star Trek*, and expensive antiwrinkle treatments because even though, obviously, she didn't have wrinkles *yet*, they were coming and had to be preempted. So that involved injections of fillers and Botox, and believe her, there was a long line of under-thirty-year-olds waiting for those services. Then there was eyebrow threading and eyelash dyeing, tooth bleaching, not to mention professionally done makeup for special occasions. On really important nights, she had false eyelashes glued on a single hair at a time. And that was just the face. The body required endless trainers, treadmills, medicine balls, and swimming pools, Pilates, yoga, Tae Bo, and weight training. All this while never getting to eat enough of anything, perpetual starvation while attending parties that featured tables weighed down with delicious, fattening food. Thank God she'd never had her boobs done—they were real, though no one believed it—but how long would they look like that? Endless waxing of underarms and legs, and of course the maximal torture that put Brazil on the map, not soccer or nuts or carnival but the tortuous waxing of the privates, Hollywood style. Manicures and pedicures and spray-on tans, and that didn't even get one out the door dressed. Sometimes she worked so hard on how she looked that by the time she was ready she was too tired to go out and be seen.

Preparing for the feast, Richard took a mollified Titi out to collect coconuts. Surprisingly, she was docile about the kitchen takeover and made no protests.

Dex and Cooked shook hands (no hard feelings) and smoked pot on the beach. Ann sat on the sand and watched the sunset while she dabbed oil over the burning wound of her tattoo. The unfinished shark had the look of an initiation rite gone bad.

At sunset they gathered for mai tais made by Dex. Loren came out of his *fare*, resplendent in a dark-red sleeveless T-shirt and a black pareu knotted around his bony hips. He had a *tiare* flower behind his ear, carrying off the whole Polynesian mixing of feminine with masculine while still looking hot. He cradled a magnum of vintage Burgundy that Richard took charge of decanting.

"In thanks for the patience of my friends. No charge for the last three days."

Titi flinched as if she had been hit with a stick.

Ann and Richard exchanged looks, the first they had dared in days. *Free* changed the whole equation, at least for the last three days. Ann wished that she had known in advance so that she could have enjoyed the time more. At the steep price they were paying per day, all inclusive, including the two bottles of alcohol a day (which meant not inclusive enough by half), even paradise could appear parsed and open to criticism: Is this worth it? This hut, this beach, this meal, this sunset? Happiness commodified?

The meal started with an amuse-bouche of tuna sashimi, garnished with a salsa of mango and Maui onion. At first, Titi and Wende served, but as the flow of food increased, Ann pitched in. Giddily she had worked out the math to convince Richard that the three free days should be added to rather than deducted from their allotment of escape. Why couldn't she get herself to do the responsible thing, pack her bag, and go back home?

As she waited at the stove for the final touches on yet another dish, she noticed Titi in the corner stirring a small blackened iron pot over a stone fire, trying to hide it from Richard's prying eyes.

"What's that?" Ann asked.

"Shark fin . . . other ingredients."

"A local dish? Are you making it for us?"

Titi gave her a long appraising look. She liked this unhappy woman whom she heard crying at night more often than making love. "Keep a secret? It's a love potion."

A couple of weeks before, Ann would have burst out laughing, but her world had been turned upside down. She could accommodate the possibility of this. "For Cooked?"

Titi nodded.

"But we all need it."

Two things had become clear in Ann's mind since they had arrived on the island: one, she did love Richard; two, she was done with their previous life. She could only guess at what he was feeling. She supposed he loved her, but he had come back to life when he returned to a kitchen. He, like Dex, had his vocation. Memo to future child: Find something or someone that makes your heart sing. Passion made you like Teflon against life's disappointments.

Ann ladled Titi's potion into demitasse cups, then put them on a tray. She would make sure each person drank his or her portion.

"What is it?" Richard asked, wrinkling his nose.

"Consommé. Don't hurt Titi's feelings."

He reached over her and grabbed a cup, critically sipping it. "Needs salt."

"Finish, or she might kick you out of the kitchen." Ann watched till his cup was empty.

More appetizers appeared: greens dressed in wasabi vinaigrette, caprese salad of heirloom tomatoes and burrata, tuna carpaccio with giant capers, shrimp in a silky coconut-milk curry. Loren, Cooked, and Dex slowed their eating, but the main courses came at an accelerated pace, a stillborn restaurant's worth of food: *maa tinito*, a mixture of red beans, vegetables, and rice that Titi had taught Richard to make; grilled calamari with marinated scallions; tempura zucchini with miso-vinegar dipping sauce; sautéed mahimahi with seared pineapple.

In a state of bliss, Richard stood at the kitchen door, watching his delirious diners. He held a bottle of wine and periodically took a deep slug. *"The discovery of a new dish confers more happiness on humanity than the discovery of a new star."*

He would not tell Ann until the night was over, but he, too, had done some soul-searching over the gas-ignited flames of the six-burner stove—like Dex and Wende, he also would leave tomorrow. His time on the island had been a reprieve, but it proved what he already knew—cooking was his life. Hopefully Ann would follow, or she would not. Now that his decision was made, he felt relief mixed with sadness.

This had been the only thing resembling a vacation that he and Ann had ever been on. His previous boredom, worrying, marking time, was now replaced by impatience that he had not enjoyed himself properly. Even as he cooked his swan song of a last meal, he wondered if he should agree to another three days since technically, as Ann argued, they would be free. He had not gone drift diving yet. Since he was cooking, contributing, getting inspiration for a whole Polynesian-inspired series of dishes, perhaps he could justify staying a bit longer? But then he thought of Javi mired in all his problems. Self-inflicted, but did that hurt any less? What kind of friend, what kind of family, abandoned his own in time of need? He was a little chagrined by Ann's callousness toward Javi. No, he would go home tomorrow.

They sat around the table, red-faced, sweating, emitting a raucous laughter that was gut-busting, rib-breaking. More bottles of wine had been drunk than there were people—Titi counted. Richard ran out, his face sweaty and red from the heat of the stove, for quick bouts of eating before he ran back to the kitchen for the next dish—Jalisco-style sweet corn pudding.

"It's good? You like?" he said.

"You could be French," Loren declared, staring down dreamily into his plate. "It is divine."

Richard glowed, in possession of himself for the first time since they had arrived. He would stay and fight for his wife.

Loren burped. "Excuse me, I was just recalling . . . Aren't there steaks in the freezer?"

Richard looked at Ann a minute. She held her breath.

"Not for this chef." He signaled to Wende, who rose unsteadily to her feet.

"Quiet everyone," she yelled from the kitchen door. "We have a surprise."

Richard appeared behind her, carrying a three-layer cake smothered under fluffy coconut frosting, burning with so many candles it gave the appearance of a bonfire. Surely he didn't put all thirty-eight candles on? Richard made his way to the table, staggering under the weight of his love offering. Wende brushed back plates and silverware with her arm, knocking over bottles, breaking glasses in her drunken haste.

"It's Ann's birthday!"

Dex stood up, holding the table for balance, and sang "Happy Birthday," jazz-style. He then sang the Police's "Roxanne," except his version was "Oh, Ann." She was living out her teenage-girl dream. This was as close to groupie nirvana as she was getting.

The cake was huge, gigantic—disproportionate to the occasion, of which there was none. It was the size of a happy couple's big family and circle of friends, of a successful restaurant and thriving law practice, of raised gold lettering on the door of a corner-view office, of a big Mc-Mansion, chemically induced triplets, fancy cars, and all the many people hired to keep the whole thing afloat—not so different, in fact, than this resort. *Not*. The cake was a lie, and even if she pretended to be happy about it, she couldn't, because even if all those things had been true, she had a premonition that these weren't even close to being enough. They were the fast-food solution to happiness. Besides, her birthday had been two weeks ago.

"It isn't my birthday," she said aloud, staring into the frosting that was so deep and thick one could drown in its curling rosettes.

"Of course it is," Richard said. "Or maybe it's the day I fell in love with the most beautiful woman I had ever seen. In her pink satin dress, scared of the thunder. I'm celebrating that day."

"No, it seriously isn't," Ann said.

"Chicks hate getting older," Dex said.

"'Chicks'?" Wende said. "You actually use that word?"

"We're here on borrowed time. Time and money we don't have," Ann said.

"What about the money bag in your room?" Titi asked.

"We're all here on borrowed time," Loren said. "'Where do we come from? What are we? Where are we going?'"

"That's original," Richard said. "Put it in a song."

"No, man," Dex said. "That's the name of Gauguin's masterpiece."

"Pass the cake, chick," Wende said.

"Hey!"

"Don't 'Hey!' me." She ate big dripping forkfuls of coconut frosting. Dieting was another thing she had done away with since she had become politically sensitized. The cake was the final straw that broke the camel's back as far as she was concerned. Look what Richard did for Ann, and look what Dex wouldn't do for her. "Did you ever hear the joke about how dogs resemble their owners?"

The table was silent. Wende was in a dark place no one wanted to follow.

"These scientists want to test out the idea. They get these three dogs. One dog belongs to an architect, one dog belongs to an accountant, and one dog belongs to a rock star."

"I don't think—"

"Let it go, Ann!" Wende snapped (Ann, the one everyone loved; they only lusted after her). "So the scientists bring the architect's dog into a room with ten bones, and he builds a pyramid. 'Wow!' the scientists say. They bring the accountant's dog into the room and give him ten bones, and he divides them up evenly. 'This is amazing!' the scientists yell. Then they bring the rock star's dog into the room and put ten bones in front of him."

"Babe, let's stop—"

Wende does not stop—the pitch of her voice cants higher. "They bring the rock star's dog into the room and put the ten bones in front of him. He pauses, licks himself, crushes the bones up and snorts them, fucks the other two dogs, then ODs."

Wende ran away from the table.

Dex coughed. "Wine does that to her," he said.

The night wore on until Titi now counted three empty wine bottles per person, a mathematically impossible reality considering that included her, and she didn't touch alcohol. Dex and Wende reconciled (apparently wine *did* do that to her because she held no grudge; she was riding a pendulum between the old and new Wende). Loren came out of his *fare* with a ring of small halved coconuts threaded through a piece of rattan.

"Birthday present. It's a shark rattle. The noise, it reminds sharks of birds feeding on small fish. They rush to join the pleasure."

"It never occurred to me to want to attract them."

"Only call when you are ready."

"It's not my birthday," Ann said, but no one seemed to care.

Wende wanted to dance, so Dex brought out his fancy satellite radio. Loren made a face at this breach of the rules, but he was in no position to police them. Dex tuned the radio to a local station, but instead of music there was an announcement:

> *"Tahiti and surrounding islands . . . preparing for a category one hurricane. The demonstration timed to coincide with the arrival of a French delegation set to hold hearings concerning reparations . . . canceled."*

"Hey, no fair listening to a radio," Richard said.

Was he the only one, Ann thought, not electronically cheating? "A hurricane?" she asked.

"Listening to music is the only way I can sleep. I put earphones on," Dex said. "Pacific Island radio has some good stations. Otherwise I tune into KROQ in LA."

"What's the difference between a tropical storm and a category one hurricane?" Ann asked.

"Nothing to worry about," Loren said. "Storms hardly ever come this far. A couple raindrops."

Dex put on some music and jumped on the table, playing air guitar. They all danced: Richard with Titi, Loren with Wende, Ann with Cooked. Perhaps the love potion had worked after all. Cooked brought out *pahu* drums made of coconut wood, and soon Dex, Richard, and he were beating out a syncopated rhythm on them. Titi did a native dance, and Wende joined. Finally, with much pulling, Ann got up. All three women, hips rocking back and forth, circled Loren, who sat blissfully in the middle of them. He closed his eyes with a smile on his lips, looking like a skinny, contented Buddha. Their hips tumbled and tumbled, keeping tempo with the accelerating and branching rhythms of the drums, faster and faster, unable to release from their grip, circling, circling, until with a great thumping climax of music, the women draped their arms around his neck.

"Now I can die," Loren said. "I've reached heaven."

Sometime during the evening, the wind stiffened and ruffled the palm fronds. By the time Ann noticed and looked out on the water, a gray woolen cloud was unfurling across the water. Wende and Cooked again disappeared, while Loren, Richard, and Ann played poker at the table. Of course Ann knew better, but still she was disappointed that the love potion did not seem to have worked.

"Where's Dex?" Richard asked.

They heard a tussling in the undergrowth. There were no wild animals to worry about on the island, so Ann went to investigate. She found Dex crawling on his stomach with the kitchen rifle cradled in his arms.

"What're you doing?"

He sat on his haunches. The farthest *fare*, Wende and Cooked's probable love nest, was fifty feet away, and light shone out between the gaps in the matting.

"In the Gulf War. Did recon. Doing a little recon again tonight."

Ann grabbed the rifle out of his arms. "What're you talking about? You already were playing with Prospero then."

Dex lowered his eyes. "None of your business."

"You weren't there," Ann said. "What a stupid thing to say. You're like a little boy." She had the urge to hit him with the rifle. "Is this thing even loaded?"

She pointed it up to the sky and pulled the trigger. It exploded, the kickback knocking her to the ground. They both were in shock as everyone came running.

"I love her," Dex whispered sloppily, drunken tears falling down his stubbled cheeks. "I can't bear what she's doing."

"Oh," Ann said—the possibility of his truly loving Wende had never occurred to her. How had she moved from potential groupie to den mother so quickly? "Poor you. I'm so sorry."

For many years, Dex had imagined what combat was like, what moving around armed felt like, so when he actually did it that night, it was an unimaginable relief. Wende didn't realize what she was doing to him, and the sadness that it had triggered.

His older brother, Harry, had been the smartest, the handsomest, the One Who Would Go Far. Dex was the ugly duckling in the family, tongue-tied and introverted. The one with acne; the one who got detention for smoking a doobie on school grounds; the one who drank too much at the school social and mooned the homecoming queen; the one who incessantly masturbated even after his mother told him it would make him go blind; the one who used raw liver for the family dinner to facilitate his bliss as an ironic literary homage, only to have his parents find out and then send him to counseling; the one neighbors thought was adopted because he didn't look like his healthy, blond, outgoing parents, or his football player brother, or even his pretty baby sister. He was like a mongrel that got dumped in a litter of golden retrievers and had to pretend to their ways.

Even though the two brothers had nothing in common, Harry took his role as older brother very seriously. At the age-appropriate times, he introduced Dex to beer, porn, cars, and girls. Harry always laughed off Dex's oddball ways: "He'll grow out of it."

The folks—conservative, Reagan-voting California Republicans—put all their faith in Harry making good, keeping up the legacy of going to Stanford, following in his father's large CEO footprints. His sister, Janey, predictably, wanted to be a teacher. Only to Dex did she confide about her secret life of partying, drugs, and sex, her voice raspy from chain-smoking cigarettes.

It was a prideful shock when Harry enlisted, though not unexpected. Men were supposed to be men in his family. All through their childhood, Dex's father had been an avid bird hunter. Along with his buddies, he had taken a young Harry out fall mornings toward Lancaster and Bakersfield to go shooting with his friends. Many of the male relatives in the family had done military service; it was considered a noble sacrifice. Dex hated guns, hated shooting, hated dead birds and war. In every way that mattered, he was a grave disappointment to his father.

Harry graduated summa cum laude and went straight into basic training just as Dex started playing in bands, skipping classes, and dropping acid. Coming home stoned one night, he overheard his father telling his poker friends about his "loser son."

After Harry was reported killed by friendly fire, his father told the preacher, "I'm not coming back to church. God took the wrong one."

Dex left home after that. No matter how famous, no matter how rich, he would always be just a slacker to his dad, a guitar player, the one who didn't die. Dex didn't contact him when his father's company was accused of being involved in a plot with a pharma conglomerate to peddle substandard drugs to the third world. Neither did he contact him when it was discovered the firm had been involved in a cover-up of the effects of depleted uranium relating to Gulf War syndrome. He did not contact him after his father's company was indicted or after it collapsed, or after his father's high blood pressure diagnosis, or after his first stroke, or the second. None of it brought Dex home. He simply had his manager, Lori, write out the checks, both for his parents' retirement home (they had lost all their money in attorney's fees) and for Janey's rehab, divorce, and monthly support for her and his little niece. He fantasized about telling his father that at least the money that they were now living off was clean. He didn't tell the old man off because he loved his mom and Janey.

He missed his big brother something terrible. He knew his life would have gone better in all kinds of indefinable ways if Harry had been there by his side. Harry loved Dex, loved his music and supported his making it. He was the definition of what family should mean, a tie where blood was only the beginning. Some of the soldiers in Harry's squad listened to Dex's first tapes while deployed in Kuwait, and Harry burst with pride for his baby brother. He understood that everyone had to play the hand that he was dealt in life.

In the years that followed, Dex began to be haunted. He felt guilty that he had not been brave enough to enlist and go fight at his brother's side. He had the grandiose fantasy that he might have saved him; more probably Harry would have been saved while looking after his inept little brother. Harry never would have allowed something paltry like death to interfere with that sacred duty. But the truth was that, even back then, Dex could think of nothing more devastating than making the accommodation in his soul that would have allowed him to kill another human being. Not even if the act was removed by advanced weapons to the level of a fancy video game. Becoming a soldier would have killed the musician in him. How did Harry—a better man than he was—make that accommodation in his own soul? They never had a chance to discuss it.

But Dex had so wanted to be brave.

Later he went to the battlefields of Iraq and Afghanistan (because battlefields, like concert stadiums, were interchangeable, he suspected), not to fight but to play his music, not in some dippy, '60s-style, peace, love, putting-flowers-in-gun-barrels kind of way, but in a strong, force-for-good way. He was brave in the manner possible for him. Every single soldier he played to was Harry. Every single soldier he played to was *not*.

Dex knew music, not guns, changed hearts and minds. He experienced it on tour, the unity of thousands at concerts. Power comes in all forms; the old man could never get his head around that one.

Rifle safely returned to its place, hours later Ann woke up on a bench by the kitchen. She found Richard asleep on the beach. She stroked the hair plastered to his forehead. In his sleep he looked as content as when they first met. Where had that Richard gone? For that matter, where had the old Ann gone? She lay down beside him. On the wind, she thought she heard voices arguing as she fell asleep.

A roaring woke her. The morning sky was a bright, glowing yellow. The silver ocean worried its way back and forth along the beachfront. Ann sat up, alone, sand in her hair, shivering.

Wende stood at the dock with a small battered valise—the same one that Cooked had carried back from their trip to town. Although Ann had grown fond of the girl and was sorry she was leaving, there was a part of her that was also glad. Wende's youth exhausted her. She didn't like her part serving as cautionary tale. Ann was tired of the girl's lording it over the *motu* with her body; tired of the haunted, panting men; tired of the bikini and breasts and the promise implied by the dazzling belly button ring that could return at any time. WILD. Poor girl didn't have the first clue. Wild could be in the heart of the most buttoned-down, burned-out lawyer. Wild was the ability to drop one life and pick up another. Wild was refusing the scratchy dry surface of things and digging into the rich loamy depths. Ann was searching for a wild far deeper and grander than anything offered up so far. She had tried to rise to the occasion, had borrowed the skimpy two-piece bathing suit to jazz up her marriage, but it wasn't her, and she knew it. Then she remembered her half tattoo. She walked to the dock and pointed to her thigh.

"You can't leave. You didn't finish this."

Wende shrugged. "You never wanted it."

"Now what am I supposed to do?"

"Dex proposed last night—you have to come to the wedding. Call me when you get back to LA, and I'll finish it."

Her words and her expression were at a disconnect.

"You don't love him."

Wende frowned. "It's time to grow up."

Ann sighed. Had this whole thing with Cooked been an act to get what she wanted from Dex? Had sweet little Wende played them all? Impossible to save another even if it was clear she was throwing away her dreams, however misguided. The girl had wanted to save sharks.

"What's with Cooked?"

He was hunched over in the gloom of a palm tree, dark and glowering, one of his eyes black and swollen shut. Titi refused to let him in the kitchen while she prepared breakfast. Later, Ann found out Titi was the one who had given him the black eye, giving the lie to the Polynesian no-jealousy policy. The human heart guided itself. Was the slickness on Cooked's cheeks from tears? He bolted from his place and ran to the water, holding a bucket.

"Go away," Wende yelled into the wind, but Cooked ran into the water and threw a bouillabaisse of cut fish around him. He raked his fingernails down his chest, drawing streaks of blood. Wende screamed. Richard and Loren jumped into the water and dragged the boy out.

"I'm sorry," Wende said. "I didn't mean to hurt you."

"I don't think he's doing it for you," Ann said.

Titi made her stately way down the path from the kitchen to the water. Cooked ran to her and fell on his knees, burying his face in her billowy dress. Had the love potion worked after all, albeit slowly, painfully, like all true love?

Wende turned away, her face pale. "Okay," she yelled. "I'll do it."

Ann was confused. Events were unspooling like a bad drug trip.

With difficulty Loren pulled the boat around in the choppy waves. The wind from the coming storm was pulling at every surface so that one had to hunch one's shoulders against it. Dex appeared with a duffel and his guitar case.

"Do you have to go?" Ann asked, more a whine than a question. The night before had been special, the whole group finally bonded, and now just as quickly it was falling apart. "We could all hang out a while longer. Our little paradise. What about the free nights?"

"Are you speaking as my attorney?" Dex said.

Ann shook her head. "As your friend."

"I don't want to lose her," he whispered.

They hugged and exchanged good-byes. Wende and Dex held hands sitting in the boat while Loren and Cooked argued; finally Cooked yanked on the hotel's official yellow shirt and got behind the wheel. The shirt soaked up his blood like a cocktail napkin, a Rorschach of heartbreak.

"I didn't think she even liked Dex," Richard said.

Thankfully, Richard appeared to be staying for now.

"Life's strange that way," Ann said.

Richard watched as they boarded and the boat pulled away.

Ann felt sorry for him. It was so easy to forget one's husband could be a hurting human being also.

Cooked was mournfully staring at Titi as if he were going away on a many-years-long sea voyage, with the possibility he might never return.

Titi and Richard turned away as the wind kicked up sand, but Ann kept watching the boat as it made its way into the deeper part of the lagoon. She alone saw Wende rise, holding the small valise, then lift her free arm for balance as she gracefully stepped over the side like a modern-day Ophelia.

"Man overboard! Woman!" Ann screamed as the others turned around and Loren ran out of the kitchen.

There was a loud cracking sound as the boat hit an underwater coral reef.

Loren grabbed his head. "I'll kill him!"

Both Cooked and Dex jumped overboard to rescue Wende. In the panic all three almost drowned. For a weird moment in the choppy waves, Cooked appeared to be yelling at Wende, and she submerged again. A miracle that they made it back to the boat, and that the boat returned to the shore before it was logged with water and sank. Their own twenty-first-century shipwreck. The luggage, including the valise, lost.

By the afternoon, rain pelted down so hard that they had no choice but to stay sequestered inside their *fares*. Even a quick trip to the kitchen punished one with a drenching. At dusk a howling began, like a never-ending freight car roaring overhead. Loren beat on each of their doors and ordered them to evacuate to his *fare*, which was the highest point on the island.

"How much higher?" Richard asked.

"One meter. Three feet. Maybe enough to save you."

Outside, the island's transformation was spellbinding. Water that had been fifty feet away, now surrounded them, and they sloshed barefoot through it. Debris floated in the sand-heavy liquid, knocking into their shinbones. This was way beyond any thunderstorm. When Richard and Ann got to Loren's, everyone else was already inside. Titi sat in the corner, chanting to herself. Cooked thumbed through a sports magazine. Dex had his arms around Wende, who was shivering and teary-eyed.

"We should have left," she said. "It's my fault."

Cooked looked up sharply at her, but she ignored him.

"The other resort would have been no different," Dex said.

"The other resort is steel-fortified," Loren said. "It can easily withstand a hurricane. Plenty of food, medicine, boats there."

"What's the safety plan here?" Richard asked.

"If the storm surge floods the island much more, the buildings will go. You don't want to get hit by debris. Put your life jackets on and head for the boat."

The stack of neglected yellow life vests sat piled in the corner. Ann did not mention the obvious—that there had been no boat since that morning.

A storm went on so long into the night that intermittent sleep finally overcame their fear. The sole light came from a battery-operated lantern, which threw attenuated, spooky shadows on the ceiling. Alternating from prayers that sounded more like plea bargains to self-recriminations (why hadn't they gone to Alsace?), Ann fell asleep on the floor and woke to the startling sensation of sitting in water. She whimpered.

"I hate storms," she said.

"I know," Richard whispered, and wrapped his arms around her, forming a Richard blanket.

It was true—Richard was the one person in the world who knew she preferred earth tones, that she liked anchovies on her Caesar salad, that she absolutely detested and loathed thunderstorms. How had she forgotten all this?

"I'm sorry," Ann said. "For everything."

"I'm not sorry for a minute of it," Richard said, and kissed her hair.

Minutes later, the water pooled up to the undersides of the rush-bottomed chairs. They would literally drown in the Pacific, their leaky life raft of an island sinking beneath them.

And then the waters retreated. Within ten minutes, the floor was no longer underwater. The force of the hurricane passed to the west.

"I've never been so hungry in my life," Wende said.

"Food," Richard agreed.

A lthough it was still raining hard, the howling had subsided the slightest degree in intensity. Celebratory after two close calls, feeling very much alive, they shoved the wet table and chairs into the kitchen. Richard cooked a large pot of linguine *frutti di mare* and served family-style.

At Richard's insistence, Titi and Cooked joined the table for the first time to eat with them. Something had been settled between the two. They only had eyes for each other and the food, which they ate with gusto. At the beach, after the near-drowning, they'd had a passionate, seawater-sputtering reunion when Cooked staggered back to solid land.

"Today I saw my life passing by," Dex said. "It's good to be back."

"You were only one hundred meters out."

"I was already checked out here." Dex tapped his ear, which in his case might indeed have been the seat of all desire. "I'm taking it as a sign."

"It's only a sign," Loren said, "that Cooked is an imbecile."

Through this exchange, a subdued Wende sat silent. Ann had been the only witness to her act.

"What does it mean?" she muttered, but so softly they could pretend not to hear her.

"The boat sinking was a gift," Titi said.

"Of course. No guilt, no remorse at all," Loren said bitterly. "It would be different if the boat was yours."

Cooked dropped Titi's hand. "Yes, it would be different. But it isn't."

The table fell into a funky silence.

Richard broke the impasse by serving a huge platter of cheeses and fruit. "'A dessert without cheese is like a beautiful woman with only one eye.'"

"Whoa, I like that," Dex said. "Did you just make that up?"

"That's the master—Brillat-Savarin."

"Cool. I think I'll use it."

Wende looked on the verge of crying. "I almost died out there. No one cares!"

Dex put his arm around her. "Clumsy honey bunny, you fell overboard. We had you covered."

Wende was about to blurt out a confession she was not ready to make and they were not ready to hear—or, rather, that Ann was not ready for them to hear, with the likely outcome that the camaraderie would again be broken. Everyone would want to leave as soon as they could. The table slumped back into inaction. So quiet that they could hear outside.

"Listen," Ann said.

Silence.

"I don't hear anything."

"Exactly."

They tumbled outside into the darkness. The island was holding them up again. The clouds had cleared away. The night sky was newly scrubbed, moon-brilliant, star-punctured.

Around them on the beach were scattered bits of rock and coral. Glistening bodies of sea life lay stranded. Fish and eels fluttered in small pools, and the guys grabbed them and threw them back into the water. The farthest *fare*, vacant, had disappeared off its finger of sand as if it never was, washed away. A lesson, Loren thought.

"We're marooned. At least till the hotel sends out another boat," Richard said.

The idea of actually being marooned sent a tingle down Ann's spine. Her fantasy was taking a majestic turn toward the real.

"It feels like the beginning of the world," Dex said. "If only you could record this feeling."

Loren yawned. "Good night, lovely people. Enough excitement for tonight," he said, and went off.

Ann felt the urge to lay out something precious before the others, to seal the evening as extraordinary. Besides, her secret had been burning a hole in her pocket for a week now. "You can record it."

They scampered through the glittering night like trick-or-treaters, kids playing hooky, whispering and giggling, sneaking kisses and gropes, tripping and falling in the sand. It was like a happy return to childhood. The beach was littered with palm fronds, and in the dark, Wende stumbled over one. Dex fell on top of her, and they rolled away, laughing.

"Knock it off," Ann said, a taskmaster. "Hurry." Her heart beat a staccato of excitement.

No reason to hurry. They had basically forever, but she wanted to create proper awe for the unveiling. The hurry also obscured the tiniest feeling of unease at betraying Loren.

The path along the island's edge was deceptively longer at night. Shouldn't they have already passed it? Richard was drinking straight out of a bottle of red wine and singing Italian opera, of all things, though he didn't even speak Italian. Dex and Wende passed a bottle of champagne back and forth. Everyone was enjoying the journey far too much for Ann's taste.

They didn't pass anything remotely familiar at the point Ann thought the camera should be. Had the storm washed it away? They went farther. Farther still. Ann walked ahead, squinting into the darkness past the feeble cone of light from her flashlight, unconfident of her landmarks. Behind her, the troops were grumbling. Richard stopped to take a leak behind a palm. Wende complained she was tired.

"There it is!" Ann shouted.

In the middle of a stretch of washed beach was her webcam. As each of them came up to it, there was an unimpressed silence.

Finally Ann said, "Here it is."

"Hmmph."

"What is it?"

"A remote webcam."

"What?"

"It films this stretch of beach twenty-four hours a day."

"No way."

"Yes way."

"Why?"

That was the question that Ann had been pondering all those mornings alone, sitting behind the camera, watching it as it watched the beach. Why do it? Who would watch it? Undoubtedly the same people who would like to be there in person but couldn't be, for one reason or another. But that didn't entirely make sense either. While the scene was lovely, so were many others, and a live scene surely trumped a videoed one any day. Were people so jaded that live experience wasn't adequate any longer?

It had to be something else. Something to do with why Ann trudged all the way there, when any other stretch of beach would have sufficed for solitude—the act of recording implied specialness. How many desires did one have independent of the constant barrage of images that brainwashed one? Was the live image of the beach any different from creating a sacred building? Did anything exist in the sacred building that didn't exist elsewhere, or vice versa? The very act of putting it in the building, or recording it on a webcam, made one take notice. One carried a photo, a rosary, a lock of hair, a seashell—the religious referred to them as relics—for the same reason one watched this scene on the Internet: it signified an inchoate longing that was getting harder and harder to access in everyday life.

"Loren did this as a performance piece," she said by way of explanation.

"Cool," Dex said.

"Loren, that old snake," Richard said.

"Right?" Ann said.

"That whole dropping out, being unplugged . . ."

"Uh-huh. But pretend you don't know," Ann pleaded, but the cats were far out of the bag. Who was she kidding? She had known that in telling them there would be a loss of control. She had accepted that devil's bargain even if Loren had not.

"Let's build a bonfire," Dex said. "So they see it. Give people a thrill. *Planet of the Apes* time."

"Fun."

"No," Ann said, horrified, but already they had tuned her out.

Dex and Richard passed a joint as they gathered kindling. Ann, defeated, went to sit with Wende. She hadn't considered the repercussions of their commandeering her secret, taking it away from her, and co-opting the situation's possibilities.

"A huge mistake," Ann said.

"I jumped," Wende said.

Ann closed her eyes. "Yes, you did."

"You saw?"

Ann nodded. Events on the island had accelerated to mainland speed, too much to process before the next thing took its place, creating a perpetual state of low-grade anxiety. She didn't want to admit she'd forgotten all about the jump.

"Are you mad about me marrying Dex?"

Ann rolled over and faced her in the darkness. "Oh, honey, I have no right to judge. You just seemed so sure of what you didn't want."

"What I almost did—it was my bon voyage gift to Cooked—but then I couldn't."

"Okay." Ann was feeling her way through the murk of Wende's explanation, unsure exactly what they were talking about but afraid to frighten away a confession.

"It feels bad. I was trying to be someone I'm not. I got scared. Cooked hates me, but I saved him. *His mother cooked for me.*"

They lay back in silence. They had formed some type of ad hoc dysfunctional twenty-first-century family unit. Ann gazed up at the stars. The heavens seemed to be spinning so fast she had to close her eyes. Yes, it felt bad. What kind of traitorous person was she, giving up Loren's secret like a party favor, like a kid trying to be popular? A blaze of fire went up and turned molten behind her eyelids. The guys were screaming and dancing like madmen. Was there sound on the cam? Oh God, yes. She was angry with them, but most of all angry with herself. She was lacking in all the qualities she admired in others.

"I keep making mistakes," Ann said.

"It's like the song 'You just keep trying till you run out of cake.'"

"Who wants to go skinny-dipping?" Dex shouted.

"I do, I do." Wende jumped up and ran away.

The old Wende was back.

For ten years the camera had recorded . . . nothing, which was the whole point, but that night the first seminal images in a decade were of the backsides of two men in the darkness, burnished in the glow of a bonfire. For an hour that was it, a burning fire, because the nighttime view of the beach and waves, even on full-moon nights, was always indecipherable. The next picture—as graven in Robinson Crusoe cam's history as the first flickering images on film—was the flame-lit figure of a naked blond woman running past the fire, laughing and giggling, being chased by a naked tattooed man with a tangle of black hair covering his face.

Dex and Wende were like children with a new toy. They sat in the sand, drinking and coming up with variety-show scenarios to stage in front of the camera.

"Leave it alone," Ann begged. "You've had your fun."

"No way," Dex said. "We're just started. Weren't you begging us to stay a few more days?"

When they returned to their water-soaked *fares* late that night, the oil lamp in the dining area was still lit, and Loren was sitting up, waiting for them like a cross father. As they walked by, Richard wished him good night, but he held up his hand to stop them.

"You betrayed my trust," he said to Ann.

Ann had regressed to her teenage years, living out all the things she had not done at the time. Having broken the rules, she just wanted the punishment to be swift. "They would have found it eventually. No one will notice."

"Viewership has exploded. It's gone to virus on the computer."

"Viral."

"Cool," Dex said.

"It's ruined."

"More people are watching than ever," Ann said.

"That was never the point. It's turned into a cheap sideshow."

Dex lit up a cigarette. "You could parlay it into advertising for this place."

"It was supposed to be pure."

"Look around. Your place is getting rough around the edges," Dex said.

"People will forget," Ann said.

Loren shook his head. "I'm pulling the plug. I want you all to leave the island."

"No," Richard answered. Ann was near tears, and even if he didn't understand, he wanted to help her get whatever it was she was after. "I'm cooking. Dex is paying. Ann is looking after you. We're not ready to leave just yet."

"Besides, there's no boat," Wende added. "We're marooned."

Loren got up and without another word walked away.

He made a big production of wanting to be alone, but once he was back in his *fare*, ironically he longed to be in the company of people. He sat hoping that someone would come and disturb him so that he could act annoyed and too busy for whatever concerns they had. Sometimes the need for solitude was real, and other times it was a mere costume. Like all true recluses, he was simply waiting to be found by the right person.

Ann barged into his hut as he was pouring himself a tumbler of rum.

"Don't be so mad," she said.

"Judas. You came and betrayed."

"What? Your public webcam? Was it really a secret? Isn't the very concept an oxymoron?"

"It's for Lilou."

"Who is that? Your wife? Girlfriend?"

"My daughter."

"You said you didn't have anyone."

"We haven't spoken in years."

"So how do you know she watches?"

"I know it here," he said, and touched his hand to his heart.

Ann threw herself into a chair. She was confused and tired; her efforts at doing good, even for herself, were going nowhere. "It was wrong. I knew better, but I was desperate. Everyone was leaving."

"You did what it took," Loren said. "You Americans, always going around fixing the world."

Ann started to cry.

"Tears won't move me."

She shook her head, unable to stop. "Me either."

But tears did move him. Loren had already sold out weeks ago when he bought the Crusoe Cam domain name, allowing it to be commodified by views, if not dollars. So he told her the history of his coming to the islands—the real, unembellished version, which he had never shared before in its unflattering, unfun entirety.

". . . After they took the girls away, I still called and wrote. It wasn't as easy as today, with email. Did their mother give them the letters? I don't know. Two years later, I received an official letter that Bette had died. Drowned in a bathtub. There were bruises on her body. My wife didn't have the decency to inform me. Lilou never forgave me for not rescuing them."

"How can you ever forgive me?"

He waved her words off, deep in the presenting of his case to an invisible jury. "Why didn't they understand? *I* was accused of a perverted lifestyle. Things that would damage a child."

"Children don't understand logic. Neither do most adults. We want a magic fix."

He slumped in his chair.

"Contact her. She has a right to know you're sick."

Loren poured another glass. "Did you know that there were a hundred thousand viewers just tonight?"

"Really?"

"And that Windy and Cooked were planning to bomb the main hotel? Titi told me while you were out on your night reconnaissance patrol. The islands are again at war."

"Why would Wende—?"

"Cooked, that idiot, talked her into it. She wouldn't arouse suspicion placing it like he would."

"So that was it." ·

"Youth is wasted on the young because they're crazy."

"You were young once."

"And as crazy as they come."

Ann woke refreshed the next morning, strangely unaffected by the copious amounts of alcohol she had ingested, the theatrics and meltdowns of the previous day. The damage from the storm had been minimal, anticlimactic compared to the human goings-on. Why did the calamities of others always have the effect of making one's own problems more tolerable? It wasn't exactly schadenfreude; it was more the relief of knowing no one's life was perfect. Everyone struggled. One was not alone. On the island she had found a camaraderie she didn't want to lose by returning to her old life in LA. When she was a little girl, her favorite game had been playing nurse—she bandaged nonexistent wounds and brought order to chaos. Here on this island, she felt that sense of usefulness returning. Was it pathological, her neediness to be needed?

Richard waved her off, too hungover to get out of bed. His face and arms were scratched from gathering kindling with Dex the previous night. His hair still smelled of woodsmoke when she bent to kiss him.

The public area was deserted, no sign of Loren, not that she had expected one, but no sign of Dex and Wende either. Not even Titi and Cooked were to be seen. The prospect of a solitary breakfast did not appeal to her. In the empty kitchen, she made a quick coffee and grabbed fruit, intending to head to her usual lounging spot behind the camera.

As she approached, puffs of smoke were rising above the tree line. When the camera came into view around the last curve of shoreline, there were Dex and Wende in front of another large bonfire. Both of them had red, watery eyes. Ann couldn't be sure if it was from woodsmoke or spliff or some diabolical combination of the two. The air was fragrant with the resiny smell of pot.

"Hey, what's up?" Dex said.

"I need a word with you," Ann said to Wende. "In private."

"Don't worry," Dex said. "We figured out how to turn the volume off the camera."

"About the boat," Ann said. "I thought you jumped to not get married."

"What?" Dex said.

Wende took her aside. "Can we do this later in private?"

"What are you guys up to?"

"Nothing. A little performance art," Dex said.

"We've been building the fire all morning."

"Okay, give me some room." Dex pulled some papers out of a beach bag and faced the camera. Theatrically, he kissed the first sheet and then let the flames devour it. The breeze blew the ashes horizontally, like a sideways snowstorm, out of frame.

"What's this?" Ann asked.

"That is the latest song I wrote."

"Why are you burning it?" Wende asked. "You never said anything about burning a new song. Is it that bad?"

"It's called 'Beautiful One-Eyed Lady.' Inspired by Richard's primo dinner last night. It's probably the best piece I've ever done."

"You have a copy?" Wende asked.

Dex fed the last page to the flames, then bowed and walked out of camera range. "What would be the point of that?"

"So that was the only one?" Wende said.

"Do you think I'm some narcissist? Faking it? It was a sign when we didn't leave the island, when you fell overboard. The universe doesn't want me to go back. This is good-bye to the band, to music. This time I'm doing it right."

Wende ran to the fire, as if by sheer will she could pull out the pages intact. "You're making a mistake."

"I feel wonderful. I'm no longer a puppet to worldly desires."

"You have no right!" she screamed.

"It's my destiny."

"It isn't. Not anymore. You involve other people. It's a gift, and you shit on it."

Dex sighed. "Women."

"You're not so pure either. You complain about Robby, but a few years back you dumped him when you thought you could go out on your own."

"You're young," Dex said, and turned his skinny back on her.

"Robby needs to make a living. He doesn't have a rich dad and a trust fund to fall back on."

"Stop it," Dex said.

"I better leave," Ann said.

"No!" Wende held her arm. "I want a witness. He doesn't like to talk about all that because it doesn't go with his image." She turned to Dex. "I've sacrificed two years with you. It hasn't been all games and fun. The best part of Dex Cooper is when he's out on the stage playing music. You're not much good any other time. I'm out."

With that, Wende took off down the beach.

Dex couldn't put out the flicker of doubt that she had ignited. She was screwing with his enlightenment. What do you do after being famous? It wasn't like being an accountant, where you can retire. The only retirement from fame was obscurity. Nonfame. As in No Longer

Famous. Thrown out of the club. Which, back to the Buddhist texts, pretty much came down to nonbeing. How did he like them apples?

Dex gave a fake bark of a laugh that sounded more like a sob. "Women."

Ann felt awkward staying but feared leaving him alone. Undecided, she sat on the sand. There was a bit of Girl Scout and do-gooderism in her that mirrored Richard's.

After a long period of silence, Dex asked, "What do you think?"

"Wende? Gone."

"I can't live without her."

Ann didn't know for sure how to take this, but he seemed sincere enough to worry. It was like reasoning with a child's outsize emotions.

"Go after her then."

He shook his head.

Pride, she thought. Men. "Start by rewriting the damn song at least. Wende is a muse, and you've insulted her."

She studied Dex. Fame had the effect of making one self-conscious of observing its object, but they had been living in close proximity for more than two weeks. Now it was hard to equate this guy with that fame. One on one, it disappeared. Dex's face was aged and craggy—he looked like a cowboy in a cigarette ad, except instead of a hat, there was spiky, dyed-black hair and an ear bolt. It was hard to explain, but somehow Dex added up to more than the sum of his parts. He oozed sexuality; he was like a human USB port, appealing to a great variety of women. Ann was disappointed to find herself ever so slightly preening.

"If things work out with Wende, do yourself a favor and get a prenup. I'll draw it up for you."

She would omit the fact that his potential fiancée was a would-be terrorist, not to mention reckless in jumping out of a boat and almost getting Cooked and him drowned.

"Never," he said.

"Why not? You've been married five times before." She knew because one night in Loren's office she had googled him and read the gossip columns. Was she stalking him?

"Six times. That would be like starting the game betting you were going to lose."

"You've never had a prenup?"

"It's glorious supporting a village."

"We better head back."

Dex nodded and helped her up. They walked along in silence.

"Richard lied to you. He didn't mean to, but he did. There is no restaurant. It's a long story . . . I took some money. We're in hiding."

"Cool, so you guys are outlaws!"

"White-collar, corporate kind of ones."

"Those are the most deadly kind. My dad was a CEO."

"So Wende was telling the truth?"

"A hell of a pedigree."

"Can't be that bad. What did his company do?"

"They made deals. Sold banned pharmaceuticals to third-world countries for record profits. Backed a supplier of depleted uranium-ammo for the Gulf War, then denied its side-effects. Were involved with financial institutions and hired a PR firm that manufactured public opinion to go to war in the Gulf. Possibly masterminded the story about Saddam's men pulling babies from incubators in Kuwait. The usual stuff."

"That couldn't be *your* father?"

"It gets better. Not only did he buy his own bullshit, he sent his oldest son to Kuwait to fight. Even after Harry's death, he never admitted he was wrong . . . I miss Harry every day of my life . . . I'll never forgive him for that."

They stood watching the waves.

"I *like* you," Ann said. "I mean *you*. Not DEX COOPER. You're nothing like I thought you were."

Dex bowed his head, flushed with pleasure.

"I lied, too," Ann said. "We did meet."

"I knew it! I never forget a pretty face."

"At the Troubadour with my best friend, Lorna. You bought us drinks. Whiskey sours? Whenever I order one, I remember that night."

"What else happened?"

"You had us drive you home. Your license had been revoked . . . You suggested things."

"Sure I did."

"You kissed Lorna, and we went home. Sometimes, over the years, I regretted it wasn't me."

Dex shook his head, smiling. "I was bad news back then."

"You're right."

"Man!" he said. "We two are seriously messed up."

"I don't feel messed up. Not right now."

Close up, Ann noticed the details of Dex's tattoos: a long twisting dragon around his arm, and a bitten apple on his shoulder (Wende's doing?). She did a double take. "What's that?" she said, using the tattoo as an excuse to touch his skin with her fingertips. A shiver went through her. The only other man to affect her that way had been Javi.

"That was a joke my first wife, Jamie, played on me," Dex said, grabbing her hand and clamping it under his armpit so Ann had to walk sideways, like her arm was being swallowed by a cuddly alligator. "Eve and the apple? Temptation. She did it in the mid-'80s when the computer company was about to disappear. How did we know that they would turn things around, that the logo would become the most recognized one in the world?"

"Funny."

"Kids think I'm pushing Apple products. Like I'd turn my body into a corporate billboard."

"Get it lasered off."

"Then I'd be cowing to the pressure of their imaging. Do they own the apple fruit? I think not."

He had extraordinarily big hands, elegantly shaped, with long tapered fingers. In another life, he could have been a concert pianist; the span of his fingers easily could cover the interval of a thirteenth on a keyboard. What would those hands feel like on her hips?

Silence dropped between them, and again there was that electricity thing from their touching, and she needed to change the mood fast.

"Is Dex short for Dexter?"

"Dex is made up. Dex is nothing. Dex is reinvention. Couldn't go by Adam Knowlton and be associated with the old guy, right?"

He brought her hand to his mouth and kissed it. Then he held her arm as he started to trudge into the surf.

"Hey, no, I don't want to go swimming."

He had her in knee-high when he let go. Before she could turn away, he splashed a wave of water with his big paddlelike hand.

"No fair." She splashed back.

"Oh, Ann, don't you know by now nothing in this world is fair?" He grabbed her from behind around the waist to drag her in deeper. "I'm the big bad shark."

If he kissed her now, she would let him. If he kissed her, she would kiss him back. She would gloss the past, undo regret, and when she was a grandmother someday, she would not be sorry that she had not kissed DEX COOPER.

She doubled over, laughing, trying and not trying to get out of his grip, when she heard a voice calling.

"Dex, honey, I'm sorry."

Wende, puffy-eyed and repentant, waded into the water with shuffling, babyish steps, totally unfazed that her boyfriend had his big pianist's hands all over another woman's semibared body. Ann was sure that a jealous girlfriend wouldn't last very long in Dex's world, what with women flinging themselves at him and making themselves available. Still, it irked her that Wende considered her beneath the possibility of jealousy. Or maybe she considered Ann too much of a friend to have any doubts of her loyalty?

"Oh, lovebug," Dex said, releasing Ann. The water frothed in his hurry to get to tear-smeared Wende. They hugged. Wende mouthed, *"I'll tell you later,"* over his shoulder. Dex picked her up, and she wrapped her golden legs around his waist. They didn't stop kissing long enough to notice Ann's hurried departure down the beach.

The somnolent morning passed. The main resort didn't have a boat to spare, so they were effectively stranded until one could be procured from Papeete. No supply runs, no snorkeling trips, no sightseeing. Worried about the cost of new repairs necessitated by the storm, Loren insisted the replacement be a used one, so the wait could stretch out even longer.

"What if someone gets sick?" Richard whispered to Ann.

"We're all healthy. Except for Loren."

When they showed up a few hours later for lunch, Dex and Wende had big smiles on their faces. Wende yawned and said she was going for a nap.

"You promised we'd talk," Ann insisted.

"Give me an hour," Wende begged off.

Revved after the friction of Wende, still tingling from his two near-deaths in the boat, chastened by the burning of his last song, Dex took a notebook and some pens and went into one of the back, uninhabited bungalows. It was still soggy from the storm and smelled of mildew, but he was glad for that. He deserved hardship. He had promised Wende he was going to rewrite "One-Eyed Lady," but before he did, there was something else he needed to do, a sort of testimonial. He was deeply committed to the idea of marrying Wende, just as he had been to each of his wives in his last six marriages; he needed to figure out how he could make her the sixth and last Mrs. Dex Cooper. He paused and took a sip from the bottle of rum he'd swiped from the bar.

**The 5 Women I Married (Before Wende, Who I Love the Most)**
In Reverse Chronological Order Because It's Easier That Way

*Giselle: I called her my Gazelle. Marriage length: 2 years. Only lasted that long because I was on tour and couldn't get to my attorney. Age difference: 21 years. Children: 1 daughter. Giselle was a model, a beautiful girl, but she had a German accent so thick I couldn't understand her most of the time. Liked schnauzer dogs. She was as tall as me and had big feet. Seriously gorgeous body. Always smelled of* expensive perfume. When I open a bottle of Must de Cartier even now I get an erection thinking of her. Terrible in bed. Hated to be touched, went rigid as a board. Don't think she liked me so much either. Definitely not as much as the schnauzers. Hated the music and the band. Loved opera, polka, shopping. Turned shopping into a competitive sport.

Micaela: Alan's (the ex-drummer's) ex-girlfriend. Marriage length: 5 years. Only that long I think so she could irritate Alan. Age difference: 15 years. Children: 3 boys. Household: 5 dogs, 3 cats, a string of polo ponies (hers). Hot and fiery Argentinean. Never didn't want to have sex, especially when we were fighting. Left many, many scratches and bites, so many that people asked if I had been in bar fights, but (see above) who's complaining? The makeup people did complain at the extra work. Had to go to the hospital one night from an infected bite and have an antibiotic shot. Much drinking and much drugging. Rehab. In, out, in, out. Hated the band (especially Alan), jealous of the music, always smashing my guitars when she sensed I'd been with other women. An effective deterrent when you are talking about Fenders, Gibsons, and Rickenbackers.

Lori: Business manager of the band. Marriage length: 6 months. Age difference: she was one year older. Helped me out of my depression after the first three marriages (see below). Both of us overwhelmed by the many problems created by the unforeseen success of the band. Motherly figure. Weren't really attracted to each other, but got fucked up together one night in Vegas, and decided, why not? Never imagined marrying someone who I liked as a friend. After we moved to the Malibu house, we rescued two Aussie shepherds and walked them every day on the beach. Question: Was Lori trying to rescue me, too? Loved the music. Diagnosed with cancer after amicable divorce. Took care of her till she was better. Still take care of her and her new

*husband, who's now our accountant. Still friends. Have dinner
at their house every Thursday when I'm in town. Made me
godfather to their son. Still my business manager. Handles the
complicated alimony payments. Longest functioning relationship
w/a woman.*

*Jamie: See below. Second time around was NOT a charm. Marriage
length: 4 months. She tried, but I was already wrecked.*

*Kelli: South African actress. Her father was a Boer and a bore.
Marriage length: 2 years. Again only because we were both too busy to
get the divorce started. Time we were together, monogamous: 3 weeks.
Age difference: 5 years. Children: twin boys. Kelli was in love with
DEX COOPER, not Dex Cooper, if you know what I mean. Had
no interest in me as a human being separate from being her ROCK
STAR husband. Only was affectionate in public, preferably with
paparazzi around. Slept with rottweiler in the bed—crowded (what
is it with me and women with dogs?). Arch conservative in politics,
listened to Rush Limbaugh (how in the world did we meet?), ate huge
quantities of red meat, especially barbecue, so she and her dad had the
grill out back fired up day and night like some outer circle of hell. Liked
to go hunting with my dad (only one of my wives he approved of),
liked to walk around the house in the nude in front of staff, band
members, whoever (best part of the relationship!). Slept with each
member of the band behind my back. Nasty divorce. Swore not to
marry again after her—broke that promise. Haha! Hope springs
eternal.*

Here Dex quaffed down the remaining half bottle of rum. He gently
stroked his apple tattoo.

*Jamie: Robby's sister. We were both sixteen. Love of my life. How
could I have known that and then made all those mistakes (see
above)? Broke, we lived in our car, in friends' apartments. We didn't*

*care. We lived for the music. Marriage length: 3 years. Age difference:*
*one month apart. She said we were twins, born in different wombs.*
*The success scared her, like it should've scared me. The band became a*
*hungry beast we lived to feed. I betrayed her brother, but also betrayed*
*her—not only with alcohol, drugs, and women, but with the music,*
*mostly with the fame. I lost myself when I lost her.*

When Dex wrote the last words, he felt like he'd stripped himself as
naked as he could without a guitar in his hands. He looked over the pages
and thought they described someone else's life, not his, although he had
certainly lived through all these indignities. Could this jumble be the
sum of his life? It seemed to describe some asshole's life. Before he
chickened out, he gathered up the sheets of paper, staggered out of the
bungalow, and made his way to the sixth Mrs. Dex-Cooper-to-be.

Wende was still sleeping, so he put the sheath of papers next to her to
be read on waking. He looked down at that angelic face—did he truly
love her? He was wild about her, but looking over those pages—was he
the best man to judge? Was his love fickle? Was his love a kind of reverse Midas touch that turned gold into shit? Whatever he felt for this
sweet girl, who was most certainly way smarter than himself, was
enough to last his lifetime. He would dedicate himself to faithfulness if
she decided to have him. But first she had to know the truth of his unlucky amorous history. At least the married part.

The affairs and casual couplings were beyond naming, counting, or at
that point recalling. In public places, he broke out in a cold sweat when
an unfamiliar woman greeted him, feeling that he probably had slept with
her at some point in the past and at least should recognize her, but it was
hard to remember, especially if she was wearing clothes.

He went back outside, ready to work on the song, but when he reached
the room again, something felt wrong. He went looking for his new
muse, Richard.

Richard had found nirvana in the kitchen, and he felt such bliss in
cooking that he didn't care if he never saw another snorkel mask,

scuba tank, or clown fish again for the rest of the trip. How had he banished himself from this joy? He had burned his wax wings against the sun—being a chef, even head chef of a star restaurant, was hard, but not nearly as hard as owning one's own place. That involved a confidence and risk-taking that wasn't in him. He should have stayed where he was, content. By pretending, he had gotten Ann's hopes up and then not been able to deliver. Dex had showed him a book of mythology from the library because it had hot pictures of naked nymphs surrounding the drowned Icarus, but the father's words to his son haunted Richard: *Do not set your own course.* No one ever told you that in the "Going for It" ehandbook of life.

He was whisking up a light béarnaise for that night's fish when Dex came in.

"Where've you been? Loren's going crazy with all the views on the cam. Half a million today. Your fans recognized you. Newspapers and TV coverage back home."

Dex felt shamed by the fact that viewers pleased him. Fame whore. He even had the very un-Buddhist thought that you can't buy that kind of publicity. He wanted to jab himself with a fork as he wondered how to find out if sales were up. "I burned another song this morning. It felt righteous. It was like a public renunciation."

"Good, I guess." Richard didn't want to be disloyal, but the drama of Dex's creative life was getting less and less enthralling.

"Wende's pissed."

"Women get like that."

"Thing is, maybe it was a mistake. I want it back. Will you hang with me?"

Richard sighed. As much as he'd enjoyed playing buddy last time, he wasn't Dex's girlfriend. He really didn't want to sit around midwifing through another long night. He had his own stuff to do.

"I'll make you a deal. Sous chef for me, then I'll come. Otherwise we're not eating tonight."

"Why can't Titi do it?"

"She says she can't spend all day cooking. Probably a blessing."

Dex weighed the idea of returning to the *fare* and working alone. "What do I do?"

The two men shared another bottle of rum as they did *mise en place*, prepped vegetables, and started the base for an angel food cake. This was Richard's favorite part of cooking, the calm before the storm, and he was glad to give Dex a feel for it.

"Can I ask you something?"

"Shoot."

"What's it like up there onstage? Singing? All those fans."

Dex took another long swig. "You know when you have a favorite song, and you can't get enough of it? You play it over and over? And then, even after a long time has passed, you hear a couple of bars, and it's like seeing an old friend? You're right back there, stronger than ever. Well, it's like that times a thousand. I want to live in that song—not because I wrote it. I wrote it because it was something I loved. It's like addiction, but not illegal."

Richard stopped chopping. "Lucky bastard."

Dex wouldn't explain how it had changed for him. He wanted to keep the legend alive. "It's like loving the right woman. I know you understand that."

Wende woke and cat-stretched out on the bed, watching the sunlight move across the wall. Everything seemed right with the world, whereas only a day ago everything was on the verge of going terribly wrong. She felt chastised and grateful for her narrow escape from being a terrorist. But in her heart of hearts, it wasn't entirely clear whether she jumped to not blow up a building or to not get married. Luckily it turned out a win-win situation. As she rolled over for her water bottle, she heard paper crunching beneath her.

"What—?" She started to read the catalog of her predecessors, and the landmine-littered yellow brick road of her probable future.

When Ann returned, jittery after her encounter with Dex, Titi had taken her aside and begged her to go see Loren.

"He only talks to you. He's mad at Cooked."

Ann was the only one brave enough to intervene. Against Loren's wishes if need be. This was exactly what she was trained to do, interfere where she wasn't wanted but was needed. First she needed to find something out.

She knocked on Wende's door.

"Go away."

What was it about the place that made them all by turns either too sociable or too solitary? That made them too easily break rules?

"I'm coming in."

Wende was stranded in her bed, blotchy-faced and sweaty.

"What's wrong?"

Wende nodded, emotions backed up so she could only gurgle and hand over crumpled, smeary pages.

"Another song?"

Wende shook her head vigorously as if she were trying to dislodge something. "Read it."

Ann wasn't surprised by what she found. A side effect of being around Wende was remembering the roller-coaster emotions, everything of life-or-death importance, that went with being in your twenties. "You knew he'd been married before."

"That's not it."

"About the hotel—"

Wende sighed and wiped her face, sat up and put her hair into a businesslike ponytail. "Don't you see? It's clear . . . he's settling for me. I thought I was settling for him, not the other way around."

"You're upset."

"I'm a muse. *I'm* supposed to be the one who is loved more."

"Oh."

"I don't want to end up like you all in twenty years. You've made compromises."

Ann could have sworn she was going to say, "Grow up." Instead she said, "We didn't intend to end up like this. By the way, I'm only thirteen years older." Pathetic that she had done the math. "What about wanting a marriage like ours?"

"I've matured. I see what I see."

"That was a few weeks ago!"

"Richard's not at fault. It's you. The way you flirt with Loren."

"That's ridiculous."

"It would be impossible to live a normal life with Dex. He doesn't know what normal is."

"*You* jumped out of a boat."

"I did." Wende folded her hands in her lap.

"Loren said that Cooked and you . . ."

"Were going to blow up some empty rooms at the main hotel?"

"It's true?"

"An error of judgment. I see that now. Sue me—I wanted to do something that mattered. Tourism is their cash cow. Kick them where it hurts."

Ann thought of Professor Faucett. He had been one of the few adults whom she knew who had kept his idealism, without going over to the point of radicalism. "What if people had been hurt? Killed? You could have been responsible."

"Give me some credit. I *did* jump out of the boat."

"Their political struggle has nothing to do with you."

"Everyone says that. Pass the buck. That's why the world is so messed up. It did get me out of getting married."

That shut Ann up. What was it about the girl that made her want to throttle her and hug her at the same time?

"I couldn't do it, and I couldn't stop Cooked. Or Dex. The only thing I could do was jump."

"The suitcase?"

Wende nodded. "Explosives."

"Christ."

Like a pretty little snake, Wende curled up against her. "You need to get Loren to forgive Cooked."

Ann hesitated, then wrapped her arms around her. "He won't listen to me."

"Of course he will. You're *his* muse."

L oren sat in front of his desktop, mesmerized. More than a million viewers in one day. For the first time since he'd come to the islands, he looked out to the rest of the world that he had shunned for shunning him. At his age he knew that much about himself: he did not have it in him to fight injustice on the large scale. Unlike Windy—dear, sweet, crass, libidinous, solipsistic, wrongheaded but well-intentioned girl of the plastic-fruit-like breasts—who was still young enough and callous enough to believe she could have some effect, that the suffering of the world could be rectified, that injustice wasn't a deeply penetrating and intractable stain impossible to lift. That's why sly Cooked had recruited her. There was still enough of an anarchic impulse in Loren to admire Cooked's misguided loyalties. He had tried to combine the flammable cocktail of lust and politics, always a hazardous brew.

After her narrow escape, Windy would return to LA and her cocoon of gated luxury among the privileged others, whose only fear was of someday being carried out of that world, kicking and screaming. Give her long enough, she would forget there was a larger world outside her own.

The reasons Loren's daughters had been taken away were beyond him to rectify. One could regret the past but not rewrite it. Unlike Windy, he would not risk sacrificing his little island of peace. Did that make him a bad man? A selfish one? Possibly. Enough for an adult Lilou to shun. Or did it just make him an average man, so overwhelmed by his own small life, so jealous of his minor freedoms, that he wouldn't forfeit them for anything past the shores of this islet.

He had just begun to have a name in the avant-garde art scene of Paris and Berlin, which was decades behind Warhol and the Factory, at the moment representation turned the final corner toward the absurd, substituting the meaningless for the meaningful. One of his best-known installations was a camcorder set up in a blank room, recording another camcorder—a serpent eating its own tail—and so the absurdity of his current situation did not entirely take him by surprise. What was new was viewers. In the exhibit, he had had a diagram to explain his intent, based on Lefebvre's idea of the transformation of space:

L'espace vécu **(lived space)**

L'espace perçu **(physical space)** L'espace conçu **(mental space)**

He had not intended the *motu*'s webcam as art because high art had to be scrupulously expunged of all human sentiment. Instead it was communion via electronics (*l'espace conçu*), not for public consumption but for private solace. For Lilou. If she watched, then his life (*l'espace perçu*) had some value. What did it mean now that their private father-daughter cyberspace had a million viewers? He studied the small map that counted hits on the website and found they were from all over the world, clustered mostly in North America, of course, because of Prospero's audience, but spreading globally, with many more viewers from Southeast Asia, Russia, and the Middle East than he would have guessed.

When he was first diagnosed, he had turned to various religious and new age remedies to try to calm the deep panic that had taken residence in his gut. The fear felt like its own tumor, a tumor of regret and anxiety that would kill him if the virus with its attendant bodily failures did not.

He didn't have the patience for any of it except meditation because meditation was what he pretty much did already when everyone left him alone, when he painted, which was his preferred state. *L'espace vécu.* He found he did not greatly miss the company of others. Illness put on the same constraints as old age for artists; as Degas said, they needed to be selfish about their remaining time in order to create. The superficial friendliness of the resort took care of all his social needs. Cooked and Titi were his *almost* family, although he didn't treat them as well as he should, but how many real families managed much better? If he didn't do something, he would lose Cooked to an unlikely combination of debauchery and idealism. Did he still have the energy to try to save the boy from his foolishness?

Loren clinched his bowels as a stab of pain, like a plucked string, reverberated through his body, but then it relented and let him out of its grip. He was losing the fight with *l'espace perçu*.

Hell was other people, but so was heaven. Loren no longer had the time to figure out which had been the greater portion of his life. During the last week, whether it was due to his worsening state or Ann's constant probing, he felt vulnerable, as if he had been skinned, as if his guests' desires and problems and petty complaints and happinesses could burrow inside him like a rash, or darts, or worms. He huddled away in his bungalow like a turtle hiding in his shell.

He studied the blue glow of his screen—the view of the beach he could see in person if he only went outside, except on screen he could also see the red pinpoints of all the people around the world who were at that same moment watching that same strand of beach, and it gave him an unexpected feeling of deep connectedness, a peacefulness, that he had not believed any longer possible. This is what he had sought and found lacking in various organized religions, a sense of the sacred, of community. Could one of the pinpoints in France be Lilou? Yes, he definitely sensed her watching. He hated Dex Cooper for cheapening his project, but at the same time he was in awe of this sudden net of connection wrapping itself around the globe. He would never have the ego to appear before his own camera—the idea of the artist entering his own creation was anathema to his sensibility; he was an old dog not willing to learn new tricks, Warhol be damned—yet secretly he could not deny wanting more, wanting six million viewers, twelve, wanting to have the attention of the whole world concentrated like prayer on this minuscule pinpoint of geography, this empty heap of dead coral, because wouldn't that love disguised as attention be the cure for what ailed them all?

Even when she was working at the firm full-time, Ann had never been on so many diplomatic missions. Now she made her way to Loren's hut, except Wende had ruined it for her by making her feel like Madame Bovary, sneaking off to a lover. If anything, she felt more than ever like a lawyer. Knocking on the door as a formality, she was surprised when she heard "Come in."

Loren was writing at his desk. He looked more energized than he had in days.

"Am I interrupting?"

"No more than usual."

She watched the rolling waves on the monitor as he finished.

"All done," he said.

"We need to talk about Cooked."

Loren frowned. "That's just what I'm doing."

"Don't turn him in to the police. You don't know if he would have gone ahead with it. He's an innocent. Deluded, but innocent."

"I'm deeding the island over to him and Titi. It's time they quit playing and married. Once he has something to lose, he'll stop this nonsense. What is the saying, 'Revolutionaries don't have mortgages'? I don't need to tell you—the world has sharp teeth."

"How will you escape those teeth?"

"It won't be my fight much longer."

Ann bowed her head. "It's a magnificent gift. A life-changing gift."

"My reparations."

"From what I can tell, you've always been good to them."

"Maybe it evens out. You know, in the big score book of life.

"Will they accept?"

"The question is, are they ready to keep the vultures away? There probably isn't time enough on earth for that."

"You mean Cooked?"

"Can be tricked."

"So stay around."

Loren grimaced. After a moment his face relaxed again. "That isn't a choice I have."

Dinner that night was fish with a fluffy béarnaise sauce, canned green beans with toasted coconut, a pudding of banana and mango—supplies were running low, testing Richard's creativity.

When Loren announced his gift, they all raised their glasses to toast Cooked and Titi.

"With this island, may you two rebuild the great power of *te fenua Ma 'ohi*, the people and the land of *Ma 'ohi*."

"Whoa, Cooked. You be the boss," Dex said.

Richard clapped. "Let me do the wedding feast."

Titi shook her head. "My family must do that, but you can make one thing."

"Name it."

"The wedding cake."

"Yes."

Cooked had been silent and put down his glass without drinking. "I cannot."

"Don't be stupid," Loren snapped. He had the tunnel vision of illness, and he fumed at Cooked's pigheadedness.

"You're buying us off."

Loren slammed his fist down on the table. "I'm giving you shelter from the storm. A decent life."

"What about the people who don't get a fancy hotel?"

"Every last one would change places with you in a heartbeat. Fool."

"You're the fool!"

Loren sat back and took a deep breath, willing the pain away. "Do you think it will accomplish anything, blowing up a few rooms? They'd lock you up, throw away the key, and forget you existed. What good would you be then?"

"He's right," Ann said.

"What's he talking about? What are you talking about?" Richard asked.

It was becoming a regular habit Ann regretted but couldn't stop—keeping secrets from Richard.

"Tell them about the pictures," Cooked demanded.

Wende nodded. "Jellyfish babies born to women exposed to radiation. Horrible birth defects. I saw the evidence for the lawsuits."

"*That* was what you were doing with him?" Dex asked.

Cooked slammed the table. "If I take this place, I'll be part of the lie, too. The military keeps us off balance so that they make money from tourists coming here."

There was silence around the table. After all, they were those tourists.

"It's kind of a *Kobayashi Maru* situation," Wende said.

Everyone stared at her.

"You know." She jabbed her chin at Dex. "Remember *Star Trek*? A choice between two bad scenarios?"

"My God," Loren said. "You people believe life is television."

"She's got a point, though," Dex said, pleased beyond reason that Wende had looked to him for help. He'd been wrong to turn her down the first time point-blank when she asked him to help Cooked. They were just kids and needed guidance. "What you need is a PR campaign. A defining action. No rogue butthead moves like you were going to do. We need to arrive at leaderless consensus."

Everyone stared at Dex in silence.

"Just sayin'."

"That's why we were blowing up rooms at the hotel. To scare tourists," Cooked said.

"No," Wende said. "That puts people on their side. Dex is right."

Ever since reading his marriage journal and realizing who was the settler and who was the settlee, Wende had seen Dex in an entirely different and more positive light. She even felt like sleeping with him for old times' sake. "What we need to do is tell a story. No one wants to watch those downer stories on the news anymore. Those depressing pictures! Bah! But if we have a face, if we have a hero . . ." Wende trailed off.

"Hearts and minds," Dex chimed in.

Maybe, Wende thought, I'll become his mistress.

Wende's father had been a used-car salesman in Boise, plagued with a consuming love for the bottle, when he met her mother. She was a hippie living on an organic farm in Oregon. Perhaps sensing the direction her future would take after marrying, she enrolled in junior college and became an accountant before Wende was born. Her father's fluctuating commissions and subsequent changes of employment led him to an irrational resentment of her mother's newfound constancy and steadfastness, which rescued the family over and over and put chicken potpie on the table. His solution was a series of get-rich-quick schemes that were made possible only by his wife's constant infusion of start-up money, which further fueled his resentment into an ugly downward spiral of penury and failure. After the fifth business closure—a restaurant-food delivery service with such slim margins and large promises (within thirty minutes or free!)—he switched to guerrilla tactics to protect his ego.

He took his wife to an expensive night out, maxing the credit card, and coaxed her into the idea of having another child with the aim of anchoring her into the marriage. Once she was pregnant, he again lost interest in the family and changed his main place of business to a local bar stool. As a cautionary tale, Wende remembered her mother putting on her old wool coat that could only be buttoned at the top due to her protruding stomach, heralding the arrival of Wende's baby sister, and trudging through the sleet and snow to retrieve him.

Wende never would understand the reason these two opposite souls came together. When they fought, he called her a commie-lib lesbian (she had mistakenly confided an experimental tryst on the organic farm), and she called him a gun-toting redneck hater. "Hater" was her mother's ultimate condemnation.

After they lost their house, his next brainstorm involved moving to the small town of Cutthroat, Idaho, in the eastern part of the state be-cause the rent was cheap and there was space. He began a last series of business blowups—mink farming that lasted six months, then bent-willow garden furniture.

Wende had been a thriving student in Boise, a star in the drama department, but the move to the boondocks shook her. The rural kids were both more innocent than those in the big city of Boise and more adult. The easy availability of drugs made her old public school look like a Catholic parochial one. The existential problem that she faced in Cutthroat for the first time in her young life was: nothing to do. Kids solved this by having sex much earlier. Teen pregnancies were the norm. Even to a fourteen-year-old, it looked like a tightening noose. Wende's solution was to withdraw to protect herself from contagion.

She stayed home, enacting dramas that she wrote for her stuffed animals and dolls way past the age when such behavior was acceptable. Her parents, in the middle of their downward slide, ignored it. Truth was, outwardly, Wende had become a nerd success story. Her grade point average was 4.9, figuring in honors classes. She *was* the drama department, whipping her peers into performances of plays by Sam Shepherd and David Mamet when all they wanted to do was *Oklahoma!* and *Annie Get Your Gun.*

Her last year of high school, her dad's borrowed used Buick stalled in a blizzard on his way home from his latest business venture, a Russian vodka bar featuring ice bar stools that you sat on with thermal cushions, which was too avant-garde by half for Cutthroat. After sliding down an embankment, he inexplicably rolled down the windows and fell asleep, freezing to death. At one a.m., no one was on the road to see or help him. The next day, her mother entered rehab. Her younger sister, Janelle, married her high-school sweetheart while still in high school and stayed in Cutthroat to raise Wende's new nephew, Petey, who came seven months later. Wende left the day after graduation, propelled as if by rocket fuel out of there.

But true happiness was not as easy as a change of venue. She waitressed while attending Valley Junior College, then transferred to UCLA for her degree. She acted, took film studies, sang in a girl rock band, but nothing clicked. Then she met Dex. That brush with celebrity was seductive, allowing her to skip the whole struggling part and just enjoy his overflow of attention, but at bottom she knew that her life with him would only be a high-octane version of staying in Cutthroat.

T he problem in the past is that the protesters have all been framed as *haters*," Wende said to the table that night. "Your story needs to be recast."

In retrospect, in light of what it snowballed into, it was hard to remember how such an outlandish plan had begun. Why hadn't the rest of them thrown out the idea immediately? Perhaps because Loren, a fatalist, was already caught up in his own personal unwinding. Titi and Cooked were pleased to get an American-style corporate makeover, though later they would be increasingly unhappy when they were pushed out of participating in their own revolution. Richard wanted to see the little man, the overlooked man, triumph at last. Dex thought of it as his brave grand adventure to win back Wende's heart. They all let the implications slide because in the back of their minds they figured the naysayer of the group, Ann, recovering attorney, skeptic, would squelch it, which she didn't, precisely because it was expected of her. She had a long history of saying no to the big idea, and what had it gotten her? Maybe naïve Wende had a point. Who would want to grow up and end up Ann? At the very least, what harm could come of such a harebrained idea?

In a partylike atmosphere, they stayed up all that night, eating dessert, then cheese, then fruit, drinking bottle after bottle of rum while hashing out Dex's idea about a grassroots PR campaign. It was dawn by the time they straggled away to bed.

At noon the next day, hangovers be damned, everyone got up for breakfast and picked up where they had left off the night before, like a prolonged game of Monopoly. The mood at the resort had utterly changed. They were on a mission, and perversely, it felt more natural than the earlier enforced leisure.

Ann dug her phone out of a bottom dresser drawer (it finally had become too ridiculous to fetch it out of its liquid plunge-pool storage each time), and Titi called her relatives to inform them of the nuptials and to pass on invitations for the wedding feast. Cooked did the same (putting Wende on for a moment to say hi to his mom).

In the late afternoon, Loren made a production of handing over a key to one of the garden *fares* for Cooked and Titi's use. Titi had to sit down on the step, she was so overcome.

"I never imagined this. I figured that all my life I would only clean these rooms."

Wende, teary-eyed, patted her shoulder. Titi flicked off the girl's touch.

"Even though I take naps in the beds during the day," Titi continued, "I take showers, use perfume left out . . ."

Quickly, the computer had gone from taboo to everyday. There was always a line on Loren's lanai, waiting to check email or surf the web.

While Richard waited for a cake recipe to print out, he sent a stealth email to Javi:

> Hope you're okay. Things are complicated here, but it's incredible, too. Don't tell Ann, but I feel guilty enjoying all this while you can't. I'm making my first Polynesian-inspired wedding cake—how cool is that?

Loren called Steve the manager to see why it was taking so long to procure a boat. Richard was driving him mad with shopping lists.

"It's on its way from Papeete. I'll have it to you tomorrow."

"We're getting ready for a wedding and a change of ownership here."

Silence on the other end.

"You should have consulted with me first," Steve said.

"It had nothing to do with you."

"Headquarters will make you a very sweet offer."

"Cooked and Titi own it."

Steve's voice rose higher and tighter, like a cord being stretched to breaking. "I won't be comfortable sending people over under those circumstances."

"Nothing will change."

"We need professionals. We need—"

"The resort is closed now. We're having a wedding feast."

"Luau style? How about I bring select guests? If you promise drums and dancers, I can charge two hundred fifty euros a couple. We'll split it sixty-forty. Romantic? Primitive? We'll get interest."

"Come near this island, I'll shoot you."

"Is that a threat—?" Steve yelled before the connection went dead.

I t was inexplicable how Wende knew exactly what to do, as if she'd been doing it all her life. Leaving Cutthroat had been nothing. Living in LA, ditto. Her life was finally taking off here on the island. For the last two years she had been observing and been disgusted by Prospero's misguided and behind-the-times marketing and anemic social media campaign, and she had ideas . . .

Inexplicable also how everyone accepted her new authority and her wish to take control of things. Dex's muse had been retired for all time. The confiscation of the WILD pendant had been prescient. Gone were the bikinis and short shorts, the leather corsets and platform shoes. She borrowed oversize T-shirts from Dex, and Ann's lady-birder Bermuda shorts. She tucked her hair up under a baseball cap. Her new outfit announced Serious.

M embers of Titi and Cooked's extended clan began to arrive. Mostly by motorboat, they came packed in tightly like sardines, wearing colorful printed dresses and shirts in celebration, carrying baskets of provisions for the feast. Dancing, music, and singing started before they stepped on the sand. Loren borrowed a boat for supply runs. Ten people arrived in the morning. By nightfall, one hundred bodies had pitched themselves inside and around the *fares*, kitchen, dining area, and beach. From splendid isolation the place morphed to happy wedding/refugee camp.

Titi and Cooked got caught up in the celebrations, and now it was Wende rather than Loren who was the taskmaster.

"We need to rehearse, Cooked," she nagged.

Her transformation included not flirting or even acknowledging their past relations, which made Titi very happy and Cooked morose.

"Remember," Wende told him, "this is for the cause."

He swayed, already too far gone on good wedding rum.

"I want a casting call. Bring all the biggest, strongest, meanest-looking guys you got."

"They will be identified by police."

"Way ahead of you—we'll put masks on them."

"It should be me," Cooked said, posing for his martyr poster. If he could push soda sales, why not revolution?

"Not you. You're the hero. You are the future owner of this resort. You can't be the bad guy."

"But—"

"I need to conference with Dex now, please." She tapped her shapely foot, dismissing him. Another surprise—how enjoyable it was to work on a purely business level and not go to the personal. Indeed, after taking meetings with Dex, Cooked, Titi, and some of the male relatives about the casting call, after going over supply logistics with a haggard Richard, who was now overseeing food service for more than one hundred and fifty people, with another hundred threatening to descend on them, Wende and Dex retired to their *fare*, exhilarated and drained, but did not discuss the schedule for the next day, as was witnessed by about twenty nosy Polynesians peeking in through every available crack in the windows, doors, and walls.

The truth was they had nothing to discuss. They were both naturals, but Wende was only just realizing that there was no aphrodisiac like a job well done. After exhausting themselves on each other, they lazed postcoitally.

Dex lay propped up in bed as Wende straddled him, kissing him on the lips, then pulled away.

"Forgive me for what I'm about to do."

"For what?" Dex asked as she hauled her arm back and slugged him as hard as she could, breaking his nose.

T he count of the wedding party the next afternoon had ballooned up to somewhere north of two hundred and fifty people. The empty strip of beach in front of the resort now resembled a squatter's slum. Tents had been erected, umbrellas and *palapas* stuck in the sand, corrugated iron roofs installed, buffet service set up in the dining area, latrines dug in the jungle center to accommodate the unaccustomed, unsustainable size of the island's new population. Islands were fragile. One took everything one needed to them, left with everything on the way out.

T he first broadcast was of a bruised—partly natural (see Wende), partly made-up (Wende again)—and fatigued Dex trussed up like a turkey, pushed along by a tribe of Polynesian men who looked a cross between scary B movie henchmen and Samoan gangsta rappers. There had been heated arguments during rehearsal: Richard and Ann thought the full warrior dress of grass shirts, anklets, armbands, and masks looked either like a historical documentary (think Rockefeller in New Guinea) or low-budget musical theater (Bakersfield dinner-house-theater version of *South Pacific*). The cast bravely elected to take off the masks and wear only headdresses. Although the main problem should have been that this now enabled them to be ID'd, instead what bugged Wende was that their peaceful expressions, their gentle prodding forward of Dex like a prized pig, gave the lie to their supposedly savage, brutal intent.

Dex chimed in that the kidnappers needed a modern, macho look— they should wear Western shorts and T-shirts, and the coup de grâce would be face paint that obscured their features and made them forbidding to look at. Unfortunately, the face paint still left them recognizable, and Cooked made an executive decision that he would not allow his friends to sacrifice themselves. Coconut masks, or the whole thing was off. An unforeseen benefit of the choice was that the eerie blankness of the masks, with their hastily gouged-out holes for eyes, nose, and mouth, made the men's appearance far more menacing than anything else tried.

Although chafing at the sudden restrictions, Wende agreed, with the caveat that the men get a little rougher with Dex while on camera. She also wanted a longer lead-in with drums to accompany their entrance. The incongruity of there being a soundtrack for a kidnapping would be ignored. "It will create tension and suspense before anything shows up on camera."

It was slipping into the realm of musical theater again, but Ann held her tongue because at least with all the distractions everyone was too happily occupied to consider leaving.

The first moments of filming showed the usual rolling waves, but the chosen day wasn't the optimal blue and sunny as usual, but gray and overcast. Moody. A shower threatened to close them down that afternoon. Out of these lemons, Wende decided to make sour-lemon martinis. Why not a whiff of Polynesian noir, the dark underbelly, the threat, of the islands? She wished, briefly, they could move to the gloomy, cannibal-rumored Marquesas for better street cred.

Drumbeats, faraway, could at first be mistaken for static, or the pulse of fear in one's own heart. As the sound became distinct, recognition turned to uneasiness. It was too loud, too insistent; this wasn't your pretty, rhythmic hula dance. It was *BAM . . . BAM BAM . . . BAM BAM! BAM BAM BAM!* It was hard and close and dangerous. A gasp—the realization that this was the sound of war drums, conjuring up every old movie where fleets of canoes, paddled by painted savages, raced through the waters to do harm.

The drum players stayed off camera—one didn't want to evoke the Copacabana—but four men, dressed in the abovementioned shorts, American-sports-team-emblazoned T-shirts, and eerie coconut masks, carried a heavy log that they proceeded to stake into the ground. Next came eight men corralling a visibly shaken Dex ahead of them.

"Why eight?" Ann asked, thinking it was overkill.

"Scarier," Wende said.

Through the whole process, Ann was mesmerized by the transformation of this young woman. All that talent and confidence had resided inside the veneer of a *Girls Gone Wild* participant. Ann had no reason to take any credit, and yet she was proud as a mother. Guess what? To the eye and the heart, if not to the brain, eight burly Polynesian men *were* better than two or three trussing up Dex, a cross-dressing Joan of Arc, to the log. How had she known that?

Right before the first rope attached man to wood, Dex made his choreographed Escape Attempt. They were supposed to let him go so far that he was off camera; he would be dragged back, kicking and screaming, for a reentrance of maximal dramatic impact.

Titi's favorite uncle, Aitu, was paralyzed with stage fright and almost missed his self-appointed cue.

He was the one who loved movies and always insisted on going to at least two or three Jackie Chan action pictures when visiting Papeete. He dreamed of being a stunt man and felt he had missed his opportunity during the most recent remake of *Mutiny on the Bounty* because he had been stung by a jellyfish the day before filming, leaving his face bloated. This could finally be his big break—he was part of the gang bringing Dex in—but he had not been close enough to even lay a hand on him, much less get a close-up. How was he ever going to get noticed enough to play a Polynesian hero, the John Wayne of Tahiti, like that?

As Dex staggered by in a dead run, head down like a football player, Aitu suddenly came to life and grabbed him, unscripted. It was stupid, he reasoned, that a man of his size, strength, and stature, a kidnapper and revolutionary, would just stand there looking good and watch this scrawny *haole* go by. In fact, it was so illogical it might make the whole sham abduction look phony. Aitu tackled Dex, who, startled, winded, hurt, looked at him with wide-open, terrified eyes. *What's this?* Right on, Aitu thought, and punched him in the gut with all the power of his two-hundred-eighty-pound frame, crumpling Dex onto the ground in a little girlie puddle.

Wende bit her lip. This was going way off script, commando filmmaking; there was no "Cut," no "Let's take that again." This was live guerrilla theater—scary, raw, but real. Besides, it didn't look like Dex would be moving on his own again for a while, so the damage was already done, might as well film it. Only after he had to be held up in order to be tied to the pole, limply collapsing unconscious against the ropes, did she begin to have second thoughts. His nose (broken by her earlier) had started to swell and bleed again. How had they managed to tie him up anyway? Kudos. It looked like the too-tight ropes were causing welts; his limbs were turning bluish. Perhaps a little overzealous in the binding?

*Let's go, people, let's go,* Wende thought but could not say aloud.

The prepared speech, delivered by the cousin of a cousin of Cooked who had gone to USC two years on a football scholarship and spoke passable English, broken enough to be even more threatening, went off without a hitch: "The reason we have kidnapped the famous Dex Cooper is to force the government to stop ignoring us. Other tourists will be in danger if our demands are not met. We demand the French government pay compensation to the veterans, their families, and civilians for health issues caused decades earlier and hidden by the government. We will hold him for twenty-four hours before avenging . . ." Yada yada yada.

Boilerplate. The original intention was that the kidnapping would be played like theater, like a reality show, and the only lure for viewers would be Dex's celebrity. They never intended for it to be taken as real. Rather it was just a way to get people to tune in and watch. A YouTube extravaganza.

For the finale, one of the "thugs" made a slow promenade to the camera, and when his menacing coconut mask was mere inches away, a gunnysack was lifted to cover the lens. The sound of a stick bashing metal could be heard, and the screen went dead. The first time the picture went blank in ten years. The act was so violent, Wende felt her mouth go dry. Her stomach was quaky inside as if she had eaten something from the fridge slightly past its expiration date. In reality, the stick was off camera, banging on a trash bin, because they couldn't risk damaging the real camera. Then Wende simply flipped the power switch off.

"Buy me a Coke and a bag of popcorn," Richard said. "We're going to Hollywood."

"That's a wrap, people. Good job," Wende said. She had the most exhilarating feeling of her young life. Nothing—nothing—compared with this. She forgave Dex all those lonely nights while he was composing.

After untying Dex, they made their way back to the resort and were greeted by crowds who were curious about the filming. The extras signed autographs. Richard went off to check food prep for the evening's meal. Ann and Wende helped the hunched-over Dex to his *fare*, where he collapsed like a loose pile of bones onto the bed, from which he would not move till the next morning. With prodding, it appeared two of his ribs were broken.

"We need to call the hotel doctor at the main resort," Ann said.

"We film first thing in the morning," Wende countered.

"A checkup. They don't wrap broken ribs anymore. Just in case you know, there's internal bleeding . . ."

Wende said nothing.

"You can't let him die or something," Ann whispered.

Dex, eyes closed, listened to the women discuss him as if he were a wildlife rescue project. A low moan came from his throat.

"Don't worry, honey bunny," Wende said. "You'll be fine."

"You're not a doctor," he said.

"Impressive job today." Ann paused. "Except . . ."

"What?" Wende asked.

Ann didn't want to be a wet blanket, but it bothered her that no one much cared about the cause the video was serving. Even some of the Polynesians seemed more caught up in the production values than the human tragedy it was highlighting. Wende puckered as if tasting something sour.

"The truth is that if we get the job done, it doesn't matter what we think."

Ann looked doubtful.

"Maybe it's a generational thing, but what's so great about earnest and ineffective? I'd rather have the job well done. If this gets the government scared of the bad PR and it finally pays up—great! Emotion? Take it or leave it."

"I better go," Ann said.

"Wait." Dex painfully moved up the pile of pillows a few inches so he was only semisupine. "Cooked and Titi's wedding is going to be a big celebration, right?"

"Sure," Wende said.

"Why don't we tie the knot at the same time? You couldn't ask for a better party. We'll get a license back home afterward."

"Great idea," Ann said, sensing it clearly was not. "I'll go discuss it with Loren."

"Wait," Wende said. She stared thoughtfully down into her unglamorous, khaki-clad lap. "I've been thinking . . ."

It was true. Wende had gotten caught up and was having too much fun in the production of their little video. She had forgotten the message, forgotten Cooked, Etini, and the rest of the clan. She felt guilty and, more important, unserious.

Ann edged toward the door.

Wende sighed. "I've decided to go home and apply to film school."

"That's okay," Dex said.

"No, it isn't. Because I need to be selfish these next few years. You're a distraction. Your life is too big."

She got up and went to him, sitting on the bed and pressing herself against his chest. Tears rolled down his face, maybe for Wende, maybe from the pain of his broken ribs—it was hard to tell.

As the wedding party settled in for a long night of drinking and eating, Wende and Ann found the "actors" from that day and paid them in dollars, crisp hundreds from Ann's bag. They had been on the island long enough that the bills took on a kind of Monopoly-money unreality. The pay was both thanks and bribe to show up again early next morning.

When they went to see Loren, he was sitting at his desk, staring at a blackened monitor.

"How's it going?" Wende said.

"My island is a disaster. My life's work is ruined. What do you think, little Windy? *Diable*."

For a moment, Wende tried to see things from his point of view, but what was the point since it got in the way of the project? "We're going on camera again at sunup. Then you're back to normal broadcasting. Waves and such."

"Nothing will ever be normal again. Do you know how many viewers we had this afternoon?"

Both women shook their heads, plotting how to leave as quickly as possible.

"Twelve million!" Loren screamed.

"Twelve?" Ann seemed doubtful.

"Million!" Loren said.

"Oh my God." Wende sat stunned. "Think about it. Our production costs so far have been about two thousand dollars. By the way, Loren, we're going to pay you for the use of your camera. Two days filming, two thousand dollars, twelve million viewers. Maybe I should skip film school and go straight into production."

"Did you watch it?" Ann asked him.

Loren nodded. "The best part was Dex being punched by that brute."

Wende shot up out of her chair. "I've got planning to do for the morning. Ann, when you're done, find me."

When the two were alone, they sat in silence.

Finally Ann asked, "Would you like an absinthe?"

He nodded, and she went to pour, carrying two glasses back.

"So what do you really think?" Ann asked. In her opinion, this was strictly home-movie stuff, amateur hour. No one would be at all interested, except maybe cult followers of Prospero and Dex. But whatever. Let them have their fun.

"It's a circus. It is your *Gilligan Island*. Who in their right mind would take any of it seriously?"

News of the abduction of the lead singer for Prospero by a lost Polynesian cannibal tribe made the front page across most major newspapers the next morning—a huge, above-the-fold picture of Dex, freeze-framed off the video, looking broken and forlorn. It had made the dubious leap from the entertainment to the news section. They had buried the lede of the story; only at the end was the disclaimer that the incident had yet to be verified. But a celebrity picture was a celebrity picture. Newspapers sold more briskly. Sales of Prospero downloads skyrocketed, as did bootlegged copies of CDs in third-world countries. It was a slow news week before the Memorial Day weekend, and the networks decided to pick up the story. Reporters camped out in front of Robby's mansion in Malibu; videos were played on YouTube; MTV aired old interviews of the band. Bogus comparisons were made to Michael Rockefeller's disappearance off the coast of Papua New Guinea, and his probable demise by headhunters, even though the circumstances of Dex Cooper's kidnapping at a luxury resort in Polynesia weren't exactly a good comparison.

It was sobering that the abduction had been taken for real.

"Should we do a service announcement stating that this is a simulated abduction?" Ann asked. "That it's a PR dramatization to bring attention to a real problem?"

"We never made claims. Ride it out," Wende said.

The writer John Stubb Byron was now being interviewed on Fox News for his insights into the troubled rock star Dex Cooper. He provided salacious details of excessive drinking and drug use that were unfortunately all true. The rest could be read in his upcoming biography of the singer, being rushed to press.

"He was my hero," Dex said.

When the White House press secretary fielded a question about the abduction of American citizens on French soil, whether it constituted an act of aggression or terrorism, he had no idea what the reporter was talking about. He covered by saying they were currently looking into the situation. Then they had to hurry and actually look into it before anyone discovered that they had not. When the French heard the press conference, they inferred that they were being insulted for not taking care of business. They jumped on the story that they assumed from the beginning was false, but now, true or false, if Americans believed it, it had negative tourist value. The first order of business was to pinpoint where the transmissions were coming from and put an end to them. If this was a hoax, people would go to jail.

Wende was geek enough to know that it would take some digital camouflage to keep the transmission location hidden for any length of time, so she contacted a guy friend, a hacker from Cutthroat, who agreed to scramble and resend the signal from Idaho to slow things down in exchange for front-row tickets to the next Prospero concert in Idaho. Done.

It shocked them that the hoax was being taken as authentic. Unfathomable four thousand miles away on a sweltering desert island to appreciate the effect as the story gained traction and grew bigger by the minute.

Ann's worries that the kidnapping video would quickly be seen as fake, a piece of agitprop theater, morphed into the more troubling fear that it would be seen as real. What exactly were the legal implications of perpetrating a global prank? She was beginning to suspect that, even if the media didn't believe in the video's legitimacy, that wouldn't stop them from acting on the story—it dovetailed nicely with the prevalence of reality shows and the meshing of news and entertainment for ratings: infotainment.

Experts in Polynesian anthropology were called in to identify from the video footage both the island and the specific cannibal tribe supposedly holding Dex Cooper hostage. News sources were totally bummed to find out that cannibalism in Polynesia had effectively ended in the islands by the start of the twentieth century. The experts were able to surmise that the white sandy beach was not characteristic of the volcanic rocky cliffs of the Marquesas, but was more likely in the south, possibly in the Society or Gambier island chains, or in the even more remote east of the Tuamotu Archipelago.

The costumes confused the experts even more, until one particularly iconoclastic female anthropologist from a university in the Pacific Northwest recognized the costumes from a Papeete dance troupe she had seen a few years back in Seattle with an ex-boyfriend. She supplied corroborating evidence in the form of promotional flyers and a captioned picture in the Capitol Hill weekly entertainment newspaper.

The French government, mired in a deflationary economy, with an increasingly hostile electorate, totally believed in the video's power to ruin consumer spending, and contacted their branch colonial counterparts to rev up the French military (*We are losing tourist euros every minute as we speak!*), intending to launch a military rescue mission once the exact location was pinpointed. If it was real, or thought to be real, they would be heroes. If it was faked, they would haul the perpetrators to jail.

The resourceful American paparazzi beat them all. Someone had a friend of a friend of the resort manager Steve, who received nice monthly payments for reporting on celebrity sightings on the island (higher for women, the most for topless), and who had nothing to lose now that Loren had screwed him over on his commission for selling the *motu* to the conglomerate that owned the main resort.

A group of paparazzi, all of whom thought the video was strictly a publicity stunt by a has-been rock band, didn't care because Dex's picture made the story lucrative to the tabloids, not to mention a free vacation for them. They pooled resources to charter a jet to deliver them to Tahiti by early morning, followed by network newscasters in their own corporate jets, who blindly aped the paparazzi for the entertainment angle to combat falling ratings, followed by newspaper reporters on Air Tahiti, riding in economy (many using their own frequent-flier miles), who were the only ones who actually understood or cared about the politics of the video, but their stories had been bumped for years because nuclear poisoning wasn't "sexy" enough. Dex's presence had just made it a whole lot more so.

From Papeete, each was on his own to discover the where and the how of finding the right atoll. Within hours, every charter tourist helicopter and boat was gone. The French military, reeling from budget cuts and layoffs, were even further behind than the newspaper reporters. Worried about looking bad and thus instigating another round of cuts and layoffs, once they caught wind of the reporters descending, they decided to send covert operatives—that is, pretty French waitresses from the hotels where the press were staying—to either find out or accompany them, carrying satellite GPS on their persons.

By noon, helicopters, amphibious airplanes, frigates, and motorboats were converging on the small, hitherto exclusive and unknown atoll.

Wende shivered in the predawn night, despite the blood-warm air, although in the bigger sense she was no longer physically on the island. Definitely not recognizably as the person formerly known as Wende, who had occupied the resort during the last two months. She ate as much as she felt like and didn't bother with exercise. Waking, she took a quick shower and clothed herself in her new roomy, comfort clothes, without looking in the mirror. As she gave up the elaborate toilette that went into being a "hottie," she realized the obvious: she could abandon her beauty now or not, but either way, it would abandon her eventually. It was a loyalty program with a built-in, guaranteed obsolescence. Time would erode her most valuable asset, so she better be prepared.

None of these thoughts greatly bothered her because she felt like pure spirit, and this pure spirit's only purpose was to bear witness to the *vision* that existed in her head, to get it down as quickly as possible before it expired or disappeared under the taxing logistics of dealing with one hundred and fifty Polynesian extras; plus the cranky principal actors, including one gloomy rock star ex-boyfriend; plus a suicidal owner, Loren, threatening to pull the electrical plug; plus the technical difficulties of the transmission to the stoned hacker friend in Cutthroat, who asked repeatedly, in texts—'SUP? nOOb—plus whatever the reaction was *out there*, back in the world.

The eight "Cannibal Kidnappers," as the *Observer* had dubbed them, showed up for their continuity check, visibly subdued even behind their coconut masks. On balance, Wende thought it had worked out nicely to let them get shit-faced the previous night. Now they had a stolidness about them that was not typical of these rambunctious, puppy-fun men, but they did look a little slow, a little dazed. Hungover rather than menacing.

"Before the camera goes on, how about a few laps up and down the beach? I need a little pep. Some energy, people!"

"Why do they need to jog?" Cooked asked, petulant at his abrupt dismissal both as boy toy and lead actor in the video.

"Trust me on this."

Dex sat in her director's chair (dug up from the yacht of a movie producer who had been a former guest).

"How you doing?" she said gently.

"You didn't care if I bled to death."

"A doctor will be here any minute. Not my fault that they couldn't find a boat last night, huh?"

"If anyone cared, one of the ones docked here could have made the trip."

Wende nodded, frowned. "The sun comes up. You give your speech, Cooked gives his, bam, we're done."

"We're done, too, that's what you're saying."

She moved in close to him. "Today, Dex, you are doing something great. You are helping people who don't have a voice. You are putting your fame to a higher purpose. You are touching on the wings of greatness. I, for one, have never been as turned on by you as I am this very minute. Think what it's going to do to your fans. Think Lennon, Clapton, Bono."

Dex blinked. "And us?"

"Let's not have things messy right now."

"You used me."

Dex had never cared so deeply now that she didn't.

The red disk of the sun rose out of the primal broth of ocean as the Crusoe live cam returned to shaky, computer-generated faux life, capturing the light on the water and the pole in front of it in a symbolically powerful crucifixion tableau. Unbeknownst to the experts, the live cam had been moved and pointed in a different direction in order to capture that very sunrise (Loren had purposely avoided such a location for its commercial vulgarity, much preferring the more subtle Japanese aesthetic of a slow lightening of sky, water, and sand to represent the passage of time), confusing the calculations of the experts and bringing the island a few more hours of splendid isolation.

The faint throbbing of drums grew louder and louder as they approached. The eight "Cannibal Henchmen" (*Daily Star*), as they were now known in the world press, came on, but this time they weren't restraining a bound Dex. They were forming an escort. Although Wende had considered dragging the whole thing out, Ann had convinced her to end the charade as quickly as possible. Dex walked solemnly between his former jailors. They had removed some of his bruise makeup and applied cover-up to the real bruises so that the damage wasn't a reminder of yesterday's brutality. Wende didn't want the audience thinking that this turnabout was coerced Stockholm syndrome stuff.

Dex stepped in front of the "cannibals," who formed a fierce backdrop behind him.

"I'm Dex Cooper from the band Prospero. As some of you may know by now, I came to the islands to rest and write music with my girl . . . my former . . . anyway . . ."

Dex coughed, looking down. Either he was lost deep in thought or he had forgotten his lines.

"The point is, I was here purely as a tourist, in love with the beauty of the place and making music, when I was abducted by this Polynesian tribe of indigenous peoples. By the way, they find the term 'cannibal' highly insulting and inflammatory. They prefer the term '*Ma 'ohi*.' More on that later.

"Of course, I was really scared at first, and then, when I realized the whole cannibalism thing wasn't going to happen, I was just pissed that my vacation was being ruined."

Wende cringed. Dex was rambling. She'd asked him point-blank if he could improvise, and he'd said yes, but he was going off message.

"Thing is, these guys are cool. They've told me about the generations

of mistreatment they have suffered under. Tomato, tomahto; potato, po-
tahto; territory, colony—far as I can tell, they're all the same. Thing is,
these people are one with their environment. They've told me about the
land being poisoned. The oceans, too. There are areas where the fish
they used to eat now make them sick. Cancer, leukemia, birth defects—
they've got them all here. In record-high numbers. And even though it
happened a long time ago, like in the '60s and '70s, the effects are as if
it happened yesterday. They kidnapped me in frustration because no
one will listen. Not the government, not the world press, and, well, you're
listening now, aren't you? Not for the right reasons, but sometimes we
have to have something jammed down our throat, have our nose busted,
our ribs cracked in order to get our attention, don't we?"

My man came through, Wende thought, and made a fist pump for
victory. She signaled Cooked to go on.

"This is one of the leading businessmen in the area, Vane 'Cooked'
Teriieroo, and he owns the buff resort where I've been staying. He's involved himself in negotiating my release. He'll take over now."

Cooked came on, wooden and nervous. "We know that the people of
the world might not believe us. They think we, to use the words of the
great Shakespeare, make 'much ado about nothing.' But the great doctor
Albert Schweitzer wrote in 1964 to our freedom leader, the great
Teariki, 'Long before receiving your letter, I was worried about the fate
of the Polynesian people. I have been fighting against all atomic weapons and nuclear tests since 1955. It is sad to learn that they have been
forced on the inhabitants of your islands. Yet I know that the French
Parliament would not come to your assistance . . .'"

Wende's eyes glazed over. She was dying a thousand professional
deaths. She'd begged, *begged*, him not to read the letter because it would
suck energy from the telecast, but no. It dragged. Should have been para-
phrased. Viewer attention span, people!

"'Those who claim that these tests are harmless are liars. Like many
other persons, I am ashamed of the Parliament's attitude on this matter.
The Parliament and the general public are sacrificing you. I feel sorry for
you and shall continue to do so . . . Who could imagine that France

would be willing to deliver its own citizens to the military in this manner?'"

Like an ace pitcher, Cooked shook off the signs from Wende to cut short. "The testing finally stopped in 1996. Its effects have not."

He read from another paper that listed the number of thyroid and reproductive cancers in the affected populations, the number of birth defects and infertilities. He listed contaminant levels in the ocean, and then hit on one of their primary concerns: Moruroa and Fangataufa, where the most intensive nuclear testing occurred. "Islands that are now radioactive time bombs."

Dex had moved off to the side of Cooked to give him center stage. He bowed his head to concentrate on the words, except that not only did he bow his head, he also closed his eyes, and started to sway ever so slightly, as if he were listening to the most uplifting gospel. A look of ecstasy passed onto his face that couldn't be caused by the bureaucratic droning of Cooked, thus inadvertently stealing the show. Was he listening to music through his earbuds? Never share the stage with children, animals, or rock stars.

Cooked continued. "We do not believe that the radioactive poisons are imprisoned in the rock. We believe there is leakage. Moruroa is nearing collapse, which will spill large amounts of radioactive plutonium into the ocean, affecting all of the South Pacific and reaching Asia and the Americas also. Why is nothing being done, except to keep people out of these areas?"

A seismic shift was happening within Cooked. His words were tamped down and bloodless on the outside because he was trying to not burst out in tears, not start shouting and parading, fulfilling the stereotype of the childish native unable to control his emotions. These words were not dry statistics to him. They were wounds. They cracked his heart open. He suddenly understood Titi's point, that his previous methods—setting bags of dog crap on fire in front of politicians' houses in Papeete, planning to blow up hotel rooms—had been wrongheaded, that the dignity of words and reason were the only path toward getting respect. In those few moments on the camera, as he bored the news networks, to the point that they would end up excerpting his speech or cutting it entirely, he had finally grown up.

"The kidnappers' demands: In addition to reparations, which have been promised but are still being stalled, they want open health records. Access to the 114 pages of blacked-out declassified Ministry of Defense documents. Open access to the supposedly 'safe' atolls used for testing, which are now guarded by the military with a twenty-mile exclusion zone."

Richard sprang up for his bit part, as if this was suddenly a press conference for tourists. "What about the American tests on Bikini Atoll?"

Cooked looked at him thoughtfully. "I do not believe two wrongs make a right."

Ann clucked her tongue. Score.

The idea by bringing up Bikini had been Wende's to forestall criticism of an American rocker attacking the French government. Forget movies, Ann thought. The girl should run for president.

"We should go," Dex mumbled.

Cooked paused, looked at him. They had gone off script. "Huh?"

Dex looked up, and there was a wicked, crazed light in his eyes, like a fifteen-year-old discovering the keys to the family car. "We should go to Moruroa."

The reasons came piling in like coins from a winning slot machine: Wende had dumped him, he was a burnout, Harry's death, his father's disapproval, the family scandal, his own banishment, all leading him to this one ripe moment of action. Why not?

*No*, Wende desperately mouthed off camera.

Dex looked her in the eye, then moved up next to Cooked.

"Captain Cook sailed to the islands to conquer, to take away. We will sail from the islands for peace."

Dex put his arm over Cooked's shoulders, and they walked off. The "cannibals" looked confused for a moment, then followed.

*And now back to our regularly scheduled beach programming.*

As soon as Cooked stepped off camera he broke down into tears, emotionally ripped, a changed man.

Wende patted his shoulder as she went by. "Don't worry. It wasn't that terrible."

Dex had pulled a fast one, hijacked the hijacking.

"Now what?" Wende asked. "We were supposed to kick it down, and you just lit the thing back up."

"You're new at this game," Dex answered. "Learn. We need strong visuals. Let's take one of the traditional outriggers here for the wedding. Leave the lagoon and board a boat out on the open ocean. Then we record the trip heading to Moruroa. Take the live cam and a satellite feed."

"It's dangerous. Radiation and stuff."

"It's symbolic. Scientists visit there all the time . . . don't they?"

Cooked shrugged.

"What about the police stopping you?"

"Wende, baby, the whole wide world will be watching. What can they do?"

"Okay," Wende said, trying to not fall behind and sound reactionary. "First of all, we need a boat."

"You'll find one," Dex said, and limped away.

Cooked stopped them. "I'm not going."

"Really? You were going to blow up a building, and you won't take a boat ride?" Dex asked. "How will it look for Polynesian independence and a safe environment for a local not to be part of it?"

"It's bad *juju*, dude."

"Come on, you don't believe in that stuff." As he said it, Dex realized that he himself did. "You'll be the George Clooney of Polynesia."

Cooked nodded, unsure yet pleased at the comparison.

The illusion irretrievably broken, Loren gave in and flipped the switch, and the whole resort was WiFi-enabled.

"You had this and kept it from us?" Ann asked.

"We use it when no one is around. Deprivation is part of the experience."

It seemed like the cheapest hucksterism to have withheld it, but now that everyone had returned to his or her portable device of choice, their previous off-the-grid status was remembered with nostalgia.

And then CNN called.

Rather, the new star girl reporter Laura Vann called. She wanted to fly a charter that hour from NYC to do an exclusive hour-long interview with Dex and Cooked.

"This is it," Wende said. "We need to clean up the island. Laura said, 'This interview is of world significance.'"

"I wonder if she'll wear a bikini," Dex said.

"I won't do it," Cooked announced. He couldn't stand going through the unbearable stage fright again.

"Remember when I said Clooney?" Dex said. "Clooney's nothing. This will make you the Gandhi of Polynesia."

Cooked nodded gravely. He understood that, beneath all the flattery, he'd become a pawn, no longer in charge of himself. All he knew of Gandhi was Ben Kingsley in the movie that he saw as a kid during a matinee one afternoon in Papeete, with Titi's uncle, the wannabe stuntman Aitu. They were there only because the Jackie Chan one had sold out. He didn't remember the story ending well.

Titi had already sped away to direct island maintenance, begging guests to pitch in with the lure that the most important reporter in the world was coming to interview Cooked.

"He'll be famous," Titi said. "He will save us with his words. So do your duty and pick up a rake."

Cooked thought she was laying it on a bit thick and left to find something to eat. As he made his way to the kitchen, relatives, friends, acquaintances all slapped him on the back or hugged him. It was spooky. By the time he came out of the kitchen, holding a supersize ham sandwich, a crowd had gathered. Seeing him, they dropped down on their knees, leaving a path for him, so that he had the sensation of walking among dwarfs. It was kind of cool until he realized the significance of the act—they were counting on him to not fuck up.

"Hey, Fineeva," he said to a first cousin kneeling by his left hand. "How's it shakin'?"

Fineeva closed her eyes and lowered her head as if she were in the presence of a deity.

He was in a world of trouble.

Cooked hurried back to the deluxe digs Loren had bribed them with, and rooted around in his boxes of junk until he found a lid of his extra-potent skunk bud. He felt it was incumbent on himself to prepare for this meeting, and part of that involved a ritual cleansing. Besides, he just needed to get high. In the old days they had used kava, but that was expensive and hard to come by. Time was short; Mary Jane would have to do. The old ceremonies and priests had long been lost, but Cooked knew that it basically involved going off alone and being in an altered state of consciousness so that he could commune with the gods and ancestors and tap into a higher source of knowledge. Beyond a doubt, he was inadequate to the job being asked of him, but he was trapped. A tool. He was no Gandhi, just another poor sap in above his head. If nothing else, at least he'd enjoy being stoned for a few hours.

As he prepared to go off, he decided to start early and rolled himself a joint to calm down. He packed nothing more than a flashlight, bottled water, power bars, chocolate, fruit (he regretted he hadn't thought ahead and made two ham sandwiches); then he decided to throw in his iPod, his iPhone, and a laptop for watching DVDs. What was he doing? He took all the electronic gadgets back out—he was going old-school—and replaced them with a book, *Colossus*, that Titi was reading. But he worried the book might bore him during the long, lonely night, so he sat on the bed and read the first few pages to make sure he liked it.

*I sit here in the child gulag commonly known as second grade. The wooden top of my desk is sticky with the collective germ-ridden, grimy smudge-prints of hands from decades of inmates before me, going as far back possibly as my dad, who attended this very same school, only to grow up, lose his hair, and become a prick to my mother and me. I believe I appear alert and to be listening to Mrs. Cornish's endless babbling . . .*

Potato chips would hit the spot about now. *What was he doing?* It was getting late. If he could just take a nap, it would feel so good. Maybe it would have been wiser to start smoking after he got to his destination.

Cooked threw the book down, intending to go cold turkey—zero entertainment. He needed peace to tap into the ancestral wavelength to know what to say to Laura Vann that would turn around the last two hundred years of exploitation of the islands. On second thought, he put his iPod back in.

He was going out the door when he saw Dex coming up the path. Like a bloodhound, he had scented good reefbud being consumed and wanted to partake.

Cooked pretended not to see him.

"Hey, bro," Dex yelled, but Cooked flashed him such a fierce, cannibalistic scowl that Dex stopped in his tracks and went silent.

Cooked had in mind a place on the other, deserted side of the island to set up camp for the night—his and Titi's favorite make-out spot, full of good mojo. What he hadn't taken into account was that an island that usually had only a dozen inhabitants now had twenty times that many. They, too, had fanned out in all directions. There were reclining forms everywhere like pairs of beached dolphins; the air was filled with soft moans of pleasure. All of it was making Cooked want to give up this whole vision quest thing and go find Titi instead, dragging her off by the hair if she resisted. At least tomorrow he would fail happy.

But as he stood there, taking out a power bar to nibble on, he had a new thought. If he blew the interview, Titi would deny him for a really long stretch. But if by some miracle, he did okay, she would be his for years because he would be the big kahuna times five. If he ballparked it, well, he would be gold for a lifetime. It was worth sacrificing a night. He continued on.

When he reached their favorite cove, shadowed by overhanging palms, it was as he suspected: occupied. Cooked stood there, indecisive, and a dude yelled, "Hey, bro, you gonna make a movie or somethin'?"

Cooked shuffled inland, stoned, hungry, and aroused, not knowing where to find shelter. Fifteen minutes later, he found himself at the sacrificial stone they had visited on that loser field trip. Until Loren had taken them there a few days ago, Cooked had never known what it was. Now that he did, it sort of freaked him out, but he didn't know where else to go.

As he had guessed, no one was there because, unlike him, everyone else knew the history. Whatever. It was a rock. The old days were . . . old. The spot was empty and filled with moonlight and made a nice place to sit and look at the sky and allow the gods to drop a huge pile of inspiration down on his head. He climbed up, laid out his supplies, and lit up his first official joint of the night. Even if divine inspiration didn't happen, it felt good to get away from everyone else's craziness for a few hours. Halfway through the new spliff, he realized that this was seriously powerful kine bud. He was seriously blazed. He lay back on the cool slab and fell up into the night sky. It was as if the universe was there for him alone. He flew. He expanded, his face covering the whole of the night sky, his breath the wind in the palms. He was spinning. He put one hand down on the stone for leverage, and his fingers probed a small worn-down cup in the stone, and Loren's words came back to him: "This is where they did human sacrifices." He lay there frozen, immobile. Horrific visions of oiled bodies writhing in firelight, stabbing their sacrifices, the bloodletting filling the basins. Although he had no actual firsthand knowledge of how they did it, it was sure to be awful, not to mention gory, kind of like a Polynesian *Friday the 13th*. Cooked sat up, spooked, and ate all his supplies, intending to hurry home to Titi, but then somehow it became sunrise. He had slept through the whole night! Cracker crumbs were stuck to his lips.

He got up stiff, tired, and stuffed. It felt like he'd wrestled the Great Shark itself, and it had showed him its teeth. With a heavy, thoughtful step, he walked back to the resort, feeling the weight of his footsteps in history, ready for breakfast.

Seven a.m. An hour passed. Laura Vann should have been there. They had radioed in that she was past Hawaii and over the Pacific hours ago. Everything was on hold; it was sweltering; people were getting jumpy. At noon, Wende got the call.

"She's not coming," Wende announced.

"Why?" Dex asked.

Wende grimaced. "The vice president is on a visit to Japan. He fell down the stairs getting off Air Force Two and broke his leg. Everyone is rushing over there to cover it. Because Laura had a jump start, she's ahead of them all. She's halfway to Tokyo."

Cooked bowed his head. The ancestors had talked to him last night, and what they had said was be prepared to be shit on. He had expected this, or not this exactly, certainly not the American vice president, whatever his name was, breaking his leg, but something like it. Look at his people's history. Cursed. Didn't this Laura Vann's change of mind also reflect on him, that he was not as interesting or worthy or important as a clumsy no-name VP? He raised his head briefly, his eyes filled, and then, embarrassed, he turned away.

"No," Dex said. Cooked's face spoke to him—a good man beaten once again by the system—and he wasn't going to have it. "No, no, no, no."

"What?" Wende asked.

Dex was bobbing his head like a possessed man. "We continue. We go on. Screw Laura Vann and her star-fucking. She just missed the biggest story of her career. Just get us the boat!" Dex yelled.

Wende sent out a request for a powerboat to make the journey across the Tuamotu Archipelago to Moruroa. Immediately offers flooded in. The best one was from a tech mogul who was also a Prospero fan vacationing on Bora-Bora. He offered his eighty-foot yacht and crew.

"Game, set, match." Wende and Ann slapped palms.

"I want to go," Ann said. "It's going to get complicated out there with the police and the media. That's my training." What she didn't want to say was that she was jealous of everyone else finding his or her purpose, doing something that mattered, never mind if it turned out badly. She wanted her shot.

"Where?" Wende was busy scanning the five thousand comments left on the live cam in the hours after Dex's "Enlightenment" episode.

"I want to go with Cooked and Dex."

"Oh . . . No."

"Why?"

"Because the power of the message is lessened. Your presence skews it into yuppie adventure travel."

Ann blinked at the jab. "That's not nice." This was her moment of self-sacrifice, of going after the greater good, and this muse was blowing her off.

Wende took Ann's hand and gave it a quick peck. "It's not who you are, Ann."

By midafternoon the Polynesian wedding party guests were whipped into a passion by the presence of a flotilla of boats. The eighty-foot yacht was anchored outside the lagoon, waiting; inside the lagoon, smaller boats circled. Loren had denied landing rights to the paparazzi so they sat in rowboats and dinghies in the scorching sun, wielding telephoto lenses and waiting for something to happen.

The French military's mission had changed en route from one of rescuing a world-famous celebrity to restricting said celebrity from making a circus and PR disaster of Polynesian tourism. Not knowing the rebels' plans to go by yacht, a French bureaucrat in Papeete calculated that by outrigger canoe the Moruroa Raid Party could drag along for weeks before getting there, with daily broadcasts worldwide, costing a fortune not only in military presence but also in lost tourist dollars, and long-lasting, radiation-like bad publicity that would continue on for years.

At first Wende had considered uprooting the live cam to record the trip, but it quickly became apparent that the paparazzi had the situation more than covered. Her job changed now to one of staging. At the appointed time, the fanciest outrigger canoe was pulled in front of the resort, and all two hundred and fifty native guests went crazy as the drums pounded. They threw flowers in the water and sang. The "cannibals" in their new roles as ceremonial rowers, now sans masks but with palm headdresses (Wende thought they needed some oomph), stepped into the boat. After a suitably long pause in which the mad drumming reached such a crescendo that the idea of cannibalism became totally plausible to the burning, sweating paparazzi bobbing in their boats, Dex and Cooked walked out of the kitchen.

Wardrobe arguments had again raged, but the final decision was to dress nonnative (because a grass skirt looked kooky on Dex and undercut the seriousness of the occasion): subdued shorts and plain T-shirts. As the men left the shady porch of the kitchen and came into full view, the lolling paparazzi started snapping pictures and digitally recording, but it wasn't till a third figure appeared—slighter than the other two, dressed similarly in shorts and baggy T and sporting a baseball cap pulled down low, but without a doubt a woman (*Look at the boobs, man!*)—that they collectively went into a frenzy.

W ende, discreetly headquartered under the shade of a palm grove, was outraged. This was her baby, and she'd emphatically said *No!* She was used to the backstabbing at home in Los Angeles that went along with being the woman associated, or hoping to become associated, with Dex and Prospero, but she had thought Ann was different. Ann was supposed to be her friend. If Wende ran out and confronted her now, the whole moment, the whole production, would be ruined. Damage-control time, and the same question was in Wende's mind as in the multitudinous military and paparazzi's collective psyche: Who was the mystery woman? Guesses were: (1) Dex's hinted-at girlfriend (which, honestly, Wende thought not credible, especially the way Ann was dressed). (2) Another hostage/tourist (this possibility reignited the military because rescuing women got a lot more mileage in the press).

But Wende beat them all to the punch when she tweeted the future tabloid headline from her iPhone: (3) *It's the Cannibal Attorney!*

Ann had worn sneakers even though she would have preferred wearing her reef shoes and saving the others for the boat, but carrying luggage would play into Wende's fears of looking like they were on a terrorist-adventure-eco-vacation. The sand was blisteringly hot. Going barefoot was not a good option since they were supposed to move in a slow, dignified procession, filled with the portent of their mission. It wouldn't have been a bad compromise to stop at the water's edge and slip off her shoes, but, again, squatting in the sand and messing with her shoes could be photographed unflatteringly and diminish the voyage's gravitas.

An hour before in the kitchen with Dex, Cooked, and Richard, she had taken Dex aside and asked to go.

He shrugged. "Sure."

"You don't mind?"

"Hey, I'm all for women's rights and being equals. But you sure you want to go get microwaved?"

Ann paused. "I think I know why you're doing it. I have my reasons, too."

She had been confused these last days, or rather weeks, or really these last years, holding all these potentially interesting ingredients to a life that weren't coming together. It was like Richard's legendary hollandaise sauce: The ingredients looked watery at first, it took forever to whisk over heat, and there was that breath-holding moment when the lemon juice was added. It either curdled or transformed into a fluffy, velvety miracle. This once, she was the exact right person to play this part. She blushed at the ego of it, but she had been born to do this thing she was about to do, whatever the consequences.

Dex nodded. "Okeydokey. Hope you don't get seasick."

Ann had never really been on a prolonged ocean voyage, so she didn't know if she had sea legs or not. She would deal with it. The hardest part of the voyage had been telling Richard.

"I'm going, too," he said when he heard.

"You can't."

"Both of us or neither." Maybe it took a crisis like your wife being microwaved to realize that life without her was unthinkable.

"No. This is mine."

He frowned. Even the possibility of Ann getting hurt made him faint with worry.

"Things could get tricky out there," she said. "Dex and Cooked aren't exactly grounded individuals. An attorney might come in handy."

"What would you say if I said no?"

"The man I love wouldn't."

"No fair."

"I'll still need protecting from thunderstorms when I get back."

Wende was wrong once again. The secret glory of middle age was the discovery that when you loved, compromise was painless.

During boarding, the metallic-insect-whirring of paparazzi and their various machines filled the air. Cooked gracefully climbed into the outrigger without any help. Next came Dex, struggling and making a little hop, accidentally stepping down on a piece of sharp coral underwater and cutting his toe. He refused to show pain, just boarded and hid his bleeding foot. The drops of blood dispersed in the water, and sharks two miles away turned and snuffed the intoxicating waterborne blood scent.

A motorboat floated very close by, but Ann ignored it as she trudged through the water, pleased with her sneaker choice after watching Dex's struggle. She figured she could take her shoes off and dry them once they were aboard the yacht. She had one leg in, one still in the water, straddling the side of the outrigger when it sloshed sideways in the wake of the passing boat. She had to hop after it. One of the "cannibals" rose and held out his hand to hoist her over. Just as she was about to grab it, a familiar voice cried out.

"Ann, is that you?"

She blinked, light-headed from the heat and all the attention, the potential of bashing herself against the skittish side of the boat and drowning in the waist-high waters. Was she simply ill-suited for the heroine life? Was she hallucinating? The "cannibal" yanked her arm, almost dislocating it, and she flew over the side of the canoe, banging her shoulder on a crossbeam. Simultaneously rescued and crushed.

"Ann! I've found you!"

The boat had raced to shore despite Loren's prohibition, and as it cut its rumbling motor, the voice became clearer. A voice she knew as well as she knew her own.

"Ann, it's me. Javi!"

# Fare Tini Atua

## (House of the Gods)

Titi watched as the outrigger canoe finally pushed away after another boat came alongside it. A man had jumped in the water and splashed after Ann. She didn't seem happy to see him, so Titi wasn't either. After a hug and some whispered words between the two, the outrigger continued to move off toward the pass. Amid the sound of drums and singing, arranged by Titi to give the voyage a worthy send-off, the man, accidental conqueror, waded through the flower-strewn waves and touched land as if all the hoopla were for him.

Ceremonies like this were rare nowadays, and Titi was happy that it was performed for Cooked's sake. He had overcome his fear and gone. People would remember him for generations.

The last similar ceremony she had attended was one of welcome rather than departure. Six years before, press had come from all around the world to celebrate a group of Scandinavian boys crossing the Pacific on a balsa raft, the *Tangaroa*, reenacting their grandfathers' victorious landing on the islands. Why did explorers only have white faces? As if her people existed solely to be discovered and rediscovered, over and over, to provide a backdrop for their exotic adventure. What if Cooked's outrigger paddled all the way to their snowy fjords—would that be news-worthy? Could Cooked say he had discovered Norway and its people?

The leader of the original *Kon-Tiki* voyage, Thor Heyerdahl, had set out to prove that the prevailing ocean currents allowed migration from South America rather than Asia as had been commonly assumed. When he landed on Raroia in the Tuamotus, he was hailed an international hero. But Titi's people had endured generations of hardship by staying in place—where was the celebration for that?

None of that had mattered to Titi at eighteen, flattered by the atten-tion, the newspaper photographs of herself with the boys. She had been picked because her grandmother had been on the beach for the official celebrations to greet the men from the original voyage in 1947.

One of the grandsons developed a crush on Titi, and she had stayed with him for several weeks. When it came time for them to leave, he had asked her to come home with him to Narvik, Norway. He described what his home looked like: forests, herds of reindeer, and thick-walled houses that burned fires inside for warmth. Although she had seen snow in movies, the reality of living in it was beyond her. The closest she could come was imagining living inside a freezer. It sounded more fan-tastical than the idea of living on the moon. He described the whiteness as being as vast as the blue of her ocean. He told her of standing on water that was frozen solid, like a giant ice cube, and how he danced on its surface with blades on his feet. "You mean like the ice-skating rink in Papeete?" she asked.

She couldn't shake the feeling that he was collecting her, a South Sea specimen, to take home. Not for a moment did she consider going. Her adult life was preordained to be spent with Cooked, on the land that gave her people their strength and identity. This had been taught to her from the beginning by her mother, Faufau, and her grandmother. During her young life, she had observed what being out of place did to Loren. Tuamotuans did not have a word for loneliness. She did not want to experience its meaning in another language.

But the land was ailing.

Faufau told the story of how she woke up early one morning and walked along the lagoon on an errand. A brilliant light flashed overhead. Not in one corner of the sky like a house on fire or the sun rising, but like a great apocalyptic flame. Faufau fell to the ground facedown, shutting her eyes tightly, sure that it was the white god coming to end the world like the missionaries always threatened. A great rumbling started, like the worst thunder, the stomach of the earth growling. The sand in front of her eyes rolled up and down like a wave, like a ripple being shaken out of cloth, then sank away. The ocean rushed to replace the land, reversing the Bible story of creation. Faufau rose, crying, and ran back home.

Faufau's father was on a nearby island, hired to do construction for the French. During a break, it was so hot he decided to go swimming. Underwater, the blue-green world that usually soothed him suddenly buckled, and a strange, awful pressure gripped his body viselike. His eardrums hurt, as if sticks were being poked through them. His head pounded as if every thought in the world was trying to crowd its way inside. He surfaced for a gulp of air, but the shiny, peeled sky burned his eyes. He saw only blackness where there was blinding white. Instinct drove him back underwater. The swallowed air seared his lungs like hot coals as he plunged back down.

A sight he regretted seeing that would haunt him the rest of his life: A large shark suspended in the water, turned inside out. Eyes popped, internal organs exploded out through its mouth and anus. The many companionable fish that he had swam among his whole life now turned monstrous.

Later the government told them that the tests were for the stability of the world, to end all wars. Destruction to prevent destruction. But these were not their wars. What about the war that now raged in the lagoon? A war that would continue on for generation after generation to the end of time?

One of Faufau's uncles worked at the test site because it paid double what other jobs did. They were told the tests were harmless. The French workmen scurried into thick cement bunkers while the Tahitians were left on open platforms, offered only the protection of face masks, which were too small to fit them. Instead, the workers played ball with them as they waited.

An enormous cloud had covered the sky, and as in a fairy tale it had begun to snow. Faufau and the other children had read of snow in their French textbooks at school and thought the teacher had brought it as a present for them. After hours of playing in the accumulating drifts, one by one the children fell sick. Faufau's eyes itched. She had a great thirst that couldn't be quenched. The drinking water in the rainwater drum was magically changing colors like a rainbow. She wobbled and thought she would throw up. Then it got worse.

Adults could not care for the children because everyone was sick. Burns bloomed on bodies. Hair and fingernails fell off like an unnatural molting.

Faufau could not know the damage had also gone inside. As a woman, she endured eight miscarriages before Titi was born.

Cooked was doing this for their future children, Titi thought.

J avi?" Richard couldn't believe his eyes.

The morning had been too much for him. He had lost his little bit of heaven in the kitchen. Ann had never seemed the martyr type, yet she was on her way to radiate herself for a cause they had known nothing about a few weeks ago. Like most people, when Richard looked at tragedy, he donated a few bucks and moved on with his life. He didn't understand the kind of person who sacrificed herself to causes. It seemed vaguely scandalous to be unwittingly married to such a person. Like a bad dream, Ann was gone, and inexplicably Javi was in her place.

Javi jogged the last few soggy feet of surf and embraced Richard. He had never felt so lost as when he didn't have his big, dopey sidekick to bully along. Then he looked around.

"Not a bad place you guys holed up in."

Wende stepped forward. "Who is this guy who almost ruined the shot?"

Richard shrugged. "Meet Javi. He's our business partner."

Javi grinned. "Nice to meet you, woman of my dreams."

"You're *el gusano*." Disgusted, she walked away.

The paparazzi flotilla had turned and followed the outrigger through the pass to the waiting yacht, so the interruption thankfully had not been photographed.

"What are you doing here?" Richard asked.

"You won't answer my calls."

"We don't have reception here."

Javi pulled out his phone and looked at the full bars.

"Until the last day or so. And Ann's gone." Like this info would make him turn around and go back to where he came from.

"Yeah? Fishing trip? How long?"

"She left for a radioactive island with Dex Cooper."

"You let her go? My Ann?"

"*My* Ann. I had no choice."

"Not if you treat her like this. I love her."

Richard rubbed his forehead. "What, exactly, are you saying?"

"You didn't treat her right from the get-go. She should have left you years ago. She would have made me a better man. At least I would have kept her busy."

Titi walked by Richard and the new strange man rolling on the sand, trying to punch each other out. When Cooked and she took over the resort, she was going to make sure there were rules against this kind of behavior. It was undignified.

In fact, the crowds of relatives and wedding guests were starting to wear on her; she had grown used to the orderly isolation of the resort. Her taste for privacy, like expensive fine chocolate, had been acquired. Cooked and she had been working alone for years, with only short breaks back to their own chaotic village. The farthest she had ever been in her life was Papeete, which was as big city as it got until one hit either Sydney or Honolulu. She was a small-island girl.

The wedding party had grown restless. Young men camped out along the beach, bored by the lack of action, were getting into fistfights. Since there was no telling how long Cooked would be away, she prepared to announce that they should return home. Wedding postponed. Her priority was to get things back to normal for Loren.

Titi's father left soon after her birth, and Loren had filled in as a kind of semi-father, crazy uncle. All this activity was too much for him in his current state. She worried that it would send him into a tailspin of depression again.

His drinking binges had been legendary. She had to bail him out of all kinds of terrible situations. Over the last year, he had hidden the signs of his illness as well as he could but had no choice but to confide in someone. No one could exist utterly alone, although Loren came close. She was steady as a caretaker because she had gone through her grandmother's and aunts' illnesses. Together they went to his doctor's visits. There came a time when her grandmother, too, had refused treatments as Loren was now doing. Titi respected his decision. The doctors took the dignity of life away, took away the soul, and everyone knew you eventually died of the poisoning no matter what. He might as well be where he wanted. Everyone said what a shame it was that Loren had never married some woman who would be there for him. He was way past indulging in men. It was unthinkable on the islands to die alone, and so his care would come down on Titi's shoulders, which she accepted.

In his hut, Loren lay in the darkness. She knew better than to try to open the windows, but left the door open to air out the fetid smell.

He smiled when he saw her, the skin drawn tight across his cheeks. Fever.

"How is it?" she asked.

"It hurts."

She nodded and patted his arm.

"So what do you think, little Titi? Are you impressed? The whole world watching us."

"What does it matter?"

"It matters because the resort will be full."

It touched her that such details could interest him.

"The wedding will happen as soon as Cooked returns," she said.

"I can wait."

"You will sit in the place of my father?"

Loren nodded. He turned away, gruffly telling her to shut the door on her way out, but he couldn't fool her. She saw the tears.

Twenty years before, their people had been thriving. People believed that the prosperity brought by the new hotels would trickle down to them, and they would all grow rich. It was still enough of a novelty to see a Frenchman that the children came out to stare, but the true novelty was the appearance of two young French girls standing behind him. They stared back at the pack of children while the man went inside Titi's grandmother's house to look for a place to stay.

While the Frenchman worked as a manager of a nearby farm in the day, Titi's grandmother was paid to be babysitter, but the way things worked was that Bette and Lilou joined a big extended family of a dozen children and twice as many adults. The girls thrived, and since Loren spent every spare minute with them, he ended up part of Titi's extended family also.

Although she had only been a child, Titi remembered a different man back then. After work, he'd come and play with the children, teaching magic tricks (to that day almost every man in the family could pull a coin out of your ear as easily as walking down the beach). He used to spin his daughters in his arms, faster and faster till their legs flew straight out and they squealed in delight; then he slowed and laid them on the earth like drunken butterflies. They giggled, tried to stand and staggered, fell back down. Titi had longed to be spun but was too shy to ask.

One time, Lilou cut her leg. They rushed her to an aunt who was a nurse. Holding her, watching the aunt stain the skin with iodine, then begin stitching, Loren cried along with his daughter. What a good father, the women said. What a good husband he'd make. He should marry, have more children, become settled. They sent attractive young women his way, but he showed no interest.

The day the girls were taken away by the French policemen was the saddest day in the village. After Loren came out of prison, not only he but the whole village mourned. They erected new stones for the girls on the *marae*. Ceremoniously, Loren gave the girls' belongings to Titi because, even if they did come back, by then they would have outgrown such things. In her young heart, Titi felt that she was being called on to replace them. The villagers decided the only cure for Loren was marriage and a new family. Once again women were brought out, not callously, but with the idea of new beginnings. Instead Loren chose old endings. Chose drink and trouble. As they found out only later, chose men over the company of women.

On the days he was still himself, he played the role of uncle to Titi. In reverse of those French fairy tales that Loren read to her, the pretty princesses vanished, and the dark, heavyset girl got to take their place. Later, when Cooked moved to the village and became inseparable from her, Loren tried to be a big brother to him also. He paid for special things they wanted but couldn't afford. He played cheerleader at their school events, and always was the prime organizer of birthday parties. He made them the wager that if they got good enough grades to get into college, he would pay for it.

As she got older, sometimes she felt they were taking advantage, as if Loren were offering himself only because of the loss of his girls, but they couldn't afford to refuse. Faufau, Grandmother, and the aunts did look after him; as badly as he took care of himself, he would have died many times over otherwise. Cooked and Titi were both in college in Papeete when news came of his sickness. Although he said it was otherwise, Titi knew it was the same wasting disease that the others had. He ate the same fruit and fish, breathed the same air, and swam in the same ocean. He'd sat at her grandmother's bedside as she wasted away, listened to Faufau's story of playing with the poisoned snow that now they understood was ash. The illness made him even more reckless; he went on drinking binges lasting weeks. It was a fluke when he won the island in a poker game. Loren asked them to drop out of school to run the hotel as if it were the most natural request in the world.

Cooked was unhappy about it, saying they would become servants of the tourists. But after all Loren had done for them, how could they complain? Without his help, they couldn't continue their studies. Once they settled down to running the resort, he became a stranger, a boss, talking to them only about business—were the rooms done, the food ordered, the plumbing fixed? He treated them as servants. Now things were changing once again.

"You don't have to turn over the hotel now," Titi said. "It can wait."

"I'm cheating you two out of your inheritance. Ill-gained as it was."

"We aren't ready." This was the truth she had been avoiding.

"Sometimes events force you to be ready."

"I want to change the name of the hotel," she said.

Loren looked surprised. Change came so fast, so hungrily.

"A name in our own language."

He nodded.

"*Mara 'amu.*"

"Trade winds. Yes, I like it."

Titi got up to leave. "I thought you should know—another guest has landed on the beach without permission."

When the outrigger pulled away from the beach, Cooked would not look back at his and Titi's relatives singing and throwing flowers in the water, a hero's send-off. In spite of his baseball cap and T-shirt, he felt like one of those ancient warriors the old people told stories about who went out to do battle against the enemy. For a proud moment, suspended over the lagoon, the sun reflecting off the water, he felt his presence in the boat was destiny. He felt brave. But when a paddle jabbed him in the back, it all disappeared. He was again scared of reaching their destination.

"Moruroa" was the spelling used by native people for the island. It meant, ironically, Big Lies. The French misspelled it "Mururoa" on purpose to make it obscure and secret. That whole corner of the archipelago was off the map for tourists, as off-limits as a locked room in a house.

Cooked knew of an old man who used to work there for the government, sorting out the three or four pieces of mail delivered each week for the foreign workers. It was a long day filled with nothing, which suited him fine. He used to swim each day in the lagoon, then catch a fish for his lunch. The day before the planned detonation, the island was evacuated, the scientists leaving behind instruments to measure the power of the blast. The explosion registered at least ten times bigger than Hiroshima before the instruments were destroyed. The old man went back with officials three days later and was shocked. All the plants gone. The little secondary island with the barrier reef disappeared. The metal tower behind the bunker on the atoll melted and lying flat like an oil slick. Not believing their claims that the island was safe, he quit his job. Those who stayed on had long since died.

The outrigger made it through the pass, surrounded by motorboats filled with paparazzi hanging out at all angles like uncouth savages, yelling at them, furiously trying to get a picture of Dex or the mystery lady's face. No one was much interested in Cooked's presence.

They pulled alongside the yacht; Ann, Cooked, and Dex climbed up a ladder. The crew's captain, Shawn, came and shook hands with them. He was young and blond, a surfer from Southern California turned captain. His job was to be ready whenever his billionaire boss got the urge for the boat. Which wasn't often. Luckily the boss was on a rare family trip, and had the boat docked while they stayed on Bora-Bora. Shawn's clothes were pressed. He and the ship were immaculate, and in comparison, Ann felt the three of them looked a little ragged. They must appear much like Loren had first appeared to her weeks ago, weathered and a bit disreputable. They stood on deck and waved good-bye to the crew of the outrigger; Shawn revved the engine and left the paparazzi in a cloud of fuel exhaust.

Cooked could not believe what he saw on the boat. Everything was trimmed in shining teak. When they went into the cabin, there was air-conditioning and a flat-screen TV with 346 channels. A refrigerated wine cellar. A full bar. A steward came and served them champagne. Dex and Ann collapsed on the white leather sofas. At first Cooked was intimidated by these surroundings, especially being waited on instead of serving. He had to remind himself that Titi and he were now owners of a resort. He would have to get comfortable in the world of guests. He downed the champagne in one gulp.

"I'd like a beer, too, please," he said.

"Coming right up, mate."

"And a Coke. With ice."

"Righto. Do you have a preference for lunch today?" the steward asked.

"Chocolate milk shakes," Cooked said. "Hamburgers, fries, and more beer."

"Could I shower first?" Ann asked.

"I'll show you to your suite. And Mr. Cooper, Mr. Garrett expressed the desire for some autographs as a memento of your stay on board. For himself and his kids. He says the autographs might make them listen to music from *his* youth for a change."

A jab, but Dex rolled with it. "You got it."

They were just sitting down for lunch when a siren went off. They went to the window to see a military speedboat approaching. Shawn came inside. There was a definite cloud on his former imperturbable sunniness.

"They're ordering us to stop."

"Ignore them," Dex said.

Shawn's voice was quavery. "They said in no uncertain terms—*torpiller*—is that 'torpedo'? They want to sink us?"

"Unbelievable!" Dex's eyes glittered. He was having perverse fun. Deep down he didn't believe they'd dare mess with him. The strength of a superstar was the ability to both mock and believe in one's own legend.

Cooked, on the other hand, was struck silent. All his life the French had bullied his people. The police could mean only one thing—bodies would be beaten and bruised, his most likely. A jail cell in Papeete probably already had his name on it.

Ann was angry. She didn't know their rights exactly, but it was clear they were being intimidated.

Shawn closed his eyes. "Between us—and I'm trying not to be a downer—the baddies always win out here."

So Cooked, Ann, and Dex were taken into police custody, regretfully before getting to eat lunch, and transported to a trawler that had been pressed into service for police use.

"I'll be here waiting for you," Shawn yelled theatrically after them.

In the meantime, the paparazzi had intercepted radio messages and caught wind of what was going on. They raced after the police boat as it pulled up to the trawler, photographing the three of them climbing the rope ladder up to the two-story-high deck. They took the dramatic footage of Dex frowning, a police officer holding his arm.

"Handcuff me," Dex said to the officer.

"There is no need for that."

Dex stopped walking.

"Come along." The policeman nudged.

"Handcuff me," Dex growled.

The policeman glanced over at the paparazzi flotilla. "*Pute* for publicity, eh?"

The paparazzi below were feasting on the dramatic showdown, which would make front page twice in one week in several papers in Australia and the United States.

"Easy, Dex," Ann said.

The pictures of the babies were in the forefront of Dex's mind. The stories of all Cooked and Titi's relatives and their cancers. He was fighting for them, but this force of oppression, this lowly policeman, was trying to stop him. *The baddies always win*, like his father, who got paid to make sure of it, but not this time. No. Dex's arm moved of its own volition, more as an extension of this line of thought than a premeditated act of violence. As he punched the policeman smack in the nose, what he really connected with was his father's legacy of deceit. No! Not this time!

The paparazzi were having the feast to end all feasts, the mother of all photo ops, living off the fat of the land. Beyond their wildest hopes, this was a career milestone. A few contemplated having the colossal amount of money they were sure to get wired into their accounts and taking the month off to stay in the South Pacific. And then it got even better.

A policeman who was restraining Cooked lifted his baton and, with a balletic half-pivot, clubbed Dex.

Dex disappeared from view as Ann started screaming.

Unscripted emotion was pure gold.

When Dex rose a minute later, a trickle of blood ran down the side of his hairline—he refused the handkerchief to wipe it off—and, yes, he was a publicity slut, playing this for all it was worth because publicity was the mother's milk of public opinion: *You know me; therefore, I am.* Maybe in the far dark past people actually did value the perfect rose blooming unseen on a deserted mountainside, maybe just its existence was enough, but in the modern age every perfection, every event, big or small, significant or not, only counted if others knew of it. Dex faced the paparazzi head-on like an inspired preacher confronting his inflamed congregation. This time his face wasn't the face of Dex Cooper, Rock Star; his face was now a banged badge of solidarity with the Polynesian people, *Ma 'ohi*, and not only with *them* but with the oppressed all over. He was the self-anointed new Bono. He was stoked, and as the police pushed him inside, away from the PR disaster this was becoming for them, he raised one skinny, tattooed arm and gave the paparazzi the peace sign.

The commandeered trawler had huge freezers belowdecks filled with thousands of frozen-solid tuna awaiting their long voyage to the grocery stores of the world. The decks were brownish and slippery, and a smell permeated the boat—a mix of public bathroom, fertilizer, and freshly opened cans of cat food.

They were held in a kind of Soviet-style conference room, with dingy Formica tables nailed to the floor and bare lightbulbs in wire cages overhead. Within the closed room, the air heated and expanded the dead-fish smell to toxic levels. The police ignored Cooked and started questioning Dex and Ann.

Cooked was used to being snubbed in his own land, a second-class citizen in his place of birth. Even during civil protests, he didn't count. Foreigners controlled them, and other foreigners, benevolent ones, championed them, but they themselves were treated like children or pets, incapable of participating in their own emancipation. Cooked turned his back on the whole proceedings, and stared at the blank scuffed wall instead.

After an hour of haranguing back and forth, Ann determined that there was no point in going farther on their trip. If they approached the off-limits zone, the police informed them, they could be legally arrested. If they resisted, their very nice borrowed yacht would be either impounded or sunk.

As the police conferred about what to do with them now, Ann noticed Cooked staring at the wall in a trance. Something had come over him—he was acting strangely.

A sailor came in from outside and whispered in the police chief's ear. He frowned. "Mr. Cooper, it appears you have a visitor."

Dex said nothing, thinking it was a trick. Sneaky police. He was thinking of various scenarios from *Casablanca* and *Blade Runner*.

"Where is the visitor?" Ann asked.

"In a boat below. We're denying boarding."

"Nice."

Dex, Cooked, and Ann went back outside under escort and looked over the side of the ship.

"Robby?" Dex yelled.

Ann saw a blond, muscled version of Dex. Robby was the golden boy of the band, the heartthrob of the good girls while Dex appealed to the bad ones.

"Thought you needed some help," Robby yelled up. "I've got our lawyers here."

"I've got my lawyer here already. Go on to the island and wait for us." No denying it—Ann was proud.

Cooked felt a strong wind wash over him. This was what he had waited for in vain the night of his vision quest on the rock, his hoped-for, Laura Vann–inspired statement. The truth was nothing had happened that night other than his own determination. Now he was literally inspirited. The ancestors entered him in the form of a shark. Without another thought he sprang up on the railing and dived overboard in a perfect arc that the paparazzi captured for all time, and that would be used for the cause of independence and later as a promo poster for the resort, and even later for tourism to the islands, and that his and Titi's children, and then their grandchildren, would hang proudly in their living rooms.

The police, shocked, stood paralyzed for a moment—did this qualify as an escape attempt?—before unholstering their guns and firing into the water.

Luckily they were poor shots.

Cooked bobbed up a few hundred yards away with only a nick on one ear. He was pretty sure he could swim all the way back to the island he felt so pumped. That lasted until he realized he was bleeding and then he began to flail as Robby's boat raced to pick him up. The police, spooked and demoralized, released Dex and Ann with a warning, and they hitched a ride with the paparazzi back to the yacht.

"You guys missed lunch," Shawn said, as if this was the most ordinary of days. "Hungry?"

Cooked, at peace after having done his bit for the ancestors, lay bandaged on the sofa, eating from a bag of potato chips while watching a ball game on the big screen.

Ann was the one who now trembled. "You could have been killed."

Cooked shrugged. "Cheeseburgers."

"You got it," Shawn said. "Where we headed to?"

"Back to the island," Dex said.

"Too bad the outrigger is gone," Ann said.

"*No problemo*," Shawn said. "I'm teleconferencing with a sweetheart named Wendy over at the resort. She said she'd order it up."

Dex sized up yet another potential rival.

Hours later, as a Technicolor sunset plastered the sky in gaudy oranges, reds, and purples, a tired Dex, Ann, and Cooked were paddled to shore. Loren had relented and allowed the paparazzi to land, and they had been partying with the wedding guests. The story was over. The reporters had been thrilled when Robby showed up earlier, and he had already done dozens of interviews talking about the band's evolving role in world humanitarian crises.

"Because we're about more than the music, right? We're about the people."

Now, the paparazzi, drunk and stoned, full of roast pork and breadfruit, dutifully marched down to the water at Wende's request (coupled with the threat of expulsion) to record the victors' landing.

As the outrigger came closer to shore, Cooked stood in the boat, an undignified wad of cotton gauze on one side of his head, to wild cheering, drum beating, and flower throwing. Even Wende approved the spectacle. When Dex made a move to stand also, Ann reached out and held him back. This was Cooked's day.

Earlier, when Robby had jumped out of the boat along with two of Prospero's attorneys, Wende just gave a short nod hello. From the old days, she suspected, rightly, opportunism on his part. A call had come in from Shawn that the yacht was headed back, and she was on her way to tell Richard and Titi the good news. Yes, she was extremely relieved—she surely didn't want them getting radiated, or whatever it was—but the impresario within her was the smallest bit disappointed in the loss of a climax for the story. As dramatic as the paparazzi's live feed of the police trawler had been, basically Dex, Cooked, and Ann had gone on a daylong joyride in a yacht. Now that Robby had shown up, stealing the thunder so carefully built up, who knew how that would affect public sentiment?

The wedding guests, despite the language barriers, were enjoying the paparazzi and their infinite capacity for alcohol, which even by Polynesian standards was truly impressive. Preparations were under way for the nuptial ceremony the next day that would last three more.

Was her project over? Wende lamented, watching the women weaving wedding mats from banana leaves. She didn't want to turn *National Geographic* and film that. There would be a feast of native foods, drumming and dancing. There would be . . . Why not a concert with Dex and Robby? A benefit concert that featured the new song, with the money it earned going to victims of the radiation poisoning and a legal defense fund seeking reparations from the government. Wende forgot all about Richard and Titi being reunited with their loved ones, and ran back to give Robby a lavish hug and make nice.

When Cooked readied himself to jump out of the canoe, the eight "cannibals" were there to greet him. They had converted tomorrow's wedding throne into a king's throne—decorated with palm fronds and a feathered headdress at the back. They carried him to shore because a hero's feet should not touch water. He was disappointed that Titi wasn't on shore to kiss him. The paparazzi, bloated with photographic riches, snapped a few pics for their personal photo albums, then went back to their carousing. For many of them, this was the best assignment they had ever been on, probably would ever be on, and they were making the most of it.

Forgotten, Dex and Ann helped each other off the boat and through the water. No one was there to greet them. A young boy was plunging tiki torches into the sand and lighting them. A young woman in a pareu walked by and offered them fruit juice. They sat in the sand and toasted.

"Today was way cool," Dex said.

Ann smiled. "It was."

"Who would have thought the thing would grow so big?"

"We accomplished something."

Wende walked up nonchalantly, as if they had been hanging out there all day. "Have fun on the boat? Robby and I need to talk with you real quick, Dex."

"Ann and I are having a moment."

"Oh. Sorry. Sure."

Wende moved off with her clipboard, which now was an extension of her body, keenly aware that in the past Dex never had cared about marking *their* moments. Strike that—*that* was the old Wende. What mattered were rehearsals. It was all well and fine to get sentimental, but it was time to move on to the next thing. And if that worked out, great, then move on to the one after that, ad infinitum. They were going to have to start immediately if they were to have a chance of performing the concert before the momentum faded.

Dex and Ann sat side by side on the beach. They faced the east, which was dark. The fiery brilliance of sunset was behind them.

"Do you think there is anything back there for us?" Ann asked.

"That's home," Dex said, waving his arm out in front of him. "That is the direction of hope, of dreams, of happiness."

A pause.

"Are you sure that's east?" Ann asked.

Wende was seething by now and wondered if they were stoned. Precious minutes were going down the toilet. Did no one want to be serious about anything?

"You guys are looking south. Nothing between you and Antarctica."

After Cooked was congratulated by all two hundred and fifty guests and even some of the drunk paparazzi, after he was slapped on the back so many times he felt bruised, after he was toasted with so many shots of moonshine that he was seeing double, Titi finally rescued him and took him away to their honeymoon *fare* at the quiet, secluded corner of the beach that was no longer quite so secluded, amid much joyful crowing and howling. When she shut the door and closed the blinds against peeking kids, Cooked experienced his first moment of peace. She unwound his bandage and discovered the tiniest divot had been taken from the top of his ear, like a mouse's nibble out of a piece of cheese.

"I'm so proud of you," Titi said, and her pareu, as if of its own will, dropped, revealing the naked, oiled gift of herself.

Beyond exhaustion, Cooked felt vanquished but in a good way. He could only stare at this girl whom he had known and loved all his life, who tomorrow would be his wife. He had done okay today, he thought. But even if he hadn't, she would still love him.

"I haven't had much rest," he said, hedging his bets.

"I'll do all the work." She smiled, the crescent of her smile glowing, an interior moon.

Cooked had been able to endure the humiliations of the past days only because of her.

She pulled him to her.

Later, when they lay in the plunge pool to cool off, she fed him cut-up chunks of Bounty bars, his favorite treat.

"It will be good after the ceremony is over and everyone leaves. They mean well, but they're trashing the island," she said.

"How will we manage alone?"

"Loren will stay. He belongs here."

"They expect us to fail. Get us to sell cheap."

"Don't worry," she said, kissing his arm, his neck, then starting all over. "Today you were my hero."

Ann sheepishly went in search of Richard, disappointed that he hadn't been waiting at the beach to greet her. She found him in the kitchen with Javi and a dozen Polynesian women, involved in the monumental production of a wedding feast. She stood in the doorway, and he and Javi saw her at the same moment.

"Ann!" they said simultaneously, turning to look at each other rather than her. Neither came forward.

"I'm back," she said, stating the obvious to the void of silence that hung between them.

"Good," Richard said, and went on stirring.

"Richard?"

He didn't move.

"What's wrong?"

"I told him I love you," Javi said casually as he kept chopping.

She looked at him, furious. "Why did you come here?"

Javi shrugged. "I missed you guys."

Lorna had straightened everything out with the creditors, the ex-wife, and the loan sharks (she had enough underground connections that this wasn't beyond her purview). Although Javi omitted the fact that he had used the money she loaned him partly for a little R & R in Tahiti and Bora-Bora before continuing on to see them, he had taken full responsibility, declared bankruptcy, and sold every last thing, even returning the beautiful new Corvette, to satisfy everyone. Everyone, that is, except for them. Technically they had spent their money at their own discretion. Was it his fault they wanted to live it up?

"I'm a new man," Javi said. "As in brand-new. No credit. I'll be working restaurants the next decade to catch up. But you guys are free and clear."

"Free," a relative term when they had just dropped a major chunk of change at a five-star luxury eco-resort for almost three weeks. Not including the sizable bar tab, first-class airfare (was it a time to go economy?), and incidentals. Everything in the restaurant had been sold off at ten cents on the dollar. The space was now occupied by a Pilates studio. There would be no resurrecting the restaurant. El Gusano was dead.

"Well, that settles that. I'm heading back to LA," Richard announced.

The "I" instead of "we" was a noticeable omission to all three of them.

"Don't blame Ann," Javi said, but Richard raised his hand to stop him, then walked out.

"What's eating him?"

Ann looked at Javi. As if the restaurant wasn't enough, he had just ruined her marriage. Of course, it had been her fault, too. At the time of the affair, Richard and she were splitting up. Sure, it had been a questionable judgment call, she had made a mistake, but people do. Ten years of good behavior afterward didn't count for anything? Life was messy, and she didn't know if she wanted to spend the rest of hers with someone who didn't understand that. She would have forgiven him. But had she?

Ann and Richard sat on the beach, surrounded by families settling in for the night, spreading blankets on the sand to stretch out under the stars. It was obvious that the simple Tuamotuan lifestyle was unavailable to them. And yet.

"It meant nothing," Ann said.

"Then why didn't you tell me?"

"Javi loves you. As much as he is capable. You and I were about to break up. You were cold and distant after your trip to France, and I thought you'd fallen in love with a girl. It happened, and then it was over. Why hurt you? We were doing fine."

"I should have been told."

"You needed Javi for the restaurant."

"Look where that got us."

"Things happen. We're adults."

Richard pounded his fist in the sand. "I'm not."

She had to bite down hard on her cheek not to smile. "Maybe I've babied you too much."

"You lied to me."

"Like you lied to me all these years about your problem with meat. That's what happened to you in France, wasn't it? Don't you think that was a pretty important detail to omit?"

"Sorry if I can't compete with almost being contaminated by radiation while hanging out with a rock star."

"What about your lusting after Wende? Your eyes almost pop out of your head every time she walks by."

"Not true."

"True."

"Nothing happened."

"If it did, I would forgive you."

"So you forgive me hypothetically, and I'm supposed to forgive the real thing?"

"What's the alternative?"

"Exactly." And like he had slapped her in the face, Richard stood and walked away.

The wedding party started early in the morning and went on relentlessly for three days. At first the food and the feasting, the dancing and the drinking, were welcome after all the nuclear showdown theatrics, and then, like other pleasurable things done to excess, it chafed and made one feel tired and bloated. The Tuamotuans never seemed to run out of energy—even the children were wound up like forty-eight-hour clocks—but the paparazzi were dropping off like flies. One had to be medevaced out for supposed alcohol poisoning, which ended up being mere exhaustion.

Dex and Robby disappeared into rehearsals, joined by the native drummers for the wedding. It was promoted as a cross-cultural event, with hot dancers brought in from Papeete, fire-eaters, more drummers, etc.

Wende, bored now with nothing to do, filmed parts of the wedding ceremony and parts of the music rehearsals, ending up with a mix of *National Geographic* rerun and a frat-house reality show. She and Ann filmed the traditional inking of his and hers wedding tattoos, the first few lines started with the traditional shark tooth and ink before a modern electric needle was used.

Ann looked down at her own dismembered fish forlornly circling her thigh.

"Can't you finish?"

"I thought you hated it." Wende grimaced as a *tiare* flower was tatted on the inside of her ankle.

"I need change."

"Change is good."

"It hurts."

"Some things are worth it, right? Let's do it."

Wende took her time and carefully worked the needle as Titi and the other women looked on, impressed with her technique. "I considered opening my own tattoo parlor a while back."

There was no comparison—the back of the shark was much finer work than the earlier front. A new maturity was evident in Wende's work as she bent over Ann's thigh and asked for the flashlight to be brought closer. She had become a perfectionist. It had nothing to do with flesh, everything with spirit, as if she had lived through lifetimes in these last few days.

When the tat was done, the women clapped, and Wende bowed her head.

"You're good to go and conquer."

W ende cringed as the production values of the wedding/benefit concert began slipping. The problem with authentic was that it didn't look the way anyone under the age of fifty had been conditioned by movies to think it should look. The grass anklets and arm cuffs looked stringy; the stumpy headdresses lacked majesty. Never mind the girls in nylon shorts and Pearl Jam T-shirts. Wende pursed her lips and drank some vodka-laced guava juice.

The highlight of day two of the wedding ceremony was Cooked and Titi being carried in from a boat in the lagoon on thrones balanced on the shoulders of six men. The thrones were lowered onto a carpet of banana leaves on which *tiare*, hibiscus, and ginger flowers had been scattered. Combined with the flowered leis of the women, the crushed petals emitted a rich perfume into the air.

At the height of the ceremony, Titi and Cooked kneeled facing each other and exchanged a single flower. The impermanence of the flower instead of something solid like gold rings was to remind the couple of the transience of their bond, and thus its preciousness. *Do not waste a single minute of this love.*

Ann never cried at weddings, but now she did. She and Richard had squandered buckets of both time and love, and had only themselves to blame.

The hope of their simple civil ceremony years ago, the small dinner party with only their parents and Javi, had seemed to portend such an exceptionally authentic life, lived on their own terms. Richard had made reservations at the best French restaurant in town, a small place with only ten tables. They got married on a Friday afternoon, and when they arrived at the restaurant with their party, they found fire trucks in front. There had been a kitchen fire. Impossible to get reservations anywhere else on a Friday night—they ended up eating at a Chinese place down the block. Ann's parents had been appalled, especially since she had refused their offer of a country club wedding. Richard's parents seemed bewildered. In the way such things rarely happen, near disaster averted itself. Javi tried to lighten the mood by ordering a round of Chinese beer. When the staff found out it was a wedding dinner, they started to cook specialties not on the menu. Richard still talked about some of those dishes, which they never found again. The owner of the restaurant came out and sang Mandarin wedding songs, accompanied by a waiter on an oboe. The brillance and oddness of the evening broke down barriers between the parents. They closed down the place at midnight. It ended up being exactly the wedding they had hoped for.

Now Ann reached for Richard's hand, and for a moment he allowed it.

L oren sat next to Faufau in the place of honor. He felt pleased looking at Titi, as if a great burden had been lifted. So this was what it felt like to make good. He'd been a cynical bastard these last years, but he had to admit feeling satisfied that night, as if he'd pulled off a slick heist. Titi and Cooked were his happy children; in the universe's obscure system of checks and balances, some kind of amends had been made.

Ever since Bette's death, he'd lived with a dread that he would continue to fail people when they most needed him. It made him shy away from all connection except what was absolutely necessary. Fatherless Titi was necessary, and yet the tie to her and her family had driven him to even more irresponsibility. *Don't think you can count on me.* In the back of his mind, he was waiting for that one time too many when Faufau at last would tell him to leave, when Titi would refuse to come to the rescue in the middle of the night, to places a nice young girl shouldn't go. Thing was, it never happened. He was ashamed to say that he got far better than he ever gave back. And so this was most deserved.

He looked around at the jubilant, hopeful faces and felt like doom. The deluded naïveté—believing that things would work out in the end—was as endless as it was maddening. Maybe that was the only way the human race could go on. Titi might as well have been wearing a "Happily Ever After" T-shirt. Cooked seemed dazed by his fast-approaching bourgeois future, resigned to it as only weeks ago he had been to the very different path of an outlaw. The world was a shark. One had to be ruthless, relentlessly moving forward; if forced to stop or move backward, one drowned. Loren fretted over these children of his, how ill-suited they were to the harsh realities of life. Titi felt his troubled gaze and blew him a kiss. Absolutely no rancor for how he had tested them these last years, no glee that now they would be calling the shots, proving his good choice.

A fter the feast was over, Loren sought out Ann. Time was running out. He needed to ask her a favor, but she would make demands in return.

"Care for a nightcap?"

In his room, he poured and they toasted.

"It was a beautiful ceremony," she said. "Be proud."

But Loren was all business. "You asked about my finger. That was so I would never forget Bette. But in my grief, I forgot about Lilou. A double sin."

He had gone back to France to court Lilou. He hated being back in his home country, hated the flat white sky, the muted colors of the land, and the crabbed people. Matilde's pinched eyes, her sallow cheeks—how was it possible he had ever been married to such a woman? Each time Matilde answered the door, she was more dour, announcing their daughter's wish to not see him. If Lilou had asked him to, he would have agreed to stay in France, even though it was like living in a sepulchre after his life in Polynesia.

He remained in Lyon for two full weeks, staying at a threadbare hotel that turned his every waking moment into a tangible longing to return to the islands. He shadowed Lilou en famille from school to grocery, from dress store to bakery, day after day. She only returned her mother's stony look.

Eventually Matilde was so exasperated by the gossip his presence caused that she forced Lilou to meet him at a café while she waited outside. This was labeled a major concession, in return for which he agreed to leave.

Up close, Loren could hardly recognize in this gloomy, timid girl the happy child taken from him.

"Titi and Faufau say hello." Nothing. Could she have forgotten? "Why do you refuse to see me?"

She looked into her lap.

"I miss you, Lou."

She stifled a sigh. "Please go away."

"Why?"

She looked up, and there was that old blaze of passion in her eyes, not dead but merely banked to allow her to survive childhood. "You let us go."

"I tried—"

"She believed you would come—"

"Blame your mother."

"I . . . blame . . . you."

After that, Loren left. He went back to the islands, never to return to France. Years later, when Lilou was an adult and Matilde passed away, the last link between them was broken. Until he got the idea of the webcam.

Would Ann find Lilou after he was gone? Tell her that he loved her and had never forgotten?

Ann's specialty at the firm had been her speed at completing an assignment. She was also good at intuiting a client's wishes even if he himself had not stated it outright. With the information Loren had given her, she did a web search for Lilou as soon as she left his *fare*. It was morning in France, and using her sat-phone, she was connected to Lilou's secretary and then was given her home phone. When Ann described the nature of her call, there was silence on the other end.

Finally Lilou said, "That's in the past."

"Understood. I'm the messenger. But I felt you should know now rather than later."

"You made a mistake."

"May I say one thing, personally, not professionally?"

"If you wish."

"Whatever happened, that's done and over. Soon, very soon I'm afraid, he'll be gone. He's one of a kind. A special man. You're a young woman, but I have a little more experience." Ann sighed. "At the end, it's the things we neglected to do, rather than the failures, that haunt us."

"You were kind to call." The line went dead.

By the third and last day of the ceremony, everyone on the island was in a state of perpetual hangover. The morning went by quietly with a breakfast setup of pancakes and fruit for two hundred and fifty, prepared by Javi.

An interesting shift occurred during the wedding extravaganza— Richard had owned the kitchen.

Although it was packed with Polynesian women doing their traditional dishes, speaking little English, Richard oversaw it all and commanded the place. Not a bowl or spoon, not an ingredient was touched without his okay. When Javi started working, Richard allowed it because the help was needed but only let him do prep. When Javi made one of his own inspirations without permission—a spicy raw fish ceviche—Richard tasted it, declared it excellent, then turned the whole plate over into the trash. The women tittered and shuffled off like a flock of beach sandpipers, averting their eyes. Men bumping noses like sharks. Javi's eyes watered as if he'd been slapped.

"Don't do this to me," he whispered. "You're like my brother."

"A brother whose wife you *fucked*!"

The women hurried out the kitchen door.

After finding out about the affair, Richard in his anxiety-ridden, wide-awake-in-the-middle-of-the-night, deepest, darkest self had to admit that he had suspected, maybe even had known, but said nothing. Why? As much as he had suspected it was happening, he also had sensed when it was over. He had married Ann because he could not imagine spending his life without her. He'd asked Javi to be his best man. It wasn't like he was above wronging those he loved. He'd allowed Ann to sacrifice for *his* dream. He'd ridden Javi's charisma toward success, suspecting that by himself he wasn't enough. What Richard had done these last years was to go into cowardly hiding. Richard had lost Richard, and who in her right mind could love that? He almost didn't blame Ann. Almost.

Cooking on the island had made him see himself with more clarity than he'd had in years. So what if he was a modest man destined for modest success? It wasn't so bad, accepting nongreatness, rejecting the siren song of fame, which required giving up the pleasures of the everyday for the possibility of existing in people's minds. What else was fame other than that? What was this thing called greatness?

Ann kept talking about Captain Cook this, Captain Cook that, from the book she was reading. When he came home to England a hero after two long voyages, his name synonymous with being the greatest explorer in the world, Cook quickly left his comfortable house, his family, and went out again on a third voyage. Richard would have kicked back, moved to the country, and taken up dairy production—come up with a killer sharp Cook Cheddar—and allowed himself to be feted by the minor gentry, agreeing to serve as headpiece at county fairs and the like. What about enjoying Mrs. Cook's company, because surely she was almost a stranger? But Cook didn't do that.

What did Cook think on his final voyage as the wooden boat creaked out into the Thames, the wood bending and pleading in the water, that last dark morning, knowing at best he would not be back for years at best?

Posterity knowing that he would not be back at all. Nope, that wasn't for Richard. There would never be a Richard Island, or Richard Inlet, or even a Richard bridge or school. Or restaurant. He could live with that.

He hated to prepare meat—he admitted it. He also hated deracinating vegetables in the torture known as French technique, and frankly, one of the loveliest things on the face of this beautiful earth was a fresh, medium-crumb yellow cake. He licked his lips. And sabayon. He'd be making a lot more of both in the future.

The resort kitchen had been cleaned, and everyone had left for the concert. Dinner service had gone off like a charm. Richard put the finishing touches on the colossal wedding cake. He was never hungry for what he cooked for others, but always made a private little dish for himself; in the double boiler, he heated up egg yolks, sugar, and red wine, plus his secret ingredient that made it out-of-this-world. The beauty of sabayon was its simplicity and temperament—if one didn't get the exact right temperature and whisk constantly, one ended up with curdled eggs instead of wine froth from the gods. This batch turned out sublime—velvety and perfumed. Richard ate the whole thing out of the pot with a wooden spoon.

Someone once told him it was foolish to love something so temporary, so destined to quickly disappear, as food, and his answer was, *find me the thing to love that will last forever.* He was going out on a limb here, but didn't loving the creation make more sense than loving its mortal creator? All these star chefs—wouldn't their tarte tatins outlast them, one and all?

It broke him up in a thousand ways, but he would leave Ann because it would be impossible to endure her disappointment in him and the man he planned to become.

To Loren's despair, Wende had turned the live cam off again and relocated it to the stage to film the concert. The period of blank screen on the Internet would only increase eagerness, she claimed. The new songs that were being donated—"The White Whale," "One-Eyed Woman," and "Tuamotuan Melody"—were already recorded and ready for purchase and download for 99 cents each online. But before they went live, the wedding cake had to be cut.

The beach was lit by oil lamps and torches, although a very expensive light set was ready once the concert started. Wende had finagled an Australian production company to donate it, hinting at future Down Under tie-ins with Prospero. Now, in the last minutes of firelight, a palm-festooned pallet was carried in and set down in front of Cooked and Titi. On it blazed the most gorgeous creation of Richard's career. At the last minute as it made its way out the door, Richard took Javi's unorthodox (but inspired) suggestion and set the cake ablaze with the long, slender candles left over from Ann's birthday.

The cake was in tiered rectangles like the stone ceremonial platforms on the islands; the base was frosted to resemble a white sand beach, with bits of sugar candy molded into seashells; the upper layers were studded with tropical flowers to form miniature jungles; on top was a thatched *fare* made out of chocolate. Inside, each bite was a treasure of custard and fruit.

"That's your masterwork, bro," Javi said.

"You're right," Richard said, not tempted in the least to be humble. He snapped pictures with a borrowed cell phone for his future bakery's menu.

Cooked cut the first piece with a sword that had been in his clan for more than a hundred and fifty years, traded from the first Europeans to land on their shores, and he fed the cake to Titi. After each piece had been put on its individual plate the pièce de résistance came: a puddle of coconut-milk rum sauce poured over it.

The concert audience, which numbered almost three hundred with press and tech help, was quiet, only a murmur of gluttony and clinking of forks audible. Besides the main cake, there were four more sheet cakes set out to feed everyone.

Ann ate her slice and knew that Richard had reached a place of inner peace.

When he walked behind her seat, accepting compliments like his own kind of rock star, she nodded her head in appreciation.

"This is delicious," she said.

He bent down and took her arm.

"I slept with Wende. When we went out snorkeling? She offered, and I accepted."

Ann left before the concert started.

The rest of the island was as deserted as it had been when they first arrived. The palms were like tall, dark back-scratchers leaning against the sky. She pushed out of her mind the knowledge that she would soon leave this place. Richard was leaving, going back to dismantle their old life. All the things in their house that she had taken such pride in, that she'd been so sure she'd miss—the wire egg baskets and chintz sofa and antique mirrors—the reality was she hadn't given a thought to any of it since she'd been away. The idea of losing things no longer bothered her, but she had never considered that Richard would be among the things gone.

Finding herself in the quiet grove by Loren's *fare*, she decided to hide out on his lanai to watch the stars. As soon as she was seated, she heard a shuffling inside. Thieves? The window covering pulled up.

"Can I buy you a drink?" Loren said.

"Why aren't you at the concert?"

"Why aren't you?"

Ann whimpered.

Loren sighed. "I'll bring the bottle."

When he came out with a lamp, she was startled by the new gauntness in his face—eyes hollowed out, dark circles underneath like he'd given up on sleep altogether.

"How are you?" she said. She had been so caught up in the circus of Wende, Dex, Javi, and Richard she'd forgotten about him.

"I long for this to be over." He grimaced as the alcohol burned the sores in his mouth. He'd been inside, making order of his things.

Ann nodded.

He coughed. "I've been watching viewer hits. The sales numbers. Already this is one of the biggest concerts of its kind. They have done more good here than I did in all these years."

They drank down their absinthe in a single gulp, and he poured another round.

"Accidentally doing good. You made a real commitment."

"Pretty Ann has the saddest face tonight."

"Richard is leaving me."

Loren shook his head. "Male pride. Eventually he will have to accept your apology. Otherwise he will lose too much."

"I'm not the same person I was when I first came here."

"I hope change includes burning that awful brown bathing suit."

"I lost it," she said. "So what are the viewer numbers?"

"Millions and millions." Loren giggled. The giggle turned into a cough.

"We should take you to a hospital."

"We're way past that." He shook his head. "Promise me something."

"Anything."

"They're going to go after Cooked and Titi. You have to help them."

"Where will you be?"

"Finishing business I've neglected."

"Lilou?" Should she save Loren the hopeless trip? No. She was a coward. "I don't know the laws here."

"There's no one else I can trust."

Trust. No one at the firm had ever needed or trusted her. She had been interchangeable.

"I won't leave till it's handled." The idea that her staying could be construed as necessary cheered her up.

The incongruous sound of an electric guitar ramped up and ripped the night apart. Then the sound of the audience screaming and clapping. The concert began, predictably, with "Best of Prospero" hits.

"A few days from now everything will be back to normal," Ann said.

"No," Loren answered. "Everything has changed."

When Ann returned to her *fare*, Javi was sprawled out on the floor of the lanai.

"Nowhere else to sleep," he said.

"Where's Richard?"

"Still signing autographs for his cake. Or hanging with his new pal Dex."

"Why did you tell him?"

"Jesus, he was letting you go get microwaved."

"Dex needed me."

"A worthy replacement. I get it."

"Richard's leaving me."

"Leaving us. No more restaurant. Can you imagine he wants to open a *bakery*?"

She had the nasty feeling one gets when it's obvious that others have moved on without you.

"You two will be together," Javi said unconvincingly. "Do you have an extra pillow I can borrow?"

"I'm going to be a divorced thirty-eight-year-old ex-lawyer."

Javi, as usual, only heard himself. "I don't even blame you guys hanging out here on vacay while I went through hell back in LA. Could you put in a good word for me with Wende? I sense interest."

Ann went inside and slammed the door.

The next morning the wedding guests, tech people, and leftover paparazzi readied themselves to depart. The island was trashed. It would take a week or more to clean it up to its former state. Mounds of garbage had been piled in the back against the palm groves. Debris floated in the water—paper, flowers, rotted food, and the occasional condom. Along the pristine white of the beach were smudges of soot from fires like blackheads across formerly flawless skin.

Again, there was singing and crying, hugs and kisses. The resort guests came down to the beach to wave off their new friends, promising to visit on other islands. Javi already had invitations from a dozen females to other villages, and a lucrative offer to be head chef at a resort in Mooréa.

Cooked, moved by the leave-taking, stood on a rock and blew the conch in good-bye. How could Loren explain that this was not a dignified thing for the new owner of a resort to do? If it wasn't dignified now, why had he been told to do it earlier? Yes, Loren definitely had done his own share of playing big kahuna.

Titi was a whole different story, as women always were. Even though she was the age of his daughters, Titi commanded a maternal authority over Loren. All he ever felt from her was a potent combination of patience, disappointment, and, once in a great while, bad temper. Last he'd seen her earlier that morning, she was ensconced behind a large table in the kitchen, processing applications from almost every single wedding guest. Many of the guests also filled out applications for family, friends, or people to whom they owed a favor. Titi looked tired. No matter who or how many she hired, she would make more unhappy than happy. Chips were being called in: *Remember when I did this for you? For Cooked? For your auntie, cousin, grade-school teacher? Your mother said . . .* She was offered bribes ranging from free food, to junkets to Papeete, to outright cold, hard francs. Titi still had not fathomed the extent to which her life had changed.

When Loren informed her he was taking off for the main resort to talk with Steve, she frowned.

"I need you here." A long line of applicants snaked out the door and around the building. Just like a man to take off when everything was at crisis stage. "We need to hire workers for cleanup. We need to draw up supply lists. I'm thinking we should look into those solar generators someone mentioned. When do we go back to pre-electric conditions? What's our new policy on WiFi?"

"You'll figure it out, Titi."

"At least take your cell phone so I can get hold of you."

Alone, Loren took a large piece of rolled-up paper and made his long, slow way around the island till he reached the camera. It had been put back in its exact spot and resumed its regular scan of the beach. Standing behind it, Loren looked out at the view that had so hypnotized him long ago, and found that, unlike him, it had not diminished a bit from its former glory. He stepped forward in front of the camera for the first time. Anathema to his aesthetic that an artist appear in his own work, but finally emotion and human need must outweigh art. While he knew there was sound available, in his imagination this was strictly a silent film act. So often the restrictions of art come from within the creator rather than from the outside world. This was simply the only way he could do it. He unrolled the paper and held it up across his chest.

> *I'm sorry, Lilou.*
> *Your father loves you.*

They stood on the trash-strewn beach, wilted flowers studding the sand, watching the last group of paparazzi pack up to leave. Loren looked at the small group assembled before him with the delicate sadness one reserved for children one was hiding a terrible truth from, but the terribleness was all reserved for him: these people, recent strangers, sudden family, would be his last guests. He already felt the nostalgia of their departure and his own.

"I'm going to hitch a ride to the main resort," he said. "I've got business with Steve about the new boat."

Everyone nodded and moved off, preoccupied with plans of leaving. None of them had slept much in days; most were contemplating taking naps for the rest of the afternoon.

Still, Ann hung back as Richard left for their *fare*, and Javi chased Wende to the kitchen.

"What?" Loren said. He'd packed a small bag with his mask and flippers.

"Maybe I'll come along?"

"No."

She smiled uneasily, studying him.

"Do you want me to bring back something for you?" he asked.

"Yourself." She kissed his cheek. "Bring yourself."

"Our time together has been special."

Ann was crying. "No. Yes. No."

She had been monitoring viewer numbers from the concert and was idly watching the regular day's broadcast (thinking with a heavy heart of when she would be watching it from back home) when Loren walked on camera and held up his sign. What were the chances that Lilou would be watching for that scant thirty seconds? The sight of his desperation undid her. Quickly Ann hit the record button. Maybe she would send the clip to Lilou? Maybe the direct message would accomplish what she herself could not?

He got the dive boat from Steve with the promise to return it in the late afternoon. The story that they were underequipped after the festivities was a plausible enough one. If there was one bit of unfinished business, it was Steve, and Loren briefly considered sinking the boat in revenge, but he didn't. It was important to be bigger than that in the end.

Midafternoon he had just rounded the north end of Kokovoko Island, approaching his favorite diving spot in all the Tuamotus: the Great Shark Wall.

The great howling silence had started with Bette's death and never came to an end. A monolithic silence, inescapable, it became the most permanent thing in his life. The cliché was a lie—time did not heal; it just swallowed other things into itself. He could laugh at a joke, or flirt with a pretty woman, or gaze at a sunset, and suddenly the loss would come down on him like a hammer blow. One day, one week, one month, year, decade—it made no difference. It was as painfully raw as yesterday. He admired but did not trust those who moved on, remained unchanged, stayed optimistic. Unkindly, he judged they had simply not loved enough. Maybe it was a French thing.

Solitude poured over him like balm, as naturally as if this had been the only life he'd ever known. As if he had been a fisherman, which in a way he had been, but the quarry was far more elusive than anything that could be caught on a hook.

He cut the motor and dropped anchor. The sun beat down like a shiny brass drum, forcing him to the absurdity of putting on a hat and sunglasses. He couldn't stand sun and heat like he used to. He ferreted out the bottle of absinthe at the bottom of his bag, nested like a poisonous green viper in his beach towel.

The first couple of swigs burned his ulcers so badly that his eyes stung, his tongue curled up like a snail touching salt, but as the diabolical spirit worked its magic, he no longer felt pain in his mouth or, eventually, in the rest of his body. No doubt it was the exoticism of absinthe that had drawn Ann, although she couldn't possibly have guessed that it was a seductor's drink. It called out to those who wished to be enchanted. He drank it neat, which was the secret of all true absinthe drinkers—one did not need all the appurtenances. The ritual of the glass, the spoon, the sugar cube, and water was strictly for initiating newcomers. He had not told Ann the whole of the Oscar Wilde quote because there were some truths one wished to keep for oneself.

The boat rocked softly. Emptiness had made him fall in love with the South Pacific. Until then, he had not fully realized the extent of his unease—how he always felt crowded by others jostling him in line, filling his ears with their thoughts. On the islands, he knew himself for the first time—the man who wasn't defined by being father, husband, artist, lover, or even hotelier. The place allowed him to take his own measure. Before, he never had paid much attention to nature other than enjoying the sun on his back while on his way to somewhere important. On the islands, the sun on his back *was* the important thing. Nature exhibited its own personality: the deep serenity of the deserted coral beaches, the shallow dreaminess of the lagoons.

He felt shame at his past years of debauchery, his cavalier attitude to the people who had taken him in as family. Despoiling his own paradise these last years, he had only wanted more tourists, more drink. The first real estate he owned in his whole life, an island won in a poker game, had corrupted him. Was his beautiful *motu* as lethal in its own way as Moruroa? It looked idyllic, one could pretend it was safe, but it poisoned one nonetheless. Maybe Titi was right. Maybe the islands had poisoned him just as much as the young men in his bed.

He was halfway through the bottle and feeling dizzy. He had brought a little food to hold the alcohol down in his stomach. He nibbled roast pork from last night's feast, as well as a few bites of French cheese. They might be brutal colonizers, but if there was one thing his countrymen did right, it was *fromage*. He had saved a piece of the wedding cake for last, washing it down with more absinthe. The cake tasted like the best kind of dream. A man capable of making a cake like that would never leave Ann. He tasted Richard's love for her in it. Other people's love gave him faith in the future, even if it was a future he would not share.

He needed a cool swim, away from the hammering sun. His love of nature had grown in proportion to his hatred of rules and laws. They were man-made, arbitrary, prone to err; they didn't accommodate reality. Nature could do nothing but be itself. Laws had caused him to lose his two girls even though in the end it was clear he would have been the best parent. Rules led to Bette's death. The bureaucrats cleaned their hands of it. *Tant pis.* A sad incident. The death of one little girl didn't matter as long as no one would be blamed. Loren preferred the regal impartiality of nature.

Unfortunately, even Polynesia was not immune—Cooked and Titi's clan, the people on the other islands, lied to and poisoned and ignored. Where were the laws to protect them? Loren might not have been the most exemplary of men, he had tried to do right and failed, but at least he never knowingly did harm. Never profited from it. He only insisted on being free. The prospect of a hospital room loomed like a jail cell. His last will and testament was to live out his life on his own terms.

He was about to throw the almost empty bottle of absinthe overboard when his cell phone rang.

Unbelievable.

He'd brought it along at Titi's insistence, not wanting to raise suspicion, and then had forgotten it. The siren song of technology—he could *not* not look at caller ID: Titi. Absolutely not. His voice would give him away. He shut the phone off. But even so the interruption had its effect.

He felt lonely where before he had felt at one with the universe. Maybe he should just head back?

He sat miserably in his deck chair, swaying. He knew what he had to do, yet he was afraid. The distraction had done just that: distracted.

Like a drug addict taking a last hit, he turned the phone back on and texted Titi:

**I LOVE YOU LIKE A DAUGHTER. NEVER DOUBT THAT.**

After he pressed send, he realized he had in all probability set panic in motion. The text would send off alarms. Ann already suspected something. His time must be measured against possible rescue. As he sat there, the phone rang again.

Doomed, vain, insatiable man that he was, he looked. It was Ann.

A tightness in his throat—he was loved more than he guessed.

Ann, who would have been the kind of woman he might have married in a different life, was easier to disappoint than Titi. He lobbed the phone as far as possible into the ocean.

H e isn't answering." Ann frowned.

They had all been napping when a boat arrived in the lagoon. Sleepy Richard and Ann came out of the *fare* and shaded their eyes to see what was causing the commotion. Steve, the manager of the resort, piloted in with a woman passenger in sunglasses and a large hat. Unlike Ann weeks ago, this woman still managed to be stylish after the long, windblown ride across the lagoon. She had to be French. Then Ann knew.

Titi came out of the kitchen, wiping her hands on a dishrag, displeased. They would have to set up a system for reservations, no constant drop-ins like this. The resort was still a mess, and they were not open to the public beyond the public that now considered itself private. Why hadn't Loren explained this to Steve? As Titi dialed Loren again, she read the text that had just come in from him, then immediately hit the call button. Instead of ringing, his phone went straight to voice mail.

"Titi!" the woman yelled as she stumbled from the boat so that Steve had to leap out to help her. She glided through the knee-high water, oblivious of her hem, which was getting soaked. In her yellow summer dress, the scene looked like something out of a movie.

Titi stopped as if she had seen a ghost. "Lilou," she said. "You've come home."

Loren was profoundly drunk and starting to feel sentimental about all he was leaving behind. He also had to piss. Maybe he'd just head back and put off the inevitable a while longer. What would be the harm? But when he lowered his bathing trunks to urinate over the side of the boat, the purplish bruises, the swollen lumps along the groin, shocked him again in all their goriness, their insistent mockery of his mortality. He had been handsome once. Desired. What would happen when he was no longer fit enough to do himself in? He didn't want to burden Titi. He refused to be warehoused with the doomed in a hospice. Was it too much to want to be remembered as a man of dignity?

He jumped over the side of the boat and adjusted the valves on his scuba tank regulator. This was his favorite location in the archipelago for diving—a reef shelf that extended from the island and then dropped off more than four thousand feet at an ocean wall. One could glide along the sandy bottom, forty feet from the surface, feeling snug and protected, and then swim to the edge and look down into the great abyss as if falling into the night sky. Looking into the far depths was like trying to see the center of the universe—an unyielding, lonely, liquid deep space.

The first time Loren had gone swimming in the lagoon, he had opened his eyes underwater and been shocked at its otherworldly beauty. In France he had watched diving on television and thought it amounted to nothing more than swimming around in a big aquarium, but when one experienced it firsthand, the effect was indescribably moving. A world independent of what went on above water—great schools of fish passed by oblivious to his human presence. Life teemed, each animal with its unique place, and none of it dependent on man, except of course on his noninterference.

In his early years in Polynesia, Loren, like any eager novitiate, swam every spare moment he had. He bought books identifying each coral, each fish. He got certified in scuba as a way to make a living off tourists. Scuba charters were part of most resorts' services. Snorkeling was child's play compared with the thrill of going deeper in the lagoon or the ocean beyond the reefs. Eventually one graduated to the thrill of the drift dives at Tiputa and Aratoru—speeding along on strong ocean currents, going in or out of the lagoon passes. It resembled rush hour in some inexplicable foreign city—a group of a hundred or more gray reef sharks, pods of humpback whales, carpets of eagle rays, clouds of Napoleon fish and grouper. Then there was the ultimate, deep-water diving. During those moments, he found he did not feel so alone, did not ache with loss.

Afterward one returned to the surface changed, less impressed with the goings-on above water. For a while, Loren walked around filled with this secret knowledge as if he had discovered a key to the universe. He could explain it in no other way than that the world seemed more vast and magical underwater.

But then, as happened to so many mystics, the worldly distracted him. He had been strong and happy while caring for the girls, but once they were gone, he couldn't muster the same faith. He was susceptible to temptation. Even though it was so wonderful down below, what could it matter with the atrocities that happened above the water? If a divine intelligence seemed in evidence underwater, how did it disappear to nullity in the affairs of mankind? The stories of radioactivity on various atolls, the poisoning of lagoons, the drifting fallout made him despair at the impossibility of true escape. His underwater universe was sadly not immune after all.

Now Loren swam along the reef shelf as if revisiting a long-lost neighborhood, nodding in pleasure at its familiar sights. The sunlight penetrated the water so thoroughly that he could almost imagine he was swimming through air. He loved how the ocean cupped his eardrums, silencing the world down to the percussion of his own heart, the beats the sound of the ocean's own pulsing life. He paused at the edge of the Shark Wall and looked out over the great wilderness of water. Tears stung at the spectacle, but tears were good. They added their salt to the ocean. From salt and back to salt. A miracle that this existed, and he felt blessed to have derived solace from it. He hoped against hope that the madness above the water would stop in time to preserve this for Lilou, Lilou's children, for Titi's children and grandchildren, for all the children of the children of the children . . .

Loren upped the pressure in his tanks and swam off the edge of the reef, diving down, headfirst, in a kind of reverse flight. A form appeared next to him, swam alongside—one of the dolphins that were found only in this area. A comforting presence, like having an angel beside him. In fact, this was the perfect companion for Loren. He looked up in adieu at the faraway surface of the water—the sun a murky smudge whose glory was unimaginable at these depths.

It was known as *"l'ivresse des grandes profondeurs,"* or "rapture of the deep." People forgot that Loren had advanced Trimix certification for depth dives. He knew the effects of narcosis at different levels. Playing along the bottom of the reef shelf at forty feet, his anxiety left him. He looked at the parrot fish munching on coral, the sound crunching in his ears like turning gravel. Manta rays hummed through the water like bees. The absinthe whispered in his ear that Titi and Cooked would manage for themselves quite well. At one hundred feet down, already there was the relaxation comparable to a glass of wine, except Loren had pretty much finished off the bottle of absinthe, and so the effect was accelerated and intensified. Gravity took over, and he no longer had to exert himself to continue down. A miracle he hadn't already passed out. He wished he could have a last taste of the green fairy now; drink was his closest companion these last years. As he accelerated down the wall, approaching one hundred and fifty feet, a silliness overtook him. He had to suck in oxygen to keep from laughing at the dolphin that even now swam at his side, not more than five feet separating them. Around two hundred feet down, Loren's air bubbles started to make a funny tinkling sound like high-pitched glass bells. A pelagic music of the spheres. Past two hundred and fifty feet, it began to grow darker, cooler. Life here existed in a perpetual twilight; the sea life had larger gills, moved less to conserve energy. He was surprised that the dolphin had stayed with him to this depth. He imagined his own skin turning gray and rubbery as his companion's. She was an attractive one. Somehow Loren intuited she was female. He imagined morphing into her mate. Side by side they would swim through the islands, having baby dolphins and playing up to tourists. Not a bad life. Possibly a beautiful life. His own movements became slower now, even though his mind raced. Every problem he thought of seemed capable of immediate solution under the laser of his expanded attention. It seemed entirely within the realm of possibility that if he surfaced he could negotiate immediate world peace. He considered taking off his mouthpiece, just for a moment, and asking the dolphin's thoughts on Lilou . . . He did not . . . Past three hundred feet, the pressure of the water began to exert itself, as if forcing him to occupy a smaller place than his body could naturally accommodate. His ribs hurt as if the stays of a corset were being tightened around him. It felt as if the blood in his veins had become effervescent. Only once before had he attempted that depth . . . The she dolphin drifted away . . . breaking his heart. He cried, but no tears came out. Probably twenty feet separated them. The dolphin was circling and pointing upward with her wandlike snout. Pointing toward light and life; fish, squid, and shrimp for all. How could he say it any other way? She was sexy. Large aquatic eyes like liquid mercury. Was it creepy to be attracted to a fish? Loren wasn't imagining it—the she dolphin was clearly disappointed in him. He knew female censure when he saw it. Perhaps she had thought they were playing a game, going on an adventure, and now she felt duped. She was going Catholic on him.

The capriciousness of revelation.

Past three hundred and fifty feet, the waters grew brighter and sunny again. Loren felt that this proved something he had always guessed, but then, in the next moment, he forgot what it was. The cold steel bodies of sharks passed, singly, like undertakers. A ribbon of yellow uncurled itself toward him like a beckoning hand. It was warm and translucent and inviting. He swam toward it as it teasingly moved away. Another tendril beckoned in pink. Then green. A deconstructed rainbow was winding itself around him like a cocoon of light. The she dolphin poked him from behind, sending Loren spinning in slow-motion through the water—arms and legs out like a tumbling blue starfish—when a thirty-foot shark turned ponderously in his direction. *May I help you?* Loren, the reticent aquanaut. The she dolphin grew agitated now. She kept nudging Loren and going away and up. Finally Loren grew irritated and slapped her side as she passed yet again. She nodded her pretty, rubbery head in hurt comprehension, and then, with a powerful flex of her muscled body like a final arch of passion, she sped upward with a good-bye flutter of her comely tail. Loren was bereft. His final chance of happiness had just swum away. The tendrils of light no longer enticed him. Their beauty was frightening, cold. It pained the artist in him that evil should hide in such splendorous guise. At his nonattention the tendrils grew faint and then went dark entirely. A truly sinister shark decided to take up new residence at Loren's side. His skin a black that sucked all remaining light. So be it. Loren shuddered out of his flippers. He almost passed out with the exertion of taking off the straps of his oxygen tank. He drank in a last sweet, deep sip of air as delicious as the fairy in its rarity and then spit out the mouthpiece. He held the tank aloft for a moment and then let it go. It was sucked downward as if by a magnet. Unable to bear the cruel face of his new companion, Loren removed his mask. Everything blossomed into a blinding white light as he took that first inhalation of sea, that first bid at a new, fishy incarnation.

So where's Loren?" Steve asked after he'd tied up the boat.

"At your hotel. Didn't you talk to him?" Titi said.

"He came this morning and took a boat for a charter. He didn't bring it back."

Titi walked away without a word.

Lilou looked back and forth between the two.

"Thank you for coming," Ann said, stepping up to her. "I'm the one who contacted you."

The men decided to break up and hit separate dive destinations to save time. Cooked and Richard would cover a private spot that was Loren's favorite.

"We'll be in touch by radio."

Dex and Javi went with Steve in the hotel boat, hitting the places one took tourists in case Loren's alibi was true and he was simply in distress. Or drunk. Or some unholy combination of the two.

Once they were gone, Titi melted down on the sand. Lilou had gone to rest, kept in ignorance of what was happening.

"What is it?" Ann asked. "What do you know?"

Titi shook her head. "I feel it in my bones. An emptiness where he should be."

As fanciful as this explanation was, Ann knew it was the right one. She had sensed something was wrong when he left. There was the mystery of his appearance on camera, but how could she have prevented his departure? If she had succeeded this one afternoon, what about all the others that would follow? As much as it pained her, she knew it was Loren's right. She sat down next to Titi and took the girl in her arms.

The hotel boat was anchored where Cooked had guessed it would be. Of course there was no evidence on the boat of Loren's fate, nothing as prosaic as a note left behind, but the final intention was beyond doubt. Cooked had liked Loren but never could bring himself to really trust foreigners. He thought in the end they would always go home. This time he was proved wrong. It moved him that Loren had made *te fenua* his final resting place. To die in the ocean made him one of them at last. The Frenchman's death frightened him. He was not ready to take on the mantle of leader, even of this small place, but he accepted that one never was prepared. It was like being born—you were pushed out into the world.

Cooked stood up in the boat and said a prayer over the water, while Richard looked down into the waves, praying Loren would pop up at any minute, as if this might still be an elaborate gag. Richard was suffering the naïve but common belief that nothing bad could happen on vacation, that the ordinary realities of life were somehow suspended. The rocking of the boat had set off a rocking in his stomach that Richard recognized as the beginning of seasickness. Despite himself, even in the hot sun, his teeth chattered. Cooked yanked the shell necklace off his neck, breaking the thread and unstringing the pieces into his palm. He threw bits in all four directions while he said another prayer.

Richard looked down, blinked, looked harder.

In the depths of the ocean there seemed to be a milky swirling, like an underwater tornado. Richard was light-headed. He distinctly felt the possibility that he might pass out. He looked up at the sky to get his bearings.

When he looked down again, the milky shape had risen and was now much closer to the surface so that he could make out distinct shapes.

"Are those . . . ?"

Cooked glanced down. "Sharks."

Now Richard was sure he would throw up.

Thirty feet below the boat, the water was filled with the galaxy-like swirl of hundreds of sharks. They made a large lazy loop with the boat as their epicenter. The water churned as some darted up closer to the surface, a few even breaking above to snatch at the air.

"What are they doing?" Richard whispered, as if he might be overheard.

"Our people believe that the souls of our ancestors inhabit the sharks. *Aumakua.* They are protecting us. Or welcoming Loren. He was one of us, I think."

"I'm going to puke."

Titi's immediate family, Faufau and thirty others, turned around and came back to the island for the funeral. Loren had not been a great benefactor to their village, he'd caused problems and love in equal proportion, but he had been family. The mourning was personal. Once everyone had gathered, they filled a canoe with dried bundles of cane, set it on fire, and pushed it out to sea. One of the elder uncles said a prayer:

*You shall mount upward*
*You shall soar on high*
*You are Above*
*You are Below . . .*

Ann stood on the beach, leaning on a long stick, and watched the boat make its fiery exit. The vessel stalled in the middle of the lagoon as it burned. She dragged the stick through the wet sand and made an enormous

to send off her friend.

Once the fiery funereal boat was mostly burned up, the mourners turned their backs to the sea and went to eat their sad feast. It surprised everyone when Steve stayed after the ceremony. They had not guessed at this unexpected display of feeling. Some of the kinder names Loren called him had been "*pute*," "*gros con*," "*fils de salope*." As the mourners sat and reminisced, Steve sidled over to Lilou.

"As the only blood relative, are you going to make a claim on the resort?" he asked. "If so, we can help."

Lilou looked at him through thick wet lashes. Although she was quite beautiful, her disdainful expression was all Loren.

*"Tu es un vrai connard!"*

"I see." Steve nodded, moved on to Titi, who was sitting with Faufau and Ann. "Loren certainly left you in a bind."

Titi looked through him as if he were a ghost.

Undeterred, Steve continued. "Corporate has okayed me offering you a check for the value that is here. Let me tell you, I had to twist arms to even get this. Poorly maintained grass shacks, outdated kitchen equipment, old generator—but corporate wants to keep the Atoll Sauvage in the family, so to speak. You and Cooked can keep your jobs, too. With a nifty little raise. I'm thinking of coming over myself to replace Loren as manager. Whip this place into tip-top shape."

"You could never replace Loren," Titi said.

"This isn't an appropriate time," Ann said.

Steve blinked, unaware that Ann had been listening. "And you are—?"

"The attorney for the new . . ."

"Mara 'amu," Titi whispered.

The old legends told that when the devil came, he would not be scary but would come disguised as a beautiful women or a handsome man. This Steve didn't qualify as either, but he also didn't have a tail.

"The Mara 'amu Resort," Ann repeated.

Steve smacked his lips. "You are a *guest*. This isn't your country, and if I'm not mistaken, you have no right to practice law here."

"Leave Titi alone or twelve of her 'uncles' will escort you back to your boat. A nighttime voyage can be perilous. Sharks."

That night Ann sat up in bed unable to sleep.

"It hurts."

Richard held her in his arms and allowed her to sob on his shirt. He was still her husband, and he could comfort her even if it was over the death of his rival. He stroked her hair.

"Nothing happened between us, in case you're wondering."

"I never thought it did." Of course he had and was relieved to hear the contrary.

"And now Lilou. I feel so bad."

"You cannot be responsible for a dish you did not burn."

Ann sniffled. "Who said that?"

"I did."

After the tears, Richard and Ann lay in bed, side by side, staring at the ceiling. Their suspended bag of money in the rafters was visibly collapsed.

"I miss the copper door, and the tables from the antique-wood place."

"Yeah."

"Do you remember . . . ?" Dangerous territory going down that path but she continued. "That restaurant in Portugal?"

"The fish stew."

"The candles in those pewter holders with the punched-out holes."

"The walls turned out nicely," Richard said. "I was against red, but you were right."

"Rome was right."

"I did learn how to make the deep-fried zucchini blossoms."

"I miss *us*."

"I lied about Wende."

"I deserved it."

How was it, Ann wondered, that everything that seemed to matter so much ended up mattering not at all?

The next morning, Lilou asked Ann to help her clear Loren's hut. It wasn't until Ann saw the rumpled sheets on the sleigh bed, the pile of books still to be read beside it, that she broke down. In three weeks, Loren had made a deeper impression on her than people she had known a lifetime.

Lilou's eyes grew big when she saw the watercolors on the door. "Whose are those?"

"Loren's."

"He painted?"

"He was an artist," Ann corrected.

"My father owned an antique shop in Lyon."

"He did installations. Avant-garde stuff. The video recorders? The Cow?!"

"Not that I knew."

"He had another life after he left your mother," Ann said.

This woman had no idea who her father was. Opening the door to the computer room, Ann waved her in and turned on the monitor. There on the screen was the beach outside. "Did you know about this?"

"What is it?"

"For you. Before we commandeered it."

She was grateful Loren had never found out that the communion with Lilou he had felt for years through the live cam was false.

"Who would this appeal to?" Lilou asked.

"He hoped you."

Lilou sat down and stared at the screen. "After what happened to Bette, I never heard from him. I wrote him letters. He never answered."

"He tried to see you."

Lilou closed her eyes. "I need a drink."

Ann went to the chest—the last two of Loren's bottles made a thin, dusty line. She would never drink absinthe again after this day. She poured it into the special bell-shaped glasses, laid the slotted spoon with a sugar cube across, then added water.

"I didn't think anyone drank this anymore," Lilou said, wrinkling her nose at the first taste.

"He called it the green fairy. I have something to show you."

She pressed play on the computer. The sight of Loren, even this sad and disheveled version, holding his sign, was a relief.

Lilou cried, sinking down to the floor, curled up into the little girl he had left.

"A part of me waited for him to come back and make things right, even though I knew better."

"I'm sorry."

Lilou sighed. "After a while, it was less painful to tell people I had no father. Then it became true."

"So why did you come?"

"You. I thought if someone cared enough about him to find me, he must not be all bad."

Titi appeared at the door. She moved around the room uneasily. Clearly their presence was an intrusion.

"Would you like a glass?" Ann asked.

"I don't drink." Titi wiped her eyes.

Ann kept pouring alcohol as they packed things away, skipping first the sugar, then the water, until they were taking it straight like pros.

Loren had left remarkably little behind, they discovered, as they went through drawers and cabinets.

"Why did he never answer my letters?" Lilou said, slurring her words.

Titi retrieved a shell that they had thrown away. "He found this years ago when we went on a picnic. I want it."

"You were good to him," Lilou said, and laid a sloppy arm across Titi's shoulders.

In a drawer, Ann found her brown bathing suit. *That devil.* She smiled, quickly balled it up and stuck it into her bag.

Titi found a crude grass skirt. "He kept that! He made it to give me dance lessons. It wasn't working so he hired a . . ."

"Dancer?"

Titi flushed.

"A prostitute," Lilou guessed.

"She danced really good. I won the contest."

All three were sitting on the floor, the packing forgotten, when Wende knocked.

"Where did everyone go?"

"We're just . . ."

"We have turned this into a wake," Lilou announced.

She regretted her decision to come, odd man out in the life of this stranger, who happened to be her father.

"Can I have a sip?" Wende asked.

An hour later, Wende was cradling a stone statue from Loren's desk. "It made me angry. Windy, he called me, no matter how I corrected him."

The other three were laughing, knowing that Loren had found it funny.

"One night Dex and I were fighting. He found me chilling out in the kitchen. He was so kind, so different when we were alone. He said, 'You should be like my daughter.'"

"He didn't," Lilou said.

Ann closed her eyes.

"I didn't even know he had a daughter," Wende continued. "He said she had a hard time growing up, but never let it set her back."

"How did he know?" Lilou put her face in her hands.

"He said, 'Make your own life. Don't let others do it for you.'"

Instead of their intended target, the words were affecting Titi.

"I read your letters, then burned them," she burst out to Lilou. "He never knew."

The three other women stared at her in astonishment.

"Why?" Lilou asked.

"I was afraid he'd leave. I thought he wouldn't love me anymore when he had his own real daughter back."

Lilou's face was unreadable. The whole nature of the last twenty years of her life recast in an instant.

"Thank you for being brave enough to tell me now," she said finally.

Each women gathered a keepsake. Ann already had the shark rattle, but she took Loren's red pareu. Lilou had gathered all the watercolors off the wall for herself, and Ann stared longingly at the pile, not wanting to take anything from someone who had already lost so much.

Titi whispered to Ann, "I have something else for you."

The men sat on the beach. Richard stared out at the innocuous waves as if they were obfuscating the fact that they could swallow up a person whole. His infatuation with snorkeling and diving was gone; he would never go underwater again. His recent experiences were irretrievably now forced into nostalgia. He would never forget Loren; literally, he was unable to stop imagining his floating, sunken body. Pure tragedy, both what Loren had done and what he'd missed by mere hours—seeing Lilou. Perhaps she would have changed his mind. Okay, Richard was being a little sanctimonious. He hadn't really gotten to know the guy very well, other than being jealous of Ann's affection for him, but now he felt embarrassed for his pettiness.

Dex came and clapped him on the shoulder. They clinked beer bottles. "Rough one, huh?"

"I can't believe how."

Robby yelled from down the beach, "BBC wants an interview in half an hour," then went back to his cell phone.

Richard did not like Robby, who treated the rest of them like nobodies, which they were in the rock world, but still. A man had died. Show some respect.

"I've known a lot of guys who died young. Best thing is to move on," Dex said.

"It makes you think, though, doesn't it?"

Actually it didn't. Ever since the ship incident, Dex had been flying high. It was always great to volunteer oneself and then not have to actually bite the bullet. Take that, Grim Reaper. Personally he thought Loren should have stuck it out, but who was he to judge another man's pain? The measure of a man's happiness in life was unknowable to others. We have to go on faith.

Richard looked over his shoulder, making sure no one was within earshot.

"Ann cheated on me."

"Yup."

"You knew?"

Dex emptied his beer and opened another. "It isn't a game changer, is it? She's amazing. I'd forgive her anything."

"I wouldn't forgive Robby. I don't like him."

"I don't like Javi, but these are the people in our lives. The rough edges that make us smooth. Were you the perfect husband?"

"Only in the kitchen."

"And me onstage. Thank God they put up with us the rest of the time."

I want another drink," Lilou said. Wende and Titi had left. When Ann went to the chest, she saw it was the last bottle and hesitated. Loren wouldn't have tolerated sentimentality; he would want the precious juice to be used up in style, especially by his daughter. After pouring, the women stared into the liquid as if it were a crystal ball.

"Loren told me this quote by Oscar Wilde," Ann said. "'After the first glass, you see things as you wish they were. After the second, you see things as they are not.'"

"What about the rest?" Lilou asked.

"Rest?"

Lilou finished it: "'Finally, you see things as they really are, and that is the most horrible thing in the world.' He used that even when I was a little girl. He learned it from my uncle."

And like that, she took back possession of her father.

"Titi tells me you two were close. Was he happy at least? Did he have happiness in his life at the end?"

"For some reason . . . we understood each other. There was sadness in him, that's true, but I also sensed joy. I did."

"My mother threatened that without her, we'd be made wards of the state. Even after she was gone, I didn't try to contact him."

"Why?"

"I couldn't accept him as he was. I wanted a different father, one like all my friends had. His lifestyle . . . I never knew what he gave up for us. That he was an artist. That would have changed everything."

Ann remained silent.

"At least I have the video, thanks to you. Maybe I'll try to find some of his installations. They must have taken pictures and done catalogs. Resurrect his name? To honor him."

"I don't think it mattered to him anymore."

"But it does to me," Lilou said. "It makes me proud to be his daughter."

Dex and Robby walked in.

"Whoa! A harem," Robby joked. He was the hustler of the band, the one who always had a one-liner ready. He winked at Lilou. "Do we have Skype?"

"Skype?" Ann repeated. Somehow, in the absinthe-soaked recesses of her brain, it made sense that Loren might be reachable via Skype.

"Why?" Wende asked. She had been following Robby to find out what he was up to. In the past, she had fought him mightily over Dex. She didn't appreciate being demoted to her old role.

"I lined up an interview on BBC News. Is that all right by you?"

"Let me set up."

Dex and Robby crowded in front of the monitor in the office and did their interview. Dex described how he had discovered himself on the island, how it had been a period of deep self-reflection (Wende jabbed Ann in the ribs at that one). He was done with rock 'n' roll for its own sake. All their future work would be tied to activism.

"We don't think we're the center of the universe anymore," Robby said deadpan into the camera.

They were leaving the islands to go back to LA and record a new album.

"But we will have an ongoing interest in the issue of reparations in Polynesia," Robby added. "These people are family."

Which they weren't, especially not for Robby, who had been there for all of forty-eight hours and kept giving his laundry to Titi and Cooked whenever he saw either one.

"We are dedicating the album to our dear friend Loren, who lost his battle yesterday," Dex said.

"Yes, to Loren," Robby said, despite the fact he had barely known him.

Ann felt disloyal sitting with Wende and Lilou on Loren's bed, listening to the broadcast. It felt smarmy, no getting around it, his death being broadcast around the world.

"He shouldn't have mentioned Loren," Ann mumbled.

"There are people who would dirty Loren's memory. Dex gold-plated him. It was a generous move," Wende, astute spin doctor, said.

Ann flinched. The sad truth was that in the modern world packaging mattered more than message, and her little Machiavellian protégée understood and accepted this in a way Ann could not.

None of those closest to Loren had known the entire man. It came down to Dex, an almost stranger, to give Loren a flash of immortality, all the while positioning himself as some kind of humanitarian. Savvy Wende was right—it would be impossible to stay within Dex's orbit without one's life becoming grist for his fame.

The guys wrapped up and came out of the office. Robby stuck out his hand to Lilou.

"Can I buy you a drink? I'd love to hear more about your father. He sounds like a visionary."

Lilou laughed, her expression of bemusement reminding Ann of Loren.

"Has Dex told you about Jamie?"

"No," Lilou said.

"My sister Jamie is Dex's ex-wife. We're all close here. I feel like we're family already."

Lilou laughed but accepted his invitation.

Life went on, as it should and must, yet it drove a stake into Ann's heart. She was moping. She longed for the spectacular gesture—Loren chopping off part of his finger as in a Greek tragedy. She, who had the least vested interest in the island, who had known Loren the shortest time, wanted some type of closure that seemed unnecessary and redundant to everyone else. They spoke of moving forward, but that was not a solution for her any more than it had been for Loren.

The idea of returning to LA filled her with dread: long lines of traffic, each car filled with a tense soul; high-rises that left deep valleys of shadow in the streets below; her hermetically sealed office with its numbing drifts of paper accumulating in her absence; the gray Brooks Brothers suits of her fellow inmates. She felt in her bones that if she remained a lawyer in that office for enough years—motivated by ambition, or greed, or self-righteousness, or even simple duty or just plain old inertia—some part of her would never *stop* being a lawyer in that office.

Wende got up to leave. "Typical Robby to offer drinks that are free."

"When Dex and you fought, I was the one who comforted you in the kitchen. Not Loren," Ann said.

Wende rubbed Ann's arm hard. "It made Lilou feel better. Where's the harm?"

Wende walked out, but Ann sat, not ready to leave.

"Because it's not what happened," she said to the empty room.

After dinner, there was for once no music. Everyone was busy packing.

Ann felt her time on the island was slipping away. She jumped at the chance to accompany Titi on a mystery journey concerning Loren. They walked in the dark to the dead center of the island, hidden from the beach by thick palms. Titi and Cooked's old *fare* was even more battered and threadbare than Loren's. Why had he not taken better care of them? But in truth he had not even taken proper care of himself.

Titi stopped for a moment on the bottom step of the lanai.

"What's wrong?"

She motioned for silence. After a minute, she smiled.

"Did you hear something?" Ann asked.

"They say it's too early, but I know he is there." She tapped her stomach.

"You're pregnant? How do you know?" Ann pictured some primitive method, a divining through stars or fish bones or something equally mysterious.

"Pregnancy kit."

Ann hugged her.

"When Loren painted, Cooked loved to watch so much that Loren gave him lessons."

Ann wasn't expecting much. Probably amateur pieces of the sort she was so afraid to make. As Titi opened the door and lit a lamp, she put on a prepared face that quickly failed her.

The walls were covered with canvases. Along the baseboard, stretcher-barred canvases were stacked a dozen deep. If one pictured the color-saturated pictures of Gauguin, these were their opposite. Whereas Gauguin had given an exoticized view of his subjects, these paintings were from behind those subjects' eyes—depictions of ordinary village people going about their lives. The originality was in turning the exotic into the mundane. The color was spare, bleached out, as if one was squinting at the scene in noontime sun. The line work was blunt, forceful, almost Japanese in its suggestiveness.

Ann felt a drag in her limbs. These were the real thing, and her recognition of raw genius in another confirmed that she would rather appreciate art than make it. That had been the nagging doubt back in Los Angeles, the antipathy for Flask's dilettantish efforts, the apathy since she had been there. Surprisingly, the realization came as a relief. So *this* was the source of rancor between Loren and Cooked. They were master and pupil, and Loren's artistic legacy would extinguish with his only student squandering his talent. What did revolution matter compared with art?

"Why doesn't he sell these?"

Titi shook her head. "He says it would be no different from selling trinkets to tourists."

"How else will people know about him?"

How could fame not matter? The whole idea of throwing away such talent outraged Ann. It also made her realize that she was as guilty of commodifying as Wende and Dex. She, after all, had been the one with the idea of renaming the website.

"We want to give you this."

It was a small oil painting: mostly white sky, tan beach, a yellowish-green palm tree with a bronzed man resting beneath it. Loren. It was stunning.

"I don't know what to say."

Titi blew out the lamp. "Thank you, I guess."

"Did you ever want to be anything, Titi?"

Titi closed the door, shrugged. "Happy."

Ann went down to the beach to be alone for a few minutes. The alone part was necessary, but so was the idea of someone eventually coming to look for her, and not a search-and-rescue team; it had to be a person who understood her enough to know why she had gone off in the first place. There was a hollowness in her stomach at the thought that the person she most needed to talk to at that moment was Loren. Like a punch to the gut, the obvious: no matter how long she sat there, he was not coming back.

In her old life, she had loved attending art retrospectives. There was a richness in being able to view an artist's oeuvre in a single show, from the newborn mewling of debut works to the death rattle of late ones. One could grasp what was usually ungraspable during the artist's evolution. Perhaps Lilou was right to try to resurrect Loren's name and save him from the oblivion that otherwise would consume his work. Even as Ann thought it, though, she knew Loren would find the whole thing hopelessly bourgeois. Perhaps he wouldn't care that Cooked chose not to paint. Maybe the island, maybe *they* were his retrospective.

Javi was allowed to cook their last meal.

He was totally stoked to try his hand at a Polynesian-Mexican luau featuring the sacrifice of a piglet he'd bought from the Aloha Pearl Resort kids' petting zoo (the Aloha Pearl hotel guests complained that they didn't want their kids stroking their dinners and creating future neuroses).

He had made special arrangements to have the piglet delivered on the supply boat, and had created a temporary pen for it in the center of the island that hopefully would lull it into thinking it had been moved to a new petting zoo rather than a stockyard. Earlier that morning, Cooked and he had taken off for the piglet's pen with a hatchet. The resort had been awakened to bloodcurdling, desperate swine cries. The ensuing silence was even more sinister, but that evening, strangely, instead of pork, a chipotle-basted fish lay on each plate.

"Hey, where's the roasted pig?" Dex asked.

Javi frowned.

Richard sat back in his chair with a twisted smile on his face and downed a copious number of mai tais, along with beer, wine, and champagne. Having Javi around again was like having a slick little brother who was destined to become a used-car salesman. While Javi treated his arrival on the island as the most-favored sibling's return to his rightful place at the center of attention, Richard emphatically did not. He had developed a liking for being the boss and refused to vacate the position. Maybe one kitchen wasn't big enough for the two of them.

Everyone was giddy at the luau, a bittersweet combination of the end of their time together on the island (with all the bathos of end of summer camp) and sadness from the events of the last few days. Of course, Robby, Javi, and even Lilou could not feel the somber absence of Loren at the head of the table as the others did. Cooked was drinking heavily, and Titi teared up and left the table at regular intervals, presumably from grief, although it could also have been from the too-spicy food.

"I put a little Yucatan, habanero spin on the dishes. I found a bag of dried chilies in the kitchen—"

"That I avoided," Richard said.

They had finished a salad of lettuce, garlic, raw onions, and dried chilies in a balsamic vinaigrette and moved on to the basted fish with sides of spinach seasoned with Calabrian red-chili oil and sweet-and-spicy baked yams.

Richard avoided the fish, but ate the rest.

Even as one ghost came to rest, another replaced it. Ever since Loren's death, Richard had started having seafood dreams that were so shameful he could share them with no one, especially not Ann, who would rightly view this as the final straw. Seafood—the last bastion of his cooking repertoire—and he'd gotten pretty inventive on the island. Thirty-six ways with grouper. Opah galore. Mahimahi forever. Tuna any way you want it. But Loren's death and the boat trip with Cooked out to that lonely stretch of water had messed with him.

Loren had told them that the early European explorers refused to eat shark because of its man-eating reputation—it would be akin to cannibalism once removed.

Richard *knew*; he'd been down there, had witnessed the sublime, mechanized violence of the ocean as eating machine. He could totally imagine it because every diver came up against the temptation eventually . . . It just seemed so natural, like a child believing he could fly after seeing birds in flight. Down below, surrounded, outnumbered by fish, one felt shackled by the mask, with its blinkered tunnel vision; the hissing, heavy tanks; the clumsy rubber flippers—all of it a barrier to being at one with the ocean. No wonder mermaids were invented; that's what you fantasized being—breathing water in and out, having a fish tail, seemed marvelous possibilities that were in reach. Poor Loren had wanted to trade in his failing, aching body for that, and it made some kind of crazy logic, although Richard would never admit that. Officially, it was a Tragedy. Officially, Loren had drowned (and the fanciful wish that he'd metamorphosed into a merman was not even capable of being uttered, no). But if Loren had drowned, and if his body floated down and down into that all-encompassing darkness, well, the ocean was an efficient undertaker, and the fish would have done their biological duty toward him. By now Loren would have literally become part of the ocean he loved so much, and there was *no way in hell* that Richard was eating any freshly caught fish.

A t the table, Titi was back but Lilou excused herself. Dex downed glass after glass of water to get rid of the burn; giving up, he tapped his knife against a glass.

"I'd like to make a toast. To Titi and Cooked. You guys have been so cool about everything. We've shared the whole life cycle from marriage to death with you. We're leaving you tomorrow but not leaving you at all. I will be back plenty. My accountants will be helping with the concert money raised. Your input will say where every dime is spent."

Robby grabbed at his stomach and left.

Cooked belched but seemed otherwise unfazed. "Can I have another helping of fish?"

"I shouldn't have," Titi said, and again she left.

"Hey, it's okay. Let your emotions hang out. We all miss our friend," Dex called after her.

Javi came out of the kitchen. He grabbed a beer and raised it. "Should we announce?"

"Yeah," Dex said. "Absolutely. So Javi's been filling me in, and I'm ready to be a silent investor in the new El Gusano."

"What?" Ann said.

"What's this about?" Richard slapped his chair down flat from its cocked position, ready to fly at Javi's throat.

"I told him what happened, bro."

"You had no right." Was it the fact that Javi had shamed him, or jealousy that he was stealing Richard's new guy friend?

Dex held up his hands in his new role as peacemaker. "Dudes. This is good. Just being on this island, all that's happened, has made me more money than if I'd been out on tour. I want to share some of that good fortune. Sprinkle a little fairy dust around for my friends."

"We won't accept," Richard said.

"Look, no hard feelings, but Javi screwed you over. He *is* the worm. But I can fix it. All I ask is for free food and a table when I'm in town. I like the idea of being in business together."

"It fixes things between us," Javi said.

Titi had returned and drank down a glass of water in one gulp.

Richard looked at Ann.

Ann . . . had no one to look at. She felt ambushed. All the things she'd already written off as not worth having were now within her grasp again. Richard obviously thought that this would put things right between them. Did it mean that he'd also forgiven her?

"We can go back and take up where we left off," Richard said. "But better."

"To El Gusano," Javi cheered and raised his bottle.

Wende got up abruptly. "Excuse me." She left at a half trot.

Robby had returned but didn't look well.

"Sorry." Titi was breaking out in a sweat and disappeared again. Then it was Ann's turn to leave, the sensation of a wave rolling through her stomach.

"Oh God." Dex ran.

Confirmed. The food had given them painful, acid-spewing stomachaches. Horrendous gas. Instead of enjoying their last night talking or playing music, they spent it spread out across the resort, roosting atop each available toilet. In desperation, Titi tried drinking coconut milk, which helped. She loaded up a tray with glasses and toured all the island's bathrooms.

Richard sat for long hours on the toilet in one of the unused *fares* as if he were doing penance, each hot, spitting explosion of spice in his gut punishment for his past inaction. These last weeks on the island that had supposedly been all about Ann had in actuality healed him. He discovered a man inside who was almost DOA, but still alive enough to be resurrected. Cooking on his own, he had rediscovered his joy, which had gotten buried underneath Javi during all those years.

Richard had changed. Hadn't he announced that he was going back to open a bakery?

So what happened to this new Richard when Javi reappeared? When he announced he'd fixed his messes, that Dex was bailing them out, that things could go back on track to where they had been before they fled Los Angeles? What had the new Richard done? Collapsed like a badly whipped soufflé. Become a yes-man. Proved beyond a shadow of a doubt that all his changes were illusory.

Javi had already been on the islands for a week vacationing in Mooréa and Bora-Bora on money he'd borrowed from Lorna. He'd been hustling a job as executive chef at the Aloha Pearl, just in case, when he saw the Crusoe cam and decided he'd better hightail it over. On top of everything, he'd gotten buddy-buddy with Dex, but Dex was Richard's friend (he sounded like a pathetic six-year-old). And then Javi made moves on Wende, not to mention in the far past he'd had an affair with Ann. Why didn't Richard just punch him out?

But the pinnacle of Richard's self-loathing was connected to the pink, hairless piglet that Javi had bought, yanking him out of the supply boat and draping the little fellow over his shoulders like some pillaging Viking. Richard wasn't a child, Richard knew the porcine score, but he had turned a blind eye *once again*. With everything else happening—the wedding, Loren, and Ann—it was easy to shove to the back of his mind the image of the cute little guy in his pen, plowing through the piles of scraps coming out of the kitchen, an animated, curly-tailed garbage disposal. Richard lied to himself that the piglet was a kind of pet, that at the right moment he would be set free. Right. On a barren *motu*, surrounded by carnivorous, luau-obsessed Polynesians, owned by the reckless, heartless Javi, that piglet didn't have a swine's chance in hell, unless it had a protector. If ever fate arranged a stage for a man to stand up for what he believed in, this was it, Richard was that protector, yet he had *almost* done nothing.

That morning they had been awoken from their hangovers by terrified squeals. Richard broke out in a sweat at the childlike screams of the restrained piglet. He knew what was about to happen; in fact he was imagining it in far more vivid, 3-D detail than he would see if he were watching the actual butchering. It was no different for him than listening to a grisly murder taking place, but he did not have the courage to jump out of bed and run to stop it. He worried about making a fool of himself. When at long last the air was still, the silence was trebly damning.

And then it happened. As if spirits had entered him and given him the strength he longed for but always fell short of, he jumped out of bed, startling Ann. He ran in his underwear to the location of the pen. He saw the piglet tied down to a rock slab; Javi stood above him with a hatchet.

"Don't you dare touch that pig!"

Richard didn't care any longer if he looked like a fool as long as he knew he wasn't a coward.

As Javi made the entire non-piglet-highlighted luau, Richard sat on his lanai, petting his new snouted companion as he rested on a bed of banana leaves at his feet. Later he sat down at the judgment table and ate the terribly overspiced food, carefully avoiding the fish. There was lots of grumbling around the table about the inauthenticity of a luau minus a pig. That's when he noticed it. Without Richard's tempering influence over the last month, Javi had lifted off into the outer sphere of unpalatable. Each bite he took was inedible, yet Richard did eat it. He didn't care. He was saved. The restaurant never would have succeeded without him.

Another foul spasm erupted from Richard's bowels. Someone was knocking at his bathroom door. He wanted privacy.

"Go away!"

"It's Titi."

"Go away, Titi."

"I brought you coconut milk."

"I can't put anything in my mouth."

"It will help your stomach."

A pause.

"Leave it at the door."

"Okay, but drink it."

"Titi?"

"Yes?"

"Thank you."

"Sure."

"Titi?"

"Yes?"

Pause.

"It was a terrible meal, wasn't it?"

Titi sighed. "The worst I ever ate."

"I should never have let it happen."

"You are too kind to that man."

"I'm a coward." What was that saying about dead lions and live dogs? Without a doubt, he was a dachshund.

Titi didn't know the details of the trouble, but it was clear that this stranger, Javi, brought agony to Richard and unhappiness to Ann, so she wanted him gone for their sake. She had dropped some leaves and powders into Javi's sauces to ensure disgrace. As penance for making the others sick, she had eaten the food also.

"Do you know what I think?" Titi asked.

"What?"

"This Javi is a very bad man."

"Really?"

"I watch him. I see. He doesn't wash his hands when he comes into the kitchen. He tastes everything with his fingers. He licks them."

"I see."

"You are a good man. Very clean."

"I appreciate that."

"Clean is important."

While everyone else retired to a toilet with a burn that extended from the esophagus to the colon, Cooked and Javi stayed at the table and drank beer, both immune to the incendiary food.

"This is a nice spread you have," Javi said.

Cooked nodded. He was very, very drunk.

"Connor over at the Aloha Pearl said it was underutilized. Do you know my buddy, Connor?"

Cooked shook his head, trying to block out Javi's voice as well as his face.

"Connor is someone you should know. I'll introduce you two. We'll go party sometime."

Cooked picked up a new beer and drank it down in one gulp.

Javi watched, impressed. "That's my man!"

Cooked said nothing.

"Anyway, his feelings were that maybe a partnership, a mutually exclusive arrangement—"

"The Aloha Pearl is a shithole. They pay below the official wage and cheat their workers."

"Maybe they have a few issues."

"'Aloha' is Hawaiian. Do you understand how messed up that is? Aren't you leaving today?"

Cooked was towering over Javi, and somehow his hand was encircling Javi's neck, not necessarily in a threatening way, unless one wanted to be picky and ask what good reason he could have for holding a man's neck in his hand in the first place. To Javi's credit, he didn't appear unduly concerned; he just ducked out of Cooked's hold to grab another beer.

"Some dinner that was, huh?"

"It made everyone sick."

Javi was tempted to try to get something negative out of Cooked about Richard's dishes, but considering the recent hand around his neck, he thought better of it.

"Well, got a long flight home, better hit the hammock." Javi gave a fake yawn. He started to leave, then did a dramatic turn back.

"Connor is probably a douche bag, agreed. But he did say Steve from the main resort would steal the place from you in a matter of months. He said they'd either buy it cheap outright, or put you in debt and take it as collateral. Just a warning. Nighty-night."

Those were just the words Cooked needed to stay up all night with the mother of all anxiety attacks.

Over time what happened—what he feared now for himself—was that most activists lost energy. They lost fight. They got older, got married, started to have too much to lose by going to jail or, worse, getting killed. They forgot. Most likely, Cooked would do nothing. Justice, if it came, would be won by others.

He didn't like his new role of being envied. Loren's gift was double-edged. It created a space between the villagers and Cooked because no matter how much he ignored it, they did not. Titi was different. She had royal Pomare in her blood somewhere way back. To her, this felt owed. The weight of stewardship was a crown to her. Not for him. No other way to look at it—the island was a rock tied around Cooked's neck, and he'd better keep swimming or he would drown.

The next morning they gathered—bums sore, eyes heavy from lack of sleep, insides still rumbling and threatening to erupt—and mutually elected to skip breakfast.

Ann sat next to her suitcase, wearing her old brown bathing suit. She would have thrown it away—it no longer fit who she thought she was—but now ironically it reminded her of Loren. Wende came and sat next to her, putting an arm across her shoulders. Less touched by grief, she could play the role of comforter. Detachment was a luxury the young had.

"I'll miss this place," Ann said.

"It'll be cool opening a restaurant together."

"Dex said you'd have your reception there."

Wende bit her lip. "He doesn't believe in my transformation. He thinks it was a fluke. That I'll go back to being his muse. That's not going to happen."

Dex was coming out of his *fare*, and Ann didn't want to stick around for that conversation.

"I'm going for a walk."

The cool sand of early morning cupped her feet in slurpy kisses. The truth was she'd stayed up all night not only from a poisoned colon but also in grief at leaving the island. Although Loren was gone, the magic of the place was still palpable. She associated it with him, but it was anyone's for the taking. Out of sight of the *fares*, she was again in Crusoe country—empty coral beaches, the relentless expanse of ocean beating up against the brittle slips of land, the desiccated shade under the palm trees. With a shift of light, it all became an indescribable paradise. The island was the ocean's soul; without land, one could not appreciate the watery vastness. No other footprints were visible; she was the first human being to set foot on the morning's newly washed sand. What a wonderful feeling of renewal each day. The thought of her old life chafed like clothes one had grown out of. Life here was pure unclothed pleasure.

Although she had not intended to revisit it, she found herself near the cove with the camera. Its power over her was gone. Loren had been right—its privacy, its secrecy, its noneventfulness had been its magic. The original people drawn to that had been its true fans. Maybe Loren being an artist made him appreciate that not every work of art is intended for the multitudes; some works are meant only for the *afición*. Even if he wasn't telling the truth about the slaughtered-cow installation (and the more she thought about it, the more she suspected he had been pulling her leg), he definitely understood this.

Other than Wende monitoring the picture periodically and the feed being shared with telemarketers who were still selling Prospero singles at a brisk pace, no one was interested in the Crusoe cam any longer. When the millions of new viewers realized the show was over, they quit watching. Hits went lower than before because the original fans had been offended by the whole kidnapping farce, coupled with the commercialized benefit concert. She did not have the heart to do the right thing, which would be to pull the plug.

Ann sat behind the camera and looked out at the same view that the camera looked out at. The green water moved back and forth teasingly, as if it were doing so only to make her departure more painful. Time was running out. The window on extraordinary in her life was closing. Would the possibility of happiness soon follow?

She was so lost in her own thoughts that she didn't register the sound of voices approaching, but as soon as she did, she was irritated. Solitude, the real kind she had here, would soon be gone—couldn't she have a few minutes more? Even inside her own house, she would not be safe from electronic invasions—rings and pings and vibrations—and even her own betraying self would always be itching to hit the refresh button just in case a life-changing email happened to float into her in-box.

Dex and Wende. Drawn to the camera like moths to flame.

"One last quickie," Dex said. "It's our last chance before the plane."

Again, as in an endless rewind, Dex and Wende were prancing amorously half-naked down the beach. Except now, not only were they annoying, they were family.

"Hey, guys," Ann said.

"Why are you here?" Wende said, as if she hadn't followed her.

"Saying good-bye."

A sudden guiltiness appeared to come over the two of them. She couldn't blame them really for moving on so quickly. It was who they were. The moment of silence went on a beat too long.

"I'd better go find Richard," Ann said.

"No, this is good," Dex said. "Since you're here, you can witness."

Now a look of panic was on Wende's face. Apparently she had taken him at his word that this was just a last roll in the sand before leaving.

Dex held her hand and dragged her in front of the camera.

Ann rolled her eyes. Another spike in viewership for the Crusoe cam. Now people would hang on for months on the off chance of it happening again. She should have pulled the plug.

"I want the whole world to know that I love this woman, Wende . . ."

"Noooo." Wende was pulling away with all her might. The skin on her wrist turned bright pink.

"Wende . . ."

"Snitzer," she said quietly.

Dex snorted a laugh, and when he let go of her hand, she bolted. He dragged her back on camera.

"Yes, I love her in spite of that stinky last name. Which will soon change. In front of the whole world, will you be my Wende Cooper?"

Wende stood there as if drugged in her anti-Cinderella moment, paralyzed with inarticulateness.

Was she undergoing some kind of trauma where she would fall unconscious any minute and they'd have to stick wood in her mouth to keep her from swallowing her tongue? She looked that bad.

"Yes," Wende said in defeat.

"All right!" Dex let go of her hand and did a victory dance like after a touchdown in football.

Wende stood forgotten at the side. She was about to get everything she'd thought she wanted six months ago—to be the sixth Mrs. Dex Cooper—but things had changed. She felt as if she was a character in a movie, and she wanted to choose a different path for this girl named Wende. Not all girls dreamed of the white dress anymore, but the pressure against them was enormous. Some girls just wanted to sleep with Prince Charming. They wanted to go off and slay dragons themselves, not be cooped up in the castle all day, tending little princes and princesses.

Dex grabbed her in a bear hug and spun her around, planting a big kiss on her lips for the on-camera finale, but when Wende came up for air, it was the new, improved Wende, 2.0, who had lagged a moment before kicking in.

"But . . ." Wende said, ducking his arm that intended to wrap itself around her waist and whisk her off camera for good. She stood square in front of the lens now in soap opera fashion and addressed her audience directly, even though the man she should have been talking to stood right next to her.

"But what?" Dex said.

"But *not* until I've made my first top-box-office-grossing film because I can't put my personal happiness first over the causes I believe in. Just like you. This isn't the '90s anymore."

"You don't believe in causes."

"Not true. Women are still shortchanged in the movies. You're either hot or not . . . working. My movies will be about empowered, strong women, and they will be made by empowered, strong women."

"I don't get it," Dex said. Clearly he would have given anything for this not to be broadcasting live.

Wende smiled beatifically into the camera. "We're going to have a prolonged engagement."

The girl was brilliant, Ann thought. Scary brilliant.

The nine a.m. scheduled departure for the main resort was delayed. After all the wedding excitement and then the tragedy of Loren's death, Cooked and Titi had forgotten to make arrangements to buy their own boat.

Since no one made an effort toward getting breakfast, Cooked decided to rustle up his own. Determined to avoid Javi, he snuck along the edge of the compound to the kitchen, but when he opened the door, there Javi was as if he'd been lying in wait for him.

"Sleeping in, big guy? Want me to whip you up some sunny-side-up eggs?" Javi slapped him hard on the shoulder, and Cooked had to resist the urge to slug him. He had to keep reminding himself that he was now the owner of a resort. He had both incredible assets ($$$) and responsibilities, such as not punching out guests on a whim. Already at the wedding, he had been hit up by just about every relative for a loan. They didn't believe that he had precisely as much cash on hand—none— as he had days before, when Loren had signed the title document over. Ann had warned him of coming liabilities (bloodsucking insects like Javi), who would try to prey on them.

Late morning they all were gathered at the dock, waiting for the boat, which was hours late. Titi had set up the special viewing telescope Loren had planned to use for the astronomical occasion that happened to fall that morning. This was her first big idea for a recreational activity, yet it wasn't working.

"It's the Transit of Venus," Titi said, goaded by their lack of curiosity. "Come on."

The Transit was the official reason given for Captain Cook to come to the islands. The English did not want to make their intent to conquer known to the other European powers. When Loren had first bought the telescope and set it up for guests eight years before, it had been a huge success. He had taken self-portraits with a date stamp to be matched with new ones in eight years. A project having to do with the passage of time. Had Loren just lost interest? Titi wondered. Perhaps he wouldn't have done away with himself before completing his project if he had remembered. Titi had overlooked the fact that all the enthusiastic guests were women who enjoyed Loren leaning over them and directing them in sighting the lens.

The clouds were rolling in heavily—they should hurry for a view—but no one was interested.

"Won't it hurt your eyes?" Lilou asked.

"Not if you wear your father's special glasses."

Lilou looked skeptically at the glasses, wrinkling her nose as if they had an olfactory presence. She shrugged and walked away.

Titi made a show of looking, but all she saw was a grainy, squirming ball, like something crawling with maggots, with a black dot slowly crossing it. This is what caused Loren such delight? Maybe it was just the idea that after the second crossing, it wouldn't reappear for 105 years? Maybe the fact of lasting long enough to see it twice was victory enough? Except he hadn't lasted. He'd forgotten. A disappointment. She had so much wanted it to matter, for it to be beautiful, so she could say, *He loved this*. No one cared. They said they'd catch an enhanced picture of it on CNN in Papeete airport.

P ast noon and no boat. The assembled group now groused and paced. They had already taken leave of one another, exchanged the vitals of email addresses, phone numbers, etc., and now nothing remained but to go. They shut off their senses to the beauty around them, as if the island itself had ceased to matter. How else could you force yourself to go? Everyone except for Ann.

The last half hour they stood in a row, looking seaward like shipwrecks, ignoring the place that had seemed so magical on arrival. All faced the ocean except Ann, who turned and faced inland. With less enthusiasm they promised one another they would stay in touch, that they'd come back, arrange reunions—why not?

When the hotel boat was finally spotted, each woman eyed her luggage and considered a last trip back to check every corner in her *fare*, but it was too late—Steve was close enough that they could see his shrimp-pink face. A man of perpetual sunburn and peeling. It was time to go home.

Ann felt sniffly and nostalgic.

Titi was throwing flowers in the water; she had nothing better to do and thought they looked pretty. Maybe they would substitute this for the conch-blowing ceremony?

"Why is she doing that?" Wende asked, pointing with her chin at the waterlogged blooms.

"So the sharks mistake the flowers for us. So we remain safe," Richard said.

The group turned in unison to look at him.

He blushed. "I just made it up."

"That was beautiful," Titi said. "Can I use it?"

The two had grown closer that night outside his bathroom door when Titi had sworn to Richard that she would take care of Piglet as a pet and let him live out his natural life.

Steve cut the motor and glided in. He jumped off as soon as he hit the bumper of the dock and threw the rope to Cooked.

"Gotta take a leak."

He was gone that fast, and they all had to readjust themselves to delay the dramatic departure yet again. When he returned, he was wiping his hands on a linen towel he'd swiped from the bathroom.

"Any chance of lunch before we push off? I've been running since early morning."

Titi stood mute. Cooked crossed his arms and looked out to sea.

"Sure," Richard said, not thinking. He was a food-services guy after all. "If it's okay with you, Titi?"

She shrugged.

"Could you whip something up, Javi?"

Javi smiled, bowed his head at the new pecking order, and left for the kitchen.

Hijacked for an even longer period, everyone put their stuff down and sprawled out on lounge chairs. Titi came out with a tray of chilled bottled water. You wanted departing guests sober and sorry to leave.

Once Steve sat down to eat, he called Titi and Cooked over.

"I begged the hotel for this boat today. That's why I'm late. I had to take care of our real guests first."

Titi nodded her head, but Cooked just looked at Steve with an expression that should have made him uncomfortable.

"They said I could have it this one time because of our VIP, Mr. Cooper here, but after this you're on your own. And we'll no longer be able to handle your supplies either."

"That's unfair," Lilou said. "My father—"

"Maybe he and you should have listened to me earlier."

"Watch it," Robby said.

"You'll put them out of business," Wende said.

Steve dropped his head down to his chest in mock shame, creating a contiguous line of flesh from chin to chest. "It's just business."

"Then business sucks," Dex said.

"I'll pass your comment on to management. Oh! I forgot—I am management." Steve looked up, his eyes squinting to their true piggish proportions (in this case not nearly as cute as the real pig, which had rather lovely damp brown eyes). "You can pass on the ride if you feel that way," Steve continued.

Dex slammed his bottle down on the table. The effect was good, but less than it could have been since it was plastic and merely squeaked and bounced away instead of shattering.

Titi delicately swayed back and forth with her eyes closed. She had known since she was a young girl that the world was simply a veil of pain, but each time its unfairness stole her breath away. Had she prayed for the wrong thing?

Cooked had murder in his eyes.

Clear to all this would not end well.

"I just want you to know I've recorded this on my iPhone. It's going straight on YouTube," Wende said.

"Nothing I've said here is illegal in the least, sweetheart."

"Don't call my fiancée 'sweetheart.'"

Wende frowned for so many reasons. "It won't exactly make you Mr. Popular. People won't come to your resort. You'll be the asshole of the South Pacific."

"They'll forget. Haven't you noticed? People always do."

Ann stepped forward. "Then the arrangement between the new Mara 'amu and your resort is severed?"

"You bet it is unless I get some cooperation pronto."

"I'm sorry, I'm being dense here—just to restate: there is no legal relationship. It was strictly a verbal understanding between the deceased ex-owner, Loren, and your resort, represented nominally by you."

Steve was changing from shrimp to boiled-lobster hue. "*Who* are you?"

"I'm legal counsel for the Mara 'amu. Which, as of this morning, is fully booked for the next five years."

Ever since Dex's appearance on the live cam, inquiries to the resort had exploded. There would be initial difficulties finding a regular supplier from Tahiti, but they could be solved.

"You don't live here—"

"A technicality, as I will soon." She had not known the truth of it till the words left her lips.

"What do you mean?" Richard asked.

"What *do* you mean?" Steve said.

But Ann forgot all about Steve now that her intention had blurted itself out. Again, Richard was the last to know. She took her husband aside. "I love it here. I don't want to go back. Can you possibly understand?"

She was too old at thirty-eight. The world's injustices could not be turned away from any longer. Surprise of surprises to discover she was a lawyer after all. She saw it then so clearly . . . She was a scalpel, but a scalpel that could be used for good or bad. She would simply retool her sharp shark teeth.

Everyone turned away, embarrassed for Richard.

"What about us?"

"That's the thing—it's a terrible thing to ask . . . but I can only imagine doing it if you are with me."

At last Ann thought she had figured it out, even though it involved leaving behind everything and grasping after the unknown. In her case, happiness might be as simple as a beach, a hut, and a man who loved her. Never mind that she would be an attorney for a multinational resort complex; lives in the twenty-first century were complicated. Even the no-nonsense men in white wigs who wrote her country's founding document understood that happiness—or at least its dogged pursuit—was important enough to equate with life and liberty as their guiding lights. They couldn't promise its attainment, or even its preservation once achieved, but Ann thought if you pursued the wrong kind of happiness, it eventually grew stale on you, disappointing, like crackers that were already soggy when you opened the cellophane wrapper. You moved on, literally searching for crisper, greener, happier pastures that didn't involve desires you were brainwashed to want. Eventually, lemminglike, you struggled blindly on and stumbled across it—the *you* that *you* are to become—and what other definition of happy could there possibly be?

S teve, irate, started the boat's motor, and the remaining passengers paired up as if they were boarding Noah's ark: Dex and Wende, Robby and Lilou, and, surprisingly, a lone Javi.

Ann, Richard, Titi, and Cooked stood and waved good-bye.

Richard had known his answer before Ann asked the question. He would have gone on his knees and begged to spend the rest of his life with her no matter where. That's just how it was. And, too, every paradise needs its great chef.

"You guys will take my calls from now on, right? We'll Skype?" Javi yelled.

A thundercloud of sharks, like a blessing, escorted them out of the lagoon.

They watched until the boat shrank to a small white dot in the universe of blue. Some of Captain Cook's men stayed behind on the islands. Each ocean voyage took a three- or four-year bite out of their lives back in England. They knew if they returned, their old lives would not

fit as well as they formerly had. On the islands they fell in love, or decided that only a permanent change of venue would suit. They stayed for
pleasure, or opportunity, or a dream, or some combination of the three,
but not a one of them failed to feel a lump in his throat as his known life
sailed away.

Ann squeezed Richard's hand. They turned their backs on the disap-
pearing boat and ran.

# Acknowledgments

A few books were invaluable to my understanding of French Polynesia, most notably *Cook: The Extraordinary Voyages of Captain James Cook* by Nicholas Thomas; *Fatu-Hiva: Back to Nature* by Thor Heyerdahl; *Representing the South Pacific: Colonial Discourse from Cook to Gauguin* by Rod Edmond; *Tahiti Beyond the Postcard: Power, Place, and Everyday Life* by Miriam Kahn; *Daughters of the Pacific* and *Pacific Women Speak Out* by Zohl dé Ishtar; and *Poisoned Reign: French Nuclear Colonialism in the Pacific* by Bengt Danielsson and Marie-Thérèse Danielsson.

A huge hug to Rabih Nassif for endless patience in reading successive drafts. For the illustrations, I want to thank my husband, Gaylord Soli. I would like to thank Hilary Rubin Teeman and Dori Weintraub for their brilliance and advocacy through three books. Lastly, to Andrew Wylie for his belief in me.